BOUND
IN
BLOOD

ALSO AVAILABLE FROM TITAN BOOKS

A Universe Of Wishes: A We Need Diverse Books Anthology

Black Is The Night: Stories Inspired By Cornell Woolrich

Christmas And Other Horrors

Cursed: An Anthology

Dark Cities: All-New Masterpieces Of Urban Terror

Dark Detectives: An Anthology Of Supernatural Mysteries

Daggers Drawn

Dead Letters: An Anthology Of The Undelivered,
The Missing And The Returned...

Dead Man's Hand: An Anthology Of The Weird West

Death Comes At Christmas

Escape Pod: The Science Fiction Anthology

Exit Wounds

Ink And Daggers: The Best Of The Crime Writers' Association
Short Story Awards

In These Hallowed Halls: A Dark Academia Anthology

Invisible Blood

Isolation: The Horror Anthology

Multiverses: An Anthology Of Alternate Realities

New Fears

New Fears 2

Out Of The Ruins: The Apocalyptic Anthology

Phantoms: Haunting Tales From The Masters Of The Genre

Reports From The Deep End: Stories Inspired By J. G. Ballard

The Madness Of Cthulhu Anthology (Volume One)

The Madness Of Cthulhu Anthology (Volume Two)

Vampires Never Get Old

Wastelands: Stories Of The Apocalypse

Wastelands 2: More Stories Of The Apocalypse

Wastelands: The New Apocalypse

When Things Get Dark: Stories Inspired By Shirley Jackson

Wonderland: An Anthology

BOUND
IN
BLOOD

EDITED BY JOHNNY MAINS

TITAN BOOKS

Bound in Blood
Hardback edition ISBN: 9781803367491
E-book edition ISBN: 9781803367521

Published by Titan Books
A division of Titan Publishing Group Ltd
144 Southwark Street, London SE1 0UP
www.titanbooks.com

First edition: September 2024
10 9 8 7 6 5 4 3 2 1

This is a work of fiction. All of the characters, organizations, and events portrayed in this novel are either products of the author's imagination or are used fictitiously. Any resemblance to actual persons, living or dead (except for satirical purposes), is entirely coincidental.

The authors assert the moral right to be identified as the authors of their works.

A CIP catalogue record for this title is available from the British Library.

Printed and bound by CPI (UK) Ltd, Croydon, CR0 4YY

This book is dedicated to the memory of
Christopher Priest (1943–2024)

"Now you're looking for the secret... but you won't find it,
because of course you're not really looking.
You don't really want to know.
You want to be fooled." – *The Prestige*

TABLE OF CONTENTS

INTRODUCTION

—◀ JOHNNY MAINS ▶—

When I was thirteen years old, my father took me to a *Blue Peter* 'Bring and Buy Fair' (table-top fair for our US friends) and someone was selling a copy of *The Thirteenth Pan Book of Horror Stories* edited by the mysterious-sounding Herbert van Thal. I *begged* my dad for that book. The spine was cracked, the covers were worn and dogeared and, inside the book, someone had folded down a couple of the pages as a reminder of where they had got to. It was a *well-read* copy.

I wanted that book more than anything else in the world. Dad had to make me promise that my mother was never to find out (she hated horror) and once he was satisfied that I was going to keep my mouth shut and no amount of torture would ever make me spill the beans, he paid 10p for the book and I took it home, putting it under my jumper so I could rush it upstairs and hide it alongside all of my other ill-gained illicit material, like copies of the adult magazine *Viz*.

Readers, I loved that book more than *anything* on the planet. I read it until it disintegrated in my hands. That book kick-started my love affair with all things horror and really brought home the joy that books could bring. I've read more horror books than any other genre on the planet. Autobiographies come a close second. I'm now in the very privileged position where I get to edit books like the ones I read in my teens, and I don't take what I do lightly or for granted. When I edit horror, I'm always looking for that same kick as when I read *Pan Horror 13*. I want the mix of shock, surprise, fear, disgust and unease that I got all of those years ago. I thought it an impossible goal, nothing I've ever read since has ever come close to that first rush of adrenaline and excitement, but the reason I do what I do is because one day, I might just reach those heady heights again.

With this volume, readers, I think I have. This is an anthology about books, about those who write them, those who read them, those who fear them, those who keep them, those who offer them to others. This is about the printed page, the blank page scrawled on by a terrified hand. This is about where books are kept, how books are made, how books are displayed, about how books are read. While some of these stories may have the feel of tales told round the campfire, they all contain doorways to places the protagonist might not want to enter. This is a volume about the contract we have, between writer and reader, between editor and writer, between editor and reader, that between us all we will do our best to entertain and be entertained in return. These are the words we read, and we are bound in blood.

If this book has come into your life and I really *hope* it's *you* – may your nightmares be plentiful and beware of the books that lurk in dark corners. They bite.

Johnny Mains
not too far from Hell's Mouth
2024

FROM THE SEA

CHARLIE HIGSON

Sent - iCloud 21 February 2024 at 17.38

Alex Furniss
From the Sea
To: Christina Marx

Hi there, Chris.

A big hello to my absolute favourite production designer!

I hope this email finds you well. You're probably thinking – long-time no ping. What does Alex want from me? He's a Hollywood hot shot now. Yeah, right. Basically, I got stuck in major development hell with Universal and after nearly two years – *surprise, surprise* – they've drowned my kittens and pulled the plugs and sent me home in a van. Which means I'm back in Blighty and can go back to that project we talked about… God, how long ago was it? It was definitely pre-COVID.

Time flies when you're having a miserable time.
I shouldn't have got greedy. The prospect of doing a big Hollywood project with

11

shitloads of dosh attached went to my silly little head. But I don't need to tell you what a bloody nightmare it is trying to work with those people – especially if you're not used to it.

Anyway, I'm glad to see that your star's risen more than somewhat since we last worked together. A quick glance at the trade rags tells me you've just finished a major project of your own, and you no doubt have something massive lined up to go on to, but I wondered if you fancied doing an *amuse bouche*? A little palate cleanser between main courses?

I'm setting up to do a quick simple shoot – bish-bash-bosh, no fucking about, done and dusted – just like the old days when we started out. The budget's just low enough that we won't have executives breathing down our necks every minute of every day, and just high enough that we should be able to do something pretty cool if we put the money in the right places. Which we're both good at. I won't bore you too much with the details here in case you don't have the time or the inclination to come on board. But it's that old Lovecraft-inspired thing that we talked about way back when – *From the Sea.* It's changed somewhat, though. I'm not doing it totally straight. As well as elements of the *Dunwich Horror* and *Mountains of Madness,* there's a bit of Poe's 'House of Usher', as well as a strong whiff of Arthur Machen. It's contemporary, though. It's as much about politics and race and paranoia and immigration and the sodding culture wars, as it is about tentacled monsters from out of space and time. Though there are some cool crab creatures at the end (which may or may not be real...)

Small cast. Contained settings. Tight storytelling. Some humour. Light on its feet and scary as fuck. No pissing about. I've got the budget to build a couple of really cool sets and some key props. Also, I was developing the US thing with an amazing new FX company who can do extraordinary things with no money, *Temple of Hekate.* The irony is they were too cheap for Universal. They didn't trust them. Wankers.

It would be a five-week shoot, early autumn, three weeks in Budapest for the interiors, a week in Ireland for the exteriors and a week in Saudi Arabia for a sort of prologue (touches of *The Exorcist*). I know that sounds extravagant but at one point we were going to shoot my Universal thing out in Saudi and I made some good contacts with the guys at Neom (if you haven't heard of Neom, look it up). They're trying to set up as the Hollywood of the Middle East and are desperate for western filmmakers to work out there. They've put together a great package of incentives, cash rebates and tax breaks that means we actually save money by filming there. Crazy, I know. Ironically, the most expensive part of filming is the Ireland leg. But I just can't find the exteriors I need anywhere else – a big old crumbling mansion on a clifftop overlooking a wild sea. Although the mansion itself will be CGI: we have to see it collapse and fall in on itself at the end of the film.

As you know, this is a script that's been close to my heart for as long as I can remember. I think God has arranged all this. He meant for the Universal thing to fall apart so that I could get on and do this. The film I was always meant to make. It'll be a blast – just like the old days – I'm gonna do it all myself, producing, writing, directing. Why work with some incompetent fucker?

Let me know what you think. I've attached the latest draft, in a spirit of insane optimism. And yes – you did read that right. It's draft 17.

Only thing is – we need to move fast on this. It would be good to push some visuals out ASAP so we can package it up and get the last of the funding in place.

Here you go.

FROM THE SEA.fdx

Cheers
Alex

. . . .

Sent - iCloud 23 February 2024 at 10.17

Christina Marx
RE: From the Sea
To: Alex Furniss

Hi there, Alex.

Karma. Fantastic timing. You're right – I think God *is* organising all this. I've just had a major project fall through as well. To tell you the truth I was slightly dreading it. It would have meant at least six months filming in Tunisia. Your five-week package tour of Hungary, Ireland and (gulp) Saudi Arabia sounds like a much better bet. Cut to the chase – I read the script and love it. I'm already buzzing with ideas – which will all probably be outside your budget (some clarification of that would help me make a quick decision).

Draft 17 indeed! You really have been sweating this one, haven't you, Alex? I thought it was *amazing*. The way that you worked all those themes into it but at its heart it's a really scary and disturbing horror film. I've got a real mad genius art director in mind to make the book and the other artefacts and come up with a look and feel for the magical/horror elements. I read the script and his name just screamed at me.

Anyway, my guy, Scott, is absolutely phenomenal. A head on him like you wouldn't believe. I don't know where he comes up with his ideas. All cards on the table, he was out of action for a long spell following a motorbike accident. In a coma for a long while and then, just as he was getting back on his feet, COVID came along. It hit him hard and he had some mental health problems. He went off the rails a bit, but he's back on top of things now and I've been trying to find a project I can use him on to give him his confidence back. This would be ideal. Some producers I've spoken to about him have been wary, but I know you won't have a problem. You always liked working with crazy people! Honestly, what you'll get out of him you

14

won't believe. Once he gets his teeth into something he is *extraordinary*.

He's fast, too. So, if you need some sexy visuals out there quick, he can do it.

So excited. Can't wait to get started on this. As I say – a budget discussion is all I need to settle any doubts I might have.

Chris

. . . .

Sent - iCloud 30 February 2024 at 11.22

Christina Marx
From the Sea
To: Scott Crompton

Scott. You know I always deliver. I've got a job that's right up your nightmare alley. It's a Lovecraftian horror thing with a twist. And a pretty decent budget.

I don't know if you're familiar with old Howard Phillips but at the core of the film is this kind of cursed book called *The Necronomicon* that crops up in a lot of his work. It's a kind of grimoire/Book of the Dead thing and plays a starring role in the film, so needs to look AWESOME. I've attached the script & I know you'll love it. I've always wanted to do something like this, where the sets and the design tell half the story and I have every faith in you to come back from the dead with all guns blazing. Just remember no live ammo on set. Joke. Is that too soon?

We *do* need to move fast – if it's a YES, we need some artwork by last week, if it's a NO you don't need to come up with any clever excuses – I'll understand.

Fingers and toes all crossed.
Christina xx

. . . .

From: Scott Crompton
Date: Sun, 30 Feb 2024 at 23:28
Subject: From the Sea
To: Christina Marx

christina you're an angel and a marvel I've read the script and you're right i
do love it but you know i have doubts i don't want to sign onto anything that
i can't pull off and see through to the end and the last thing i want to do is let
you down when you have such faith in me can we get together and talk this
through before I commit?

Scott

. . . .

Sent - iCloud 03 March 2024 at 18.45

Christina Marx
From the Sea
To: Scott Crompton

Hi Scott,
It was great to see you on Tuesday and I'm so glad I was able to persuade you
to take on the job. The first thing we need are some concept visuals for the
book and a poster that clearly sells the idea of the film in your inimitable style.
I'm happy to take this thing in stages. They need selling visuals for the Sheffield
Horrorcon 11/12 May, Cannes right after and then Frightfest at the start of June.
I hope that is do-able. If you can at least give us artwork for that, and come up
with an overall look, then hopefully that will give you the confidence to push on
and commit to the actual film.

I've attached a rewrite of the opening that Alex just sent me – it focuses even more on the book. Which is apt, because, let's face it, it's the star of the film.

Love
Christina

. . . .

BLACK SCREEN.
The cold, depressing sound of flapping wind, churning waves and rough weather.

A caption comes up - stark white letters.

1. THE SEA

Now the opening chords of Vaughan Williams' *Sea Symphony* blast out. And the chorus explodes...

CHORUS (O.S.)
Behold - the sea...

CUT TO:
1. EXT. ENGLISH CHANNEL - DAY
A miserable seascape. Scummy waves under a dull grey sky. Drizzle in the air, whipped all directions by the wind. There's a big swell - the whole surface of the sea undulating chaotically.

The music continues as we skim along the surface, just above the billowing water. There's a black dot in the distance, tiny and insignificant against the power of the sea.

As we get closer, we realise it's a makeshift rubber dinghy. Packed with young men, mostly dressed in black, huddled together, frightened. Their backs to the sea. Hoods up and heads down, sheltering from the cutting wind and the rain. A YOUNG MAN is steering at the back - grey-faced - haunted - desperate.

The whine of the outboard motor sounds pathetic. Useless. The boat is barely afloat. There's no sight of land on either horizon.

We move in closer and focus on one of the passengers. ABSHIR, a young Somali man. He looks seasick. He's clutching something against his chest, trying to protect it from the elements. It appears to be a large, rectangular object, wrapped in layers of plastic. There's dried blood on the plastic, but the rain is washing it off. Abshir's hand wipes the last of it away.

We focus on Abshir's eyes. He's not here in the boat. He's thousands of miles away...

Abruptly the sound of gunfire erupts.

CUT TO:
2. EXT. SUDAN - DAY
A very different scene. Hot. Dry. Dusty. The sun beating down relentlessly from a cloudless sky. We're in a flyblown desert town, ravaged by war.

In the distance are several Arab soldiers, firing aimlessly. There's no great sense of order or purpose. They look almost bored.

FOUR AFRICAN MEN - coughing, choking, gasping for breath - hurry across fallen rubble and throw themselves against a protective wall. Almost all that's left of a partially demolished concrete building. The men are wearing western-style clothing and carrying backpacks.

A bullet snaps and whines, throwing up more dust from the top of the wall.

OLDER SOMALI MAN

    We will have to go another way.

YOUNG SOMALI MAN - BEYDAAN

    There is no other way.

OLDER SOMALI MAN

    There is always another way. We will go back and work our way around them.

YOUNG SOMALI MAN - BEYDAAN

    Without our guide we are lost.

OLDER SOMALI MAN

(he spits)

    Puh - he was no use to us. He deserved to get his brains blown out.

ABSHIR

    I agree with Beydaan. It is too dangerous. We should wait for night.

ZAKARIYA

    Don't stop. Don't go back. You can make it. But not me...

The others turn to ZAKARIYA. He is the oldest of them. More Arabic looking. He looks worn out. Sweating heavily.

ABSHIR

    What is it, Zakariya? What's the matter?

ZAKARIYA pulls his jacket aside. His shirt is drenched with dark blood. More blood is pouring out of his sleeve, wetting his hand.

ZAKARIYA

This is the end of my journey.

The others accept it. There's no point in arguing with him. ZAKARIYA painfully shrugs his backpack off and starts handing out the contents to the others - 2 bottles of water - some cans of food - a packet of dates - a wad of grubby cash - and finally - the rectangular object, wrapped in its protective plastic covering.

As he takes it out, his blood smears the plastic.

ABSHIR

What is this?

ZAKARIYA
(forcing the book on ABSHIR)

A book. Take it. It's valuable. If you get to England, there is a woman at the British Museum. Her name is Maggie King - the details are with the book. If you take it to her at the British Museum, she will give you a lot of money. It was to be my future. Now it is yours.

ABSHIR

What is the book?

ZAKARIYA

The white men call it Al Azif. They believe it was written by a man called Abdul Alhazred. That is not a real name. And that is not the real name of the book. They say it is filled with the names of the dead. Do not try to read it. I was told that by the man who gave it to me. This morning I looked. To try to see if my name was there... I think it must have been...

He puts a hand to his bloody chest and the light goes out in his eyes. He's given up. ABSHIR looks at the book. The older Somalian grabs his arm.

OLDER SOMALI MAN

Throw it away, Abshir. The man was mad...

ABSHIR thinks. What should he do? He makes a decision and stuffs the book in his backpack.

. . . .

From: Scott Crompton
Date: Tues, 05 Mar 2024 at 05:17
Subject: From the Sea
To: Christina Marx

aaargh you know me too well I am stoked about this I've been up all night working on stuff listening to the music mentioned in the script FULL VOLUME the Vaughan Williams sea symphony and the walt whitman poem its based on and now its like an invisible force is guiding my hands hahaha you joked at lunch that you and the director guy alex felt that god was behind all this I THINK ITS CTHULHU! hahaha horrors a great genre to exorcize your demons LOL first thing tomorrow or is it today already I am going to get on the case and scare up some research material

Scott

. . . .

From: Anthony Newsome
Date: Mon, 11 Mar 2024 at 10:32
Subject: Books Enquiry
To: Scott Crompton

Hello Scott,

Thank you for your enquiry regarding the Necronomicon. I'm sure you will understand that you are not the first person to ask about access to the book and our university library archive, and we are obliged to tell you what we have to say to everyone else.

I'm afraid there is no such book and there never has been. We do have many ancient texts here at Miskatonic, and our collection is world famous, but the Necronomicon is not part of it. The works of H.P. Lovecraft are pure fiction. He made up everything in his books, including the Necronomicon itself. Frankly, we have been plagued by fans of Mister Lovecraft arriving at the university over the years, insisting they must be allowed to see the Necronomicon and accusing us of lying when we explain that it doesn't exist. In fact, we have dedicated members of faculty whose job it is to deal with these people and explain to them the reality of the situation.

Mister Lovecraft used our university in his books (and used our library for research), but its representation in his work is entirely fantastical. I'm afraid, in creating your version of the Necronomicon, you will have to do what H.P. Lovecraft himself did and use your imagination.

Regards,
Anthony Newsome

Anthony Newsome MLS
Associate Librarian Rare and Manuscript Collections
Miskatonic University Arkham Mass.

. . . .

Sent - iCloud 12 March 2024 at 21.55

Hildred Castaigne
The Book
To: Scott Crompton

Hi there Scott

You don't know me. And I aim to keep it that way. My name is not Hildred Castaigne, that's a pseudo – a false identify, proceeding from the heat-oppressed brain.

Here's the thing. I was passed your name by a circuitous route. Bullet point version – a junior librarian at Misk is dating a buddy of mine. She told him about your inquiry. He passed it on to me. No names. I have to inform you, my friend, that the Misko staff are not playing straight with you. They're not totally capping you but neither are they giving you the full FACTS OF LIFE. It's the truth they don't have a copy of the Necronomicon. They told no word of a lie there. Because there's no such artefact. But what they didn't tell you is that Lovecraft based the Nec on another book. A real book that sits locked away in the vaults of the Miskatonic U. Library. It goes by many names – De Legibus Mortuorum, Almulik Biallawn Al'asfar, Canticum Domini Muscae, Tragoúdi Tou Árchonta Ton Mygón, Rex in Luteum… … But none of them is its actual factual name.

Why?

Because it has no name.

Thing is, they don't want it to get into the hands and the heads of their spaced-out students. So it rots down there with a few more recent banned books, arty porno, paedophilia, terrorist manuals, textbooks on drug making, that sort of shit. Everything and anything they don't want on their hallowed shelves, but which nevertheless is still pretty valuable.

Me and a group of like-minded people, including some ex-students and even some ex-faculty, have set up a group dedicated to trying to prise this tome out of their cold dead hands. Nobody's seen it outside of the library in many years. But there are some facsimiles. There are photos and copies of some of the pages. Now, we want this to be more widely known, and this movie of yours might be a key or a lever to try to get things moving.

Here's the pitch. We can let you have a peek at some of this material. But this is dangerous for us and keeping our organisation afloat costs a few beans. So, if *you offer us* some beans, I can offer you a little private dinner. A taste. This way, I'll know you're serious.

Obviously keep this under your chapeau for now.

Castaigne

. . . .

From: Scott Crompton
Date: Tues, 12 March 2024 at 21.55
Subject: The Book
To: Hildred Castaigne

OK sending you money proves that I'm serious but how do I know that you're serious??? your email looks suspiciously like a shakedown a scam if im going to get on board with you and this becomes a business arrangement your going to have to show me something to prove that you have what you say you have

scott (real name)

. . . .

Sent - iCloud 13 March 2024 at 23.14
Hildred Castaigne
The Book
To: Scott Crompton

Fair enough, Scotty. I'll show you mine if you show me yours. If you're cool with what I send then we'll exchange account details.

Zapping you a link which shows the cover and three random spreads. If I had the wherewithal and the whatever I'd send you a link that expired and a *Mission: Impossible*-style self-destruct mechanic that burst into flames and sent out smoke the second you'd read it. But no matter what I do, you could just screengrab it, so I got to trust you.

But let me tell you this, brother Scott – if you play straight with me I will not look for you, I will not pursue you. But if you don't, I will look for you, I will find you, and I will kill you. LOLZ.

So, let's play. Beware though, Scotty, over the years, this tome has been called evil, haunted, possessed, the legend goes that if you read it you get sucked into its pages never to escape!

Mwah-hah-hah-haaaargh!!!!! Gurgle gurgle choke death rattle.

Beam me up.

Castaigne.

. . . .

Sent – iCloud 08 April 2024 at 10.42

Alex Furniss

OMFG

To: Christina Marx

Holy Cow, Chris,

You did not lie. The stuff that's coming down the pipe from your man Scott is extraordinary. I've never seen anything like it. It reminds me of the first time I saw Giger's designs for *Alien*. We'd never seen that before in a movie. I didn't think there was anything else you could do that hadn't been done, but this artwork, Jesus I can't put my finger on it, why it's so disturbing. It's hypnotic. You don't want to look at it, but you can't look away. I mean there's nothing particularly explicit but, Jesus H.P. Christ, I worry that we won't get away with it. That they won't let us use this stuff. But – hell – don't stop him. Keep it coming.

The cover and the pages of the Necronomicon that Scott's shared are out of this world – appropriately! I've seen this kind of book done so many times in movies and Lovecraft adaptations, *The Evil Dead*, whatever, but they're always a bit cheesy. Nobody would ever accuse Scott of cheese – his stuff looks – well, it looks genuinely evil. Depraved. And he's working so fast. I can't believe how quickly he's moved on from drawings to actually making the book.

I've shown some of Scott's visuals to the guys at Hekate and they are going NUTS. I can't remember ever working on a project like this where everyone on board is so up for it, so into it, so wanting to go that extra mile to make it sensational.

I can't wait to unleash this artwork and this movie onto an unsuspecting world.

I'm working on another rewrite. Scott's input has inspired me to really make the script live up to his visuals.

Cheers

Alex

. . . .

From: Scott Crompton
Date: Thur, 18 Apr 2024 at 04:27
Subject: Are you OK?
To: Christina Marx

sorry sorry sorry you know I didn't want this to happen I warned you tho it might but I worked so hard when I started its burned me out I'm I've come to a bit of standstill sorry I haven't sent anything through in the last 10 days or is it more???

i think its this flat working on this working on the artwork and making the book trying to do it all at here it's not ideal but the flat you know Ingrid left me she left me when I was ill after the bike smash she was good at first she nursed me

I know she did

the real nurses told me she was there she was always there and when I came around it was me and her but it was bad stuck together locked up together in COVID and I couldn't sleep and I couldn't concentrate and I had headaches and I couldn't remember things it made me angry I got aggressive with her I should never have been aggressive I could see it in her eyes the way she looked at me she was starting to pull away starting to hate me and as soon as she was able to leave when lockdown lifted she did

I couldn't I wanted to stay in the flat I wanted to stay here in canterbury I wanted to stay in the flat but its wrong everything here reminds of her it made me angry angry at myself angry with her angry the world angry with the car that pulled out without looking

your the only person I can tell this to
doctor archer – so called dr archer was useless he was worse than useless

27

trying to put me on all drugs trying to convince me I was damaged I was crazy he's the crazy one

i did go crazy the other night tho smashed up smashed up the living room tore up some art id been working on which is why ive not sent you anything last few days

i do have idea loads of ideas too many ideas im sending you some thoughts – no images just ideas – to clear my head – unclutter my thoughts and empty them onto the page

i have to move can't stay after in this place suffocating me I will go stay at my mothers place in suffolk in the past have done some of my best work there in the sun lounge overlooking over the looking over the sea so much light clear my head

itll be appropriate being there on the north sea not far from dunwich should have thought of it before the real dunwich how neat is that??? do you know the story of dunwich??? In the middle ages it was really important port as big as london but the east coast is eroding falling into the sea even back then was a big storm half the town sunk under the waters they say on some nights you can hear the church bells if I don't get the inspiration there to finish the job I wont find it anywhere

you know there's a lot of villages out that way sank under the waves hundreds of years ago and its still going on today COVEHITHE – EASTON BAVENTS – RUNGHOLT over the sea and up in yorkshire are more RAVENSER ODD and COLDEN PARVA

the seas are rising england is falling

trust me please trust me I will do this I want to do this I think the artwork is the best stuff ive ever done you asked me where I was getting inspiration getting references from what my sources were I can't tell you christina im sworn to secrecy all I can say is its costing me money and if you were able to transfer some to my account it would be really helpful

28

sorry to end on a begging note but you said how much your director liked what I was doing it will only get better once I move to suffolk my head will clear and ill get everything done

bless you for thinking of me and your kindness

Scott

. . . .

Sent - iCloud 27 April 2024 at 11.55

Christina Marx
RE: update
To: Alex Furniss

Hi there, Alex.

Here's the latest from Scott, it's just notes, ideas and a few rough sketches, I'm afraid, but interesting material nevertheless. As I said on the phone, he had had a bit of an upset, but I called him and we had a looooong talk and I think I was able to calm him down. He's such a sweet guy, but he gets lost sometimes. Anyway, he's moved to the countryside now and I hope it gives him a fresh lease of life, and a new burst of energy.

Anyway – these are some of the notes he sent about the thinking behind the designs he's working on. I've tidied them up a bit and cut out some of the stuff that just didn't seem relevant, and added some punctuation! His writing can be erratic to say the least.

```
I don't know if Lovecraft knew it, or he was
channelling something beyond himself, but his
description of Yog-Sothoth is weirdly similar to
```

descriptions of angels in the Bible, which aren't the beautiful, majestic, winged magazine models of Renaissance art. They're a lot more fucked up. This is from Ezekiel 1. (I'm just picking out the relevant bits – Ezekiel goes on a bit and he repeats himself all the time, like my mother when she had Alzheimer's.)

'And I looked, and, behold, a whirlwind came out of the north, a great cloud, and a fire infolding itself, and a brightness was about it, and out of the midst thereof as the colour of amber, out of the midst of the fire… came the likeness of four living creatures.

As for the likeness of the living creatures, their appearance was like burning coals of fire… and the living creatures ran and returned as the appearance of a flash of lightning.

Now as I beheld the living creatures, behold one wheel upon the earth by the living creatures, with his four faces… and their appearance and their work was as it were a wheel in the middle of a wheel.

As for their rings, they were so high that they were dreadful, and their rings were full of eyes round about them four.

And when they went, I heard the noise of their wings, like **the noise of great waters**.

I looked at the living creatures (cherubim), I saw a wheel on the ground beside each creature with its four faces… Each appeared to be made like a wheel intersecting a wheel… Their rims were high and awesome, and all four rims were full of eyes all around. And their whole body, and their backs, and their hands, and their wings, and the wheels, were full of eyes round about.'

You see - *wheels within wheels*. Covered with eyes. It says somewhere else they're the colour of crystal - just like Yog-Sothoth - crystal spheres within crystal spheres. Lovecraft describes Yog-Sothoth as a conglomeration of 'malignant globes'. 'All-in-One and One-in-All of limitless being and self - which has no confines and which outreaches fancy and mathematics alike. A squirming mess of intersecting, luminescent spheres, or bubbles.' Or crystals?

Were the Old Ones in Lovecraft simply *Biblical angels*? One and the same? Yog-Sothoth is the key to the gate, whereby the spheres meet. Yog-Sothoth knows the gate. Yog-Sothoth is the gate. Yog-Sothoth is the key and guardian of the gate. Past, present, future, all are one in Yog-Sothoth.

Do you know John Wheeler's theory of the one-electron-universe?

Basically, it's a mystery why every single electron in the universe is identical, with the exact same charge and mass. Wheeler suggested it could be because they're all the same electron, travelling forwards and backwards in time – from the beginning of time to the end of time – from the beginning of the universe to the end of the universe. Going backwards and forwards over and over and over so that it fills the universe with what appear to be numberless different electrons – but which are actually all the same one. When it's going forwards in time it's negatively charged – it's an electron – when it's going backwards it's a positron, the anti-matter opposite of an electron. That could be an explanation of how Yog-Sothoth works? He's matter and anti-matter, travelling both ways through time. Existing in all places in all times all at the same time. He knows the beginning and the end.

Past, present, future, all are one in Yog-Sothoth.

The Bible and physics. They're both the same. God, my Catholic roots are showing. I need to bleach them out. This place is full of my mother's Bibles. And her pictures of the Pope.

You can't help but think about the sea when you're here. The smell of it. What's under it.

The beach this morning was a mess, covered in a foul black substance and littered with thousands of dead things – crabs, starfish, razor clams, mussels, oysters, lobsters, like a scene from Hieronymus Bosch.

They're claiming the black stuff is sea coal, it's not like any coal I've ever seen. And the shellfish - the crabs - lying there, twitching, half dead, dying, dead, as if the sea had vomited them up. It stank of decay, necrosis… I can't get the script out of my head.

The crustaceans, *The Mi-Go*, the crab creatures, the giant walking lobster things garlanded with seaweed and barnacles, that take Maggie and Abshir at the end of the script? I have some ideas for how they might look – a bit different to how they're described in the script? Are they inspired by Leviticus? '*Anything of the swarming creatures in the seas and of the living creatures that are in the waters that does not have fins and scales is detestable to you. You shall regard them as detestable. You shall not eat any of their flesh, and you shall detest their carcasses.*'

You can sense Yog-Sothoth and his kind by their **smell.** Do you remember that news story about a spurned wife who hid a load of dead prawns inside her husband's hollow curtain rails and screwed the ends back on, when he kicked her out of the house? The man was haunted by a terrible stink and had no idea where it was coming from. What does Lovecraft say in *The Dunwich Horror*?

'*By Their smell can men sometimes know Them near, but of Their semblance can no man know, saving only in the features of those They have begotten on mankind. They walk unseen and foul in lonely places where the*

Words have been spoken and the Rites howled through at their Seasons. The wind gibbers with Their voices, and the earth mutters with Their consciousness. They bend the forest and crush the city...'

As I say, there were pages of this, Alex. I've just sent you some of the less wild stuff. I don't understand physics at all, I'm afraid, but I thought you might find that bit about time-travelling electrons interesting. Scott tends to think a lot about all this stuff. Always makes sure anything he draws or designs has some sort of mythological, religious, scientific, archaeological or historical underpinning. Expect more twisted imaginings from him soon! And time-travelling prawns...

Here's hoping he gets the last of the artwork to us soon.

Chris

. . . .

Sent - iCloud 30 April 2024 at 14.30

Hildred Castaigne

Pieter Van den Berg

So long

To: Scott Crompton

Now listen, Scott, fun is fun but that's it.

We're turning off the pump. You don't miss your water 'til the well runs dry. And you have scraped the barrel. Sucked at the teat 'til the titty is empty. There ain't no more – that's all folks. We just hope you get this stuff out into the world so as we can bring a valuable artefact into the light.

You got more than enough stuff to make your fake Necronomicon, and I think you get the style now, so if you want to mock up some more pages of your own we ain't gonna stop you. Our aim is to serve, and we have served and are shutting up shop for the night.

Night night, sweet dreams.

French-Canadian bean soup.

Castaigne

. . . .

Sent - iCloud 30 April 2024 at 09.55

Christina Marx
RE: spoke too soon
To: Alex Furniss

Hi there, Alex.

I should have had patience! Just got a torrent of stuff from Scott. So much of it I'm sending you a WeTransfer link. I have to say, it's the most extreme stuff he's produced. Some of it may well be too extreme. I don't know how it fits exactly with the film, but if there's some way you can use these new elements, they're pretty mind-blowing. I'd say it's perhaps even worth updating the script? I mean, you've only done 18 drafts, after all! Another one won't do any harm!

I've also attached my latest designs for the sets, but, I don't know, they feel a bit mundane compared to what Scott's doing. If it's OK with you for me to change things, I'm thinking of visiting him and seeing if he can give me some input on how to make the sets as strange and disturbing as the visuals that he's produced. I want to do justice to his version of the Necronomicon, and all the magical props and paraphernalia, not to mention the monster designs.

Yog-Sothoth – bloody hell – wow!

That'll keep you awake for a few nights!

Best

Chris

. . . .

From: Scott Crompton
Date: Wed, 1 May 2024 at 04:14
Subject: Are you OK?
To: Christina Marx

christina christina I miss you I need you

I shouldn't have come back here

my dead mothers house

the crosses the pope the bibles
the sea rising smashing into the sand cliffs

when I talk to you on the phone it all makes sense i understand things to get
my head above the water but as soon as you go as soon as i don't have your
voice in my ear things fall apart the sea levels rise

i sit here in the sun lounge listening to vaughan williams & looking over to the
sea so much light too much light too much of it coming in coming in at me white
and cold numbing my eyes and the SEA that great old cold see pushing clawing
gnawing at the cliffs eating its way through some nights you can hear the cliffs
fall crumble and crash

as if CTHULHU wakes he stirs and thrashes the water waves his tentacles making waves hahaha i don't really believe it THE OLD ONES i don't believe it someone has hidden prawns in my curtain rail I think

but know the sea is going to get me i don't know where to go i look in the book the book for clues youl think im cracked a mde up book no such thing as the NECRONOMICON now it's not its name let's put it to the prop making the prop the prop the necronomicon crop pop prop I mustn't get angry and I mustn't get scared im making all this stuff its surrounding me the pictures on the walls the pictures I've made the pictures from the book that castaigne sent me he says he's not sending me anything more but more keeps coming if not him then WHO??? who is sending me the pages now????

I want it to stop i have enough i don't want to read see anymore of it I don't want to read anymoreofit the first pages he sent I don't know what no i don't know what language is written in i asked him this no one knows perhaps some lost middle eastern language but the pages but its new set of pages he sensed the clear i understand them better I CAN READ IT NOW i go back to the first pages he sent and i can read them now all starting to make sense but it's not a sense I want to make I DON'T WANT TO UNDERSTAND IT insinuated itself into my mind its poisoning me making me made out everything doubt myself doubt everything doubt the world doubt everyone i meet doubt you

I mean don't get me wrong im not going crazy im really not starting to believe that tentacled beings the old ones the old gods cthulhu and his gang of ancient pensioners are going to come crawling out of the waves like deformed crab creatures crossword squid whales and octopus basatan and the mi-go

dunwich

you know there's a lot of villages out there sank under the waves hundreds of years ago you know the legend you can hear the church bells ringing did I tell you that???? did lovecraft base his story on that the dunwich horror that where he got the name from the horror of drowning of being submerged I feel it sometimes as if im drowning on dry land in my bed cant go to bed for fear of drowning

i try not to blame you i do i really do but you and the director and Alex the director you the two of you got me into this i think sometimes i try not to think it but sometimes i think you did it DELIBERATELY you spoke to doctor archer lovecraft said YOG-SOTHOTH moves backwards and forwards in time in space and that every magician every wizard and sorcerer every witch in the world was just yog-sothoth passing through on one of his passages like a future electron or a positron sometimes I think I know I shouldn't think I think I think I think I think you and alex your your your magicians positively and negatively charged but i know your not it's just im not safe here

they're upstairs they're upstairs again I can hear them I don't know how many of them are maybe there's only one of them can hear him walking around walking walking walking clump clump clump WHAT ARE THEY DOING UP THERE????and the sea sounds closer every day as if the sea levels are rising minute by minute inch by inch foot by foot the waves they just hammer one after the other like some great machine thump thump thump thump thump thump the footsteps the waves the waves the footsteps I can't sleep fingers won't work three days and nights ive been awake now I wish I could think straight

who will save me who will save the boy

the drowning boy

. . . .

Sent - iCloud 2 May 2024 at 07.45

Christina Marx
RE: Are you OK?
To: Scott Crompton

Scott,

I've tried to call you. I tried calling first thing. Maybe you're asleep. I notice you sent your email in the middle of the night. Looking back, I've noticed the times on all of them. Do you never go to bed?

I'm sorry. I don't understand half of what you said. I don't know where to start. I don't understand about the people upstairs walking around. Have you been up to look? It's probably just the wind banging a window.

Listen, there's nothing I can say here. There's too much to process. Please just call me. We can talk. As you say, things are better if you talk. I think I should come down to visit you. Can you give me your address?

Love

Christina xxx

. . . .

From: Scott Crompton
Date: Thurs, 2 May 2024 at 14:44
Subject: Are you OK?
To: Christina Marx

I live in a bungalow
you dont need to know where it is

. . . .

From: Amanda Westwood
Date: Fri, 3 May 2024 at 09:36
Subject: reaching out

To: Christina Marx

Hello Christina

I'm sorry for emailing you out of the blue like this. You don't know me. I'm a neighbour of Scott Crompton here in Suffolk. Scott has mentioned your name to me several times and mentioned that you were a production designer. I looked you up on the Internet and managed to get this email address from your website. If I have the wrong Christina Marx, please forgive me and ignore this email.

If I have the right Christina Marx, then I wonder if you could perhaps let me know that this has got to you. I never can trust emails on websites and don't know if they're always monitored. But, as I say, if you do get this message, I would be very grateful if you could call me. As I say, I'm a neighbour of Scott's, one of the few neighbours left in the village. I expect Scott has told you that we are all slowly falling into the sea. I knew Scott a little from before. He used to come and look after his mum towards the end, when she wasn't well and really struggling with her dementia. Since then, the cottage had been deserted for a long while. The ones on the cliff road are really not at all safe. When Scott first came back here, I used to see him out and about in the shop and the little cafe. The pub long ago closed down. He seemed preoccupied, wrapped up in his own thoughts, but he would still say 'hello' and chat. Lately, though, he's become increasingly, I would say, agitated. I know he had an accident. We talked about that a little bit. But he's become increasingly distant and reclusive. Then yesterday I was walking the dog in the evening, and there were loud noises coming from his bungalow, all sorts of crashing and banging. I knocked on the door to check that he was alright, and he assured me that everything was fine, but I could see that he was very distracted. It was clear that he didn't want me to come into the house, so I asked if he wanted to join me on a walk along the coastal path. It's quite set back from the cliffs now. We can't get too close and every year the path is moved further back.

He said he'd like to join me as he needed some fresh air to clear his head. We talked as we walked. Actually, he talked, and I listened. I'm afraid he came across as being very unwell, paranoid and obsessive. He kept looking fearfully at the sea as if he expected something to come out of it. I have a sister who suffers from bipolar disorder and Scott very much reminded me of her when she's in one of her manic phases. I don't believe Scott is bipolar, he's never mentioned it, but it's possible that he hasn't fully recovered from his accident. He mentioned that he had been in a mental hospital for several weeks but scoffed at his treatment and said that the doctor who looked after him was a charlatan and should be struck off. Scott insisted that there was absolutely nothing wrong with him. As I say, he also mentioned you a few times. For the most part, he told me how much he respected you and relied on you, but then sometimes a change would come over him and he seemed to be blaming you for some unnamed slight or insult, as if you had done him wrong in some way. If I hadn't known otherwise, I might have thought he was talking about more than one person. As I say, one moment he was singing your praises, telling me how you had saved him, and the next he was saying it was your fault that he was in a bit of a pickle now. That you had poisoned him in some way. He also went on about somebody who I think is called Henry or Harold Chastain. I don't know how he spells his name, but Scott said the two of you had been in league against him. Even at one point suggesting that this Chastain character was some sort of pseudonym of yours.

Oh gosh. Sorry for such a long rambling message, but I thought I ought to tell you the way Scott's mind is working. I was considering talking to someone, a doctor, or even contacting the police just to warn them, but I don't want to get him into any trouble, and I felt that if he was visited by someone in authority it might tip him further over the brink. As I say, he seemed very paranoid and unstable, on edge. On what I would describe as a hair trigger. I wonder if you, as a friend who will know him better and know his medical history a bit better, might know the best thing to do?

Yours,

Amanda Westwood

A. Westwood

Chair: Alfkethill Village Soc.

Alfkethill. Suffolk

. . . .

Sent - iCloud 3 May 2024 at 19.17

Christina Marx

Re: a big favour

To: Daniel Isaacs

Hi Danny, hope all is well with you.

I'll be brief. Are you still based in Diss? I know you used to have your workshop
there, but you may have moved. Just I need someone to do a favour for me.
Do you remember Scott Crompton, the art director who had the motorcycle
accident? He's living in Suffolk – a village called Alfkethill, not too far from you
– and I need someone I trust to check in on him. He's not answering any of my
calls or replying to emails. Frustratingly, I'm stuck over in Hungary on a recce
and just can't get back for a couple of days.

If you've moved from Diss or can't help, no problem at all, but please do give me
a call when you can. I'm on the same number.

Christina

. . . .

Sent - iCloud 4 May 2024 at 18.39

Daniel Isaacs

Re: a favour

To: Christina Marx

Chris.

So, I drove down to visit Scott in Alfkethill. His nosy neighbour was right. He's not in a good place. He's become fixated on you. But I couldn't figure out what his problem was, what he thinks you've done to him. He was being very cagey. I have to say I didn't really feel safe in his presence. He was jittery and pretty incoherent. Plus there's a weird smell coming off him like someone who's spent too much time indoors by themselves, not washing or changing their clothes. There's something else to it as well, kind of a chemical smell, a bit fishy, pretty unpleasant to be honest with you. I didn't really want to spend too long with him. I know you said on the phone you wanted to visit him but really, Chris, I would advise against it. Some of the things he said about you were pretty unrepeatable to tell you the truth. I know Scott. I know he has no history of aggression or violence – except for that one incident with his girlfriend that got him sectioned after his accident – but, as I say, he's not well.

The whole house was full of drawings and paintings and models and he had something on a table in the middle of all the chaos, covered in a sheet. He was really protective of it and it was clear he didn't want me to go near it. It was all pretty out there – like a bad dream. The bungalow feels like some kind of insane art installation or one of those scary horror attractions where you walk through dark and dingy rooms and people dressed as zombies or chainsaw-wielding gimps jump out at you. The atmosphere was totally oppressive. Claustrophobic as fuck. Some of the imagery is really quite intense and some of the images were disgustingly violent. Upsetting and visceral in a way that's hard to describe. And God knows what that thing he's got on the table under that sheet is. I really don't want to think about it.

Christina, I'm serious, don't go there without someone to look after you. I can go with you if you want. I remember Scott from better times. When are you back from Hungary?

Danny

. . . .

From: Scott Crompton
Date: Tues, 7 May 2024 at 03:46
Subject: coverd in eyes
To: Christina Marx

listen bitchcunt im coming for you don't think i wont I might be outside your
house now looking at you watching you i know what your doing you and your
warlock lover alex you set me up you poisoned me and now you're sending
your spies REALLY???? that woman with the dog???? that was pathetic you
think I didn't see through it & danny isaacs that talentless wanker coming
here sniffing about the place i know what you want you want to steal the
necronomicon not pay me for all ive done youv used me as a stooge as your
familiar I know where you live christina im coming there im there I can see
you on the web on CCTV cameras I can see through them all I am 5G i can
see you christina

listen no listen
i am become mine own brother he dwelleth within me Jesus O Jesus save me
help me save me christina daughter of christ I need you cain has got into me the
book has taken control of me the music is there always there whitman's words

thou art calling me o vast rondure, swimming in space coverd all over with
visible power and beauty alternate light and day and the teeming spiritual
darkness unspeakable high processions of sun and moon and countless
stars above below the manifold grass and waters with inscrutable purpose
some hidden prophetic intention now first it seems my thoughts begin to
span thee

all distances of place however wide all distances of time all souls all living bodies
though they be ever so different all nations all identities that have existed or may
exist all lives and deaths all of the past present future this vast similitude spans

them and always has spanned and shall forever span them and shall compactly
hold and enclose them... yog-sothoth

time and space and death

save me christina
you cannot save me christina
save me christina
you cannot save me christina
save me christina
you cannot save me christina
i cannot save you

O THOU TRANSCENDENT NAMELESS THE FIBRE AND THE BREATH LIGHT
OF THE LIGHT SHEDDING FORTH UNIVERSES THOU CENTRE OF THEM

. . . .

Sent - iCloud 7 May 2024 at 11.17

Christina Marx
RE: coverd in eyes
To: Scott Crompton

Oh, Love. Oh, Scott,

I feel so sorry for you. I do. I so do. You're confused. So lost. I know you didn't
mean to say the things you did. I can see underneath it all what you were trying to
say, trying to tell me. You have to stop and try to sleep. I can help you, believe me.
You're still the dear sweet Scott I always knew. So passionate. So fired up by your
work. You're such a clever man. You just have to stop your mind from racing.

Just on one thing – I checked with Alex, we've looked at the accounts and the bank statements. You've been paid up to date. I promise. And the extra for your research material. If that sets your mind at rest. Stop working now. Don't do any more. You've been pushing yourself too hard. Rest, sleep, eat, go for walks, drink water. God, I know I sound pathetic, like I'm trying to be your mum. But I care deeply for you, Scott. Hold on. Help is at hand. Please just hold on.

All my love,
Christina xxx

. . . .

THE TELEGRAPH

Long stretch of coastal road and several houses fall into sea as storm batters Suffolk

Red weather warnings from the Met Office came too late as the storm developed so rapidly it gave local residents little chance to prepare.

Keith Schott 8 May 2024 • 4.36pm

People are being warned to stay away from a mile-long stretch of the Suffolk coast around the village of Alfkethill, after a substantial chunk of land collapsed onto the beach during powerful storms overnight that swept sea defences aside, brought down power lines and destroyed five properties.

After a tranquil, spring day of clear skies and calm seas, residents of Alfkethill turned in for the night with no inkling of the perfect storm that was brewing far out in the North Sea. But by four in the morning winds were raging at over 90mph and the storm-whipped sea surged to an unprecedented high tide.

When power lines were downed the sudden loss of electricity plunged the area into total darkness as water crashed into many homes in the village.

Alfkethill, which is home to around 200 people, has suffered from severe coastal erosion in recent years with many properties abandoned as the cliffs continue to slip away. Only one of the houses that fell onto the beach was believed to be occupied and police are searching the ruins for bodies.

Amanda Westwood, chair of the Alfkethill village society, said she had spoken to the homeowner, a Mr Scott Crompton, only a few days ago and he had expressed concerns about erosion and sea levels.

'It's very sad for us villagers to be here watching this happen,' she told us. 'It's not nice for anyone.'

The whereabouts of Mr Crompton are not yet known.

MIRROR

Two bodies found in Suffolk house washed over cliffs in freak storm

Police are still searching the remains of a beach-front bungalow following the discovery of the bodies of a man and a woman

By Kelly-Ann Carpenter, News Reporter & Tim Winder

9 May 2024 • 10.20

Residents of Alfkethill, Suffolk, still reeling from the loss of part of their coast road and several properties during overnight storms on 7 May, were shocked to discover that the hurricane force wind and mountainous waves had taken the lives of two people when the property they were staying in collapsed onto the beach.

Most of the houses closest to the sea were abandoned and boarded up but one bungalow was still occupied. The identity of the two bodies has not yet been disclosed as the investigation is ongoing.

Det Insp Andrea McGowan told reporters: 'The conditions of the ruined property where the bodies were found means that there are going to be some delays, while we allow for meticulous forensic examination of the scene and determine who the individuals are.'

She added that the beach and cliff top would be out of bounds to the general public over the coming days.

Coastguard Pete Bierce, who has been helping with the clear up after the storm, told the Mirror: 'The house has been totally demolished. No way anybody inside when the storm took it would have stood a chance.'

It is estimated that the tide raced three metres higher than predicted and some residents who braved the intense weather conditions report seeing waves of over 80ft.

Local councillor Andy Forrester told us 'I've never seen anything like it. It's almost as if the sea was alive, like some great monster attacking the shoreline. It sounded

48

like a war zone. I've never been so terrified in my life. I really feel for those poor souls trapped in that building.'

Since the start of October, at least 1.8 metres (6ft) of the Alfkethill dune has been lost to the sea – and it's feared that after the events of 7 May worse is to come.

Coastal erosion is a natural process as waves pound beaches all along England's eastern coastline, but stronger storms and bigger waves are striking fear in local residents like never before. These are the first reported deaths in the area due to collapsing cliffs.

. . . .

METRO

Home>News>UK

Mystery of dead bodies found in ruined beach house after storm devastates coastal village

Sara Briggs

Published May 10, 2024, 1.34pm

Police are treating the deaths of a man and woman discovered under the wreckage of the bungalow as suspicious.

Police in Alfkethill, Suffolk, have released the names of two people found dead on Wednesday morning in the hope that someone might be able to help them piece together events leading up to the tragedy that took place on the night of May 7th.

They are 39-year-old Christina Marx, a production designer for films and TV, who lived in Oxford, and Daniel Isaacs, 45, a carpenter and scenery construction manager from Diss.

This morning Police released this statement. 'Wounds sustained by these two individuals are not consistent with what you would expect to find if they were the result of accidental damage caused by the collapse of the house. We believe a person or persons, as yet unknown, caused the injuries to both parties that led to their deaths, before the building was demolished.'

The owner of the house, Mr Scott Crompton, who also worked in the film and television industry, has been missing since the night of the storm. There is speculation that his body may have been washed out to sea.

Police are urging anyone with any information to come forward and help them with their enquiries. And that if Mr Crompton is still alive, he should make himself known to them at the earliest opportunity.

. . . .

THE SUN

FEATURE

News > UK News

WHERE IS HE? Weird loner is chief suspect in 'Bodies On The Beach' double murder investigation

Tom Keaton
Published: 23:38, 12 May 2024

At first police assumed that the two bodies found in the ruins of a clifftop bungalow that had collapsed onto the beach at Alfkethill in Suffolk were victims of the freak storm that ripped the village apart on Wednesday night. But closer investigation by the forensics team has revealed that the man and woman had been brutally murdered.

The Sun Online looks at the chilling things we know so far and asks 5 key questions.

WHO WAS THE OWNER OF THE DEATHTRAP COTTAGE?

Scott Crompton, the man who had been living in Sea View Cottage has been described by locals as a 'weird loner'. The property had previously belonged to his mother. Crompton, who works in TV and films, had only moved into it recently, but in the short time he had been there he had aroused the suspicions of local residents.

He worked all hours of the day and night listening to strange music at a deafening volume, and could often be heard shouting and screaming. Locals had commented on the amount of bottles and cans he'd been leaving out for recycling in the days leading up to the storm, and there were reports of him behaving in a drunken manner around the village.

One resident, who preferred not to be named, said Crompton 'Gave off a weird vibe and smelled like a tramp.'

WHERE IS SCOTT CROMPTON?

Crompton, who spent some time in a mental hospital following a motorbike accident in 2019, has completely disappeared. Police are working on the assumption that his body was washed out to sea in the storm. But they have stressed that if anybody has any information about him, or what exactly happened on the night of 7th May 2024, they should get in touch. They are warning members of the public, however, not to approach him as he is potentially highly dangerous.

DOUBLE MURDER – BUT WHAT IS MOTIVE?

The murder victims have been identified as Daniel Isaacs and Christina Marx. Mr Isaacs, a set builder for the film industry, died from repeated blows to the head with a blunt object. Police have described it as a savage and unrelenting attack. Miss Marx, a successful and attractive set designer who has worked on movies starring Daniel Radcliffe, Keira Knightley and Robert Downey Jnr, suffered lacerations and puncture wounds that could only have come from a sustained assault by a sharp blade. *The Sun* has learned that the pattern of the wounds were not random and show signs of being arranged in a ritual manner.

Locals have described the crime scene as 'eerie and disturbing'. Before the police cordoned off the seafront, drawings and paintings, believed to have been made by Mr Crompton, were found strewn across the beach. They apparently showed evidence of Satanism and black magic rituals.

WHY DID THE HOUSE FALL INTO THE SEA?
Sea View Cottage was one of five properties that slipped over the cliff during the storm. It was built in the 1950s when the area was a popular seaside destination. Originally it was nearly 100 metres from the cliffs and Scott Crompton's mother had been delighted by 'the best view in Suffolk.' All of the other properties on Sancroft Road were abandoned and vandalised. One local resident told *The Sun* that 'Crompton was insane to move back into that place. It was an accident waiting to happen. But then, judging by what's happened, it looks like he was insane.'

HOW SCARED SHOULD WE BE THAT SCOTT CROMPTON HAS NOT BEEN FOUND?
The chilling discovery of two murder victims underneath the ruins of Crompton's house sent shock waves through the close-knit community of Alfkethill. Already suspicious of Crompton, some have shared with us that they had been scared of the eccentric loner. 'Not only do we have the aftermath of the storm to contend with,' said Donald Livesey, owner of the small village shop, 'but we also have the shadow of this man stalking us. I wouldn't be surprised if this wasn't the end for Alfkethill.'

. . . .

My brain reeled as I saw the mighty walls rushing asunder – there was a long tumultuous shouting sound like the voice of a thousand waters – and the deep and dank tarn at my feet closed sullenly and silently over the fragments of the 'House of Usher.'

Edgar Allan Poe – 'The Fall of the House of Usher'.

FOOTNOTES

A.K. BENEDICT

The college library was up three flights of stairs but felt like four. Aisling, out of breath by the second flight, plonked herself, wheezing, on the window seat, bag of books at her feet. The mullioned window ballooned out as if centuries of thoughts pressed their faces to the glass, wishing for release.

Outside, a weeping willow dipped its tresses in the Cam. The wind swished them up, shampoo ad style. A crow flew by, craaking. Huffing on her blue inhaler, Aisling watched two students walking over the bridge, huddled together. Loneliness pinged inside her.[1]

Aisling was long used to being unnoticed. People often seemed surprised to find her in a room she had been in for hours. No one asked her for her help, or for her love. Before she came to Cambridge for her doctorate, Aisling's aunt[2] had told her that this was the time she'd find her tribe. A month in, however, Aisling had scuttled between the city's

---

1. Loneliness is less of a pang than a ping, a high-pitched keen under the skin; the 'ee' a stretched fake smile, the 'ih' of the last gin. A pang is too round a sound for the ice and a slice that unsought alienation brings.
2. Auntie Maeve, who had a fifty-three-year-old sourdough starter, three parrots, and a moustache that resisted waxing, plucking and hair removal cream.

libraries, her set,[3] and the staircase gyp room,[4] without once making an enriched connection.

As Aisling stood, readying herself for the last staircase, a woman of no fixed age loomed up the stairs. She turned towards Aisling with her whole body, as if her spine was clamped. Dressed entirely in black leather, when the woman raised her bowler hat she resembled an ambulatory exclamation mark.[5] The only skin showing was the parchment of her face. 'You're late.'

Aisling looked around as if the woman could be talking to someone else. 'I think you have the wrong person. I'm just returning some books.'

'You are Aisling O'Connor, otherwise known as Ash. We were due to convene at two o'clock and, as it is gone half past, you are overdue.'

Aisling's brain stammered. 'I'm sorry, I didn't know.'

Bridget's gold embossed eyes flashed. 'Your ignorance is not an excuse.'

'Are you my new supervisor?'

'You could call me that, but I'd rather you called me Bridget. Now, follow me.' Bridget loped up the stairs, two at a time. Her legs seemed too long for her body.

Aisling hesitated for one moment, then did as she was bid.

Inside the library, Bridget sent dust motes scattering as she swept past students bent over tables like desk lamps. Aisling scurried after her, book bag banging against her shins. A sense of excitement was opening inside her. For once, she didn't know what was happening.

Bridget snaked through the stacks. At the far end of the library, in the history reading room, she pressed a green button on the wall, and a leather-lined panel swung back.

She stepped into a dark room, lit by candles. 'This is your office

3. Some of the older Cambridge and Oxford colleges have 'sets' – student accommodation of two connecting rooms, study area, and bedroom. Draughts through ancient windows often make sets fucking freezing.
4. A gyp room is a basic kitchen in Cambridge student accommodation, in Aisling's case it served all six 'sets' of rooms around Staircase C in the college's Great Court. Aisling made soda bread and brioche in this kitchen, hoping that she would befriend one of the other residents, even leaving out loaves on the countertop with a calligraphed sign – *please help yourself!* – *Aisling, Set 4*, x. Her bread, like her, remained untouched.
5. Bridget wore a high neck shirt, slim-legged trousers, black gloves, boots, bowler, and a long coat that skimmed the floor – all in soft, black leather.

from now on.' A lamp came on, bent over the desk like a student, but brighter.

'My office?' Aisling took in the room: the bookshelves; the smells;[6] the oval rug spiralled with symbols; the carved desk; three armchairs by an open, lit fire; a kitchenette in the corner; a locked cabinet; and the brass-domed ceiling that reflected the swaying flames.

Bridget strode to the centre desk and, after pulling back the chair, indicated that Aisling should sit. 'You're the apprentice Inscriber.' The capitalisation of the initial 'I' was clear in her voice.

Aisling settled into the chair, which was more comfortable than it looked. 'I am? What does that mean?'

'In exchange for a financial sum that will, to you, seem beyond sense, you will assume a role passed between women scholars for centuries. We share the role for now but when you're ready, and I have completed my role, you will fully take over.'

Bridget slid a key from her pocket and, on unlocking the cabinet, manoeuvred a large book from its depths. She held it to her chest as if letting it rest and get its first breath. Bound in dark leather, they looked like mother and daughter.

Aisling, feeling like she was intruding, looked down at her desk, tracing the grain in the wood with her finger.

Bridget slowly held out the book and placed it in front of Aisling. 'This is *The Cailleach*.' Her voice was soft, caressing each vowel and kissing each consonant. Her eyes shone with tears that seemed green in that light.

Curiosity twanged in Aisling.[7] She reached without thinking for the book, but Bridget slammed a cow-skin fist down on Aisling's hand.

'You must take the Inscriber's Oath before you make contact with *The Cailleach*.' Bridget clamped her hand round Aisling's and bent back her

---

6. Smoke; waning wax; dark chocolate; and Bridget's neroli, labdanum and laudanum perfume.
7. Now curiosity *is* a pang. It has the round sound of cymbals that reverberate through the body and into physical action; the sonic depth of an ache that cancers bones and haunted houses the heart.

arm, lifting Aisling's palm to the domed ceiling. 'Say after me: "I, Aisling Robin O'Connor".'

'I, Aisling Robin O'Connor.'

'Swear allegiance to the goddesses, to—'

'But I'm agnost—'

'To the faithful interpretation of their word,' Bridget continued, ignoring Aisling, 'and to the Sistership of Inscribers that turns from one woman to another across time.'

The book seemed to slowly pulse, as if a lethargic heart was hidden within. Fighting the urge to look inside, Aisling clung to her reason. 'I don't even know what I'm agreeing to.'

Bridget simply repeated the oath, and then again at every one of Aisling's objections. Aisling felt her weak arguments melt like a tallow candle. She had never felt so compelled to do anything, or be anyone. She longed to hold the words in her mouth.

'This is what you were born for,' Bridget said, with a kindness that made Aisling want to cry. 'You've never felt important before, I know, Cerridwen told me. But that is because you have never had such purpose. Now, you are fulfilling not just your own potential, but a prophecy.' As she spoke, Bridget winced, gloved hand holding onto her shoulder.

'Are you okay?'

'I will be. Are you ready to break cover and emerge from your static life?'

The path was already written in her brain, and as she said the words, it was as if they were wrapping a jacket around her, binding her together. Giving her the spine she'd never had.

'I am.'

Bridget almost smiled, one sharp tooth showing. 'Now you are fit to hold *The Cailleach*, and may it hold you forever.'

As Aisling touched the cover, both she and the book began to shiver.

'I'll leave you to get acquainted.' Bridget loped to the door.

'But what am I supposed to do?' Aisling asked, self-soothing by stroking the book's frontispiece.

'Your thesis is on the *Pythia*, correct?'[8]

Aisling nodded.

'Then you are familiar with the process of prophecy. You will be the medium for the goddess that chooses you.'

'I research it, I don't *do* it.'

Bridget bent over at the waist, creaking, to place her face near Aisling's. A tattoo twisted up from under her leather collar and stopped just under her earlobe. Aisling wondered how far the tattoo travelled beneath the clothes. 'Time to stop reading and writing,' she whispered, snapping back up, then turning away.

'But how do I—'

'*The Cailleach* will tell you, if you ask it nicely,' Bridget called back as she left the room. The leather panel slid into place, and it was as if no door, or library beyond it, had ever existed.

Aisling thought she'd be panicked at being left alone, in a silence so thick it rivalled the O.E.D.,[9] but instead she was as calm as if she'd slipped into the chapel during evensong. Her breath was slow and even, no wheezing.

Opening the manuscript, she found it was a series of books, handwritten by different women. Each was dedicated to a Celtic goddess and carried its own scent.[10] Every section was written on different vellum – some of the paper was so soft it could be creased with a nail; another type of paper was dark brown with indigo ink; one book was made from paper so thin and brittle it was like crispbread.

Some of the writing was so faded it could hardly be read, even with the magnifier Aisling found on the desk. A few pages were so cracked that words fell into deep ravines; more were torn, sentences lost or held together only by glue and wax paper. Most of the books, however, were

---

8. The Pythia was the high priestess of the Delphic Oracle at the Temple of Apollo in Delphi. The priestess made prophecies, ostensibly given to her by the god Apollo, for those who visited the temple.

9. *The Oxford English Dictionary* is a twenty volume, 21,728 paged authority on a millennia of English language development. A good lunchtime for Aisling as a teenager would be sitting in the corner of the school library with volume 1 on her lap as she fed on 'A-Bazouki'.

10. Damana's scent was a jammy rose that lingered in the nose; Aine was vanilla, pear and cinnamon; Epona sniffed of daffodils, bread, hay, and horse breath...

legible, containing the accounts of previous Inscribers and those to whom they had provided prophecies. Predictions ranged from the wild to the mundane,[11] but there was no indication as to what Aisling should do next.

The panel in the wall careered to one side, and a woman with long, curly hair stumbled in. 'Are you the Inscriber?' she asked. The whites of her eyes were sunset with red, her foundation showed the path her tears had taken.

Aisling sat the woman down in an armchair. 'What's your name?' she asked, placing another log from the basket onto the fire.

'Felicity. I'm here to ask about—' Stopping, she put her hand over her mouth. Her cuticles were nibbled back into raw pink strips. 'I'm not supposed to say, it's giving you too much information.'

A tannin-strong urge to stand up and run out of the room swept over Aisling. She didn't have to be here, in fact, she didn't know how she'd even ended up in this situation. 'I'm sorry,' she began to say on the way to the door, then Felicity blinked out four more fat tears. Her breath came in laddered blocks as if holding back sobs.

Aisling walked over to the mini kitchen. 'Can I get you a cup of tea, Felicity?'

'Yes, please. Strong, milk, three sugars. Are you going to read the leaves?'

'No. At least I don't think so.' Aisling hoped that Felicity wouldn't notice her hands trembling as she filled the kettle and readied the cups. 'Did Bridget tell you about me?'

Felicity frowned. 'Who's Bridget? I just got an email telling me to come to the back of the library, press the button, and wait for the Inscriber to divine an answer to my question.'

Teacups full on the side table, biscuits piled on a plate, Aisling sat with Felicity by the fire. *The Cailleach* lay on her lap.

Felicity swallowed. 'What happens now?'

Aisling placed her hands on *The Cailleach*, feeling the curve of the 'C'.

---

11. The wild – 'Elizabeth Verspringen will marry a man with a cock larger than his arm. Their children will not be his, but neither is his cock' – Rhiannon: 3 v. 7. The mundane – 'India McMahon will think she has run out of clean underwear on 25th April, but there is a spare pair of knickers under the dog food' – Machu: 2 v. 19.

Please help me, she silently asked it. *I want to help this woman, but I don't know what to do.*

The book quivered under her fingers.

The fire sparked red and purple.

Sudden incense spiced and thickened the air.[12] It was coming from Aisling's mouth.

She reared back, her spine lengthening, her shoulders broadening. Her hair grew, glinting red and gold in the firelight. Above, the brass dome blazed.

Power volted through Aisling. She breathed out smoke that came from somewhere so vast she could only feel the scalding edges of its beginnings.

'Oh fuck,' Felicity said, curling back into the seat. 'What are you?'

'You are here to ask me if you will ever have another child,' Aisling said, but recognised neither her voice nor its source. 'As your last babies died inside you. You want me to release you from the pain you carry as you carried them.'

Felicity doubled over, keening. 'Please. Help me.'

Pity coursed through Aisling, banked by mountains that looked down on all. 'You will have your babies, but you will have to fight. I know of war, and I know of fertility, this is what the land has allowed me.' Aisling stood, her limbs strong and long as she held *The Cailleach* up to the dome. Her arm itched as if being scratched, as if it could do magic.

'What do I do? How do I fight?'

'You must rid yourself of the man you are with. Leave him, kill him, it matters not to me. It will take all your resolve and strength but do this and you will be rewarded with what you long for, and they will be rewarded by not having a cunt as a father.'

Felicity laughed, then covered her mouth, then laughed again. She stood, hand on her stomach. Her eyes carried a spark of the fire.

Aisling collapsed back in the chair, the last of the smoke bellowed out of her. All the power she'd felt had gone, all that remained of the experience was the itch on her arm. She pulled back her sleeve. '*...not having a cunt as*

---

12. An incense of red musk, frankincense, clove, plum, and dragon's blood.

a father' she read. Her forearm was etched with the fortune she had just told.

The itch had gone by the time she went to bed that night. Sleep, though, did not come. It was too dull compared to what she had felt, the colours she had heard when the prophecy came through.[13] Her body had felt sound, had smelled music, had been alive in a way that made her dead before and after. Felicity had hugged her with such force and love, thanked her with everything she had. Aisling had made that happen.

Aisling was ready when the next fortune seeker came, and then the next. Rachel Downey sought counsel for a lost love, Billy Ren a lost mother, Unwin Ridgeback a lost plague pit. All found them, with the goddess's, and Aisling's, blessing and help.[14]

Money flowed towards her as words cascaded through. And all that power. Aisling felt as if she flew when pelleting the goddess's thoughts, a corvid soaring over Cambridge and beyond.

The cost only seemed to be the real estate of her skin. Each prophecy inked more of her body but, as no one saw her naked, not even her if she could help it, she didn't care. She had only thoughts of love towards the source. *Who am I communing with?* she asked each time she talked to *The Cailleach. Who are you, my goddess?* The goddess, though, did not reply.

One morning, as Aisling strode into the history reading room, she stopped. Bridget was leaning against the panelled wall, fighting for breath. She was barely a slim volume, bent at the spine, lungs crackling like crumpled pages.

A student stared at her in disgust. 'Can you go somewhere else?' he said. 'I'm trying to work.'

'Get out,' Aisling told him. The goddess glared at him, through her.

Scrambling to his feet, he backed away, knocking books off a shelf. 'Sorry. Don't look at me.'

Happy to comply with his request, Aisling turned back to Bridget. Bridget's face was now almost entirely tattooed in flowing ink, words

---

13. A motet of mauve, scarlet, plum, garnet, indigo, and black.
14. Occasionally, a petitioner came that Aisling was less happy to help – such as Stewart Ridge, who was looking for his brother's will in order to inherit his house. As he had killed his brother, the goddess had bestowed Stewart with impotence, and no will.

crossing the bridge of her nose and lining her lips. One blank space was left on her right cheek.

Putting her arm round her bony, leather-bound shoulders, Aisling was about to help Bridget into the office, but Bridget stopped her.

'I just came to say goodbye,' Bridget wheezed. 'And that I am sorry.'

'Sorry? You've given me everything! Words flow through me, I channel life and love and war and peace and all that lies in between. I have never felt so strong.'

Bridget shook her head. 'I know. But you will end up like me.'

She winced, her gloved hand going to her cheek.

'But you are magnificent! How many people have you helped?'

'Hundreds.'

'And think how many more you'll help when you're better.'

'Only one more. And I can't get better.' Bridget placed her hands on top of Aisling's. 'Listen to me. You have a choice. Give up your role as priestess now and you will have a good life. You will find your person, the one you want to connect with; or you can keep going here and be your goddess's scribe.' Each word was scratched on her cheek, climbing her cheekbones. Each word made her more breathless.

'Three years, five hours and thirteen minutes from now,' she continued, 'the next Inscriber will come into the library, and you will induct her into the job. Soon after, you will meet your goddess for the first and last time.'

'And I must choose?'

'This is my last word. Sorry.' Bridget's gold eyes stilled. As the word '*Sorry*' took up the last space on her skin, Bridget collapsed onto the floor. Only Bridget wasn't there, only a tangle of leather and dust motes.

Aisling carried the clothes into her office. The only thing she knew to do was consult *The Cailleach*. Placing her hands on the cover, Aisling silently said, *Please, Goddess, show me what all this means*.

The book opened of its own accord and flicked through its pages to the last segment. Aisling hadn't seen this part before. '*The Book of Cerridwen*'. The lettering was edged with gold leaf, the paper thin, and it smelled of neroli and labdanum, leather and laudanum. The last page, curved up as if written over a hillock, ended with '*This is my last word. Sorry.*'

Bridget had scribed Cerridwen's words, and her own skin was now part of the book. She had used her last piece of skin to warn Aisling of her fate.

Aisling backed away from the manuscript. This was where she made a choice. Bridget had said she would get what she had always wanted, a person to love and connect with. Or she could stay and inscribe until she was paper.

She thought of a life beyond the library and its books, where her skin could touch other skin, and live a life before she died.

The goddess breathed incense inside Aisling and raged at the thought of losing her. 'You are mine.'

The panel slid back, and a woman entered. 'Help me, please,' she said.

The fire sparked red and purple.

'Sit down, please,' Aisling said, and wondered which piece of her skin was next.[15]

---

15. This extract is taken from The Morrigan, last book of *The Cailleach*.

THE HOUSE WITCH

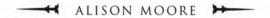

ALISON MOORE

'*Human beings must love something, and, in the dearth of worthier objects of affection, I contrived to find a pleasure in loving and cherishing a faded graven image.*'

Charlotte Brontë
Jane Eyre

She had a fantasy. She imagined a man – a handsome colleague, a friend – no one she knew in real life; she imagined herself and this man somewhere nice, nowhere that really existed, somewhere snug like a public house, an olde worlde inn with an open fire, or somewhere discreet like a private members' club, though she had never been inside one and didn't really know what they were like, or a bistro, she thought, something like that, though she wasn't quite sure what it meant. She imagined a pleasant hour, clever conversation; she pictured them laughing, herself and this friend, or something more than a friend – it was always a man and, though he didn't always look the same, he was always good-looking; and she herself looked smart, poised, happy.

It wasn't like that though. The office in which she'd been working for nearly a month was on the outskirts of the city, where there was not a lot of choice. There were pubs, but no one had asked her to go to one, and she hadn't asked them either. Besides, she didn't really know the area, didn't know the pubs; she'd looked into one on the day of her interview, but when she opened the door, everything went quiet, and the interior was very small, and she hadn't wanted to go in. She was yet to discover a private members' club, and there was nothing that called itself a bistro.

The office building had a staffroom, and at lunchtime some people went there. They sat beneath the fluorescent light, in the hum of electricity, eating their sandwiches and their microwaved soups and bad-mouthing the boss. They said to her, 'What are you reading, Ruth?' and, 'Anything good?' and, 'You're quiet.'

She looked up at the faces hanging over her, with their harshly lit skin, their droops and wrinkles; they were waiting. She said, 'It's about a man who—' It was hard to say, though, what it was about. She looked back down at the book lying open on her lap, waiting for her thoughts to collect, for the answer to come. She said, 'It's good, I think.'

'It sounds it,' said someone, and someone else laughed.

The artificial light gave her a headache. There was a window, but it faced a wall. The spider plants on the sill looked sickly, yellow.

————◆————

It had belonged to her mother, who had been gone for years. Ruth remembered the handsome book in her mother's hands; it had seemed to live there. She remembered it being carried around the house and held on her mother's lap. And yet it had seemed natural when, in the wake of her mother's departure, Ruth found the book in her own bedroom, left behind like a goodbye note.

It was harder and harder to remember what her mother had looked like. Ruth could recall her mother's clothes, and the way she stood, the way she moved, and even her smell, but she wanted a face, with all its specific details and particular expressions. It was gone though. It had been cut, neatly, from their family photographs. Ruth could recall her mother sitting at her bedside with a storybook, perhaps a fairy tale – she could see her mother's knees, and the freckles on her forearms, and her long hair hanging loose – but her voice, too, was lost.

Ruth could more vividly picture the man her mother had gone to and was inclined to forget that she had never actually met him.

On what had seemed like an ordinary morning, her mother had driven away in the family estate car, with the sunlight bouncing off it. They only understood later that she would not be coming back.

It was just the three of them now – Ruth and her younger sister and their father – apart from the extended family: there were plenty of cousins, even if they no longer saw them.

They had a new, or new to them, somewhat smaller family car, which Ruth and her father shared, at least in theory; she never saw her father driving these days. He rarely went out and never went far. He worked from home. He had what he called his office at one end of the dining table. He had online meetings and, in the evenings, online game nights with old friends; there was a constant gallery of faces on his laptop screen.

Almost anywhere Ruth's sister might need or want to go was within walking distance: she walked herself to and from school and did not even need to cross the road; she walked to and from Girl Guides and the local park and the swimming pool. She was not allowed to stay out late. 'Not yet,' said their father, who liked her home before dusk. 'When you're older, you can make your own decisions.'

Ruth was not so much older than her sister, but sometimes she felt like her mother. She got her up on school mornings, made her breakfast and packed her lunch, combed the knots from her hair. 'Don't forget to brush your teeth,' she said as she headed out, leaving her sister and their father at the breakfast table, and driving off in the family car, which she increasingly thought of as *her* car.

There was a car park behind the office building, but you had to get there early or you would find there was no place for you. From time to time, they took away a space or two – they were widening the road – so it was like musical chairs. She had what she thought of as *her* parking place, though it did not belong to her. There was nothing special about it – it looked out over a stretch of wasteland – but she'd chosen it anyway. Sometimes, by the time she arrived, her space was already taken, and she had to park elsewhere. It made her whole day feel wrong.

Ruth locked her car and crossed the car park, which lay, at this hour, in the shadow of the office building. She worked on the ground floor, in a long, open-plan office. She was not the first one there: walking the length of the room to her station, she was flanked by half-asleep and washed-out faces with unfocused eyes. The coffee machine hummed and beeped like life support.

She put her bag under her desk and logged in. Her work was not very interesting, but it was easy enough, data entry, tracking the usage of public buildings and community facilities – swimming pools, libraries, art galleries, museums. The footfall in some of these places was so low it hardly seemed worth paying someone to open up, to turn on the lights, and she wondered what would happen to them, if they would be allowed to continue, unvisited, or if they would be closed down. And if they were closed down, she wondered what would happen to the art, the artefacts and the relics, the collections, whether they would go elsewhere or be stored somewhere or what. If there was nowhere for them to go, would they just be kept in storage forever? Perhaps someone like her would keep a record on a computer, so that they would not be lost.

She supposed that, in due course, this work – her work – would become automated; she would become redundant. In the meantime, it was better than nothing.

She spent the morning filling in spreadsheets, entering figures into their cells, aware of her bag nudging her feet while she clock-watched. She should have put her sandwich in the fridge, but she did not like going into the staffroom, with its unnatural light and sickly spider plants and constant buzzing. There were days when, unable to face spending her lunch hour in there, she did not take a lunch break at all.

It was her view of the car park that made her think of eating her lunch out there. When the lunch hour arrived, she fetched her bag from beneath her desk, went out to the car park and got into her car. The sun was on this side of the building now. It was almost midsummer, and already, just after midday, it was uncomfortably hot. Eating her chicken sandwich, she thought of her sister, in the school dining hall, eating the same sandwich.

Startled by a looming shape in her peripheral vision, a change in the light, she looked up and saw Carol, close up, her face framed by the window. Carol was in data entry too, doing similar work to Ruth, but she had been there much longer; she was like a permanent fixture. Ruth could imagine nothing worse than being stuck for years in a dead-end position.

She was waiting. Ruth wound her window down and Carol said, 'Here you are,' *as if I were a child,* thought Ruth, *wandering off without permission.* 'What are you *doing* out here?' she asked, as if it might be something illicit or indecent. 'It's too hot to be sitting in your car,' said Carol, as if Ruth were a baby or a dog. Carol had done Ruth's induction and showed an interest in her well-being. 'It's going to be awful by the end of the day. By home time, you'll be in an oven.'

'Yes,' said Ruth.

'What's your book about?'

Ruth looked down at the book in her hands. 'It's about a house which—' she began before pausing, struggling to say exactly.

'A house witch? What's a house witch? Oh my god, it's so hot. Don't tell me what it's about, I might read it after you. You know the staffroom has air conditioning, don't you?' Ruth did know; it would be icy in there, humming like an old fridge. Carol stood up straight and looked towards the office building. 'I'm going back in,' she said. 'Don't stay too long, you'll cook.'

Ruth watched Carol, in her rear-view mirror, retreating to the shelter of the office building, and returned to her book.

—◆—

The upper floors of the office building were occupied by other departments – Accounts, Human Resources, Management – and on occasion Ruth was required to go up there. If she was in a hurry, she could take the lift, but she preferred to take the stairs. She liked the exercise, stretching her legs, and she liked the view from the big window in the stairwell. She stood there for minutes at a time, looking out.

Beyond the car park and the wasteland, there was a lake, or a pond – it was hard to judge the scale and, besides, she wasn't entirely sure of the difference. Anyway, there was a body of water. It wasn't visible from the car park or from her office window, from ground level, but it appeared when she was in the stairwell, on her way to or from the upper floors, like a mirage on the horizon. She wondered how she might get to it.

She mentioned it at home, and her father said, 'We had a pond here, in our back garden. It was your mother who dug it out, or had it dug out; it was her project anyhow. But I had it filled in when you were little. You don't want a pond when you've got a little girl running around.'

'I might try to get there,' said Ruth, 'in my lunch hour.'

'You could go with a friend,' said her father. 'Have you got friends there?'

'Of course,' said Ruth.

'Have you got a boyfriend?' asked her sister.

Ruth laughed, but it sounded shrill and made her think of monkeys.

Her sister said again, 'Have you?'

'There's a man called Harry Harlow,' said Ruth. It sounded nice, that double H, and she thought of Marilyn Monroe, who'd been told that the double 'M' was a lucky omen.

'Is he your boyfriend?'

Ruth smiled. 'Perhaps I'll run away with him.' She felt the atmosphere change. She wasn't sure why she'd said it, any of it. She wasn't planning on doing anything of the sort, but now just the thought of it put a twinkle in her eye.

———◆———

In fact, when she tried, the following day, to get to the lake, or the pond, or the pool, she found it was terribly easy once she found the way. It took her a while to walk there, and – she was mindful of her allotted hour – it would take her a while to get back. The path, if you could call it a path, was so overgrown that it would not be obvious, she thought, to anyone else.

It was even hotter today, quite relentless, and she had no protection. It was blissfully quiet there, even if it was not exactly beautiful: it was no boating lake; it was no lily pond. She stood at the edge of the water, peering into the murk, looking for signs of life. She saw something moving in the shallows: a rat, just glimpsed and gone underwater.

The path that encircled this body of water would be slippery, she supposed, at times, but now, in this heat, the mud was dry and cracked. On the other side of the path, weeds had grown tall and gone to seed. There was not the slightest breeze, she realised, looking at the dandelion clocks. She would not pick one. As a child, she had been unnerved by how they devoured the hours as she blew away their seeds, another hour lost with every breath; and she had never lost her childhood fear that it was touching them that made her wet her bed.

There was a lone bench at the far end, towards which she walked. She was expecting to see a plaque – *In memory of_____ who loved it here, Rest in peace* and so on – but there was nothing like that. When she sat down to eat her sandwich, a squirrel appeared, a grey one, and she spoke to it, feeling like a Disney princess communing with the animals, like Snow White or Sleeping Beauty. She tried to feed it, although some people said you shouldn't feed grey squirrels.

Two women were walking along the path towards her. She recognised them from the office. When they reached the bench, they sat down.

'Hardly anybody knows about this place,' said one.

'It's nice,' said Ruth.

'Well,' said the woman, staring out at the expanse of stagnant water, 'it's not *nice*.'

The other woman said, 'Do you come here often?'

'No,' said Ruth, 'it's my first time.'

'Where are we anyway?'

The first woman knew: 'This is Catcher's Water.'

'Is it a lake or a pond?' asked Ruth, but no one seemed to know.

'What's the difference anyway,' asked the second woman, 'between a lake and a pond?'

'A lake is deeper.'

'How deep is this?'

No one knew.

The second woman said to Ruth, 'I like the look of your book.'

It was a very attractive book, with a worn leather cover.

'It has an unusual design.'

'Yes,' said Ruth, running her fingertips over the book's face.

The two women leaned in for a closer look.

'Is it any good?'

'Yes,' said Ruth. 'I think so.' She had read the book many times. Each time she got to the end, she started again.

'What's it about?'

'It's about a young woman,' said Ruth. She started to describe this young woman, but it was as if she were only describing herself. And there was a man, she said, who might have been her lover. She was vaguely aware that he, in her head, was conflated with her mother's lover, except that the man in the book was the same age as Ruth was now. And there was the house, a lonely old house which was in the middle of nowhere; there was a WELCOME mat, and the door was always open. It wasn't easy, Ruth told the women, to say exactly what the house was like; they didn't care to know about the house though, they wanted to know about the man.

'Is he handsome?'

'Yes,' said Ruth. 'I believe he is.' But now she wondered if it was like Mr Rochester, who she could only ever see as handsome, however many times she was told quite clearly that he was not. 'He's charming,' she said. 'Or at least captivating.' Beyond that, she was not sure – he was somehow faceless.

'We heard *you've* got a fancy man,' said the first woman.

'Are we going to meet him?' asked the second woman.

'Maybe,' said Ruth. 'Yes, I expect so.'

—◆—

'Are you coming, Ruth?'

She looked up from her work. Robin was standing beside her desk, holding his coat. 'Coming where?' she asked.

'To the pub, where else? It's payday. Come on. It's Friday! It's five to five!' He looked at her expectantly.

'Which pub?' she asked, even though she did not really know one pub from another.

'The local. Come on, we'll be there for happy hour. We can do the karaoke.'

She always went straight home. Her father would be expecting her. If she was late, he would stand at the window, waiting to see the car pull into the driveway. She had to cook their evening meal; she had to supervise homework and screen time and the brushing of teeth. But she was tempted; she was still young.

'Now or never,' said Robin, putting on his coat.

'Yes, all right then,' said Ruth. She wondered if she ought to let her father know, but she wasn't planning on being hideously late. She logged out of the system. Her sister's unsmiling face filled the screen, a passport photo set as wallpaper. It was old now; everyone asked if it was her daughter.

She shut down. Somebody switched off the coffee machine and someone else turned off the lights. Ruth put her jacket on and lifted her bag onto her shoulder. Her sister would be walking home from school around now, after one of her clubs: Spanish club or chess club or book club. Ruth had never belonged to a club and wondered if she had missed out.

Robin had gone already, and Ruth had to hurry to catch up, with him and Carol and everyone else, their boss at the front, leading the way, setting the pace. They went out into the warm afternoon, bustling along the pavement, merry in the sunshine, heads turning to look back, faces with rosy cheeks and sparkling eyes and teeth like pearls; they were shouting, 'Come on!' 'Keep up!' and 'Last one there's a rotten egg!' They were laughing and chattering like schoolchildren released from the classroom, and Ruth thought briefly of her schooldays, of walking in a crocodile and No Talking.

They could hear the music as they approached the pub, growing louder as they opened the door. Ruth was the last one in, and the door slammed shut behind her.

The pub was warm, and someone was singing and someone else joined in. They found a table big enough for them all, and Robin said, 'What are you having?'

Ruth asked for a cider, and Carol said, 'Are you still reading that?'

'She's always reading that.'

'What is it?' asked Robin.

One of the women from Catcher's Water said, 'I think it's a love story.'

'Is it a dirty book?' asked Robin. 'Are you reading a dirty book, Ruth?'

'Leave her alone,' said Carol.

The chattering was very distracting. Some of them were signing up for the karaoke, asking Ruth what she wanted to sing. The pub was full of people, full of noise, and it was too warm.

In any case, she had just found something interesting in her book. She was surprised she had never noticed it before, this description of a landscape that was just like the wasteland, and a body of water that was so like Catcher's Water, and beyond that was the house. It was like a map drawn in words. There was no biographical note – not even a publisher or publication date was given – but now it seemed the author might be local or at least had local knowledge, and perhaps there really was, past Catcher's Water, a house just like the house in the book. Ruth had thought there was nothing much out that way, but of course there had to be *something*, even if it was just more wasteland. She tried to recall the view from the window in the stairwell in the office building, but could picture nothing beyond Catcher's Water, as if the world ended there. Well, either way, she would have to go out there and look.

'Have you decided yet?' asked Robin, sliding the menu of songs across the table towards her. Someone on the little stage was singing 'Could You Be Loved'.

'I'm not staying,' said Ruth. She put on her jacket.

'You're not going already, are you?'

'Do you *have* to?' said Carol.

'Stay,' said Robin. 'Have another cider.'

Ruth thought of her father and her sister who would be expecting her home. 'I have to go,' she said as she walked to the door.

With a pleasantly softened feeling, the taste of cider lingering, the noise from the pub receding behind her, she walked towards the car park, half empty now. It was a warm evening, too warm for a jacket; she took her jacket off. It would be light for hours yet. She thought about the wasteland and Catcher's Water, and beyond that the enchanting house which was waiting for her, with the WELCOME mat out and the door standing open.

———◆———

It occurred to Ruth, as she crossed the wasteland, that all this land might be his, and at the same time she wondered vaguely what 'his' meant, who 'he' was. She felt she was failing to separate, in her mind, the author and the man in the book; they ran together, like the self who is dreaming and the self in the dream. Either way, she was going to his house. And were there not even more layers, more personas: there was the author and the narrator and the man in the book; there was the implied author, and the unreliable narrator; there was an implied reader, which made her feel as if even she, reading a story, might not be real.

Catcher's Water lay preternaturally still, showing no signs of life beneath its surface, but Ruth remembered the rat, which might be in there somewhere, or in the undergrowth nearby. A dark cloud of gnats or midges hung over the path and Ruth moved through them without breathing for what seemed like an impossibly long time.

Past the far end of Catcher's Water and the bench that was not a memorial bench, where Ruth had previously seen or at least remembered nothing, it was all fields. There was no fence, no locked gate, not even a sign saying KEEP OUT. Beyond the lush grass waiting for sheep were breathtaking acres of lavender – she might have been in France – and extensive fields of blue flax and rape and an extraordinary display of poppies which brought to mind Flanders fields: *We are the Dead. Short days ago / We lived*— She could remember no more.

She trusted – as she passed from one field to the next, through all the colours of the rainbow – that she was heading in the right direction, though there was no house in sight. She trusted the book which was guiding her. She must have walked miles, she thought, but then she looked at her watch and saw how little time had gone by.

She felt its presence before she saw it, or perhaps she saw its great shadow out of the corner of her eye. She had been looking at her feet, at her work shoes flattening the grass, treading a new path, pollen clinging to the toes. When she looked up, a lone house had appeared in the field, and the path she was treading would lead to its steps which led up to the door which stood open. Ruth felt a tug of recognition, as if she had been there before, as if she had always known this house. But of course, she reminded herself, it was because she knew the house in the book and this was the house from the book – she found herself thinking of it that way, as if the house had stepped from the book into the real world, but of course she knew that, in reality, it would be the other way around: the author had written his house into the book.

Ruth could not imagine a finer place: it was a house fit for the lord of the manor – though it might just be a bolthole – and surrounded by fields for as far as the eye could see. *Bucolic*, thought Ruth, though the word always sounded bad to her, bringing to mind colic and bubonic, pain and infection, illness and disease.

She climbed the steps and paused on the WELCOME mat. She knocked on the open door to announce her arrival but at the same time she was stepping inside, into some kind of reception room. Her footsteps were deadened by a luxurious carpet with the kind of busy pattern used in pubs to hide the dirt. The walls were hung with olde worlde things such as she'd seen displayed in pubs for decoration: obsolete farming implements and archaic medical equipment whose original purpose eluded her.

In spite of the warm day, there was a roaring fire; the room was stifling. On a table in the middle of the room, a drink was waiting to be drunk. *He might be in the very next room*, thought Ruth; *he might come in at any moment*. She felt terribly thirsty. She touched the glass, felt how warm it was. There was a bowl of salty snacks. Was this hospitality, for houseguests? There were no chairs, no seats of any kind. She would wait for him, but she didn't want to wait too long.

She took her phone from her bag. Her battery was unexpectedly low. She sent a text to her sister, saying not to wait for her, that they should eat without her.

You're not coming home?

Not now.

Did you leave me the book?

Had she?

It was in my room.

Ruth looked in her bag and saw that the book was not there, but perhaps she did not need it anymore.

What's it about?

What *was* it about? There was a lover of some kind, thought Ruth, and a beautiful house, or *was* it a beautiful house? There was a house anyway. And she remembered a lake somewhere, or a pond, or a pool, and a rat.

I guess I'll find out.

Ruth was typing her reply when her battery died.

She should make her presence known, she thought, as she made her way from the reception room into an adjacent room, going deeper into the house. This room was even hotter than the last, despite its great length, its high ceiling. Above the fireplace, where some homes, some establishments – a fine manor house or a certain type of members' club or gentlemen's club – might have hunting trophies, there was some kind of art. Ruth thought at first that she was looking at something abstract, but on closer inspection she saw that they were faces; they were like the cover of her book. And they were not only over the fireplace, they were hung on every wall. There were a great many of them – it was an extensive collection – though the room was so large, there was plenty of space for more. She wanted to touch them – she felt that if she touched them she might understand what they were – but at the same time she thought she should not. Studying them in the otherwise silent room, she could imagine herself watched by an attendant.

She was thinking she would go no further, but it seemed, in fact, she had no choice: this was all there was. The house had seemed so much bigger from the outside. Ruth had expected a living room, and maybe a library, and surely a bedroom, a kitchen, everybody had to eat. But there was nothing like that.

There was only the warm drink, the salty snack, put out like an offering. She returned to the reception room. She had always liked the idea of putting out milk and bread for hedgehogs to eat in the night, but her father had told her it would attract rats, and besides, he said, milk and bread was no good for hedgehogs; it made them ill. Ruth looked at the drink on the table. She thought of her cold cider, how refreshing it had been. She thought of Carol singing 'Bad Romance'. Ruth's throat ached with thirst. She lifted the glass and took a sip of the room-temperature drink.

Through the doorway, she could see the still-blue sky. It would be light for ages yet, but, she thought, she wouldn't wait forever.

She could see the field across which she had walked, but the path she had trodden was gone. It was difficult to get her bearings, to remember where home was. There were no landmarks to help her; there was nothing beyond the horizon.

It would be cooler out there now. She looked around for her jacket, thinking she might need it when she left, but she appeared to have lost it. *Well*, she thought, *never mind*.

She felt a presence in the room, and the lightest of touches on her bare skin, and turned to smile.

WHATEVER REMAINS AFTER YOU LEAVE ME

ERIC LAROCCA

I

It's my wedding day when I first realize that my skin starts to itch every time someone takes a picture of me.

The recognition occurs to me quite gradually over the course of the day. Of course, in my quiet, private moments I had suspected something was wrong—something I couldn't define, something I was incapable of understanding, something that lingered on the periphery of my perception and whispered to me when I wasn't fully attentive. The realization doesn't fully occur to me until one of my cousins pulls me aside and mentions how red and tender the skin on my wrist looks. I glance down, humoring her, and recognize how swollen and sensitive my flesh has become. I sense my cheeks heat red. Whether from nerves or embarrassment, I cannot be certain.

"Have you been picking at your arm?" she asks me, twisting my wrist so that she can get a better view.

I laugh nervously, shooing her away.

"Must be just—wedding day jitters," I tell her, hoping she'll release me and drop the whole thing.

My cousin, Esther, has always been overly protective of me. Naturally, her defense borders on the humiliating from time to time, but I certainly can't fault her for showing concern for her only male cousin. Her *younger* male cousin, more specifically. I especially can't criticize her fretfulness

79

when she's been so supportive of my engagement to Raul for the past seven months. Naturally, there were family members who expressed their disapproval. Their disdain had nothing to do with our queerness, but rather our swiftness to tie the knot. Some of them hurled around words like "impetuous" and "nonsensical." But Esther never wavered in her support of us. I'm not quite sure why that surprises me. After all, I know how much she cares for me, and I know she realizes how much I adore Raul.

Skin itching as another camera flashes in my direction, I pull my sleeve down to hide more of my exposed wrist. I weave through the crowd of guests bobbing back and forth on the dance floor we've assembled in the recreation hall. The music pulses with such violence and, for a moment, I wonder if I can hear the blood throbbing in my head. I'm patted on the back by an uncle I haven't seen since childhood. I'm congratulated by an aunt dressed entirely in velvet burgundy who supposedly had mixed feelings about attending the ceremony, according to Esther. After I drift through the seething crowd of guests, I arrive near the bar and realize I still can't find Raul. I've always hated formal gatherings. I especially detest the idea of wearing a suit. It feels like casketing yourself in a tiny pine box. It feels like attending your own memorial service.

Just as I'm about to skirt outside, a little boy—a distant relation from my father's side of the family—ambushes me and takes a picture with a Polaroid camera. The camera whines like a disgruntled animal and then prints out the photograph. While the little boy studies the picture, I sense the skin around my wrist curling—a terrible itch. I slide a finger beneath my sleeve and scratch myself for only a second, so I don't attract too much attention. The little boy seems to notice my scratching and furrows his eyebrows at me.

"What are you doing?" he asks.

But I don't answer him. I'm already peeling away from him and sprinting toward the door when I crash into Raul. He holds me tight, perhaps a little unsettled.

"I was looking for you," I tell him. "I have a headache. I wanted to step outside for a bit."

Raul doesn't hesitate. He loops an arm around me and together we drift outside, petals of moonlight dripping all around us like droplets of rain being poured over a bed of drowsy hydrangeas.

II

It's early in the morning. Raul and I still haven't gone to bed since we left the party. Instead, we've made love three times. I penetrated him for the very first time, and he mounted me twice until I brought him to orgasm.

As we curl up against one another, the hotel television playing muted pornography, I sense Raul soften a little. He doesn't grip me and hold me as confidently as he did when we were fucking. Of course, I suppose there's a certain level of roughness that usually accompanies lovemaking between two men; however, I've never encountered him to be so cold and distant before. I wonder if I've done something to upset him. Usually, he prefers to be the dominant one, and I can't help but wonder if I've unspooled some of his confidence by manhandling him the way I had in the passion of the moment.

"Thinking about something?" I ask him, running my fingers along the curve of his collarbone.

He forces a smile and kisses me. Then he pulls away, straightening and moving toward the bureau arranged near the doorway to the washroom.

"There's something I want to give you," he says. "I've been thinking about whether or not I should."

I wonder what he could mean. What could he possibly have for me that he's already thought twice about? I straighten, pulling the sheets up to cover myself, and I watch him as he drags out a large leather-bound book from one of the bureau drawers. He pushes the drawer closed and then creeps back toward the bed, spreading the book out in front of me. I glance at him and notice he's staring at me with such intensity, such longing. I think to ask him why he's gazing so unreservedly at me, but I don't. Instead, I tip the giant book open and peer inside. It's a collection of photographs of the two of us that Raul had printed and arranged in the transparent sleeves on each page.

I let out a surprised cry and then I begin flipping through the pages. I come across a photo of Raul and me on our very first date at the small Vietnamese restaurant where we had eaten. I turn a few more pages and I arrive at the photo we had taken on our first trip to the zoo when we posed in front of the giraffe exhibit.

"You kept all of these?" I ask him, too astonished to utter anything else.

"How could I not?" he says, taking my right hand and kissing each of my fingers.

I continue flipping through the book, admiring page after page of our photos, our most precious memories. It's not long before I realize the room is completely silent. Raul says nothing. He merely stares at me, watching me—almost as if he's waiting for me to realize something he had hidden.

"It's perfect," I tell him. "I can't believe you second guessed yourself about this."

It's then I notice how Raul's eyes lower, almost sorrowfully—the same way a doctor might address the parents of a poor child in hospice.

"There's something I want to tell you," Raul says to me, his voice starting to thin and shrivel.

I'm surprised at how somber things have quickly become. Only just a few moments ago we were wrapped in one another's arms, our firm cocks growing limp and drained of all fluid. There's something decidedly different about how Raul addresses me now. He doesn't address me as a husband— or even a lover, for that matter—but rather as someone who could save him, someone who could prevent something awful from happening to him. *What on earth could that possibly be?* I wonder to myself.

"There's something wrong?" I ask him.

Even though I ask the question, I already seem to know the answer. It's more than apparent in the way Raul's eyes avoid me, the way he nervously fumbles with his hands and the way he perspires. There certainly is something wrong with Raul—something he hasn't told me.

"I didn't want you to worry," he says to me.

But I'm already well past the state of worrying and now easing into the area of blind panic.

"Worry about what?" I ask him, grabbing his hands and forcing him to look at me.

Raul is quiet for a moment. Then he does something that surprises me. He starts to chuckle. Softly, at first. Then a bit more forcefully, as if to make certain I'm paying full attention to him.

"I want to be with you all the time," he tells me, clearly laughing at himself. "I can't bear the thought of ever being without you. I wouldn't want to live."

I press my fingers into his arm, leaving little pink bruises there. "Yes. I know."

"I'd join you in the bathroom to watch you shit if you'd let me," he says.

I'm a little surprised by his vulgarity, his crudeness, but it doesn't really bother me. I know how much he loves me and cares for me.

"What's the matter?" I ask, begging him to throw a glance in my direction.

But he won't. He keeps his attention away from me almost as if he's guarding himself, almost as if he suddenly needs to protect himself from what he loves most of all—me.

"I did something I can't undo," he tells me. "It's the only way the two of us could be together. *Really* be together, I mean."

I pull him so close to me that I begin to feel the rhythm of his heartbeat inside my own chest.

"We *are* together, darling," I remind him. "Nothing will ever change that."

Raul shakes his head, pulling away from me and smearing some dampness from his eyes.

"Have you been seeing someone else?" I ask him. "Another man?"

It's the only thing I can think of. It's the only thing that would explain his unexpectedly bizarre behavior.

"No," he tells me. "Of course not. I would never."

I relax, lowering some of my guard. At least I know he's telling me the truth.

I watch him begin to pace the length of the room, shaking his head.

"I think I'm just needlessly worrying," he says to me. "I shouldn't have said anything."

I think to put the pressure on him and ask him if he's sure, but I don't want to upset him any further. I can tell how hard this was for him to even admit.

I peel the bedsheets from me until I'm standing naked in front of him, my thigh and stomach slimed with the fluids we had emptied from one another earlier.

"I was going to take a shower," I tell him. "You want to join?"

Raul shakes his head. "I think I need a cigarette."

"I can wait," I say to him.

But he shakes his head and encourages me to go on without him. So, I obey him without much prodding.

I skirt into the bathroom and close the door behind me. Even though Raul had expressed his desire to accompany me every time I relieved myself, I've never been quite comfortable with others in the bathroom. After all, I struggle using public toilets and have always been that way since I was a child. When I finish using the toilet, I flush and climb into the shower stall. I twist the faucet and hot water sprays all over me. After I adjust the water temperature, I sniff one of the expensive-looking soap bars on the shelf and I swipe it, starting to lather myself until I'm completely covered.

As I clean myself, I think of the photobook that Raul had given me. There was such a painstaking attention to detail in the way he had presented the book to me, almost as if it were a sacred artifact uncovered at an excavation site in Jerusalem. The way he had arranged each photograph, the way in which he had lovingly labeled each picture with the appropriate event and day—it was obvious to me that he had put so much care and attention into creating the photobook. However, I can't help but recognize that there's something more sinister lingering between the pages. After all, he had delivered the book to me with such seriousness, such mournfulness. I can't help but wonder if Raul's desperately trying to tell me something.

Just as I'm about to turn off the shower faucet, I hear what sounds like a champagne bottle cork popping in the bedroom. A vulgar thud—like a heavy bag being dropped from a ledge—follows immediately after. I turn off the water, snatch a towel from the nearby rack and dry myself as quickly as possible. As I open the door, I inch out of the bathroom and into the bedroom.

"Raul?" I say. "Did something fall—?"

But there's no response. The room is silent.

I skirt around the corner and it's then that I find him—my beloved Raul, his lifeless body slouched in the leather armchair situated in the far corner of the room. He's gripping a small pistol in his right hand. The wall behind where he was seated is splattered with his blood and little bits of tissue. I stare at him blankly for a moment, my eyes going over him again and again—trying to make sense of what he had done to himself and why.

I start to scream and it's not long before there are forceful knocks on the bedroom door, voices begging me to open up. But I cannot move. Instead, I stand there, shrieking until I'm hoarse, as I regard my husband's lifeless body and all the secrets unraveling from him—the tiny wraiths of smoke whispering from between his lips like all the unsaid things he never had a chance to tell me.

III

It's nearly three weeks after Raul killed himself that I start to realize that my toes curl, tightening uncomfortably, whenever someone says, "I love you."

It's the same sort of gentle realization that arrives on the periphery of my perception just like when I noticed how my skin would itch whenever someone would take my picture. Of course, it's been several weeks since the wedding and I haven't had my picture taken in a while, so my skin is safe. However, Esther keeps checking on me now that I'm staying with her for an indefinite period of time. Her idea. Not mine.

She'll be folding laundry downstairs and quite suddenly I'll hear her bolt up the stairwell. She'll burst into the guest bedroom where I'm napping and she'll say to me, "I love you, David." I keep my feet hidden under a blanket, so she can't tell that my toes curl whenever she does this. But perhaps she can see the reluctance to answer permanently etched onto my face—the hesitation I feel whenever any loved one tells me how sorry they are for my loss and how they'll keep me in their thoughts and prayers.

In fact, in the three weeks since Raul's demise, whenever someone tells me how much they love me and how they continue to think of me, my toes curl so exaggeratedly that I wonder if they might snap in half. Esther can plainly tell that I don't wish to be disturbed for a while, so she promises to let me sleep and offers to make me tomato soup and grilled cheese when I'm hungry again. Even though I want to sleep—I yearn to sleep, to be cast away on some invisible conveyor belt in the constellations of twilight—I can't seem to close my eyes. It's as if they've been propped open with metal wires and tiny invisible filaments.

Although I know I probably shouldn't because it will upset me, I dig through my suitcase and locate the photo book that Raul had given me the same night he died. I curl onto the bed and spread the book out in front of me, flipping the cover open and gazing inside at the first page of photographs. I haven't told Esther about the photo book yet and I wonder if I ever will. It would hurt too much to talk about—a blood-splattered relic from the night everything in my life forever changed.

As I flip through pages, I notice how some of the photographs appear to be somewhat distorted—almost as if the camera lens were blurred with filth. I squint, trying to comprehend. After all, when I had first glanced at these photos on the night Raul had died, I hadn't noticed anything wrong with the quality of the pictures. In fact, they had looked clear and bright.

However, now they seem to be grainy and processed through a million filters. It frustrates me and makes me wonder if, in time, Raul's memory in my mind might dim to a mere smudge on a blurry Polaroid. I loathe to think of that and how easy it might be for me to eventually forget Raul. After all, he had loved me and cared for me so earnestly. It would be a shame to think of how I could eventually forget him or fail to conjure his likeness in the privacy of my mind.

It hurts to realize that the very thing I had depended upon—the photobook Raul had given me—won't fill the immeasurable void that he had left in his absence.

I wonder what will.

IV

It's late in July when Esther invites some of her neighborhood friends to the house for a small cookout in the backyard. Children play games like hide-and-seek and tag while their parents mill about on the porch and drink wine or beer. I offer to help Esther with some of the barbecuing, but she says that her husband, Frank, is more than capable of grilling the hamburgers and hot dogs. She encourages me to mingle with the guests and to drink some of the wine. But I don't feel like drinking right now. I certainly don't feel well enough to chat with people I hardly know.

So, instead of following Esther's guidance, I sheepishly make my way over to a corner of the porch where nobody is, and I stand there like an awkward teenager at a school dance. I pull my phone out of my pocket and start thumbing through the several social media apps I keep meaning to delete. I haven't posted much since everything with Raul occurred, so my notifications are minimal at best. I exit out of social media, and I open the camera app, wondering how haggard and bedraggled I look today. I aim the cover above me so I can hide my double chin and I'm not terribly upset with the way I look. In fact, I look well for the most part. Usually, I'm quite critical of myself. Not when Raul was here, however. He always told me how handsome I was, how much he wished he could stare at my face and take note of my beauty all day.

I click the button and the camera snaps at me, capturing my image in an instant. I sense my skin start to itch. For a moment, I scratch. Then I click on the picture and let it fill the screen. I sense my stomach curl when I gaze at the picture in its entirety. I'm positioned in the foreground, forcing a half-hearted smile; however, there's a dark shape—a tall figure with dark hair and skin that appears as if it's been covered in soot—lingering on the porch beside me. I squint, looking closer at the figure and, for a moment, I think I recognize the face—it's Raul. But he doesn't look like he once did. Instead, he appears as if he's been caught in a permanent state of agony—his mouth open in a muted screen, his jaw extended impossibly like a snake does when it feeds on larger rodents. I shake my head, wondering if I'm seeing the picture correctly. *This can't possibly be true*, I think to myself.

I decide to test myself and take another picture. I thumb the photo away and return to the camera app. My face fills the screen. I tap on the button and the camera clicks. A quick flash. Once again, my skin starts to itch. I press on the photo I've taken until it balloons out and fills the entirety of my phone screen. Once more, I'm positioned in the foreground, smiling awkwardly at the camera. The dark figure of Raul loiters behind me, his fingernails as long as spindles and his dark hair sebaceous and greasy looking.

Not fully convinced of what I'm seeing, I sprint inside the house and make my way into the small office on the first floor. I close the door behind me, and I amble over to the printer arranged beside the oak desk in the center of the room. I click on the photo and press "Print." The printer whirs alive suddenly and begins to reproduce the photograph. I slide the paper out from the tray once it's finished printing and I regard the image on the page. It's exactly the same as the photo I had taken on my phone—me in the foreground and the dark entity that resembled Raul hovering in the background.

I decide I'm too tired to return to the party outside, so I make my way upstairs to the guest bedroom and lock the door. I hurl myself onto the bed and realize I've absentmindedly landed on the photobook that Raul had gifted me. I pull it out from under me and flip the first page open, regarding the blurry photograph I can hardly recognize. I think it's perhaps the picture of Raul and me at the local zoo, but I cannot be certain. The uncertainty vexes me like nothing else. I think of throwing the photo book aside, but I don't out of respect for Raul. Instead, I push the new photo I've printed inside one of the empty sleeves near the back of the book and close the page.

I think of the picture I took and how unsettled I was at first by the sight of Raul so disheveled, so unkempt. However, I realize that my apprehension soon softened to admiration for the thing that resembled Raul. *How could that be? Why wasn't I frightened of the thing in the photograph?*

Realizing there must be something wrong with me, I peel the book open again and arrive at the page where I expect to see my face centered in the frame and Raul's ghostly shape lingering in the background. Instead, I'm met with something entirely different. I'm in the foreground, of course, but the shape that was once Raul is now more defined. He looks like his old self—his olive complexion, his beautiful dark hair, his shimmering eyes. He doesn't resemble the monster he once did when I first examined the photograph. Raul looks perfect. Even more astonishing, he has both of his arms wrapped around me and he's kissing the nape of my neck.

I shake my head in total doubt. I can hardly believe what I'm looking at. *Raul? Can that* really *be you?*

Before I allow myself to covet the photo too sincerely, I slam the book shut. I sit for a while in silence, holding the photo book in my lap. I can hardly move. I'm fearful I might abruptly undo whatever magic I might have conjured in order to bring Raul back.

I tip the book open again and arrive at the page where I left the photograph. But this time, I'm met with disappointment. The photo is now blurred like the others, as if the two of us were standing beyond a rain-battered window.

I knew it wouldn't last, I think to myself.

But something suddenly occurs to me: I was able to conjure Raul's likeness in the image after I printed it out and set it inside the photo book. I realize that he'll always be with me as long as I have my picture taken and keep the book close to me at all times. Of course, there's the added discomfort of the itching that seemed to appear, as if out of nowhere, the very day I had married Raul. But I'm more than happy to keep that minor ailment as my cross to bear—my penance for being able to keep Raul alive in some little way.

I realize that I won't ever have to be apart from Raul if I constantly take pictures of myself. Naturally, he'll appear distorted and malformed at first, but once I tuck the printed photograph inside the photo book, he'll come to life for me once more. Just for a moment. I'll need to keep doing it. Again, and again.

I hold the camera high above me, turning the camera on so that my face fills the entirety of the phone screen. I press the button and there's a brief flash. I thumb my way to "Photos" and I click on the most recent one. As usual, I'm in the foreground and the dark shape of Raul—skin black as ink and tongue drooping from his unhinged jaw—hovers in the background like some obscene spectator at a lavish banquet.

I sense a familiar itch. I scratch my arm, a little harder this time. In fact, I'm so careless that I don't realize that I've broken some of the skin and I'm bleeding.

Once again, I travel downstairs to the office and print the photograph. I'm back in the guest bedroom in a matter of seconds with the new picture. Just like before, the photo is different. I'm centered in the frame and Raul—effervescent-looking and boyishly handsome—remains behind me with both arms draped across my shoulders in a giant bear hug.

I stare at the photograph for a few moments and then tuck the small picture into another one of the empty cellophane sleeves inside the photo book. I can't seem to pull my attention away from the photograph. I know for certain that once I close the book, the picture will become blurred— just like the fading memory of Raul and I together.

Just then, I wonder if I've correctly heard a voice—delicate and impossibly small—whisper to me, "*I love you.*" I'm quite certain that's exactly what I've heard when all the loosest parts of me begin to curl.

CHOOSE YOUR
OWN ADVENTURE

NADIA BULKIN

Philippa's Psychic Shoppe was Michael's idea.

But Elle liked to think that he had seen her lingering on the *Weird and Wonderful Spinriver* page in the hotel guidebook and had decided to give her what she could not provide herself: permission. They were walking down Spinriver's Main Street in search of stores that they could both enjoy when Michael pointed out the purple sign with the gilded "P" and said, "Hey, that might be fun, huh?"

Her heart galloped as he opened the door and let her enter the stuffy cloud of patchouli and lavender first. Her parents would have grounded her if they caught her sneaking into a place like this while living under their roof—there was a store in the Northcourt Mall's old wing with plaster gargoyles and blood red signage that she and her cousin Kayla used to go out of their way to pass without ever daring to enter—but the whole point of this trip was that she was no longer groundable. She was a married woman. She—and her husband—could choose her destinations herself.

Inside they inspected gemstones and animal skulls, sniffed candles, batted dreamcatchers. They giggled at blurry photos of purported auras and steered clear of the many boxes of tarot cards—there was something about the figure on the cover of the decks, the so-called "magician" with his right hand raising a wand and his left hand pointing down (*to hell*) that made Elle dizzy—and in one of the cluttered aisles they were cornered by the proprietor of the psychic shoppe, Philippa herself.

Elle didn't know what exactly she expected from this Philippa woman, but was marginally disappointed to see that she could have passed for any of the middle-aged cookie-baking church ladies back at home. "Hi there," she said, and there was a rockiness in her voice, a precarious fatigue, like a hill prone to avalanches. "Can I help you find something?"

"Say, you got any love spells or anything?" Michael joked, prompting Elle to gasp in mock indignation and real embarrassment. "Something to inspire real undying passion?"

Philippa's eyes darted down to their ringed hands, then back to their faces. Just as she had while standing at the altar of Eternal Eden Church on her wedding day, Elle found herself anxiously wondering what the woman saw when she looked at them: a well-matched pair? Or a man straight out of an upscale suit catalog and a clown-woman trying to keep up? "I have just the thing for you," Philippa said.

What she had for them was a closet. A broom closet? The door had been removed, replaced by a thick purple curtain that was presently tied back by a tasseled rope. Inside sat a wheeled stool and a small writing desk upon which lay a closed book. "A new find," Philippa said. "A very special one."

It looked like a hardbound vintage children's book, at least based on its slim size, the wear on its corners, and the simple, cartoonish cover. *The Mill of God*, the title read in playful script. Below the title, a dopey boy in overalls stared up at a barn fitted with what looked like a gigantic, fiery, upright wagon wheel.

"Um..." Michael was trying to be polite but couldn't keep down a boyish chuckle. "It's a... book."

"It's a book of destiny," Philippa corrected him, and then elaborated: "They tell you your future. They're very rare, and this one's only half-spent. You're just in time."

Reading the book would cost them twenty dollars each. "Although you're not so much reading the book as the book is reading you," Philippa said as she exchanged Michael's fifty-dollar bill for a ten.

Philippa pointed them to the closet. Elle tugged pleadingly at the collar of Michael's shirt, as if to say, *please go first*. Michael swung his gaze into an exaggerated eyeroll, as if to say, *my wife for you*. Philippa sat him on the stool and had him sign something—Elle couldn't see exactly what, a liability waiver?—and then drew the curtain shut.

Michael re-emerged within a few minutes, looking a bit befuddled. Elle was about to ask him what fortune he'd received when Philippa put up her finger and said, "Ah ah ah. No spoiling the surprise." It was the first time Elle saw any light in the woman's eyes, and she found herself smiling, speeding toward the closet, thinking of her mother whom she had to admit she missed.

Once she was sitting and flipped open the cover, she saw what she was supposed to sign: the inside front cover. The spattering of letters and names in various colors and inks must have been what Philippa meant by being half-spent. She found Michael's initials in the middle of the page, added her own, and then jerked as she heard the curtain rings slide behind her, left to right. And then they were alone, she and the book.

The Mill of God told the story of a nameless Youth who, on his way home from school, encountered a magical gristmill that turned grains of wheat not into flour, but into gold. The Youth started producing his own gold to buy a horse, and then a new house for his family, only for the horse to run away and the house to burn down, leading him to destroy the mill and make his living as an honest farmer. When locusts came, his resourcefulness saved his village from starvation, and the Youth traveled to a castle to be personally thanked by the King—a greater honor than any gold could buy.

It left her feeling... odd. Like she'd unexpectedly heard her own voice after picking up the phone. She wobbled around on the stool and noticed that the purple curtain was dusty, maybe even lightly stained.

"So why don't you tell each other," Philippa said, "how your story ended?"

"He finally finds the cave of wonders on top of a mountain." Michael shrugged. "It doesn't show what's actually *in* the cave, though, so I guess I just have to assume he gets enlightened."

Elle thought he was joking at first. "Cave of wonders? What happened during the locust plague?"

Michael shook his head. "There weren't any locusts. He got the gold. He traded it in to get the key to enlightenment, which turns out to be a map to a cave, which turns out to be on a mountain." He turned to Philippa, as if expecting her to reveal the secret to her trick and said again: "There was just the mountain, and the cave."

—◆—

Michael said *The Mill of God* was the most expensive book he'd ever bought, and he didn't even get to keep the damn thing. The use of a swear jostled Elle, despite knowing Michael had been the closest their small school had to a "bad boy," but not as severely as it might have had she not been distracted by the fear of their imminent split. They'd said *'til death do us part* less than four days ago and already, they'd been proven liars.

She was going to end up in a castle. He was going to end up in a cave of wonders.

She was quiet for the rest of the afternoon, and he brought it up during dinner. He was proud to have gotten them a table at the best restaurant in Spinriver—The Tiger & The Sable, a bustling steakhouse—and seemed disappointed that she didn't seem impressed. It was nice that he wanted to impress her. She forced a smile. "Just thinking about that book again. Thinking about what it meant."

"Don't tell me you believe that thing predicted our future. God's the only one that knows that."

She clucked her tongue in an irritation that bordered on nervousness. Fought the urge to look behind her in case someone in the corner of the restaurant was watching, waiting, peeling back the theater curtains that walled off her interior thoughts. "No. I know. Only God knows. That's not what I'm... but... but it's reading you, right? It read us."

Michael's scoff was an unmistakable signal that she needed to back off; she was annoying him. Maybe the wine was dulling her response time. "Yeah. Sure. Like a mood ring. So what?" He took a bite of steak and then pointed the knife at her. "Oh. I get it. You're pissed that we got different results."

Even in high school, even in *middle* school, he'd been able to do this—cut straight into her soul with a single observation. It would be disturbing if he were a lesser man.

"Just because we're married," Michael said, patiently, "doesn't mean we have to have all the same favorite things. You have your favorite color, I have mine. You've got your hobbies, I've got mine."

She wanted to object, to explain to her new husband that she was afraid—afraid that their radically different endings might be an indication of some deep incompatibility that hadn't been surfaced by the church's premarital counseling—but when she lifted her head to share her cobbled-together words, she saw that Michael's gaze had veered to his left. Even before she got confirmation of what had drawn his attention, Elle felt her insides freeze. Yes, there she was. Red hair. Black skirt. An open, doll-like face with fluttery eyelashes and half-parted lips like something straight out of a Botticelli. She was taking a nearby table's order. Laughing, her body loose and open and free.

Elle excused herself to stop herself from screaming. Making a scene, she knew, would do no one any good—she was not a child anymore. Instead, she hurried to the bathroom to splash water on her face as her mother had advised her, and reminded herself to be thankful that her Michael was a normal man.

He's a man, her mother had said when she bemoaned that she had caught him ogling her admittedly very pretty coworker Melissa while picking her up at the office. *You should be glad he's normal.* And yes, she knew that even the elders noticed the young-and-beautiful – to expect otherwise was to demand blindness—but there was something about the *way* he looked, wasn't there? An intensity? An intent?

In the mirror, she tried to mimic the waitress's toothy smile, her butterfly eyes. But it was like her face just wouldn't open that way. Had Michael ever been with someone so plain, she wondered. She had long prayed for a husband like him: charming, handsome, "mission-driven" as he put it. But she knew for a fact that he could not say the same of a wife like her, because his gaze never used to linger over her when they were in school. And as this thought washed through her, the panic she felt when she watched him watch the waitress was replaced by something else—something closer to guilt.

When she got back to the table, though, he was smiling warmly; he'd poured them both another glass of wine and ordered a bowl of strawberry ice cream to share. Her favorite.

That night she dreamt of Michael in the arms of the redheaded waitress in the cave of wonders, which, in her imagination looked less like a mountaintop cavern and more like the small limestone cave tucked in the overgrown heart of Arrowhead Park, where kids with more lenient parents—kids that had included Michael, she knew—spent their summer nights learning how to drink.

Elle was not a drinker; even in college she hadn't learned how, because she went home on weekends. Which meant she'd gone straight to sleep after they meandered back to the hotel and was still woozy when Michael woke her up the next morning with a soft but insistent shake of the shoulder. "It's nine," he said as she struggled to get herself right-side up. He'd already gone for his morning run, his hair still glistening with beads of shower water. "We've got those riverboat tickets, remember?"

In the bathroom, Elle pinched the folds of her belly, imagining the power of a knife. She turned to her side to see exactly how much she'd like to slice off and saw something odd tucked beneath the toilet tank—a crinkly plastic bag from a local drugstore. Inside was something soft, something blue—Michael's shirt from the day before. Why hadn't he put it into their shared laundry bag? Why was it under the toilet? These were the thoughts that picked at Elle, as she let the bathroom fill with steam.

◆

Elle did nothing more than worry about the fated end of her marriage until her cousin Kayla posted about Mercury being in retrograde. She asked Kayla, privately, if astrology wasn't out-of-bounds considering the sinfulness of divination, and Kayla said astrology had nothing to do with

CHOOSE YOUR OWN ADVENTURE

divination—it was making sure you knew what obstacles might stand in your way on your path to God.

This reinterpretation unlocked a door in Elle's mind that she had not known existed and allowed her to spend hours on the internet searching for confirmation that would give her the permission to dig deeper, do more, act first. Details of future events, she came to understand, were forbidden knowledge. Manipulating fortune was the domain of God alone. But at least a few sources suggested that destiny was different. Destiny was a culmination of a human's actions, essentially a preview of the verdict that would be passed down on Judgment Day. Destiny could be shaped. Destiny could *change*.

So, she vowed to bring hers closer in line to Michael's the only way she knew how: moving through the world like he would. She did sprints through the neighborhood toward what she imagined to be Michael's destiny, past the house of the pretty gym rat who always turned Michael's head, past the house with the giant Bennington flag mounted on the garage. Back home, she washed off the sweat with the cold showers that Michael always said got him "mission-ready." At work, she crept into Melissa's office while everyone was at lunch and took her pink stapler. She considered sneaking behind the door and spending the rest of the afternoon tucked behind Melissa's long trench coat, as Michael would have done as a frat boy on a panty raid—but just as she was wondering how she would explain herself if Melissa caught her, a chitter-chattering group from sales passed by, spooking her. Still.

And then, once she could think of nothing else to do to tap into her husband's soul, she put on one of Michael's flannels and drove back to Spinriver the next time Michael went out of town.

Philippa's Psychic Shoppe was much busier than it had been the day she went in with Michael. An ice cream vendor had even set up outside, to catch the tourist overflow. Once Elle pushed her way inside, she realized that the main source of the clog was the broom closet, and the line of patrons that snaked out of it. Most of them were teenagers—the group directly ahead of Elle was still in braces—but there were middle-aged hippie couples too, and what looked like a bachelorette party, and lone wolves in leather jackets. And yet none of them, Elle realized when she passed a baroque mirror, had her wide dilated eyes and tense stone mouth, what looked like *frenzy* leaking out of her pores.

Philippa wasn't pleased to see her at the front of the line. "For you, thirty dollars."

She ponied up and took her spot in the broom closet. She signed her initials again—the inside front cover was so much fuller now, a forest of hard lines and curlicues—and then began to read. Once again, the Youth used the gold to buy a horse and house, though this time he lost neither. He continued to accumulate gold and eventually became the town mayor, then a nobleman, then a king with a castle, which crumbled into flour upon his death. But there was no mountain. No cave of wonders.

She was still staring at the last page when Philippa pulled the curtain open. Until this moment, she realized, a tiny part of her had been holding onto the obscure hope that *The Mill of God* had been a parlor trick. "This is the same book?" she asked, though she already knew it had to be.

"Did you check for your initials?" Yes, she had, and her original signature had been there just where she left it, nestled next to Michael's. She remembered still being unaccustomed to signing herself EP instead of EK—there were trembles in the black lines, like hesitation marks. "Then it's the same book," said Philippa, and made an exaggerated sweeping gesture toward the shop, the light, the line of people waiting to take their turn in the closet and then the world beyond.

She ate lunch at The Tiger & The Sable, to torture herself, but the redheaded waitress was not in sight. On Main Street she thought she saw her, then and again, a pink sundress bleached yellow by the sun, but when Elle tried to get a closer look the late summer crowds would spin until she had to stop and grab for something steady. A stop sign, a brick wall, a shuttered ice cream stand. A lamppost, once. On that lamp post fluttered several tattered pieces of pastel paper: piano lessons, a missing dog, a missing woman.

Red hair. Doll eyes. She felt sick suddenly, imagining them running off together. Climbing their mountain, nesting in their cave of wonders, all *enlightened.*

Why were you trying to act like him tho? Kayla asked, later that night. *Eloise, LISTEN. You are the yin to his yang. Marriage is all about balance! That's what the book is trying to tell you!*

A fair point, Elle thought. But hadn't she balanced herself against Michael plenty? She'd even changed her name to suit his desire to not be married to an "old Victorian lady." Besides, what did Kayla know about marriage—she was still trying to find her twin flame, whatever that was. Elle put the phone down and went to carry out all of Michael's outstanding errands—taking out the garbage, changing the lightbulbs in the garage, checking the status of the poisoned gopher tunnels in the backyard.

The third time she went to Spinriver she got caught in westbound traffic—an accident of some kind, it was just debris by the time she passed it—and arrived six minutes after closing time. The drive itself was a last-minute decision, precipitated by a burst of stomach-chewing anxiety about her and Michael being flung to the opposite ends of the Earth when the seven trumpets blared; now she was afraid that God was telling her *no*. The store was dark but she still rattled the handle, making the little *closed* sign shake as if flipping it over would turn on the lights and unlock the door and grant her a third opinion by *The Mill of God*, because she knew that Michael would be back first thing in the morning and she couldn't hang around here until 9 a.m., and she had to, she just had to, *she absolutely had to know.*

She was looking around for a rock to throw when she heard a car chirp. Peeking into the nearby alley, she saw Philippa loading a box into a small mud-spattered car.

"I'll give you forty," Elle said, and Philippa clicked her tongue. Rolled her eyes in the dark.

Once Philippa unlocked the Shoppe, Elle was stumbling toward the broom closet even before Philippa had a chance to turn on the light. "Haven't you heard that you should never go to a psychic twice?" Philippa called after her. "Let alone what you're doing."

With the light on, Elle could see that Philippa was bruised up all along the outer edge of her left eye socket, the purple a perfect shadow of a punch. Some people, she said, could not accept a fortune that didn't come with a decoder.

"I blame video games," she said, though she didn't sound like she meant it.

Elle decided not to pry. She grabbed the book and squeezed in a third EP in the far corner of the inside cover, where a half-inch of virgin paper had been spared amid the dizzying mess of smoggy handwriting. "What happens when you run out of space?" she asked.

Philippa shrugged. "Then it's over, I guess." The ease with which she spoke of this likely loss of an income stream made Elle wonder if perhaps Philippa longed for the book to die. She imagined its funeral—buried under trees on a moonless night, burned and scattered into the river, pulped and bleached and reborn as something innocent.

That time the Youth told some unscrupulous friends about the magical mill before he had the chance to use it, and upon losing control of it, decided to pass the rest of his life foraging alone in a forest.

<hr />

After her third time having her destiny read by *The Mill of God*, Elle gave up. She didn't have the stamina to make that stop-and-go drive into low country again, just to drag her disappointment back home. Michael, for his part, was getting tired of her constant need for reassurance—she could tell by how often he was staying late at work, and the shortness of his comments when he was at home—and driving her husband away was not how she wanted to make her own destiny. So she folded up the urge to reconcile her anxiety, neat as a fitted sheet, and shoved it in the back of her mental closet.

And then she found the plastic bag that Michael had tucked under the toilet back in Spinriver, still containing the shirt he'd been wearing the day they went to Philippa's. It was in the shed with the gopher poison; she'd seen a couple new mounds pop up in the backyard and wanted to be proactive, as a favor to Michael. Heart beating hard, she laid the crumpled shirt on the plastic bag and started looking for... what, exactly? She had no idea until she saw it, at which point she could see nothing else: a long delicate strand of red hair.

Had he been trying to hide it? Was she ashamed? She ran her fingers around the cuff of the sleeve where the hair was hugging the fabric,

CHOOSE YOUR OWN ADVENTURE

tracing the spot where he'd be shackled if marriage was such a burden, imagining his explanation if she asked him: *she was beautiful but she didn't mean a thing to me.*

Another flutter of red pulled her attention to the front placket, where another hair had wrapped like a most insidious vine around the mother-of-pearl buttons. She followed its thread until her eyes landed on something else, something she couldn't make sense of—a two-inch dried splatter of faded red.

For an unknown period of time, she simply sat cross-legged on the floor of the shed, staring at the shirt. Her phone eventually roused her—it was her mother, telling her that people were starting to inquire about her delay in sending out wedding gift thank-you cards. "Are you all right?" her mother ended up asking, so she must have sounded wrong. "Where's Michael?"

Her mother loved Michael. Elle had been nervous at first that Michael's "wild youth" —the trouble he got into breaking into neighbors' houses, the girls he chased—would be off-putting to her parents, but her mother saw it differently. Said it meant he'd had a taste of sin and had now chosen a godly life.

"He's at work," she said, hoping that was true.

"This late? Are you taking good care of him, Eloise?"

Taking care. Care-taking. Yes, she needed to take care of him.

"Don't worry, Mom," she whispered. "I've got it."

With renewed purpose—with *mission*, as Michael might say—Elle took the shirt inside the house and prepared it for cleansing. There had been an unsuccessful attempt at spot-cleaning the stain—probably with hydrogen peroxide, if she had to guess—but Elle knew another way, a rougher way to separate these particular proteins from the fibers of the cloth. She made an ammonia mix and rubbed it into the red with her toothbrush, then turned the shower on and drowned the entire thing. As the cold water turned faintly pink an energy overcame her, a sort of giddiness that she hadn't felt since she was a child—calling ducks in November for her father to shoot, he said he'd never heard such a skillful lonesome hen—and she got into the tub with the shirt, pausing only for a moment before getting out of her clothes so she could fully be with the liquid streaming out of Michael's shirt. His detritus. His wake.

101

What had Kayla said? *Marriage is all about balance.* The calm in her stomach told Elle that this was true; the trick was understanding exactly who she was balancing. She would have to thank Kayla later.

Michael found her sitting by the fire pit later, wrapped in the blush-colored sweater he got her for their first Christmas as a couple.

"Could you tell me, again," she said as he took a seat on the bench and put his arm around her, "what ending you got in that book in Spinriver?"

He took a small swig of his beer. "Jeez. You're still on that?"

But he was smiling. She could see in the soft folds around the corners of his mouth that there was a mildness in there that he had chosen to share with her, a certain restraint. He used to call her his mission, when they first started dating—after he'd graduated college and finished a real mission trip and returned to their hometown ready to start a family, ready to choose a wife. She remembered how flattered she'd been when he sauntered up to her after Sunday service and cracked a joke about their pastor's new haircut. She was not accustomed to being chosen, and especially not by someone like him. She had to admit, it felt nice.

It still did.

"I just want to know what's going on in that head of yours," she said.

"You're such a weirdo," Michael said, fondly. "Fine, fine. The kid goes to the city with the gold and tries to decide what to buy with it. He realizes that material things won't make him happy, and what he really wants is enlightenment. So, he finds a wise man and buys the key, which is actually a map to this cave on a mountain. He spends the whole rest of his life trying to find the right cave, and the right mountain. I think it's one of those metaphors, you know?" He moved his fingers through her hair, tugging gently. "You know: it's the journey, not the destination."

◆

Even before she got into the car, she knew this would be her last drive to Spinriver.

She'd replaced the shirt in Michael's closet—he'd worn it again since, giving her a big kiss goodbye as he walked out the door in it—and deep-

102

cleaned everything they took with them to Spinriver. Not just his things, but hers too; they were in this together, she was sure of it now. With every action she imagined herself stitching up a hole that had been torn in the double gauze future she'd been so patiently stitching since she was a child.

She just needed *The Mill of God* to see it too.

It was 2 p.m. on a stormy Wednesday when she got there—great weather for a psychic reading—but Philippa's Psychic Shoppe was closed. No, not closed; it was shuttered. No felt stars and paper spiders in the empty window displays; no tables of tarot decks, no cash register, not a single stone that hadn't been dragged in on the bottom of a moving man's boot. The broom closet that had once served as the dark home of *The Mill of God* was wide open, and empty.

"You just missed the sale," said a voice behind her: an old man fighting off a hunch by locking his hands behind his back. She must have looked confused, because he added, "The going out of business sale?"

"That doesn't make sense. Last month there was a line out the door."

The old man made a noise of indifference. "Fortune changes fast."

He walked off chuckling to himself. Elle peered back into the empty storefront, wondering for a moment if someone else now possessed *The Mill of God*—but she had a feeling that Philippa would have hung onto a book of destiny, even if she sold all her other little hand grenades.

Having vowed to make this her last visit, Elle had prepared. She had found Philippa's home address online, suggested by a reverse look-up site and confirmed by county property records. As Michael's wife, she knew she would have to be resourceful—the same way her mother patched up hurts left by her father, assuring those he'd injured that he'd meant no harm. It was quiet work, soft work. But such silent, careful sanding down of rough edges was exactly what kept the world safely spinning round.

Philippa lived far from the cobblestones and gas lanterns of Spinriver's tourist district. The streets were broader in Philippa's neighborhood, bumpy stretches of patchy asphalt rimmed with weeds and bungalows fenced off from each other with wire. Elle confirmed that the muddy little car she was parking next to was Philippa's, and then rang the doorbell.

Philippa's face was healed, yet Elle could still see the ghost of a shadow around her left eye. Like something was missing there now. Behind her, *The Mill of God* sat before a roaring afternoon fire.

"This is the last time," Elle promised, handing over a fifty-dollar bill.

"It better be," said Philippa, stuffing it in her shirt pocket. "Because I'm about to burn that book."

Elle frowned; it seemed unfair to blame the book for whatever misfortune had struck Philippa. She was tempted to tuck the book under her jacket to save it from this fate, but when she opened it to sign her name, she saw that the inside front cover was practically black. A brief territorial fantasy sprang up of painting a huge EP over all of those petty little signatures, a tag to defeat all tags, in white correction fluid, or sparkly blue nail polish, or blood.

"It's spent," Philippa went on. "I'm spent, too."

This time Elle did not read the book of destiny in private. She sat with the book on her knees on a lumpy couch catty-corner to Philippa's recliner and slowly, carefully flipped each page.

And this time, she—the Youth—reached the mountain. Like a key grabbing onto the teeth of its one true lock, she turned the last page and found herself face to face with the cave of wonders. There were still differences between her reading and Michael's—her Youth didn't set off for enlightenment but for inner peace—but those were minor details. They both closed the book standing at the mouth of a sparkling abyss; that was the most important thing. The only important thing.

She pressed the book to her heart, gave it a murmured thank you, and then relinquished it back to Philippa—who immediately and heartlessly began ripping out its pages and flinging them into the fire.

"You know what the title means? 'The Mill of God'?"

Hypnotized by the way each paper curled like an insect in death, Elle shook her head. She added "No" because Philippa wasn't looking at her, and was surprised to hear her voice crack with—what, sadness? She wasn't sad. No part of her sad. She self-consciously batted at her eyes, wiped away the hints of moisture there.

"The millstones of the gods grind late, but they grind fine." Every time Philippa tossed another page into the hearth, the fire in her eyes would gleam just a little bit brighter. "It's Greek."

Philippa had said "gods," but Elle thought about God—the one true God, vengeful and exacting and mercifully final in His judgments. Sometimes the final swing of that divine axe was the most peaceful destiny Elle could imagine. "That's true, I think," she said. "At least I hope so."

This time Philippa did look at her, though her hands kept ripping. Tossing and ripping. Elle slid her arms into the sleeves of her jacket as Philippa said, "Four times you read that book and you never once asked me what any of your endings meant. Yours or your man's. That's usually the first thing anybody wants to know. What does the valley mean? What is the sea supposed to be? Is this a good ending? Am I a good person? It drives them crazy. But not you."

Elle wondered for a moment about the sea—neither she nor her Youth had been to one—before zipping her jacket up to her chin and giving Philippa a tight smile. One of her mother's smiles. "It doesn't matter," she said. "You take care now."

BROKEN BACK MAN

◄◄─── LUCIE McKNIGHT HARDY ───►►

It's quiet for a Saturday. Usually there would be at least a couple of large groups – lads out after the rugby, celebrating or commiserating, or a dozen pissed-up lasses on a hen-do, glammed up to the nines and screeching like angry crows. They're the sorts that normally wouldn't be seen dead in a place like The George, but they'll call in now for *Happy Hour! Two-for-one cocktails and shots!* Neither you nor Lise know how to mix cocktails, but nobody complains when you upend a can of Bacardi Breezer or Smirnoff Ice into a glass and chuck in a little umbrella. It's that kind of place.

Even the old lads are missing today, the ones who usually bring a sense of tranquillity to the place: Tony and Mikey and Ivan, the old-timers who have been regulars since long before you started working here, whose long service is repaid by each of them having their own spot along the bar, and woe-betide anyone who takes it. They'll make a half pint last a couple of hours, and barely make eye contact with you when they order another drink, just mutter, 'One more, Jack.' They'll sit morosely with their own thoughts until closing time when they'll shuffle off without a word. Theirs is a calming presence, and you hope they'll be in later. As barman, but also unofficial bouncer, you don't much like working the Saturday shift: the casual yet insidious threat of violence, the simmering bad tempers brought to boiling point by the addition of alcohol.

It's blowing a gale out there. The front door is shut and the curtains are closed against the ravages of an early November evening, but you can still hear the wind howling along the street, even from where you're standing behind the bar. The dishwasher's packed up again, so you're taking out each glass in turn and wiping it dry before placing it on the correct shelf – pint pots under the bar; wine glasses in the racks that hang next to the optics; shot glasses on the mirrored shelf. That shelf desperately needs dusting, but you're buggered if you're going to do it. That's Lise's job, and if she'd have turned up for work on time today, it might have got done.

You don't mind doing the dishwasher, though. There's something soothing about the repetitive process: pick up glass, wipe with tea-towel, place on shelf, repeat. Meditative, although you'd never use that word out loud in a place like this. The George isn't really a place given to meditation; it's a back-street boozer, the old sort, entirely ignored by the gentrification process and virtually unchanged since it was – reputedly – frequented by small-time crooks and criminals in the 1960s. The wallpaper is testament to this: brittle woodchip, stained with smoke that's long since been outlawed, and prone to flaking. The carpet is a marvel of psychedelic engineering, a variety of brown and orange swirls, pockmarked like the cheeks of an acne-afflicted youth with the evidence of decades of cigarette ends. Even the bar itself is unchanged – it's exactly as it is in the photo that hangs next to the inglenook, a long, L-shaped dark wood affair, panelled, robust and, despite the sepia tones of the photo, evidently as battered and scratched as it is today.

You've just hung up the last wine glass and have helped yourself to a packet of pork scratchings when the door crashes open and Lise bounds in, a flurry of dripping auburn hair and turquoise scarf, her long skirt whipping around her ankles as she tries to rectify her inside-out umbrella. Her usually pale face is flushed with the exertion of the act, and she's frowning, but when she's slammed the door behind her she looks up and sees you standing behind the bar. She flashes that beautiful smile, and you swear you can feel your heart flutter. You think it literally skips a beat, and as a student of English, you do not use that word lightly.

The wet hair suits her, and you're about to tell her this when you realise how lame it will sound, so instead you lift up the flap at the end of the bar and go to help her. You take the umbrella from her and manage to turn it the right way around, close it. Lise shuts her eyes, takes in a deep breath and runs her hands through her wet hair, but she's still smiling.

'Jack, my saviour,' she says in her gorgeous Geordie accent, and your heart skips another beat; at this rate you'll be dead by closing time.

'It's nothing,' you manage, still fumbling with the umbrella, because looking at her is just too much to bear. You can feel the heat creeping up your cheeks. It's fair to say that you've adored her ever since she'd joined your tutorial group at the beginning of your first year. Not only is she beautiful – russet-haired, eyes the colour and depth of the sea on a stormy day – but she's whip-smart, too, and can hold the entire room in the palm of her hand when talking about the role of nature in Romantic literature, or madness and decay in the Gothic novel.

She takes off her coat, a long, billowing, green velvet garment, and hangs it up in the little nook behind the bar. She shakes out her hair and runs her fingers through it, freeing the auburn strands. Then she goes back around to the other side of the bar and shuffles herself onto a stool: Mikey's usual spot.

'Pint, please,' she says, grinning, and you smile back at her, even though you know you shouldn't. The cider fizzes orange as it cascades down the side of the glass, and all the time you keep your eyes focused on it, unable to meet her eye. When it's full, you have to look up at her, and she's doing her usual amused face. You put the glass on a beer mat in front of her and she lifts it, sips it daintily, nods, then downs half of it in one swallow.

'Thanks, Jack,' she says. 'You're the best.'

Ostensibly, Lise is employed at The George as a cleaner-cum-bartender. You'd been working here for a couple of months when Scab, the sour-faced, irascible, Glaswegian landlord, had started making noises about how he was too old for this shit, being on his feet all day, at the beck and call of customers. He particularly hated what he called the *physical hardship* of running a pub – the constant hoisting of crates and bottles, the changing of barrels in the cellar. 'D'ye know what one o' them things weighs, laddy?' he'd ask you, a rhetorical question because the answer was immediately forthcoming. 'Fifty-eight kilograms! One hundred and thirty pounds! That's just over nine stone!' At this point he'd already delegated the changing of barrels to you, so you didn't know what he was complaining about, but still he'd said he was going to advertise for staff, and he'd got as far as putting a postcard up in the window: *Staff Needed. No experience necessary. Not much pay either.* He'd thought it was funny, and reasoned that only people who really needed a job would reply, thus filtering out the idiots and chancers. What he didn't realise was that you'd taken down the postcard within minutes of it going up and taken it to class the next day. Lise had been saying for ages that she should really get a job to supplement her student loan, and when you showed it to her, she'd given one of her enigmatic smiles and said she'd think about it.

She'd shown up at The George the next afternoon, just as you were starting your shift, and had charmed the usually taciturn Scab into giving her a job. Trouble was, Lise didn't like to work. She'd announced on her first shift that she was going to 'ease in' to the role and 'watch and learn' before taking her place behind the bar. 'There's no point in me going in all guns blazing and getting it wrong, is there?' she'd said. 'I need a training period. You don't want me pouring a pint wrong and scaring away the customers, do you?' Scab had grunted at that, but shuffled off up the stairs to his flat, and you knew it would be up to you to pick up the slack. Even though you'd shown Lise half a dozen times how to pull a pint, she still preferred to stay on the other side of the bar. But you don't mind, not really.

Gradually, the place starts to fill up. First a group of crusty types – students, probably – who order pints of cider-and-black like it's 1998 or something, and sit there, unspeaking, meticulously rolling cigarettes then taking it in turns to go outside to smoke them. They're harmless enough. A dozen women come in – all fake tans and heels, their pink veils and penis-shaped fairy wands marking them out as one of the hen-do's. They'll leave soon enough, dragging their paralytic bride along to the next pub on their list, so you'll tolerate them, as well, for now. The group of estate agents – arrogant, smug bastards in suits come in for the cheap beer and to look down their noses at the debris of The George; of them you are less tolerant, but you can't make them leave until one of them does something to justify it. It's just a matter of time.

And it's only now that you notice him. You didn't see him come in – you're sure you would have noticed the palaver of trying to get a wheelchair through the narrow door of the pub. He's sitting with his back to you, slightly hunched in the wheelchair, which has been pushed up against a corner table. He's ignoring the chaos around him, and you see that he doesn't even have a drink in front of him. There is a faint whiff of familiarity about him, and you think for a moment that he might be one of the regulars taking up a new spot in the lounge rather than up against the bar itself, but it's not that; you can't place him. His shoulders are narrow, and even through the dark wool of his coat, you can tell that underneath he's scrawny and fragile. Dark, tangled hair curls down his neck and sits on his collar.

'Who's that?' you ask Lise, who follows your eyes over to the corner.

'Dunno. Not seen him before.' Then she clocks the wheelchair. 'Should I go and see if he wants a drink? He's going to have trouble getting up to the bar, the state of those lasses.' One of the hen-do women is belching out the tune of a Taylor Swift song.

'Yeah, could you?' For some reason you're glad that Lise has offered, even though you suspect it's a ruse to justify staying on the punters' side of the bar. You watch as she approaches him, leans down, speaks to him. He appears to answer her question, because she comes back to the bar, lifts the flap, and proceeds to pull a half of mild. There's almost as much head as there is beer, but you don't say anything.

'Poor feller,' she says. 'Can't talk properly. Sounds like he's had a stroke or something. Didn't want me looking at his face, either, put his hand up over it when he answered me.' You glance back at the man in the wheelchair. The air of familiarity is stronger now, but just as elusive, and you're about to go over and see if you recognise him when you notice the book on the table in front of him. The worn brown leather cover shouts at you. Surely not? You sidle over towards him – not too close, you don't want him to see you, but you have to make sure that the book is what you think it is.

It is. It's the diary you thought you'd lost.

The dreams had started when you were about sixteen. At first, you'd thought it was real, that you'd actually woken in the night to the gentle tapping noise and what followed it, but after a few weeks of the dream recurring, and becoming more intense, you'd convinced yourself that it was a nightmare, or some sort of sleep paralysis.

The tapping would be quickly followed by a scraping sound, a soft sliding rustle which would increase in volume as it got closer to you. Even though you knew – felt *certain* – that you were still asleep, it was all too real, and each time you could smell it, too – that sweet reek of rotting flesh and bile. Eventually, the sounds and the smell would become too much and you would force yourself to look out from beneath the bed covers and confront it. Each time it was the same.

A man, illuminated by the light from the landing, writhing, worm-like on your bedroom floor. Rotating himself onto his stomach, grunting with the effort, he would turn his face up towards you, but it was cast into shadow by the light from behind him and you could never make out his features. Propelling himself forward on his elbows, his useless legs dragging behind him like those of a rag doll, always the deep agonised groan, followed by a hoarse rush of breath from the effort. The landing light would flicker on and off – once, twice – momentarily throwing your bedroom into utter darkness, followed by a sudden burst of light which would reveal him ever closer, advancing across the floor towards you.

And each time, just before you woke screaming, begging for dawn to arrive, he would reach up to you, a gnarled, sinewed hand, the nails nicotine-yellow, pleading.

In a voice barely audible through the pain, his face still obscured by the darkness, he would implore you. 'Help me, please. Help me, please.'

You called him Broken Back Man.

It's always been a sort of unwritten rule, since you started at The George, that changing a barrel is shorthand for going for a quick smoke. Sure, sometimes a barrel will really need to be changed, and on those occasions you'll go down to the cellar and have a few quick drags on your ciggie, pinch the end and put it back in the pack, before attending to the actual task of hoisting down a new keg and switching it for the empty one. At other times, when it's busy and you're finding it hard to stay awake – usually after pulling an all-nighter to finish an essay – you'll make it an excuse for the punter who's waiting for their pint. You wouldn't try it with one of the regulars – they'd know straight away what you were up to – but the students and the out-of-towners, they would never suspect.

You're thinking about doing exactly this now. You're finding the presence of the man in the wheelchair strangely perturbing and feel the need for an escape, albeit a temporary one. It's the sense of familiarity that bothers you, the sense of déjà vu that creeps across the back of your neck like a cold, damp hand when you catch a glimpse of him. He's barely touched his drink, and instead has occupied his hands – dirty, yellow nicotine-stained fingers – with inspecting the book, flicking through the pages of what you're convinced is your diary; he seems riveted by the contents. You've been making excuses to get out from behind the bar, to sidle over to him, try to catch a glimpse of his face, but he keeps his head turned resolutely away from you. Sometimes, as you go around collecting empty glasses, wiping the tables down, even though that's Lise's job, you think you can detect that familiar sweet reek of decay.

Lise seems to sense your discomfort and is making more of an effort to serve drinks, to keep up with the clamour of the Saturday night clientele. She keeps shooting you worried glances, but she doesn't say anything. It's even busier now, customers jostling for attention at the bar. You're putting the empty glasses down when one of the estate agent types taps you on the arm.

'When you're ready, mate!' he barks into your face. His breath is meaty and sweet and for a moment you feel nauseous. Lise looks at you and it's as though she can read your mind. She jerks her head in the direction of the cellar door and winks.

'Just got to change the barrel,' you tell him, and fumble your way back behind the bar and into the nook, from where the door to the cellar leads.

On the way you rummage your cigarettes and lighter out from your coat pocket. The steps are old and dilapidated, and the wooden treads groan under your feet. You descend in darkness; the light switch, for some unknown reason, is at the bottom of the stairs, but the light thrown down from the nook upstairs is enough for you to position your feet carefully on the steps. Your heart is like a pneumatic drill in your chest.

———◆———

You'd started keeping the diary as a way of maintaining control. You may not have been able to make out his face, but if you could log the visits Broken Back Man made to you in your dreams, you could at least look back on them and tell if they were becoming more or less frequent. As the months, and then the years, of his nocturnal visits proceeded, the entries in your diary became more intense and greater in frequency, the dates closer in proximity. The small, leather-bound journal became more and more dog-eared, the handwriting fainter and less assured as your confidence in your own mental health was eroded. You became withdrawn, avoiding your friends, sitting in your bedroom at night getting drunk or stoned, anything to try to dull the terror you felt at the prospect of going to sleep and the inevitable visit from Broken Back Man.

And then you started at uni, and met Lise, and it was as though a tap had been turned off. Perhaps your brain was too engaged with the fantasies you concocted around this beautiful and unattainable woman in your tutorial group, and couldn't accommodate thoughts of both her and Broken Back Man. You didn't know. You only cared that the dreams stopped abruptly after you met her, and the relief you felt was almost as intense as the fear he had instilled in you. Over the course of the next couple of years, during the chaos of the various moves you'd made between halls of residence and shared houses, the diary had disappeared – misplaced, no doubt, among the cardboard boxes and general detritus of student life – and you had been glad.

But you'd never forgotten that outstretched hand, and the fragile voice pleading, 'Help me, please. Help me, please.'

When you've reached the bottom step you flick the switch and the strip light blinks once, twice, above your head, before illuminating the cellar in a harsh, yellow light. The walls down here used to be white, you think. Now they're grey and stained with mildew, and damp has encroached up the walls, tendrils rising, as though trying to escape from the pitted stone floor. The ceiling is low and curves down at each side, like a vault, and it's only in the middle of the room that you can stand upright. A rank of metal barrels is lined up to your left, each attached to a pipe and then a pump, which in turn will push the beer up to the bar above. Each is labelled with the brewery's logo and, scrawled in marker pen, the name of the particular ale or lager it contains. Against the other wall is a metal rack containing the full barrels, the spares, the ones that you'll have to hoist down when you really do need to change one. They are stacked horizontally, the dull metal of their fat bellies gleaming reluctantly in the strip light. A metal clip is firmly positioned at the end of the rack, holding them in place and preventing them from slipping and crashing to the floor.

You take your time with your smoke. Now that Lise has the hang of things she can take over while you're down here. You lean against the wall and inhale deeply, once, twice. There's a tiny window looking out onto the back yard, which sits a storey below the ground floor of the pub, where the land falls away behind it, down towards the river. The glass is smeared and filthy, and you can just about make out the shape of your face, a pale oval suspended against the grey of the wall behind you, but all detail is lost in the decades of grime that have accumulated there. Your features remain obscured.

'Jack? You down there?' Lise's voice reaches you from the top of the stairs. You can just make out a flash of red where her hair hangs down. You step forward and see that she is leaning over, her hair hanging clear of her face in a glorious conflagration, a waterfall of fire. But her face is even paler than usual and she's frowning.

'It's that weird guy,' she says, her voice high-pitched and pinched. 'You know – the guy in the wheelchair? He's just collapsed. Keeled over onto the table. I think he's unconscious. I don't know what to do.'

115

He looks like a heap of old clothes, lying there unmoving on the table, his face turned away from you, arms sprawled across the sticky surface. A shapeless bundle made up of a dark coat and a woollen beanie hat, like a scarecrow or a Guy Fawkes ready for the bonfire.

A small crowd has gathered, but no one seems to be doing anything. You urge yourself to take control, to help him, but you can't even bring yourself to touch him. You tell Lise to call an ambulance and she just looks at you in panic, so you pull out your own phone and dial 999. You are set apart from yourself, as though suspended above this situation, looking down at what is happening. Reality is flickering, on-off, on-off. The dispatcher tells you to inspect his airway for obstructions, and you relay this information to Lise, who looks horrified but then reaches around to his face and places her fingers in his mouth, making no attempt to conceal the disgust that is evident on her face.

'What's that?' she says, and she removes her fingers, leans in, places her ear next to the old man's mouth. She listens, intent, and holds up a hand to the onlookers, in a request for silence.

'You're hoping Jack can… what?' she asks with a frown. She looks up at you, silently begging for help. 'He's saying he hopes you can do something… but he's not saying what he wants you to do.'

Even before you push her gently to the side and force yourself to lean into the old man, even before you smell the sickness and decay on his breath, you know what he is saying. Revulsion squirms in your stomach, but you have to know. The man's lips purse together, ancient leather mottled with phlegm and saliva, preparing to say the words that aren't *hoping Jack can*.

You keep your face turned away from him and position an ear against his mouth. He lets out a groan, a fragile exhalation of breath, and then he whispers the words you have been dreading.

'Broken Back Man.'

—◆—

You've just managed to kick out the last of the punters and have offered to wipe down the tables in the lounge bar. The pub had returned to an approximation of normality fairly swiftly after the ambulance had arrived and the paramedics had stretchered the man out into the night. You'd found yourself unable to watch, so instead you'd flicked through the diary – *your* diary – that you'd picked up and pocketed during the chaos of the incident. Even though the entries are largely identical, the language that of someone recalling a recurring incident without resorting to originality or nuance, they are more chilling for that, serving to reinforce the indelible, unchanging nature of your dreams, and their inevitability and the sheer power they hold over your nerves.

The last entry you remember writing was the night before you left home for uni, and you read it through, feeling the familiar chill but gaining reassurance from thinking of it as a milestone, a marker on your journey away from Broken Back Man. But then you turn the page and see that there is one last entry. It's one you don't remember writing, yet there it is, written in your fountain pen ink, in what is undeniably your handwriting. There's no description of a dream, no words at all, other than the heading. Written in your familiar spidery scrawl, and underlined neatly, the same as for all the other entries, is the date. Today's date.

The ring of your phone from your coat pocket in the nook behind the bar makes you look up. Lise is wiping out glasses behind the bar and she looks at you, one eyebrow raised, and cocks a thumb in that direction, as if to say *Shall I answer it?* Normally, you'd let it go to voicemail, but something tells you this might be important, so you nod at her, watching while she retrieves your mobile. She puts it to her ear and instantly her face folds into a frown. She turns away from you, her hair falling around her, concealing her face. Unnerved, you stride across the room and place the glasses on the bar, trying to see through her hair, to read her expression. She nods and presses the phone against her shoulder, muting it. She takes a deep breath and turns to face you, tucking her hair behind her ear.

'It's the hospital.'

Even though you know what she's going to say, you nod at her to go on.

'The old man? The one who was in earlier? The one in the wheelchair?'

Of course I know who you mean, you want to say. *He's back. He's come to torment me again, after letting me think he was going to let go, to leave me in peace, to stop inhabiting my dreams, somehow he's back. Except it's worse now. He's real. You've seen him, an entire pub full of people have seen him, even an ambulance crew has seen him. He's real. It's Broken Back Man.*

But, of course, you don't say any of this. You stand there, mute, as Lise tells you that there was nothing they could do, they tried to resuscitate him in the ambulance and again at the hospital, they did everything they could, really they did. But he died at a little after ten o'clock.

Help me, please. Help me, please.

There's a gale kicking up in your ears, a whooshing sound that is louder than the wind in the street outside, but through it you can make out Lisa saying that he had no ID on him, no means of identifying him whatsoever, and so the hospital are calling you on the number you gave the ambulance crew, on the off-chance that you might know who he is. You hear her mutter that you seem to be in shock, and that she'll ask you to call them back, and her hand is on your arm, her soft, warm hand, on your arm.

Help me, please. Help me, please.

But you can't deal with this; you need a cigarette. You push past her, grab your fags from your coat pocket and open the door to the cellar. Even though it's dark, you remember how to place your feet on the treads, the groaning sound they make revoltingly familiar. As you near the bottom, you turn on the light and the first thing you see is the window in front of you. It reflects an approximation of your body – tall, lanky, gangling – and your face, which you can only make out as a rough, watery shape in the filth of the glass, your hair appearing as a dark, matted halo around it, curling around your neck and onto your collar. You place your foot on the bottom step, and the wood gives a louder groan that usual, and buckles under you. You fall forward, the weight of your body smashing against the beer barrels which lie stacked horizontally on the rack in front of you. Finding yourself lying on your front, you try to push yourself to a standing position. You see your face one more time in the window, the features incomprehensible, made invisible by the smeared glass. And that is the last thing you see before you hear the click of the catch which holds the barrels in place, and you hear the slide of metal over metal as the first of the barrels rolls towards you, carrying the weight of eighty-eight gallons of beer directly onto your spine.

You feel no pain at first, but your legs are useless as you try to crawl towards the stairs, to call for Lise to help you. You hoist yourself up onto your elbows and place them one after the other on the hard, damp cellar floor, dragging yourself to the foot of the stairs. When Lise appears at the top, her mouth open, her hand up to her face, you raise your hand to her, your fingers out, pleading. Your voice sounds fragile, agonised as you plead with her.

'Help me, Lise. Help me, Lise.'

THE WITCH'S PILLOWBOOK

◄◄ PRIYA SHARMA ►►

Estelle told me to write to myself, and to Ollie. She calls this the pillowbook
exercise. I was doubtful at first, but she's right. It's helped me to order my thoughts.

I want to say to Ollie: How can I miss you when you're right here?
We've fallen into routines. I thought moving would remedy that but we're
the same, just in a different town. Your hand reaching for me in the dark
used to be a nuanced question. Now it means comfort, and I'm comforted,
but I want more than absentminded affection.

It not about sex. I'm not wishing us young again. It's about feeling
alive. Keeping our demise at bay.

◄◆►

The neighbour was at their door before the removal men had finished
unloading. Mel and Ollie were unpacking in the kitchen. The woman
called out, then stepped into the hall.

"She's keen," said Ollie, under his breath.

"Come on through," Mel beckoned. "I'm afraid we're in a state."

"I'm Petra. I live next door."

"Want a drink?" Ollie motioned to the kettle.

"No, thanks. Is it just the two of you? No children?"

"No."

"Martin and I weren't blessed either," Petra went on, warmed by a misplaced kinship around their mutual lack of progeny. "Come over for Sunday lunch."

Mel and Ollie paused so long that a refusal would seem rude.

"That's lovely," Ollie said finally. "Thanks."

—◆—

Later Mel asked, "Why did you say yes?"

"I panicked."

They both burst out laughing.

"We might as well get it over with. I'm sure she's harmless enough."

It was pleasantly strange to be in their own bed, but in a new room. Mel wriggled closer to Ollie, and he put his arm around her. His chest hair was still damp from the shower, the skin on his belly endearingly soft and warm. Her hand strayed lower.

Mel had become erratic of late. She experienced unpredictable pangs of want and then malaise. She was on the cusp of change.

Ollie kissed the top of her head.

"I'm up for christening the house tonight but *he* might not be so willing." There it was. The forced joviality. Sex spoken of in euphemism and his member in third person. "I'm bloody knackered."

Mel lay awake beside him, sweating. Unsure if it was the furnace of desire or a menopausal flush.

—◆—

"I've lived in Lambshead all my life."

"That's not a virtue, Petra," said Martin, her husband.

He moved around the table, filling glasses. He paused at Petra, touching the back of her neck. She shifted, is if he'd done something unwanted or unseemly. Or perhaps she was just annoyed.

"Why Lambshead?" she asked Mel.

"We passed through here when we were in our twenties. It charmed us. We recently got to a point in our life when we could move, so we thought of here."

122

"You were lucky. Houses go fast. The primary school here is excellent. The local church isn't what it once was, but you'd be welcome."

"The high street is so much better than we remembered from when we viewed the house." Mel was keen to change the subject.

"There's been an influx of new shops recently." Petra pulled a face. "The art gallery and the deli are okay, but now there's a tattoo parlour and a lingerie shop."

Mel stifled the urge to ask if women in Lambshead didn't wear knickers.

"They're all, you know," Petra dropped her voice an octave, "*sex people.*"

Mel barked with laughter until she realised Petra was serious. She saw it then. It wasn't just sex. Petra had never lost herself in the throes of anything.

"It's common knowledge." Petra raised her chin. Her pale cheeks pinked up.

"Are you ready for dessert?" Martin asked.

"We'll help clear."

"You stay there, Melanie." Petra busied herself.

Mel found herself alone with Martin when Ollie excused himself with a joke about insulting the porcelain. She could hear Petra running taps in the kitchen.

"It's good to have you here. Petra can get odd ideas. You'll be a good influence on her."

Mel bit her lip. She hadn't moved one hundred miles to be saddled with this woman.

Martin glanced over his shoulder, checking Petra was out of earshot.

"It's hard when you get to our age and realise that you're not in love anymore."

It was an unexpected, unwanted confidence. From the look on Martin's face, Mel guessed it was much worse than just falling out of love. He found his wife ridiculous.

—◆—

I heard the door close as you came in. You carried in your new printer, talking about the traffic and the ruckus at customer services when someone was making a complaint. You didn't look at me. Not once. Not properly. There was a time when you couldn't take your eyes off me.

The first thing you do when you wake up is pick up your phone and start scrolling. The worst part about it is that I do the exact same thing.

You once told me that a man should kiss his wife's navel every day. I took this to mean that love takes effort. Practice. Patience. How do we do this, now that we are older and tired?

⸎

It was a short walk to the shops. Mel followed the lane that ran between the backs of the cottages towards the high street.

The seasons were turning, summer shrugging off spring. *I've been asleep far too long.*

She stopped by the low fence of the last garden. Dead crows and rabbits were strung up in the trees, but it wasn't them that brought her up short.

A bare-chested man worked in the sun. Mel had known Ollie's body all her adult life. It gave her pleasure and comfort. This was the opposite. The shock of the new. This man was younger than her but not inappropriately so.

He worked the skin that was stretched on a wooden frame. Mel watched him move a blade across the taut surface. She recognised the haptic skill retained in the arm of a craftsman. His movement emphasised the tattoo that ran across his shoulder and down his arm.

Her appreciation was coupled with a distant arousal that got closer to her core with each motion of his shoulder. Then he turned to her. The ESP of knowing oneself observed. He didn't smile. Nor did she. There were no questions in their gaze, just mutual appraisal extended beyond decency.

Then he bowed his head as if in fealty, which startled Mel, her legs moving like a skittish colt's, carrying her on.

⸎

I saw a man today. He stared at me with such intent. And I stared right back.

I can't lie. I look at other people. I extrapolate the simplest contact into carnality, but I don't want them. Not really. Fantasy is never about the object of desire. It's about what's missing in yourself.

There's a dichotomy in long-term relationships; the tension between novelty and comfort. I only want Ollie, but we've fallen into the same patterns in everything. Familiarity undoes the intensity of living. I can't carry on with everything being the same. It's like slipping underwater and letting myself drown. I'm done with stagnation, others' expectations, and people-pleasing. I want to take life by the throat. I want to tear loose and fly to the moon.

⬥

The main road ran down to the bottom of the hill, where it split around the old jailhouse. The solid limestone building now housed an art gallery.

The ubiquitous minimart that Mel remembered was now a delicatessen. She was drawn to the blue awning and carefully stacked vegetables outside. A teenage girl sat on a stool, reading a book. Her denim apron was embroidered with a golden wheatsheaf. She jumped down to open the door for Mel.

Lambshead appeared unmarked by recession. It was busy and people were buying. The abundance within made her extravagant. At the counter she asked for a focaccia studded with salt and rosemary.

"Welcome." The woman serving her paused. "You're new, but I think you're one of us."

She filled a paper bag and handed it to Mel. "Roasted almonds from Spain. On the house. I'll be seeing you again."

Mel stopped at the florist. A foreign impulse as she never bought herself flowers. A sign in the window read *Under new ownership*. She dithered before the joyous blooms within.

A tall woman with blue hair was arranging a bouquet of gladioli.

"I love your tattoos." The words popped out, unbidden. "I'm sorry, that was personal."

The woman's body was a garden. She was decorated from the neck down, from what Mel could see. Ivy wound around her limbs. Roses opened amid the foliage, eyes at the centre of some of them, that stared at her, unflinching.

Threaded through it all was the diamond-back of an adder, its head coming to rest on her left wrist.

"Don't apologise. That was a lovely thing to say. Thank you. Let me pick some flowers for you."

She deliberated and then chose a bunch of pink tulips, the buds closed tight. "These are so underrated. Europe went crazy for these in the 1600s. Do you like them?"

"Yes," Mel said, because she realised she did.

"You're new, aren't you? You're in one of the old cottages. The flowers are on me." Her smile produced a dimple. "I insist."

The tulip heads lay in the crook of her arm, their petals pale pink and silky. A sly thought insinuated itself. They were a bouquet of glans.

Ollie would be waiting for her at home. They could make love on the living-room floor. She could surprise him with more than focaccia. She could buy something new, as much for her as him.

The lingerie shop was at the bottom of the hill. The window was dressed to look like a bedroom. Celadon wallpaper featured giant white cranes, accented in gold. A wardrobe without its doors revealed sheer items on padded hangers. Embroidered slippery things were left in artful disarray on a chair as though abandoned mid-seduction.

A kimono caught Mel's eye. Grey silk draped softly from a hook, distorting the swallow pattern. Her own towelling dressing gown made her feel thick-waisted and frumpy.

The bell over the door sounded as she entered. The window's promise was fulfilled within. It was a shop for Knightsbridge, not the English countryside. There were open armoires and mahogany display cabinets, not generic racks. Fat-headed peonies graced console tables.

Mel picked up a sheer black bodysuit. Embroidered serpents coiled up the sleeves and over the chest panel, but it wasn't designed for modesty. It was the garment of a woman who relished sex. Who relished herself.

There were inky blue bras and thongs stitched with silver stars, French knickers in cream voile, black satin bustiers, and seamed stockings. Did all the women of Lambshead go around in these exquisite fantasies? No wonder they were so happy and expansive. Well, all except for Petra.

Mel buried her face in the swallow kimono when she found it.

"Isn't it gorgeous?"

Mel turned. A woman uncurled from an armchair. The thought of being watched made Mel flush.

"I'm Estelle. Give me a shout if you need help. Browsers are positively encouraged."

"Thanks. I'm Melanie."

Estelle's hair was a waterfall of silver, platinum and steel. It refuted Mel's mother's mantra that older women should cut their hair short and dye it. It didn't age Estelle. She looked powerful.

On impulse Mel picked up the snake bodysuit. "Do you have this in large?"

"Of course. I'll put it in the changing room while you're looking around. May I be bold, Mel?" She said *Mel* like they were friends. "I'll leave some other things in there for you to try on. No pressure. Only if you like them."

—◆—

I've tried every variation of HRT. It's not a panacea for everything. It's not given me a youthful vagina or relieved the brain fog that makes every day a chore.

The worst thing is my skin. I'm accustomed to the flushes, but the itch is infernal. At first I thought it was shingles, then a reaction to my washing powder, but it's not. Antihistamines don't help. Now it's all over. Sometimes I think I'm on fire. I scratch in my sleep. I'm amazed there's no blood under my fingernails or on the sheets.

I asked Ollie to check my back for a rash and he said I looked like I'd been scrubbed with a wire brush.

—◆—

"I'm going to run a bath. Care to join me?" Mel kept her tone light.

"I'm going to finish setting up the office. You go and relax."

Mel languished in the suds, and still Ollie didn't come. She unpacked her new finery.

Petra had seen her from her lounge window when Mel came home. The woman's wave faltered when she saw the distinctive glossy shopping bags. *Sex people.*

A card was clipped to the receipt. *Estelle Ellcock. Relationship and intimacy coach. For couples and individuals.* She put it in her knicker drawer.

Mel lay back on the bed, dressed in the serpent black bodysuit. She heard her husband's tread on the stairs.

Ollie laughed as he stood in the doorway.

"Am I funny?"

"No, no, I was just surprised, that's all. I didn't know this was on the cards."

Her mood was curdling. She wanted him to say *Let's have sex. Let's make love. Let's fuck.* Or even better, not say anything but be overcome by need.

"I didn't know I had to book an appointment."

"I'm getting older. I need a little advanced notice."

"Get over here."

He took off his trousers and lay beside her. He still wore his socks. She wanted to rip them off. She leant over and kissed him instead. His kisses were reserved. Almost delicate. She wanted him to crush his desperate mouth to hers. She pushed her fingers deep into his back, seeking the real him beneath his skin. He gasped. She took his earlobe in her teeth, wanting to bite and make him bleed. She wrapped her legs around him, grinding against his groin.

Something crackled beneath them. He pulled out the garment tag that she'd left on the bed. He turned it over and saw the price.

"Bloody hell, Mel. How much have you spent?"

⸺◆⸺

They were both considerate at breakfast as if to reassure one another that all was well.

⸺◆⸺

I walked miles today, taking the turnstile at the bottom of the hill, leaving Lambshead and the disastrous night with Ollie behind.

It was a glorious day, warm but with a pleasant breeze. I buzzed, as alive as the meadow with its ox-eye daisies and ragged robin. On impulse, I took off my trainers and socks to ground myself. It was the first time in a long time that I'd curled my toes in the grass. I held up my arms to the sun and he smiled back, making me squint. A buzzard wheeled in his company.

A voice called out to me. I turned, annoyed at first. It was the young woman who'd opened the door of the deli for me. She waved, with full-armed enthusiasm, and jogged towards me.

"I'm Hester. I work at the shop in town."

"I remember. My name's Mel."

She fell in beside me. She kept glancing at my face. Her curiosity made me shy.

"May I show you something?"

"Lead on."

She chatted away, telling me about working for her mother and wanting to be an artist.

"There."

The field ahead had been ploughed and seeded. Shoots pushed through the velvet furrows which all seemed to point to a green mound, an anomaly in the flat field.

"That's Long Sally's Tump."

"It's a barrow." A neolithic construction to house the dead, where the living could visit.

"Yes." She smiled, pleased that I knew. "Come on."

We took the path that edged the field, brushing past nodding cow parsley. The green mound's opening was constructed of stone, a heavy lintel along the top. It looked like the Pi symbol. A sacred geometry in the landscape.

I followed Hester in on my hands and knees. We had to stoop once inside. It was cool and dark. I fumbled in my pocket for my phone and turned the torch on. I shone it into the side chambers, which had been sealed with iron bars.

"The remains of about twenty people were excavated just before the First World War. They were buried in the churchyard, except for the skeleton of Long Sally. The giantess. Nobody knows where she went."

I imagined her long bones nestled in this mausoleum and the fingers of her progeny touching her with care, telling her of the sun eclipsed and the yellow moon.

The weight of stones and packed earth above were heavy on me. I went from darkness into light. I have been asleep far too long.

Sunshine hurt my eyes. Hester led me to the top of the barrow. She stretched out on the grass. Her top rode up revealing the tattoo encircling her navel. A snake eating its own tail.

I lay down beside her and let the day's warmth penetrate my bones. The strangest thought came to me, and it's with me still: This land is my body and these are my children.

◆

Estelle's consulting room was at the back of the shop, decorated in pale wood and textured neutrals. Mel sniffed the tea Estelle handed her.

"I blend it myself. It contains truth serum and hallucinogenics. I'll give you some to take home."

Mel giggled. Estelle had spark. A therapist who was therapy herself.

"I've never done this before."

"Let's just have a chat and see where we go. Why did you move here?"

Mel opened her mouth, the answer she'd given Petra ready. Then she stopped.

"I was at a self-service till and the bacon wouldn't scan. The machine kept saying *Somebody is coming to help you* and I cried because I knew nobody was. I was suffocating in my own life. I went home and told my husband that I wanted to move."

"How did that go down?"

"Ollie's a very considered person. It took him a while to process, but he understood."

"It sounds like you're good friends."

The word *friends* made her sigh.

"Yes, but I'm scared we're losing all the other parts of our relationship. I wonder if we're going through the menopause at the same time. I mean, the male menopause is a thing, right? Tiredness, waning libido, apathy. I'm scared I've uprooted us and nothing's different."

"What needs to change?"

"I love him. I just can't carry on as we are. And I can't explain it to him until I understand it myself."

"Let's try and figure it out."

Estelle pulled out a box from a drawer and placed it on the coffee table between them. She knelt before it, her fingertips resting on it.

"I sense exciting things in you. Once you've freed yourself, you'll be astonishing."

Estelle took off the lid and laid it aside with care. She took out a parcel and unwrapped it. She presented it to Mel.

"This is for the pillowbook exercise."

The cover was soft leather. The vellum pages crackled as Mel turned them.

"I want you to write in this every day. Fragments of your day. Dreams. What you want to say to Ollie. Streams of consciousness. Anything. Don't censor yourself."

"It's too good to waste on me. I have notebooks at home."

"It's an important book for an important purpose. This was made by Callum. He lives here. He's the last vellum maker in the country."

The bare-chested man. Mel knew without being told.

"Writing reveals your subconscious. It'll help you materialise what you want."

"Wish fulfilment."

"Exactly. Rituals, spells, prayer. They're just a way to actualise our inner life."

Mel flicked through the book. There was a mark on the corner of one page. It looked like a flourish of sorts. Like the curl of a K. It wasn't on the surface but a pigment within, like a tattoo.

"What's this made from?"

"Human skin."

They both burst out laughing.

I had my third session with Estelle today. Callum was in the shop when I arrived. Estelle introduced us. He ignored my outstretched hand and leant down to hug me. He must've felt my heart banging. I was acutely aware that we were surrounded by the trappings of sex. If Estelle and Callum were amused by my discomfort they hid it.

Up close I could see Callum's snake tattoo. Callum saw me looking.

"It represents renewal and healing."

I couldn't stop staring at him. It's strange to write such private thoughts on something he made. The shock of him goes through me as I write.

"You're the vellum-maker."

I watched his mouth as he explained his craft. How he washes the skin in water and lime to soften it and remove the hairs. How he stretches it on a frame called a herse, then scuds it with a lunellum. The crescent-shaped knife I saw in his hand that day, when he was working in the garden. A ritual item.

He told me that the best quality vellum is made from the skins of the unborn.

Callum's mouth was wide and full. He laughed easily. He looked at me in a way that nobody has in a long time. Like he was enchanted.

"You'd better be going." Estelle sounded peeved. "Mel and I have things to talk about."

It was clear that they were lovers from how Estelle kissed that full mouth.

"Aren't you going to kiss Mel too? We're friends now, after all."

I laughed, but they didn't. I expected him to protest, but he leant in. His mouth lingered on mine. My lips parted, despite myself and I felt a rush of heat between my legs.

I resented Estelle in that moment. Older than I but able to command someone like Callum. I don't know if I envy her Callum's kisses or her power over people.

Mel sat in the corner of the café, writing in her book. She kept her sessions with Estelle and the journal a secret from Ollie. The illicit liaisons with the page had become an essential part of her day.

She drained the last of the coffee and put the book away. It was only then that she saw Petra, who was sat with two other women. They all looked the same, with their shiny hair, and their uniform of linen skirts and strappy sandals.

There was nothing for it. They were right by the door. Mel picked up her bag. It seemed childish not to say hello. They all turned to look at her. Petra put down her mug.

"Lyndsey, Hannah, meet Mel, my new neighbour."

Lyndsey suppressed a smirk. Mel was conversant in playground cattiness, having been the butt of it. She could tell when she'd been the subject of discussion. Heat prickled up her spine and across her back. It started to burn.

"Well, I better be off."

Mel could breathe again once she was outside. She looked back, despite herself. The women's heads were together in a conspiracy.

Bunch of curdled-faced trout, she thought.

A wasp landed on the inside of the window.

Go on, darling. Do your worst.

Galvanised by Mel's magical thinking, the wasp took flight. It landed on Lyndsey, a dark blot on her unblemished cheek. All three of them were on their feet, swatting at the assailant. Too late. Lyndsey screamed. She had been stung.

—◆—

I dreamt that I went outside while you were sleeping. It was early and you were tired, Ollie. Are you tired of me? I don't know anymore.

I'm scared to ask you in case you say yes.

I stood on the lawn. It was unbearably hot. I peeled off my t-shirt and my knickers. The night was fragrant. I could see all the colours of the night, dark blues and blacks, swirling like the contents of a cauldron. It made me feel electric. The flesh I was born in is a miracle. Why have I always just tolerated it? I held up my arms to the moon, who governs menstrual blood, amniotic fluid, tears, and the sea. She turned her face to me, illuminating what's written on my skin.

I am a book, waiting to be read.

Petra was at her bedroom window.

Stop looking at me. *She's always watching me. If go into the garden, she's there, head over the fence, always commenting on what I'm doing or complaining about something in the town. I hate her scrutiny.*

I'd like to put her eyes out.

◦

Martin brought Petra home from the hospital today. She woke one morning, screaming fit to raise the dead. We heard her.

They can't find a reason for her blindness. She's had all kind of tests, even a psychiatric assessment.

Petra put her hand on Martin's shoulder as he walked up the path. She was a pale, blind ghost at his side. He was whistling to himself. He sounded remarkably cheery.

A thought came to me, unbidden. I did that. *It was accompanied by a stab of glee.*

◦

Mel dabbed cream around her eye sockets with the tip of her ring-finger. Ollie was undressing for bed.

"We should go and see Petra and Martin."

"Why?"

"To see how she is. I'm making lasagne, so we can take them a portion. I can pick up some flowers."

"She won't be able to see the flowers. It'd be a waste."

"She'll appreciate the thought. She'd come over if something bad happened to you."

"You bet she would. She'd be here like a shot."

"If not for her, for Martin."

"Sadly for Martin she's not lost the power of speech too."

134

"What's got into you?" Ollie raised an eyebrow.

"When did you care so much about the neighbours?"

"She's just gone *blind*. Why are you being so malicious?"

"Not malice, Ollie, I'm just not a hypocrite. It's all bullshit."

"Decency isn't bullshit." He paused.

"Go on. Say it."

"I'm just wondering if you need to try HRT again. Or antidepressants."

"What?"

"Coming here seemed to help at first but all that fury's back. But it's worse. I can't keep up with you. We moved for nothing."

"I thought you wanted this too."

"I didn't, but you did. You were struggling."

"*We* were struggling."

His face was grey. "That's news to me."

"Really?"

He sat down, winded.

"Life is so humdrum. We never talk about anything important. And you don't tell me that you love me anymore."

"I didn't know you needed reminding. Love isn't about what you say. It's about what you do. I uprooted my whole life because you wanted it."

"What a martyr, Ollie. Am I going to have to live with that for the rest of our life?"

<hr>

Do you remember our first night together, Ollie? We shared a single bed in my student digs. We wanted each other so badly, but we were both shy. Surprised by one another. Your dogged attention never overwhelmed me. It was a promise.

I don't know how long we slept that night, if at all. It was a twilight world of touching. Even then, you were the most attentive of lovers. You made me feel beautiful. Seen.

You were different by lamplight. You were animal, all scent and secretions. I never knew that you, so awkward when you danced, could be so coiled and graceful. Your timing immaculate.

We *were animals in heat. It wasn't a sordid thing, but a true expression of ourselves.*

I'd have you like that again.

---◆---

Mel slid her hand across the mattress. Ollie's side was empty. The sheet was cold. She dressed and went downstairs.

Ollie was waiting for her. The crumpled cushions and bunched up blanket evidence of his night on the sofa. His face was blotchy.

"I'm sorry. About what I said. About everything. I'll do anything. Anything you want. Look, I'm changing."

He dropped to his knees before her, hands gripping the backs of her thighs, sniffing and snuffling at her crotch. His hot breath penetrated the thin fabric of her skirt.

"Stop."

The blood was in his cheeks and clearly elsewhere. He tried to pull her to the floor, tearing her clothes. She didn't want Ollie like this. She couldn't see the man she'd trusted with her body all these years. He frightened her.

"I said stop."

He was Ollie enough to hear the fear in her voice. He sat back on his heels and started to cry.

"It hurts, Mel." He pushed his fist against his sternum. "Why does it hurt so much? I want you so badly that it's a physical pain."

He covered his mouth with his hands, choking on his sobs. He was in pieces. The moment of threat had passed. She guided him onto the sofa, pulling a cushion onto her knee so he could lay his head there. She stroked his hair, making soothing sounds like a mother to her child.

---◆---

Mel woke with neckache. She'd slept at an odd angle, her head lolling against the back of the sofa. The summer night outside the window was a rich dark blue.

136

The dog, its head on her knee, was familiar. It was a yellow labrador, darker at the tips of his ears. He tilted his broad head, brown eyes below a prominent brow. The look he gave her was both noble and indignant.

The labrador sat up, whining and pawing at her.

"Who are you?"

Mel fussed him, his loose pelt moving over his frame as she rubbed his back. His coat was short and dense, both dry and strangely oily to touch. He shook his head sending his ears flapping.

She knew him.

"Ollie?"

He cocked his head, his nose quivering, then started to lick her face.

<hr />

Mel tied Ollie up in a pool of lamplight, outside Estelle's shop. He whimpered and strained at the leash she'd improvised from a nylon washing line.

Mel was prepared to rip the door off, but it was unlocked. The interior looked like a butcher's locker in the dark, the oddest cuts on hangers.

A soft light shed on the stairs from above. Mel took the steps two at a time, calling out. Blood pounded in her ears.

It wasn't the chic apartment she'd expected. It comprised of one long room. The floor's black varnish was scuffed and gouged. There was an altar along one wall, dressed with a set of mirrors and candles. The matt dark walls sucked up the flickering light.

Estelle lay on a chaise, the only other piece of furniture in the room. The velvet upholstery was dirty and stained. She held Mel's pillowbook.

"Where did you get that? It's private."

"Martin. He got it while you were asleep."

"He's been in my house? Why would he do that?"

"Martin's my brother-in-law. Between us, he's a very weak man." Estelle licked her forefinger and turned the page with a flourish. "'I'd like to put her eyes out,'" she quoted. "Well, aren't you just full of surprises?"

"I didn't know it would happen, I promise. And I didn't know Petra was your sister."

"Don't be sorry, angel. I needed to deal with Petra at some point. You've done me a favour. And how. Who knew you'd be so gifted?"

"It can't have been me. Not just from writing it."

"Oh, it can."

"And Ollie?" To say aloud *my husband has become a dog* was ludicrous.

"Martin said you have a new pet. It *is* Ollie."

Mel knew it was true.

"How do I turn him back."

"Transmutation is permanent. You can only go forward. Become."

Estelle's sharp teeth that had seemed attractive now looked dangerous. "Become?"

"You're in the final trimester of your life. The expectations of child rearing are behind you. Life has no further plans for you. You're free to go about your true calling."

"Which is?"

"To wield power."

Mel's blood ran so fast there was barely a pause between heartbeats. Her legs buckled and she crumpled to the floor. Estelle sat beside her, rubbing her back.

"The pain will pass. I promise. This will all make sense soon. The land is calling to you."

"My parents are Latvian."

"That doesn't matter. We are rivers of blood from the world over, all running together. It's just some people are too stupid to know it. Our symbol is a lion and a unicorn. One's from Africa and the other is a fantasy."

Estelle cradled Mel's face. She was too weak to push her away. She couldn't locate the pain. It was everywhere, all at once.

"What's happening to me?"

"Come and see."

Estelle helped her to her feet and walked her to the mirrors. The candlelight hurt Mel's eyes.

Estelle stood behind her, looking over her shoulder, arms around her to undo the buttons of Mel's top. Mel tried to resist but then saw herself as she was revealed. Her blouse dropped to the floor. The rest of her clothes followed.

"While you've been writing in the book, it's been writing on you."

Mel was reflected in tryptic. She was marked from every angle. Words and symbols glowed red as if lit from within. The pulse of pain at her core made the calligraphy on her skin throb. Mel was the word made flesh.

"You've no idea how long I've waited for someone like you. You're the perfect vessel."

A vessel. I'm no more to her than a jug or a vase. Mel felt a surge of power through her, like flexing a muscle. The writing on Mel flared bright. Her multiple reflections confirmed her new skill.

I am tired of being passive. I will never be passive again.

Estelle's court filed in. The deli-owner and her daughter. The tattooist. The florist. Martin guiding Petra, a marble-pale Madonna. Bloody tears coursed down her cheeks. She didn't lift a hand to wipe them away.

Finally there was Callum, leading Ollie. Ollie's claws made a clipping sound on the floor. He strained at his makeshift leash when he saw Mel. When Callum yanked him back, he trotted on the spot with excitement.

"Isn't she wondrous?" Estelle displayed Mel like a specimen.

Mel held up her head. She wouldn't tolerate Estelle for a moment longer. She pulled the woman close. It was an embrace made of light. It was blinding. The others turned away, shielding their eyes. Ollie's barks rose to a frenzy.

A dark thing came out of the bright column. Estelle, transformed. She was a crow. Her black plumage was shot through with feathers of grey and silver. She opened her stout bill and cawed.

—◆—

Estelle doesn't understand that the written word is dynamic. It illuminates everything, from one generation to the next. It casts light into the darkness but the stain of night is always with me. Cut me in half and it runs through me like the words in a stick of Blackpool rock.

I am miniaturised in a vast landscape. Its barrows crowded with kings' bones and an armoury of longbows, arrows, swords, and Nintendos. Eagle standards and a Windrush of faces shine by the light of comets. And when I dance, it's to Ska.

I am temperate. I am hills, forests, and the enclosure. I am winterlight in black boughs. I am the heath and common and oak. I am the hole in the hagstone. The mulch and the mud.

I am the chalk horse, the plough and seed. The blaze in the furnace and the fingers crushed in the loom. I am King Arthur and piers and smackheads and cream teas.

This land is my body and these are my children.

<hr />

Estelle-crow flew against the window, striking the glass in a panic. She landed heavily, one wing flapping, the other one broken. Mel's hands closed around her. She spoke to Estelle in soothing tones, looking into the bird's bright gaze. Then she wrung Estelle's neck with a quick, decisive motion. She dropped the corpse and went over to the chaise. Mel was a queen in recline, finally at home in her own skin.

Callum released Ollie, who raced to pick up the dead bird in his mouth. He looked up at Mel with adoring eyes, then lay down beside her, his tail thumping the floor.

BOOK WORM

ISY SUTTIE

I

I always called him Roger, never Worm Man. The Worm Man thing was started by Jamie and Lee, and it came from the time they'd sneaked into the allotment at the end of the school field and got all the way to the end, only to find Roger standing in the blackberry bushes, staring at them, screaming GET OUT OF THE ALLOTMENT, and – importantly, and apparently – his hair was not in fact made of hair, but worms. Alive worms, grey and purple, attached by their tails, wriggling frantically for their lives. Worms with slime dripping off them onto the blackberries and Roger's trousers.

Personally, I think it was all to do with the fact they'd got told off for being in the allotment by Miss Harper. Claiming they'd seen a man with hair made of worms was an attempt to make themselves bumbling innocent kids, and Roger inhuman. I never saw him as inhuman. In fact, he's probably the most human human I've ever known.

Worm Man as a name caught on quick, and became what all the kids in the village called Roger. One of the reasons I couldn't bring myself to do it myself was because he lived across the lane from us and I saw him almost daily. It would seem so two-faced to start referring to him as this name behind his back, when he said good morning to me and David every day, and waved to Mum if she managed to make it down the shops for cigarettes and vodka, which was nice, because some people didn't bother to wave to Mum at all anymore.

Roger's house was an old two-up-two-down, just like ours. His was next door to a car mechanic's that always had a trio of grease-covered men in blue overalls tinkering with engines outside it. I'd have to step round rusty car parts to get to school, while they stood sipping tea and smoking Mayfairs in five or six puffs, sucking them dry and flicking them towards the little brook behind them, their smoky breath billowing out like speech bubbles.

It never occurred to me to worry about the cigarettes being around petrol, because they were adults, and I was not. It never occurred to me to worry about much at all, and the fact I often arrived home from school to find I'd need to put Mum to bed because she'd drunk too much with Sue – or without Sue – and that she'd been crying again about how Dad had gone, it was just something I had to do. Nothing to question. Putting her to bed gave me the best chance to get my homework done and make some toast for myself and David before it all began again the next day.

The only thing I hated was when she cadged cigarettes off the mechanics. It made me want to change my name and move David and myself into a place of our own.

The mechanics were the reason I first saw the sign in Roger's window. I was walking to school with David, and he recognised the Nissan badge on the car they were working on. The men loved David because he knew all the car badges off by heart. 'Nissan,' he said, and pointed. 'Nissan,' they chuckled. 'Nissan,' said David again. 'Nissan,' they replied. 'We've got a Dodge in the back,' said the biggest man, the one with a red beard. 'It'll be out in the next few days.' We never ventured into the garage to look at the cars, even though it was all open, a big metal shutter raised right up. We always waited until the men worked on them outside. As David stepped forward to give the Nissan badge a little stroke, the biro-written sign in Roger's window caught my eye:

Wanted: assistant to help old man with community venture – apply within (in this house)

'Roger's starting a library,' said the biggest man. They didn't scoff, because they knew starting a library wasn't an easy thing to do. They weren't like that. No one was. The pride in the village came before anything else. Say a man left and moved to Texas and became a serial killer, he'd still be 'one of us, but fallen on hard times'. If a man moved in from outside town, even from the next village, he'd always be 'so-and-so from such-and-such-place'. They'd almost be *waiting* for him to move to Texas and become a serial killer, revealing his true colours. So, because it was Roger starting a library, it was just a fact. He was starting a library. Correction: he *wanted* to start a library, but he needed help.

II

I'd never been in Roger's house before. I'd knocked on his door twice in my life – once because Jamie had dared me to, but then we'd scarpered to the brook before he opened it, and the other time with David when we were trick-or-treating. We hadn't made much of an effort – I'd had a real spider in my hand, which was my 'trick' – and David had bunged a Superman cape over his school uniform. Roger had given us a digestive biscuit each, and I'd opened the hand that didn't have the spider in it to accept mine.

In the hall, it smelt musty and of cat food and there wasn't much light. Roger led me into the living room where a black and white cat lay on a tatty brown sofa with its eyes closing. The thickness of the carpet meant you couldn't fully open or close the door. I perched next to the cat whilst he told me his plan, his eyes gleaming.

'You won't remember this, but there used to be a library on Goyley Bank,' he said. He had grey stubble that grew so far up his cheeks it almost reached his eyes. 'And I've been thinking it'd be nice to start one from my house. Just for locals, just to come in and borrow a book. Since Aileen died, they've all been in boxes. It bothers me, seeing them lying there. It's like they're asking to be read.' I'd never met Aileen, and I'd been born there. 'How many books have you got?' I said. I was totally unsure of what my role would be in this venture, and I was surprised at my forthrightness. 'About forty,' he said. 'We'd have to write down in the front cover of the book when the person'd have to return it. Neatly, like. Then, in a big book, we could write down who's borrowed them and when they're returning them. It'd just be in this room. Different shelves for different sorts of books.'

I noticed he was already using 'we'. This sounded like a lot of work. What would I do with David? 'Have you had anyone else come?' I said, gesturing towards his window sign. 'What do you reckon?' he winked. 'I can only do after school,' I said, 'and my brother David'd have to come, too. He's not a bad boy as long as you tickle him every so often.' 'Sounds like he's got his head screwed on, does David,' grinned Roger. 'Now, when can you two start?'

III

As it turned out, all the books were Aileen's, and they were all romance. I went from knowing nothing about the woman to knowing one thing about her: she loved books about women with long hair falling for men who wanted to 'romp' with them. As I slid the last book onto the shelf, which I'd decorated with paper hearts to signify that this was the romance section, Roger stood back and sighed. 'We're too limited here,' he said. 'We need more books.' We replaced his window sign with a new one:

Bookworm Library, open 4pm – 6pm Monday to Friday. Large selection of romance novels. BOOK DONATIONS URGENTLY REQUIRED.

The mechanics were the first customers. They each solemnly took a book from the romance shelf without examining them at all, and then Roger asked them to queue up. I was to write their names in the large black book Roger had given me to keep track of who had borrowed what. The biggest mechanic was first, the one with a red beard. He looked at me blankly, clutching the book to his overalls. It had a picture of a woman in a long flowing dress stroking a horse. It felt awful to ask his name, unconscionable. 'Just put Derek,' called Roger from across the room where he was watching 'the first borrowing', as he was calling it, clenching his fists in excitement. The next man gave his name as Derek, too, and the third one just said, 'next door'. I wrote down what they said, and put the titles they were borrowing: *She-Devil*, *The Wind in her Sails* and *If the Walls Could Talk*. Then I wrote, 'return by 15th October or pay a fine'. 'What's the fine?' chuckled the red-bearded one. 'Ooh,' laughed Roger, 'you don't want to know.'

After they left, he said, 'well done, kid,' and we started jumping for joy and David danced in the middle of the room even though he didn't understand why we were so excited. The cat fled off the sofa in fear.

When I got home, Mum was still asleep on the stairs, so I put her to bed, and while I did that, David fell asleep on the sofa watching TV with his head on his Superman outfit. I left him there for a bit while I did my homework, then I carried him up to our room and I lay next to him trying to get to sleep. I couldn't, though. I kept picturing the looks on the men's faces as they'd queued up, so respectfully, how they'd watched my hand move the pen as I'd written down the book titles and their names next to them, how they'd immediately trusted mine and Roger's system. I couldn't believe how easy it was to just start a library in your own house by laying out some books and putting a sign in the window. What were all the people in the world doing, just walking about and moaning about the rain and the price of fags and hair dye? They could be starting libraries in their living rooms, shops in their front yards. They could be dancing in their backyards and screaming at the moon. But no one did. No one did anything in that village. And now we were doing something.

IV

The second night, I had to take David with me again as Mum was out with Sue. He sat with the cat on the sofa and drew on a pad with 'Basildon Bond' on the front that Roger got down from a cupboard. David liked to think he was writing down important things for the library, too. Of course, it was all complete gobbledegook but we acted like he was the head librarian, with his Basildon Bond pad and digestive biscuits.

We had more customers than the first night, and I was given a specific place to stand with my big black book, next to the living room door. At one point, there were eight people in the room, and two women were after the same book – *Lights Out*. They came to a tacit agreement that one of them could borrow it before the other on the condition that the first one gave the second one a free Bailey's – she worked behind the bar at the Boat House.

Neither of us intervened until they started to discuss how the first one would hand over *Lights Out* with the Bailey's, saying how it'd be a nice book to read in the pub. 'It'll have to be returned here first,' I found myself saying. 'We've got a system.' I held up my black book with a flourish. The first page was now completely full of book titles, names and return dates. 'You want me to return it here before I give it to her?' said the first one, laughing. 'I go back years with Roger.' I looked at him and he willed me on with his eyes. 'It's just for the system, madam,' I said. 'We don't make the rules.' 'Who does, then?' she asked. 'Him?' she pointed at David who nodded solemnly, and I went over and ruffled his hair before returning to my book. 'I remember when you was nothing but a twinkle in your ma's eye,' said the first one, winking at me, but she gave me her name – Brenda – and I told her she could have it a week. 'Won't need it a week,' she replied, winking at me again, 'Only a night.' She gave us both a Black Jack from her bag. Mine was very squashy, and I thought it could be old, but I still unwrapped and ate it as they left, then I unwrapped David's for him.

Roger brought in more digestives and I was glad, because all Mum had left in the kitchen for our tea was a small block of cheese and a few slices of bread. David wolfed three down in a row and I was more restrained. 'We've done well,' said Roger, his cheeks rosy. At five to six, as he was about to turn the sign to closed, Brenda rushed in with two carrier bags overflowing with books. 'Here you go,' she said. 'They've been lying in the attic for years.'

As she left, we tipped the contents onto the carpet. In an instant, we had three new sections – cookery, biography and adventure – and I stayed behind to log the books and arrange them on the shelves as my brother crunched his way through four more digestives. The cat watched me as I did it, her eyes flat and her fur gleaming in the lamplight. 'This is it,' Roger kept repeating, stroking the cat behind her ears which always made her purr. 'This is where it all begins.'

V

He was right. By the end of the second week, we had about a thousand books. On one of the days, everyone who came in to borrow a book donated at least a bag in return, and we'd had some old shelves from someone. That Saturday, Roger and I decided we had to rearrange his living room to accommodate our increase in stock. We moved the coffee table into Roger's kitchen and stacked the books in the middle of the living room as well as along the sides. It felt like a real library. 'This *is* a real library, kid,' Roger said. 'We just had to have the books to prove it.'

After the first few weeks, when our success was much bigger than we could have predicted and I had to move on to a second big black book, I told Roger to start taking Sundays off from working on the stock. I could see he was getting tired out. It didn't stop people turning up though, despite him drawing the curtains in every room and reading all day, nestled on the sofa with his packet of digestives and the cat by his side. People would pound at the door with their armfuls and bagfuls and boxfuls of books. When nobody answered, they'd just leave them on the doorstep and Roger would take them in on the Monday morning. Even if they'd been rained on or nibbled by a fox, he never, ever rejected any books. 'It's invigorating me,' he kept saying. 'The first thing since Aileen went. I used to read all the time and believe that *I* could have those sorts of adventures and then, when I got to being a teenager, I just stopped reading, started drinking with my mates, and all that space in my

147

head went away. All those worlds I could have known.' 'Well, you know them now,' I said. He grinned and nodded. 'Yes, yes I do. Books take me away, you see. Hours can go by. They take me away.'

He stopped washing, I think. His stubble became a knotty beard and his hair started standing on end like real worms. Nobody minded. It added to the experience. He talked so deeply to customers. He really took an interest in their little grumbles. He'd say things like, 'Well, as Tolstoy would say, you can't pay a plumber unless he's sorted out your u-bend.'

Still the donations came. The two upstairs bedrooms were now packed with books. We'd tried to sort them into categories upon arrival but it was no use. There was no space to do it. It reminded me of the end of a game of Tetris when all the bricks pile up faster and faster and there's nowhere for you to fit them into the wall, and then you die.

I put a sign in the living room window saying '**no more book donations**'. Roger couldn't see it because the window was so full of books. I got David to sneak through the gap at the side and tack it onto the glass. But nobody took any notice whatsoever. If anything, there seemed to be more coming than ever. We'd only been open two months, and I swear we had more books than the school library.

'Aileen would have found this very funny,' Roger said. 'Me having to weave my way through a book maze.' There was a path about two foot wide, which curved its way from the bedroom doorway to the bottom of Roger's double bed. Roger was showing me how he had to twist and side-step through it to get to bed every night. He laughed as his head brushed against some Penguin Classics, which I wished we could display downstairs, but downstairs was the same as up here. People couldn't pick up a book without sending ten flying, and God forbid you should try and take one from anywhere other than the very top.

'Good excuse not to change the sheets,' he said from behind the book wall. I hovered in the doorway. It didn't smell like he'd changed the sheets for a long time, but I never said anything. Everyone treated me like I was an adult when I worked at the library, but not in that grand and fake way some adults do when you're a kid. It was just like I was a worker. They didn't bat an eyelid at my skills, like you wouldn't a normal librarian. I'll always be grateful to Roger for that.

That night, David noticed the cat's spine was visible through her fur, and we started feeding her Black Jacks – Brenda had given us a whole box. The cat dwelt on David's lap, her eyes grey and half-open, trying to swallow one of the sweets. I called Roger through. 'When did I last feed her?' he said, running his hands through his hair so that it looked even more like worms. David and I started feeding her after that. Roger said he would, but although I knew he wanted to mean it, I didn't believe him.

VI

We decided to have a Christmas party. All the mechanics said they'd come, and Roger said fine, as long as you smoke outside, as smoke will damage my books. We temporarily moved some of the books into the kitchen, and had to move even more throughout the night, as so many people came to join in.

Roger wore a suit with holes in it and a shirt with a pointed collar. He asked me if I thought he looked smart, and I said yes. 'Aileen would be proud,' he whispered. I didn't like the smell of him when he stood close to me. It was an even more intense version of the musty smell in his hall. I didn't move away though. 'She would,' I said. 'I can't stop reading!' he laughed. His eyes took on a strange look, as if he was seeing into me. I didn't like it and it reminded me of how Dad had used to look. 'I can't stop reading and I never will.' He clapped me on the back.

I didn't feel the same about reading. I liked it, and sometimes thought about stories when I was in bed, but I mainly liked working at the library because I was in charge of the big black book. I liked printing the names and dates neatly on the lines. I watched Roger whisk Brenda off her feet and twirl her around before pouring her a glass of wine. He was so different from the Roger I'd first met that I felt like one of them must have been a lie.

There was no space in the living room for any more than five or six people, so everyone spilled out onto the street, and the mechanics opened up the garage and let the guests use their toilet. Brenda started dancing under the streetlamp even though there was no music, with everyone clapping around her. She picked David up and spun him around, and let him touch her hair, which was sprayed rock-solid. Mum came out groaning about the noise, but Brenda's friend took her back inside. I was scared when Mum came out. I hadn't mentioned the library to her – I'd just said, when she'd asked (which was twice) that I was helping out Worm Man. She knew he had no wife and she didn't ask for any more details. I wanted it to be my thing. I didn't mind that David knew. He had to know, as he was too young to be left alone with Mum. He didn't understand anyway. He was just grateful for the Basildon Bond notebook and the biscuits and the fact that the cat liked to sit in his lap and eat treats from his podgy little hand and knead – he called it *stinch* – her paws on his clothes.

VII

It was David who found her when everyone had finally gone home. He found her not by her presence, but her absence. He knew her pattern. She was always on his lap in the evenings, and that evening, after we'd gobbled down the late-night fish and chips which Roger had bought the three of us as a celebration, she was not there. She was not under the sofa either, her favourite hiding place. She was not down at the skirting board, and she was not on top of the fridge, or lapping drips of water from the tap next to the pile of dirty mugs.

David was small enough to crawl into the tunnels in the living room and to see that the biography tower in the far corner had toppled over. One of the guests had probably leant on it and it had given way, volumes of hardbacks about cricketers overcoming their injuries and boxers overcoming their upbringings and actors becoming estranged from their parents cascading down into a dark corner, which just happened to be the place where the cat was feasting on a biscuit David had dropped there for her, sensing she was nervous in the presence of so many people shouting and laughing, singing and chanting.

I was very proud of David because he carried her crushed body out, his tongue poking out in concentration, and on some level he knew she was dead, even though he was saying 'she sleeping'. He put her down on his little sofa square and tried to feed her a chip. Her nose was still shiny and wet, and I found that fact very disturbing. It made my stomach ache, in fact. 'She's too sleepy for chips,' I said to David. He was stroking her head like he always did. He tried to get her paws to *stinch* his leg. 'She's too sleepy for that, David,' I said. It seemed odd that she was as she always was, black fur with a tiny white mark under her mouth – 'that's a kiss from God,' Brenda had said when she'd first seen it – not more *dead.* There was no blood.

David put his head right down onto hers and rubbed his cheek on her ears. I didn't know if this was a good idea, but it was something he'd always tried to do when she was alive, and she usually wriggled away from him, so I thought it best to let him have his moment with her. At this point, I turned and looked at Roger. He was surveying the room, counting the books. 'Roger,' I said. He started picking books up and scanning their titles, smelling them, clutching them to his chest, breathing them in. 'Roger,' I said again. 'She's…' I didn't want to say 'dead'. 'Look at her,' I said. He turned his face to me, and I'll never forget the look in his eyes. It was the same look Mum had when she got a new boyfriend who promised her the world. 'We've got thousands of books,' he murmured, his hair standing on end. 'Kids, we've got thousands.'

VIII

We buried the cat at the end of our titchy garden, next to what had once long ago been a square of sandpit. I used the old red plastic spade Dad had bought us in Cleethorpes. It took ages to dig a hole big enough. David and I shivered before the heaped mound of earth, with David's rusty toy digger lying beside the cat's body, which we'd placed in the hole. It was absolutely freezing and the sky was thick black. The lane was totally silent. It felt like the kind of night where the world next to ours is loosened at the seams.

I looked behind me to Roger's house, unsure whether to go ahead and cover the cat with the sand. All the curtains were tightly drawn but the lights were on. David and I had tried to bury the cat in Roger's backyard, but it was impossible to find any place soft enough and he'd only given us a teaspoon to dig with. He'd wandered around the house humming, gathering up armfuls of books and moving them from room to room as we'd hacked at the dry earth with the spoon. I wondered if the cat reminded him of Aileen's dead body, and if that was why he couldn't really take it in. I noticed that my sign asking for no more donations had gone from the front window. Roger must have taken it down.

'Let's just wait for two more minutes, see if he's coming,' I said quietly. We gazed at the cat lying on her side. Her eyes were open, and I wished they weren't, but I didn't know what to do about it. Touching them was unimaginable. Why hadn't I seen before that they were open? Or had they opened on their own? My heart beat fast in my throat.

David held my hand loosely and I noticed his lip was trembling. 'She's too cold,' he said, suddenly leaping forward, knocking the red spade away and scrabbling at the earth. 'I'm stinching her,' he said. I had to hold him back and he started to scream and claw at my arms. I prayed out loud to God that someone or something, even some evil creature, would take the cat away. I wished adults were in charge, like when Granny got taken into the crematorium to burn. I couldn't possibly start to cover the cat with sand while David was like this. He would try to leap into the hole with the cat.

Eventually he lost his power and collapsed into sobbing and Mam opened the window and shouted, 'What the bloody hell is going on out there? First the dancing, now the screaming. It's nearly midnight.' That's when I saw Roger's bedroom curtains were open. All I could see were books, stacked in a wall like bricks, with no gaps. It was like they were laughing at us. I looked at the cat's little head, and I knelt down and grabbed fistfuls of sand and covered it first, so I didn't have to look at her eyes. David was kneeling down too, shaking his head, but he didn't try to stop me. As I was covering her body in the same way, I noticed something in her fur. Lots of tiny lines. At first, I thought it was worms, but as I looked closer, I could see they weren't moving. I stopped grabbing at the sand. They weren't worms. They were words. Written on her fur, in white writing, was:

Return by December 20th at midnight or pay a fine.

December 20th. Today's date. I looked at my watch. 11.58 p.m. I cried out and looked at Roger's house, but the tableau was the same: just the books, watching me, noting my every move. 'Help me, David!' I shouted, and he reached into the sand too and we covered the body as quick as we could, panting in the darkness, not daring to look back at the books.

IX

I went over the road the next morning. I knocked at the door and counted to one hundred while I waited. David asked if he could see the cat if she was inside Roger's house. I gave him a conker that Jamie had given me at school and he turned it in his hands as I knocked again, then rapped on the living room window, then told him to throw the conker at Roger's bedroom window. It missed, of course, so I had a go. David was giggling and his cheeks were pink. I didn't know what we were going to eat that night if Roger didn't answer. Mum was away somewhere with her new boyfriend Graham, and she hadn't said when she was coming back. When I threw the conker the third time, the curtains in Roger's bedroom parted a crack. Even through the crack I could see that the books were engulfing him. I could only really see his hair and his eyes. His hair looked like it was moving, and his eyes were alive and dancing. I waved and he waved back. I motioned for him to come and let us in. He closed the curtains. We waited for half an hour then went home. I found a can of out-of-date baked beans at the back of the cupboard and we ate them together in David's bed as we were so cold. David was still talking about the cat, but eventually he drifted off to sleep. I had one last look across the lane before I turned out the light, but Roger's house was dark apart from the round glow of a lamp behind the curtains in his bedroom. At least he was reading.

X

The customers banged on the door so much that the mechanics had to come out and tell them to stop. He wasn't answering the door and that was it. And no, they couldn't leave their book donations or the books they were returning at the garage. It was, after all, a garage. It had been fun, but everything ends. Move on. Twenty per cent discount on a car service though, if that was useful to anyone.

I watched it all from mine and David's room. I didn't want to go out because customers associated me with the library. Even if I could get into the house, which I couldn't, how would I begin to find my big black book and start to tick off the books people were returning?

They knew him in the police station. 'Someone's been round,' the man at the desk said, 'but if he don't want to answer the door, he don't want to answer the door.' I didn't know what to say, so I walked out and down the steps without saying thank you. I felt that they were sniggering behind my back, so I went back in. 'I want you to write it down,' I said. 'That I've been in.' They said they would, and I insisted on giving my full name, including my middle name, which I didn't think I'd ever said out loud. The man wrote it down and told me not to worry. 'It's only Worm Man,' they said. 'He'll be alright. Old blokes are tougher than people think.' 'He's Book Worm now,' I shouted as I left again. 'Not Worm Man.'

When I got home, Graham was there. He was okay, and due to him, Mum had started getting dressed and wearing eyeliner and brushing her teeth. His thoughts about us seemed to amount to 'if they don't bother me, I won't bother them'. He worked as a window fitter and suddenly that week, when he moved in, there was milk in the fridge and fish fingers in the freezer and

I didn't have to think about begging from the chippy every night. Every time I looked out of the window, Graham said, 'Don't be hankering after that old weirdo. Let him live with his books, your mum says.'

XI

'A new start,' Mum kept saying. 'It's a new start. Graham's sister lives in Hull and we can stay with her while we get ourselves together.' 'Can I come back and see Jamie and Lee?' I asked. 'Yeah,' she replied, glancing at Graham. 'When you're eighteen!' I didn't like it when they laughed at me.

They thought I didn't get time to say bye to Roger, but I did. I had a photo of me, him and David that Brenda had taken the first week we opened. On our last night in the house, I took it out and wrote on the back:

I liked doing the library a lot. I've tried so many times to see if you are okay, but I've run out of options and now we're moving to Hull. The cat is buried next to the old sandpit in our garden.

I took a digestive from our kitchen and put it in an envelope with the photo, and sneaked out once everyone was asleep to post it through Roger's letterbox.

YEARS LATER

David and I managed to get back to my village just before I was eighteen, when Mum and Graham decided to take a trip on their own to Lanzarote. The two of us got a coach back, which took two hours, and we got off at the market square, crossed over the little brook, and came up our old lane. The mechanics' garage was still there, and the one with the red beard was outside. He looked older and bigger. He greeted me and David if we'd only moved to Hull yesterday, and asked David if he knew the badge of the car he was working on. David had moved on from car badges now, but he was always a good lad and, sensing it would please the man, enthused about the Vauxhall in the middle of the path.

While they were talking, I let myself do the thing I'd come here for. I walked on a few metres, not daring to raise my eyes until I'd positioned myself squarely in front of Roger's house. I don't know what I was expecting – for it to have been bought by someone new and changed completely, modernised, with shiny window frames and neat lace curtains, or perhaps for it to have become a ruin, a wasteland where people dumped bed frames and sofas. However, it was neither of those things. It was still standing, and it hadn't been bought by anyone else. But there was something off about it. Something terribly wrong. I took a step closer, and then another, to check that what I was seeing was real.

And it was. The house still stood, but it was no longer a house. There were no bricks, no roof, no door. The entire outside of it was made up of thousands and thousands of books, packed together like sardines. There were no windows left, apart from a tiny pane of glass in what was Roger's bedroom. The others had been swallowed by the books. Around the walls, single pages lay scattered in the overgrown garden, rustling gently in the breeze.

I took another step closer, my hands shaking. I could hear David and the mechanics chatter about cars, but as if they were very far away. Where the living room window used to be was a sign saying '*donations needed*', made out of printed letters ripped out of books and glued onto a sheet of paper. Next to it, something caught my eye. Something I recognised, jammed into the wall. The photo of me, Roger and David I'd posted through his door the night before our move.

I heard a voice shout, 'Stop! Don't go any further. It's dangerous.' The mechanic was by my side, and his voice was urgent. Roger hadn't lived there for years, he explained, nobody had, the house was unsafe and due for demolition, and I wasn't allowed to go closer. As I stumbled backwards and looked up one last time, I saw a face. I saw a face I knew, for a split second, cross the tiny pane of upstairs window that was the only vaguely house-like thing left about this house. It was a grinning face surrounded by worms, and even through the blurry glass, I could see that the worms were not in fact struggling but dancing, dancing from his scalp like they didn't have a care in the world.

THE MAN WHO COLLECTED BARKER

—◄ KIM NEWMAN ►—

Sally Rhodes let Wringhim pick her up in the Dealer's Room, and willingly accompanied him back to the house in Lodovico Street. He matched perfectly the description the Australian's people had given her, down to the sharkskin suit, watery eyes and William Powell moustache. She spotted him straight off, flicking through a stack of *Spicy Mystery Stories* magazines at one of the stalls. She had done enough research in the past week to pass herself off as one of these bizarros, and engaged him in conversation. He was only too keen to brag. She had the impression he hadn't ever talked with a real, live girl before. That gave her an advantage. He was too pleased with her interest in him to question it. She dropped a few names, and he stooped for them.

'Dennis Etchison? Now, there's a thing. I have every story he ever wrote, in the magazines they originally appeared in. Men's magazines, mostly, if you get my drift...'

Sally smiled. 'That must give you an unbeatable pickup line.' He didn't get it. 'You know, "come up and see my Etchisons"?'

He still didn't get it. She decided to abandon irony as a tool in this case.

Wringhim started to tell her about the three issues of *Vault of the Strangler* missing from his collection. He seemed to take their absence personally. His eyes glowed like neons, and his voice took on the exact

159

lascivious tone of the husband in *Gaslight* talking about the hidden rubies. He recited the names of obscure pulp writers in an unholy litany, 'Seabury Quinn, Arthur Leo Zagat, Justin Case, Otis Adelbert Kline, Robert Blake...' His long fingers played over the yellowed edges of the stack of pulp magazines in front of him, curving into claws as he flicked an issue open to scan a contents list. He all but slobbered over a faded cover picture of a voluptuous girl, clad in two cobwebs, being consumed whole by a hungry plant. Unmarried, the file had said, no personal ties. It was easy to see how he had sublimated his procreative urges.

Later, in Lodovico Street, Wringhim produced a huge keyring and dealt with the triple locks on the door of the Collection Suite. She expected a dusty morgue with piles of ancient, rotting books, and skeletons of long-missing persons scattered on stone floors. She got a striplit, modern library, with freestanding shelves of bright-spined paperbacks arranged alphabetically by author, while the more dour hardbacks were behind glass against the walls. Many of the spines had embossed skulls, ghosts, severed hands, full moons behind clouds, bats. Titles were written in dripping blood, or green slime, or monkish gothic script.

'I have every book Arkham House ever put out, all personally signed to me by the authors.'

She thought that wasn't possible, but merely nodded, trying to look interested.

'And here, Miss Rhodes, I have a complete set of Ramsey Campbell's works.'

'The books look a bit... well, scruffy,' she said.

'Yes. I've coated them with dirt from the gutters of the streets in Liverpool where Campbell was living when he wrote the books. It's personalised touches like that that make any given item unique. You notice the red smudges on the binding of that American *Incarnate*?'

Indeed, she had. 'Yes, is that...?'

'Strawberry jam. Smeared by Tamsin Campbell, the author's own daughter. That would nearly triple the worth of the volume, of course. As I was saying, the personalised touches always add to the value.'

'Hmmn, interesting,' she murmured. The profile the Australian had put together didn't quite convey how many cowboys short of a posse Wringhim was. He had no record, but that didn't make him clean. He had independent means, which covered a multiplicity of indulgences. She was beginning to get a feeling about this lead. Not a nice feeling, but a useful one. Perhaps she would be able to report back to the Australian tomorrow after all.

'What's through here?' she asked, indicating another multiply-locked door.

'Ah, that's the centrepiece of my collection. That's where I keep my Barkers.'

'Clive Barkers?'

'Of course. He's the most collectible of the moderns, you know. There are so many special editions, so many variants…'

'And your collection is complete?'

He smiled, and she noticed his ratty little foreteeth poking out from under his double-slash of a moustache. 'But of course, Miss Rhodes. You must come and see.'

More keys ground, and the door was unsealed. The windowless room beyond lit up automatically, like a fridge. The light was ghostly, slightly glimmering.

'Special conditions operate in here. The lighting is calculated not to fade the dustjackets. All my Barkers are mint, Miss Rhodes, mint.'

It was cold. Doubtless, another preservative measure. Three walls were a neutral battleship grey, the fourth consisted of a ceiling-high set of bookshelves. Neon strips hummed on the ceiling. Opposite the shelves was a divan. She got the impression that he spent a lot of time on the divan, just looking at his collection.

'Come in, come in.' She followed him into the Barker room.

He stood by the shelves and indicated a set of books apart from the rest, on a shelf by themselves.

'Here I have all the editions of the *Books of Blood*. The first three volumes, of course. The others are down there. To a true collector, volumes four to six are immeasurably less interesting. I have them, but they aren't quite the thing… aren't quite special, if you get my drift. The first three books are where the action is. And I have all the action in the field, all the action.'

He was evidently proud of the accomplishment.

'Surely, there can't be that many,' she prompted.

'Ahh, but there are, Miss Rhodes, there certainly are. These are the original 1984 Sphere paperbacks with the twisted photographs on the cover. The first United Kingdom edition. Signed, of course, in red ink, inscribed personally to me, and dated before the official publication. As it happens, these are the first three copies to roll off the press...'

Gently, he pulled one off the shelf, and opened it to display the inscription. 'To Dave, thanks for your enthusiasm, Clive Barker,' it said. There was a picture of a zombie with a pencil moustache and no eyes under it.

'What's that smudge?'

He looked again. 'Ahh, an interesting story. When he was signing, Clive used my pen. I have an antique fountain pen, and the nib slipped a little. He cut his finger and bled onto the page. You've no idea how much more collectible that makes this book. No idea at all.'

Sally could have sworn she heard subliminal organ music under the eternal whirring of the extractor fan. This room didn't feel like a tomb, it felt like a morgue. And Wringhim was displaying his books as one necrophile coroner might show off his latest conquest to another, pulling out the gurney and throwing back the stained green sheet with a magician's flourish.

'And here are the reprint paperback editions, with Clive's own covers. And the Sphere library hardbacks, and the Weidenfeld and Nicolson general issue hardback. This is a set of the 1985 Weidenfeld and Nicolson limited edition, boxed and signed naturally. And the American Berkley editions, paperback and hardback, with variant covers. This is the Berkley uncorrected proof of *Volume II*, with the plain spine, put out in April 1986. This is the 1988 Sphere trade paperback omnibus volume, and the 1988 Ace/Putnam American equivalent. These are the two variant cover Scream/ Press editions, 1985 and 1986. And, of course, there's *Libros Sangrientos* from Spain, *Das Erste*, *Das Zweite* and *Das Dritte Buch des Blutes* from Germany, *Tunnel van de Dood* and *Prins van de Duisternis* from Holland,

Livre de Sang from France, and the ideographed Japanese editions. The one in the can is a special German edition with a warning sign.'

'And those books to one side?'

'Ahhah, my special prizes,' his eyes shone again, with all the fervour of a scientologist describing the earthly manifestation of L. Ron Hubbard. 'These are all the special signed, numbered, limited 1985 Scream/Press edition, illustrated by J.K. Potter, bound by Kristina Anderson. Soon after, something horrible happened to the bookbinder and she hasn't been heard from since. The edition is in full leather red Niger Oasis Goatskin and embossed with gold, signed and dated, with zombie doodle and personalised dead baby joke inscription. The underspine is veined manuscrift calf vellum from Germany, dyed red. The signatures are sewn in red linen thread. The endpapers are handpainted with a Roman horse and English carnival motif, the top edge is stained yellow and painted with a Grand Guignol clown's head, the endbands are handsewn in red, yellow and black silk on linen cores, there are tissue overlays on all illustrations, and the title and copyright pages are splatted in human blood and red acrylic paint.'

'Very nice.'

'But there's more. Look, here...'

He pulled out yet another copy of the first *Book of Blood*, also leather bound, also embossed, presumably signed, dated, doodled and dead babied.

'Something must have gone wrong there,' she said. 'It looks a little rough.'

'Ah yes,' he said, his eyes shining again, spittle clinging to the ends of his moustache. 'This is a special special edition. It's bound in human skin.'

'Human skin? Isn't that illegal?'

'Not in Tijuana. The publishers found a doctor who could recommend locals who, although young enough to have unblemished skin, were dying of incurable diseases. By offering to pay a sum to the survivors of these poverty-stricken unfortunates, they were able to convince the patients to have the title, author's name and publication information tattooed on their chests and backs while they were still alive. Then, after the inevitable took its course, the grateful families handed over the corpses for a surgical flaying, and a skilled bookbinder was brought in to prepare a special special edition of five sets of the *Books of Blood*.'

This was beginning to sound both unhealthy and suggestive. He opened up the book at random, and she saw red printing on thick pages.

'They found several reams of unmarked papyrus from the Museum of Antiquities in Cairo. They were reckoned to come from the tomb of a High Priest of Seth who was expected to write his memoirs in the afterlife. There's supposed to be a curse on anyone who defiles its whiteness, but Clive Barker is a notorious iconoclast and the reams were used in the preparation of these volumes. The tooling is done in gold melted down from an Aztec sacrificial idol that miraculously survived the conquistadores. The top edge is stained with the hymenal blood of an Arab princess kept fresh in a phial after her seduction by Sir Richard Burton, and traced with blasphemies in Sanskrit, Hebrew, Coptic script and Pig Latin. It's signed, inscribed, and doodled on, of course...'

'For the text, did they use...?'

'Human blood? No, it clots too quickly. This, sadly, is just red ink. Although, funnily enough, by some strange coincidence, when he was signing his zombie drawing...'

He turned to the page with the picture, and Sally saw the familiar stain.

'Would you care...?'

He handed the book to her. Gingerly, feeling it in the soft meat of her fingertips, she took it. The unique binding gave slightly as she squeezed. It was deeply tanned, and she saw a scattering of moles. The title and author's name stood out. She expected it to smell, somehow, but it was perfectly cured.

'The bookbinder unfortunately had his eyes put out shortly before the volumes were complete and was therefore unable to appreciate the wonder he had created. One of life's tragedies, Miss Rhodes.'

'You have all five sets?'

'No,' he replied, 'only three. The other two are in the hands of...' he spat unconsciously, 'another collector. Thus far, he has resisted all my offers. But I am certain that I shall eventually prevail on him to part with them.'

'But I see five sets in that section.'

'Ahh, yes. These two are different. An even more special special special edition.'

She saw now that these two sets, three uniform volumes each, were lighter in colour.

'What could be more special than human skin?'

'Blood, Miss Rhodes, blood...'

She remembered her research. '"Everybody is a book of blood; wherever we're opened, we're red."'

'I beg your pardon?' Wringhim looked astonished.

'The epigraph. The epigraph of the *Books of Blood*. Remember?'

He looked faintly irritated. 'Oh, yes, of course, I was forgetting.'

'I'd have thought you would have known the books backwards by heart by now.'

'No,' he said, 'sadly not. I have no reading copies of the *Books of Blood*. Each of these is unique, a collectible. I couldn't risk reading them, turning the pages, breaking the spines. Ugh! I took the books out of the library once, and read most of the stories. Very good, I thought.'

His fingers strayed along the shelves to the lighter volumes.

'Blood,' he whispered. 'Blood.'

Sally was shivering in the cold now. Even the dead skin of the book in her hand had gooseflesh. Being Mexican, the former owner probably wasn't used to the chill. That organ she couldn't hear was playing 'Tequila' now.

'This set, Miss Rhodes, is a unique prize, unique by virtue of blood.'

'Go on,' she said, knowing she couldn't stop him, 'tell me about it.'

'A cousin of Clive's, a distant connection, of course, but related by blood. I happened upon this fellow in a Cardiff pub one night. Evidently, he was something of a black sheep of the family. Always cadging drinks by the virtue of his name and trying to impress barmaids with his relationship to a distinguished author. Clyde Barker, he was called. In his cups, he made the mistake of falling from a dock. He drowned.'

'Drowned?'

'From my point of view, most fortunate. If he had walked under a bus, he would have been no use at all, don't you see?'

'The skin…'

'Would have been irreparably damaged, yes. Clyde Barker died without means, and so I took the liberty of arranging for his funeral. I had to settle outstanding bills with several bookmakers and drinking establishments. I saw to it that he went to his grave in as good a suit of clothes as he could hope for. Of course, I wanted something in exchange. But the skin is perishable. It goes first. A good suit will outlast the skin in the ground, any week of the year. So, this edition is bound in the skin of a blood relative of the author's, printed on the palimpsest parchment of a twelfth-century black magician's grimoire, signed in red ink, with a watercolour self-portrait of the author as a rotting zombie on the inside front cover, personally inscribed to me, an original still-unpublished sixty line poem called "Rotting Love" scribbled on the title page, endbands handsewn in hemp thread pulled from the noose used in the execution of Dr Crippen, a spine of weapons-grade plutonium sealed in lead, a booklock that was once part of the famous Iron Maiden of Nuremberg and finally bled on in a Rorschach pattern by Clive Barker himself. The bookbinder accidentally had his hands severed in an accident with a printer's guillotine and will sadly never work again.'

Sally had to take charge of the situation now. Wringhim was raving, too far gone for the police to deal with. She produced her licence. 'I'm a private investigator,' she said. 'The Australian hired me. He's expecting four more books and three movies…'

He turned at last to the final set of the *Books of Blood*, edged in gold, bound in what she knew to be human skin.

'…a lot of people want to know where Clive Barker is, Mr Wringhim…'

He pulled out the first volume, and presented the cover to her. The nose was flattened, the lips and eyelids sewn shut with thick black thread, but the face was still recognisable.

'And this, is the special special special edition of the *Books of Blood*.'

She pointed her little ladylike gun at him. He ignored it and opened the book to the redly-blotched title page.

'The hard part, Miss Rhodes,' he said, 'came after the books were bound. The hard part was getting the author to sign them.'

BLOODHOUND

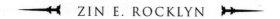

ZIN E. ROCKLYN

I dreamt her.

Not *of* her directly, but she was there, tucked away neatly during each nonsensical vignette. She said nothing, only stared at me with a slight smirk nestled in the corner of her mouth, eyes drilling into my right temple, my dreamself too slow to turn in time to see her full on. When I could feel my body reaching towards consciousness, she mouthed something, her voice a feather on the wind.

It didn't reach me until I woke up. Two words.

"Burn me."

And I knew my sister was dead.

All the girls are born with a gift. My mother's was dreams. She dreamt most often of death so asking was inviting dread. Before last night, I'd never dreamt in my life. My gift is even less tangible than the stories of your subconscious and one I share with my sister. My sister managed to use hers towards a career while I let mine consume me in ways that resulted in being institutionalised four times.

"Georgana, do you have anything to add, anything you'd like to fortify your case with?"

I look up from my clasped hands. They're ashy. Have been for the last two weeks. I'm tempted to etch my sister's face into the black of my hand. I'm beginning to forget the angles, so much like mine; warped memories of childhood and fake mirrors mixing and melding.

This is my fifth stay.

"No," I choke. My voice sounds odd to me, more like an echo of my sister, certainly not me. I look up from my hands and into the concerned face of Dr Meldano. Her ice-blue eyes widen ever-so-slightly, her lips part, and she sits back perhaps a fraction of an inch. I've startled her, and so I ease my muscles, soften my stare, lift the corners of my mouth. "No, Dr Meldano, I am... done. I have no further rebuttal." My voice is not my voice, and I can only hope my panic isn't showing.

Dr Meldano returns to her practised, cold demeanour. She's new at this, a fresh, pretty face in a rotten environment, trying to make a difference to feed her ego through a toughened exterior that falls apart the moment she leaves the parking lot.

I'd seen her. Once. Crying until her pale face was crimson with the exertion. She hadn't made it to her car then, just kind of collapsed at the doorway between departments. No one else was there. Just me on good behaviour duty, her silent wailing, and the lingering smell of vomit and piss. I didn't wait for anyone to collect her, I'd imagine she did it herself, but I did leave her dignity intact by allowing her to command my sedation the very next day.

It was a rough day.

But I promised no more of those. Hence us sitting here at my third evaluation in a deadlock of manipulation.

"Thank you, Georgana," she says, her voice cracking. She clears her throat, looks away with a tick. "Please, step into the hallway so we may discuss your case."

I nod, forcing myself to stand and round the chair, my grippy socks squeaking on the polished floor all along the way.

Neither of us breathe until the door is closed behind me.

It's colder than when I was admitted and when I check my wallet for the hundred Ray slipped me, I discover it has mysteriously disappeared. I chuckle, my breath leaving me in clouds, and a shiver hammers its way down my back. I want to turn back because I know who did it, but decide it won't be worth a sixth, so I step forward and head home.

◄◆►

Three bills and an eviction notice greet me as I struggle with the key in the lock. About fourteen roaches scurry from the hallway light, effectively fucking up my surprise party as I throw the envelopes and sheet of paper on my kitchen counter. I flick on the light and twenty more run for the crevices of the ancient building. It's an efficiency, a dorm room in a halfway house for the slightly unstable consisting of a bed, kitchenette and a sliver of a bathroom with a standing shower. Luxury compared to most, but I don't treat it as such. I ignore the sting in my nose of unwashed dishes and fast-food containers and plug in my phone. As it glows with its greeting, I contemplate cleaning up a little, but then notice the empty dish soap bottle and mouldy sponge and decide to use the last forty bucks I have on some supplies, maybe something to eat because I am hungry—

My eyes land on the six benzos next to the kitchen sink. The only leftovers I now care about.

I'm supposed to stop taking them, switch over to the escitalopram sitting in my pocket, but that shit doesn't help with sleep. I'd lied and said I took the whole bottle when I truly hadn't meant to take as many as I did in the first place.

I just wanted it to stop, that dread, that ache in the centre of my abdomen making everything, every movement feel like trudging through molten lead.

Before I can think on it any further, my phone screams at me from the bed. A little Halloween joke between me and Ray that my panties now regret. Plus, Halloween was a week ago, time to change it. It screams again, this time louder it seems. Then again. And again. I stand rooted to the spot until I feel something scurry over my fingertips. I flick it away, my eyes still on the glowing screen twenty feet in front

169

of me, letting the phone continue to scream at me until my neighbour yelps, "Hey!"

I snap out of it and rush to the bed, grabbing the phone and quickly unlocking its face to put it on vibrate. But it continues to scream, screaming each time it receives a message, an email, a Facebook message, and there dozens of them by the way this poor broad is screaming, screaming, screaming her last and final until I tap the text and see—

BURN ME.
Once. Just one text. Just one email.
BURN ME.

Just one Facebook message, the little circle entrapping the face so much like mine. I attempt to trace the cheekbone that could cut flesh and accidentally open the third message from my dead sister:

burn me.

"Okay, Alexandra," I say to the phone, my hands trembling. "I will burn you."

◆

Instead of hitting the ground running and calling my brother-in-law, I sleep. It is a normal sleep, the sleep of pure exhaustion, though all I've done is walk out of a hospital.

No dreams, no screaming phones.

I'd clearly passed out, my Carhartt damp with sweat as the setting sun curled its fingers around the blinds. My phone is still in my hand, my feet on the floor and my back twisted at an angle its forty-two-year-old spine doesn't appreciate. I rub at my eyes with my free hand and ease into the sitting position. I arch my back and stretch, my phone still glued to my palm. Finally, I look at the screen, ignoring the fist forming in the base of my belly, and open its face.

It's fully charged. Other than that, there is no change.

I grow a bit warmer, my hands pooling with sweat as I open my texts. Alexandra is not the last conversation. In fact, it's Ray, unopened and bold,

170

though no notification had gone off. So I scroll. And scroll. And scroll. Until I see 'twin' from three weeks ago. I open it.

Looks like I'm headed up your way, sis. Got a lead on a beautiful edition of The Dark Dancer and lo and behold, it's in Hardwick. Join me?

I hadn't answered. Typical. We weren't exactly on the good terms her text implies. Still, the sourness of guilt licks at the back of my throat and I'm nauseated. Desperate for water, I stumble to the sink and grab the last clean glass, immediately filling it with tap and gulping it down. I pour more, gulp it down. I repeat until I feel less like a raisin in the sun.

My phone goes off.

It's Ray. I open the line.

"Beer?"

"Fuck yes."

<hr />

It wasn't exactly a secret, our gifts. We used it to our advantage, but only enough to fly under the radar. A tent at a freak show here, running numbers on a Friday night there. Most of us thought it a blessing. Most of us flourished. But some…

I used to be a cop. Before that I was studying to be a lawyer. I had a breakdown, flunked out, then thought law enforcement was the next best thing. It was something I could put this *gift* to use with, ease that fucking knot. But it didn't. All it did was get me into fistfights with grown men who were supposed to be my Brothers in Blue. Then again, I couldn't, or wouldn't as my former union rep said, keep my mouth shut. And they were some shady motherfuckers.

So I became a PI. Business went well enough for a middle-class suburb in Northern New Jersey. Until I found out why sixteen-year-old Chrissy Sadler was disappeared by her own father, a goddamn deputy. I tried to continue after that, but a crusted wound had been opened and I found myself wanting the world to stop just for a day or two or three. Have the world right there in the palms of my clasped hands as I slept time and space away.

Alex, on the other hand, used her gift for hunting books. The rarer, the better. For her ego, for the payday, didn't matter which, she made a life out of it. She married a man just as obsessed with the past as she and they have one daughter, my niece, Jasmine. So ordinary, so perfect.

I asked her once if she felt it, that heaviness, the despair.

She blinked at me as if seeing me for the first time.

"No," she lied.

And we never talked about our gift again.

"How'd it go this time?" Ray asks as we sip our third Guinness. The first two are always in silence; well, as silent as a dive bar can be. The silence doesn't last long and neither do the first two pints. There's no awkwardness between us to blab away. We met in silence at a buddy's funeral seven years ago. The repass was in the very bar we sit in, and we just gravitated towards each other. While others wailed or joked or played pool, we sat in silence drinking. On the third drink, we clinked glasses and exchanged numbers, only to run into each other everywhere in this small town. We discovered we were neighbours back before I resorted to crashing at my PI office and would sit on his porch for hours, commenting on passersby for a chuckle or two, but mostly in silence.

He's my best friend.

"My sister apparently came to town," I blurt out instead of answering. I hear him choke next to me, but keep my eyes ahead. "Well, Hardwick."

"Close enough. She know you were on vacation?"

I shook my head. "They never know."

"Mm." No judgement, just acknowledgement. He keeps the silence.

"I have a… weird feeling," I say. I rub the condensation with my pinky fingertip. Bring it to my lips, but then decide to smell it. It smells of blood, though it is clear. I frown.

"Call Jason," Ray suggests.

Just as I open my mouth to answer, my phone screams. Long and loud. The entire bar is on alert and I'm hot with embarrassment. Ray chuckles.

"Change that shit. Halloween's over."

"I already did," I mutter and it's not the right notification sound anyway because as I pull it out of my coat pocket, I see it's a phone call, not a message. Before it can scream again, I open the line. "Hold on, Jason." I cover the microphone. "Order me another," I mouth, then walk to the front entrance where most of the smokers huddle outside. Exiting the cloud of nicotine, I bring the phone to my ear and say, "Have you heard from Alex?"

There's a pause on the line and I wonder vaguely if I'm being rude. Then I remember I don't care. "Nice to hear from you too, Georg," he says, that nasally voice oddly sad. He blows out a breath. "And no, I haven't heard from Alex. It's been a very strange day, but I don't suspect anything to be wrong. Well, at least until I saw you called. You never call me. What's going on?"

"When was the last time you talked to her?"

"Yesterday, last night when she got where she was going. She said goodnight to Jasmine and told me she'd be home by the weekend. Why?" His voice is waking up, becoming more animated and tight as he talks. He's worried. I'm making him worry.

I ignore it all and pass a hand across my lower stomach. "Did she mention anything about seeing me?"

"No, she said you never responded to her text, so she figured you were still mad at her, Georg, what is going on? You're scaring me."

"What about the book?"

"Georg, stop. Answer me."

"I… can't. I just got back from, uh, vacation and I just want to talk to her. I'm not mad. Anymore," I say, though I doubt I sound convincing.

I can hear the phone shift. "Vacation, huh?" And there it is. That smugness that I fucking hate. "Didn't you borrow five hundred dollars from Alex a couple of months ago?"

I clench my jaw. "Not sure if you're aware of the economy these days, Jason, but five hundred ain't dick for long so—"

"Typical Georgana," he mumbles and I want to go through the fucking airwaves at this dickhole.

"Anyway, can you tell me about where she's going? Or where she went?" Silence. "I want to pay her back."

That works. He rattles off that she was headed to Hardwick, New Jersey, to some estate sale for a rare book she wanted to keep for herself.

"It was the first book written by a freed enslaved woman," he continued. "Most copies were burned when a white scholar labelled it blasphemous. No one is sure of its contents, but witchcraft was whispered about."

I scrunch my face. "*Witchcraft*? Isn't that a bit late for witch trials?"

He snorts and I feel my free fist tighten. "Last trial in Salem was 1878, Georg, this was way before. The book and the woman who wrote were quite controversial. Did you know—"

"Can you get me that address? Of the estate sale, I mean," I say before he can start in on his day job, lecturing.

"Uh, sure, you sure everything's all right?" he asks, the snootiness gone, concern rising once again.

Burn me.

I shut my eyes tight and there she is, as plain as the day being swallowed up by the black of night dressed in a pair of distressed jeans and a plain white tee. Both designer. Her feet were bare and caked in grey mud. Her hair up in a casual bun, white-girl style with Black-girl permed hair. She smiles, her teeth coated in the same mud.

Burn me.

"Yeah, yeah, everything's fine," I lie, then ready myself for the hunt.

—◆—

In the morning, Ray lets me borrow his truck. "I can't go with you," he says, trying to convince himself. He won't meet my eyes and his brow hasn't stopped furrowing since he dropped me off the night before.

"No, Ray," I say, "you cannot go with me. You are a contributing member of society, unlike me." I grab the keys. "Go to work, Ray. I'll see you when I get back."

He looks at me then, grey eyes tired. He wants to say something (*no, you won't*), but he stops himself. "Yeah, I'll see you when you get back," he says instead. "Remember, the heater—"

174

"Two smacks and a rub," I say, winking at him. I slide into the driver's side and slam the door shut.

Dread is a knot so thick, I wipe my chin of drool.

———◆———

The house isn't impressive, but bigger than I've ever lived in. I'm guessing five beds, four and a half baths. Backyard with an above-ground pool. White with black shutters. The estate sale is over, so it won't be simple getting in. I can only hope someone is home.

I knock and luck is on my side in the form of a harried new mother with a plump and fussy infant on her shoulder. "Can I help you?" she asks, accusatory. She is a severe-looking woman, angular and crane-like. She eyes me from head to toe, taking in stats and keeping her cell phone on the ready.

I put on my best smile. "Hi, yes! My name is Georgana Mosley and I'm looking for a book. My sister may have—"

"Ah, yes, *The Dark Dancer*!" she says, relaxing and opening the door wider, but not enough to let me in. Only enough to show off the finest fashion from J. Jill. "I thought you looked familiar! You two could be twins!"

My smile falters a bit. "We actually are!"

"Oh, neat! I was hoping this one would be a twin, but it looks like she ate her instead!" I shift uncomfortably in my size eighteen pants and hope this little one has enough attitude for the both of them. "C'mon in!"

I step into the home and mark the lack of difference in temperature from the outside. It's unseasonably warm, but not warm enough to not turn on the furnace.

"This is my mother-in-law's place," the woman explains as she shuts the door. "She passed away six weeks ago and we're just getting to all her junk. So much memorabilia. Some not so... *politically correct*, if you get my meaning. Follow me." I smile a little harder as she looks at me, then let it drop as soon as she leads the way. "I knew we couldn't just do a yard sale, too many valuables. I had some appraised while she was in hospice and refused to let it be haggled down to a five buck sale, know what I mean? So my husband tasked me with the responsibility. Your sister was great! Really communicative and passionate about this, so I decided to give her a discount." She stops in the middle of the hallway which is just past the family room and faces me. "Two-fifty, instead of the original six hundred. Isn't that amazing? Such a steal."

"How do you know it's valued at six?" I ask, then want to kick myself. I don't give a shit about prices, I just want to find Alex.

For a moment, she looks perplexed, then she recovers. "Lucky guess, I suppose. Your sister was grateful and she paid three, but then left the book. Weird, right? She was reading it in the basement, but then left it there and said she'd be back this morning for it."

"Have you heard from her yet?"

She frowns, then, as the realization hits her that she has a stranger in her home, turns to suspicion. I smile.

"I was hoping to surprise her with it. She's having a bit of buyer's remorse. Her kid needs braces," I say. It's not like I'm damning Jasmine to buck teeth, genetics will take care of that eventually. "So I wanted to buy it for her and tuck in the extra cash." I wink and it actually works. The woman eases and grins right back.

"Haven't heard from her yet, so you're in luck!"

And we head to the basement.

—◆—

"I'll leave you to it," the woman says as she hands me the calfskin novel. The book hasn't been taken care of, I can see that much. The pages are brittle and dry, the cover splitting, but it is legible and I almost feel giddy holding it. If only I could follow through on my lie, Alex and I would definitely be sisters again and I wouldn't be such a disappointment.

"Thanks," I say. I'm tempted to open the pages, find out what intrigued my sister so, but that fucking dread slams into me so hard just as I open the cover, I spit up on myself. I immediately turn from the steps and away from the woman's prying eyes.

"You okay? Would you like some water?"

"Uhm, no, thanks!" I call back, wiping at my chin with the sleeve of my coat. "I promise I'll be out of your hair in a few minutes."

"No problem! Take your time!" she says.

No spittle has hit the book and I'm thankful. And tempted yet again, so I follow through, swallowing back bile as I read an author's note:

Dearest Reader,
Partake under the bright moonlight and let the words dance
across your nightly visions.

I ignore the instructions and flip further into the book, letting my eyes skim over the contents. This freed woman was well-educated. The prose is more graceful than most of her peers of the time. I look at the author's name: Marilee Mosley.

I don't think about it. The likelihood is slim, considering the book is nearly two hundred years old and Mosley isn't an unpopular name. I tuck the book into the breast of my Carhartt and jog back up the steps while trying my hardest to think up a story for the missing three hundred dollars.

"You know what?" the woman says, popping up in front of me as I exit the basement. "Why don't you just take the book?" I frown, not meaning to, but what? She waves at me. "Your sister is a lovely person, and you strike me as…" Her eyes roam and her disgust is hardly hidden. "The same. I'm already three hundred dollars richer from it, no need to be greedy! Where is it?"

"Uh, well, I've got it right here," I say, trying to laugh off whatever awkwardness was to come as I unsheathe it from my coat. I don't look at her as the silence thickens.

"Get out of my house," she growls.

"Gladly."

———◆———

"So she bought it but she didn't take it," Ray says over the phone later that evening. He'd booked me a B-n-B in the heart of Hardwick when I said I didn't feel right coming back without her. Upon entering, I immediately took a shower, then a bath, then slept.

No dreams.

"Yeah," I mumble as I pick out my little afro. I contemplate starting my locs again as I look for the book. It's on the nightstand, right where I left it when I thought about reading it before my impromptu nap.

"Are you going to do what it says?" he asks.

I snort a laugh. "What? Read it under the pale moonlight? Uh, no, it's below freezing tonight and—"

"You've got a window, I'm sure," he rushes. He sounds anxious, off-kilter. This is unlike him.

"You okay, Ray?"

"I dunno, man, this whole thing weirds me out, to be honest. I mean, where the hell could she be?"

There's a knock at my door and I blurt out, "No fucking way."

"What?"

"Someone's knocking." And I'm wondering if I ever left that hospital.

"I gotta go. My gun's in the glove box." He hangs up.

"What good that's doing me," I mumble, then put the phone down on the desk.

The person knocks again. I take in a breath, stride to the door and open it.

And nearly collapse.

—◇—

"Walk with me," she says, holding out her muddy hand.

"Alex, what the fuck?" I breathe.

She's smiling, her teeth individually highlighted by more mud. Hand still extended. At least she's wearing a sweater and jeans. No shoes.

"Aren't you cold?" I ask dumbly.

"Stop delaying the inevitable, Georg, come with me. And take the book. There's not much time left."

Again, I'm wondering if I'm sedated by something stronger than haloperidol, but when I think about it, the dread is easing, my belly isn't in knots for the first time in years. Perhaps this is real.

So I grab the book and walk out into the moonlight with my dead sister.

＊

We've been walking for an hour along the Appalachian Trail, not on it, but by it, traversing the damn-near sideways terrain of underbrush. I'm struggling while my sister floats along, gliding barefoot and snapping twigs like it's nothing. The moonlight slices through the trees, casting an eerie glow about the place. We've passed other hikers, most already holed up in their tents for the night. One older gentleman warns us to set up camp soon, though he clearly notices our lack of gear by the look on his face.

Alex grins at him and we simply keep walking.

Until we find the clearing.

There are remnants of a stone chimney on one side of the creek, the side my sister crosses over to. Even the trees seem to breathe differently around here. There is an undeniable energy permeating every plant, every creature. I cross the creek and my sister finds a stump to sit on. Like the obedient little sister by fourteen minutes, I sit at her feet cross-legged, looking up at her as the moon glows her a halo.

"I used to live here," she says. "When I was freed." She looks about her, a soft smile on her face. Her face so different to mine. Yet the same. Same nose, same lips. Same burnt umber complexion. But wholly and completely different to the child I grew up with, to the woman who slapped me just four months prior. Her hair, no longer permed, stands out from her head, proud and reaching for the moon itself.

She reaches forward, caresses my face, and for the first time in years, I feel safe. I melt at her touch.

"Forgive me," I whisper.

"I already have," she says. From the palm of her hand, a match alights.

It hurts less than I expect it to.

BELL, BOOK AND LAMP

◄ A.G. SLATTER ►

'Frederick Alsop Windermere Bell, you are the luckiest turd I know.'

Algernon Bell almost spat out the petit-four along with his cousin's name. But Algy was no amateur and it would take more than irritation to remove food from his possession, so somehow it remained in his cavernous maw, damp and masticated. He kept his voice low – even the Gilgamesh Club had its limits for profanity, especially in the dining room. Red velvet walls and gold brocade curtains, enormous portraits of founders and benefactors, a barrel ceiling painted with various coats-of-arms, a truly glorious chandelier and the imported padouk wood tables a precise four and a half feet away from each other to allow for privacy, waiters moving as elegantly between them as prima ballerinas.

'Steady on, cuz. It's not my fault the rest of you couldn't be bothered with her.' Though his forties were creeping closer and writing snippy notes to his face, Freddie's grin was wide and white; he was particular with dental hygiene to the point of obsession. His smile, as cousin Diamanda had once said, was as if someone had opened the curtains at dawn when one had a spectacular hangover. 'Just a little investment of time whenever the old girl came to London. Out to dinner, museums and parties, some gossip about the rest of you, gambling until the wee hours and then off to an all-you-can-eat brothel.'

'What sort of man takes their great-aunt to a brothel?'

'The sort of man who's just inherited their great-aunt's very large estate.' Freddie couldn't stop grinning. He'd seen the solicitor that morning, listened to the reading of the will along with the other cousins, and signed everything required as fast as he could while the rest complained loudly about *The Unfairness*. But no one could argue when it was pointed out that he'd been the only one of the grand-nieces and nephews to give Great-Aunt Vina Bell the time of day. And he hadn't minded the old stick – was warmed by the knowledge she'd accepted him for what he was – but couldn't deny that the inheritance had been his endgame. Had felt no need to hurry things along because she was already teetering on the edge of her grave and he had a decent enough (survivable) allowance (secret) from his mother after his father had ostensibly cut him off. Say what you will about Freddie Bell, whatever his other faults (and they were numerous) he wasn't unnecessarily greedy, and he *was* generally patient.

'Have you seen the house?'

'Never been there. She'd always come down to London and stay in the Arlington Street townhouse. Entertain there. An interesting bunch at her table, old explorers and scientists – when I say scientists I mean nutters who'd tried to reanimate frog corpses – some graverobbers amongst them, I'd wager. Lady artists with no interest in men, folk who'd spent fortunes either hunting creatures to extinction or hunting things that probably didn't exist outside of drunken conversation or legends told to scare off intruders.' Freddie shrugged, came back to the actual question. 'Have *you* seen it?'

Algy frowned, forehead wrinkling, eyes narrowing. 'I think, when I was very young, Father took me to Ardhaven House as it was called – Vina was away, and he'd been asked to check in, make sure the servants weren't slacking off.'

Freddie snorted. 'Sounds just like Vina!'

'The place was – is – big, obviously, well-maintained. But she could never keep staff after she'd stopped travelling, moved back for good – start of every year, a whole new batch sent by agencies, regular as clockwork. Well, except for that butler, he's been a constant.'

'I'm told there's a butler down there now and a housekeeper and some maids. Not that I'm inclined to make it my primary residence – too far from anything fun – but since an immediate visit is one of the terms of my inheritance, I do need to go down there.' Freddie shrugged. 'Well, if Paris was worth a mass, then Great-Aunt Vina's fortune is certainly worth a night in a country estate.' He grinned again, a blinding flash of teeth. 'I'll sell, I think, her Arlington Street place – a bit fusty and fussy – buy somewhere more interesting. Keep the manor, of course, but only for occasional retreats with *special* friends.'

'You turd. You lucky, lucky turd.' As Algy knew the sort of company Freddie, given his druthers, kept, it was fortunate this was the worst thing to come from his mouth.

'Now, now, Algy. Keep speaking like that and I'll not invite you to my London dinner parties. The first thing I'll be employing is a French pastry chef – shall I poach Her Majesty's?' As he recalled, the staff in the townhouse was skeletal but stable, the same servants for years; much to be said for a good position in London rather than at a remote estate, and with a mistress who only appeared in town every six months or so.

Algernon pursed his lips, pinching off another utterance of the word 'turd', and contented himself with stuffing in another mouthful of food. 'You couldn't afford it, not even with Vina's fortune. She may not pay well, but there's cachet in working for the Queen, even a widowed one who spends half of her time hiding from the world. Cachet's something you don't have, Freddie.'

'Not yet. However, where money goes, cachet will surely follow.'

'When are you off?'

'This evening, late train, overnight, into the wilds of Hibernia.'

'That's Ireland, you idiot. You mean Caledonia.'

Freddie shrugged again, rising. 'If you'll excuse me, Algy, I have matters to which to attend before I go to *my* estate. And don't worry, I'll settle the account.'

'Who said we don't live in a time of miracles? Take care, cousin.'

As Freddie made his way from the dining room, Algy's eyes caught the younger man's narrow back one final time, thought the suit a little ill-fitting, noted with pleasure that Freddie's girth might be expanding. Almost unbidden the words slipped out: 'Utter, utter turd.'

Outside, in the miasmic air of London, the sky overcast, the noise of the madding crowd swelling up to meet him, Frederick Alsop Windermere Bell paused on the stairs on the Gilgamesh Club and took a deep breath. It stank, but he didn't care. He was a rich man or soon to be, he was young enough to enjoy for a very long time all that his great-aunt had left him, and he had didn't need to be at St Pancras for several hours. *And* his preferred house of joy was located not more than two hundred steps to his left. Madame Eugenia always welcomed him – thanks to Vina's paying his monthly bills there, because there was only so much one could expect Mummy to cover – and the girls were fresh enough to excite him, but inured enough to tolerate the pain of what he did to them, and disposable enough that their demise (accidental or otherwise) could be smoothed over by the liberal application of funds – of which Freddie was now (or soon to be) in glorious possession.

Freddie headed left.

The train trip was uneventful, Freddie'd slept the sleep of the innocent – proving that Morpheus bestows his favours unfairly – woken, dressed and breakfasted before arrival. The fine-boned girl he'd enticed from the third-class carriage (emptied as they'd proceeded norther and norther) had been travelling alone. Unlikely to be missed, unlikely to be found until the return journey and only then if someone was eagle-eyed enough to notice the body he'd thrown from the window as they'd passed over a bridge high above a river.

Ardhaven Station itself was barely more than a stone hut, barely more than a pitstop – twelve poor cottages and one inn – but stop the train did and Freddie fairly danced down the metal steps onto what could only generously be termed a platform. A taciturn turnip of a man with a pony and trap – hardly the magnificent conveyance Freddie had expected – waited outside and barely enquired as to Freddie's identity. Fair enough,

Freddie supposed, since he was the only person disembarking. What were the chances of another well-heeled gentleman appearing *here*? Fortunately, he'd packed light, nothing more than a Gladstone bag – it would have been a disaster had he been a woman with a trousseau, or a man more devoted to fashion. The rattling trip was accomplished with minimal conversation, mainly Freddie reminding the man to collect him the very next day for the return journey, and contenting himself with taking in the highland scenery. Summer, but hardly warm, and he was glad of his astrakhan overcoat.

Twenty minutes later, he was deposited (having never learned the name of his driver) at the door of a very large manor, its three wings constructed of dark grey stone, windows with almost a greenish tint to them as if they kept an ocean contained. Freddie scanned the small, surprisingly sunny glen, the gloaming of the forest surrounding the house, the emerald slope of the hills as if forming a secondary wall around the estate, and the ribbon of the road on which the man and his pony and trap were making impressive speed as if to flee. Freddie, calling a reminder about being collected tomorrow, received no acknowledgement. Somewhere, beneath the clip-clop of the beast's hooves and the clatter of the trap, was the sound of very much nothing. Behind him, at last, the creak of a door, which sent him swinging about.

'Master Frederick, I presume?'

The man who spoke, standing in the doorway of Tiamat House, was nothing if not cadaverous. Freddie wasn't actually sure he could bear to look at him for any extended period – too much like staring upon looming death. Not that Freddie had anything against death, he just preferred it if he'd caused it and could leave very quickly afterwards while someone else cleaned up the mess. But this man…

'Ah, yes. Frederick Alsop Windermere Bell.' And he wasn't sure why he was introducing himself to the butler – *his* butler by all accounts – as if the man was an acquaintance of consequence, someone he wanted to impress. He cleared his throat, put some ice into the tone and said: 'And you are?'

'I'm Fielding, sir. Miss Bell's butler.'

Mine, Freddie almost said, but managed to restrain himself. Fielding stepped from the threshold and took the three stone steps down to where Freddie's hold-all sat. It almost seemed as if the shadows from the foyer followed him. Freddie blinked, shook his head to clear the illusion. By the time he focused again the butler was back at the entryway, the leather bag in hand.

'Are you well, Master Frederick? I do hope the trip wasn't too arduous.'

'Oh no, just arduous enough.'

'Quite. Miss Bell has, I'm sure you've been informed by the solicitor, left very specific instructions for your first day here – after that you'll be free to do as you wish, but the mistress was very particular.' Freddie wasn't especially delighted to be told what to do by a servant, but until he knew better the situation, he would smile and nod. 'Shall I show you to your room first? You can freshen up and rest…'

'Thank you, Fielding, I'd appreciate that.'

The décor owed rather a lot to the British Museum, in fact to myriad museums Freddie had visited with his great-aunt. Filled with so many antiquities that it appeared a curator had been stealing display items for a very long time indeed. On reflection, and recalling how many explorers and amateur antiquarians had graced Vina's table over the years, Freddie had no doubt that quite a few of his great-aunt's decorations had an uncertain provenance.

Corridors lined with marble columns and pedestals, the latter topped with busts of bronze and gold and even more marble. Rooms – not one, but many – filled floor to ceiling with shelving and leather-bound volumes, titles on their spines picked out in silver and gold, and at intervals lacunae into which had been inserted smaller items: ancient lanterns covered in verdigris, frameworks hung with primitive jewellery, crystal balls, daggers, statuettes of indeterminate deities, and a bewildering array of phallic *objets*. Other chambers housed entire stone structures, removed from some Middle Eastern ruin and rebuilt in the middle of a drawing room in a grand house in the remote highlands – he thought he glimpsed a displayed hypocaust as he passed, almost pristine in its entirety. In other areas still, there were the altars – all manner of them – Roman and Greek, Sumerian and Babylonian, Mithridatic and Egyptian, Hittite, Parthian, Nabatean, others he couldn't recognise. Freddie had not realised exactly how much knowledge he'd taken in at Vina's knee, but he'd always been a sponge. Some of said altars, he thought, had either not yet been fully assembled – or perhaps they'd been destroyed more recently; he couldn't be sure.

Through a great hall lined with mammoth statues, all goddesses, scraping the ceiling, all of different origin. Cow-horned Hathor; winged Nike; Diana with her bow and arrow, a hound at heel; grieving Demeter, a veil obscuring most of her face; Inanna trampling a lion; Ereshkigal and her clawed feet; Yemọja, a pedestal of blue and crystal beads flowing like waves; the Cailleach, a beara-wife, clutching a sieve to churn the storm-waves; Guanyin holding a jar and a willow branch; Angrboða, mother of monsters, the heads of her three children climbing up her body, Loki, Iormungand and Hel.

As he tripped from the hall with a lingering look, Freddie's head turned to see where he was going and he almost ran into a monumental sheela-na-gig, almost smacked face-first into the gaping hole he'd spent so much of his life yearning after and love-hating.

The butler paused, mid-stride, raised an eyebrow.

'A bit—' Freddie began, then ended with a whine '—confrontational.'

'Quite, sir.' Fielding continued on, leaving his charge to quick-step. Freddie's developing certainty that dear old Vina might have been more than eccentric, and something of a graverobber, grew stronger.

◆

The second-storey bedchamber was almost monastic, which surprised Freddie. Given the positively sybaritic décor of the rest of the mansion, *this* seemed little more than an oversized pantry. Grey wallpaper, thin dark carpet, a narrow bed with an equally narrow bedside table, wardrobe and matching tallboy. Musty yellow curtains.

The butler must have caught his expression. 'The mistress said you might find this space a little… deprived but bid me offer her apologies: we've not had visitors for a very long time, and so the guest rooms have not been kept up to standard. However, she did not think you'd like to sleep in the suite where she breathed her last. You will, of course, make

187

arrangements for redecoration more to your own tastes, Master Frederick, as soon as you wish.'

Freddie smiled, thought about how much the antiquities almost overflowing from the place might add to his fortune. 'Very considerate. Are you the only member of staff remaining, Fielding? I'd heard there was a housekeeper, maids?'

The man nodded as he carefully placed the overnight bag on the plain chest at the foot of the bed, then said, 'No. Or not anymore. Your great-aunt let everyone go as she faded, her requirements grew fewer, and she saw no need to be attended by an army in her dying. I was sufficient for her. She thought it best they be able to find new positions as soon as possible.'

This seemed considerate and quite out of character with the great-aunt who couldn't keep staff. With his hopes of a young housemaid to warm his evening expiring, Freddie pouted out: 'Quite.'

'There is a water closet through that door.' Fielding gestured. 'I would suggest you spend the day resting – your great-aunt was very specific about the timing of this activity. I will deliver luncheon at midday, then return to collect you around four this afternoon. There are some books to keep you amused.' He pointed to the stack on the bedside table; Freddie caught familiar titles, volumes of Graeco-Roman myths, Babylonian and Sumerian epics, things read to keep Vina happy. 'The house can be a labyrinth until one knows its ways, so please wait for me to accompany you, sir.'

'Thank you, Fielding.' As the man reached the door, Freddie felt one last spark of hope flare. 'Fielding? I don't suppose there are any young ladies close-by? For after-dinner entertainment purposes?'

The man paused and Freddie wondered if there might be a disapproving expression when the butler turned, but found only thoughtfulness. 'There are a few crofts in the next glen, tenant farms with daughters. After you're settled to fulfil your great-aunt's last wish, shall I – source – some company, sir?'

Freddie smiled, faith renewed, appetite sharpened.

Freddie, neither tired nor feeling like he needed to freshen up, gave it a polite fifteen minutes to ensure Fielding was properly gone from his door, down the corridor and the long stairs, back through the strange rooms with their looming statues and doubtful artefacts, back to wherever the man spent his days. While Freddie waited, he listened – to nothing.

Not a sound in the house, or at least his current part of it, not a murmur of life – reasonable, he supposed, given that there were no other staff members. Just himself and the butler. None of the usual noises, the murmur of voices, the shuffle of shoes along carpets, tapping on polished floors, the gentle susurrations of cleaning and tidying for a finicky old spinster.

Freddie levered open, with difficulty, one of the glass doors, and stepped out onto the small balcony. The sun felt surprisingly warm, there was no breeze to move the trees or grass. And, again, no sounds out here either, no birds chirping, not even the babble of a stream. As if he was in a bubble – a vacuum. Disconcerting.

He stepped back inside, shut out the external silence only to feel the inner silence settled on him like an oily coat. He shuddered. Shook himself like a dog flicking off droplets of wet noiselessness. He looked at his pocketwatch, observed time pass sluggish as an ice floe. At last, he went to the bedroom door, grabbed the handle, turned it.

Met resistance.

An old house, not maintained, he told himself, just required a bit of elbow grease.

Freddie pushed and twisted, insistent. But the door resisted still, and he came to the realisation that he'd been locked in.

Like a child. A bad one. Like a prisoner.

Not like the rightful heir.

Not like a grown man with his full liberty.

Locked in this room, in this house, by a bloody butler.

He shouted for a while, then gave up, knowing it for a waste of energy.

Once more out onto the balcony, but it was far too high to jump, and there was nothing he could identify or was willing to risk as hand and footholds.

Freddie, pressing his nerves down, lay full length on the bed, fully clothed, stared up at the ceiling, pondered his revenge.

In another ten minutes he was asleep.

The sound of a key turning, the rattle of a doorknob, the creak of hinges which he'd not noticed upon entering the room, were all things that woke Freddie several hours later. The change of light through the window, to his blinking gaze, told him that he'd slept much of the day away.

He wished he'd been able to swing upright immediately, look as angry and affronted as he felt, but it was a slow rising and he caught sight of himself in the mirrored door of the wardrobe. A pale, wispy man with a distinct paunch on an otherwise slender form, eyes puffy, face too, with the engorgement of slumber, hair askew, suit crumpled. Hardly an intimidating master.

'What the deuce do you think you're doing, locking me in here?'

'Sir?' Both eyebrows went up slowly but inexorably and Freddie felt foolish even before they'd reached their apex.

'I tried the door after you left, it was locked.' Freddie realised he'd admitted his own perfidy: after all, he had agreed to stay where he was.

'Was it, sir? Locked, sir? I'm not sure how – there's no key for this door, lost many years ago. Sometimes the knob does stick, however. At any rate, I do apologise for any inconvenience.'

The apology, lightly given, a little dismissive, was nevertheless an apology, and Freddie felt his rage bleeding away even as he followed up with: 'You said you were going to bring lunch, you blighter!'

Fielding pointed wordlessly to a small round table in a shadowy corner, a seat next to it, a silver tray perched atop, a covered plate, a goblet of what looked like red wine, a smaller plate of bread and a dish of butter curls. 'You were asleep, sir, when I came in. I didn't want to wake you. You'd had such a long trip and, if sir will permit me to observe, there is also the element of grief.'

'Grief?'

'It affects us, sir, even if we aren't especially aware of it acting upon us. Even the least sensitive will feel it in some way.'

Freddie was caught between taking to the man task for implying that Freddie was insensitive, and his own embarrassment to find the promised luncheon waiting, his own accusation shown to be false. In the end, he went for a spluttering apology. 'Deuced sorry, Fielding, that was unfair of me.'

He didn't recall ever having apologised to a servant in his entire life and wasn't too fond of the sensation.

'Think no more of it, sir, I certainly shan't.' Fielding retreated into the corridor. 'Are you ready, Master Frederick? Do you need more time to prepare?'

Freddie shook his head, purposefully avoiding his image in the mirror. No one else was here. It didn't matter. Best to get it all over and done with as soon as possible. He followed the butler, smoothing his askew hair as he went.

But he was *sure* he'd heard a key in the lock. *Sure.* But it wasn't worth pushing the matter, not when he had no proof and there was nothing to gain in doing so. Perhaps the man was just playing a joke; Fielding, knowing he'd have no place here with Freddie as lord of the manor, was simply getting in a cheap shot while he could. Well, Freddie was well rested now. He would remain awake all night, until the man with the pony and trap returned as instructed to collect him for his return to Ardhaven Station. Freddie would have done his duty by then, and besides, he needed the butler as witness that he had indeed observed the instructions of Great-Aunt Vina's will. The butler was his means to riches, so any revenge Freddie sought would have to be delayed. Freddie was patient. He could wait.

<hr />

Entering yet another space filled with them, Freddie found himself thoroughly sick of books, but this one was a library proper – 'The Library' as Fielding put it, having explained that all the other rooms with tomes were merely 'storage'. *This* was where Great-Aunt Vina had taken her ease most nights, to read and drink and converse when she'd summoned company, explained the butler as he led Freddie along a series of twists and turns between towering bookshelves, their footsteps echoing on polished parquetry. The ceiling was lost in shadows, but he could see his way, passably well, so light was coming from somewhere.

No surprise, Freddie supposed, that the shelving wasn't a straightforward arrangement, but rather something of a maze in keeping with the nature of the house. It would be irksome to own a place that one couldn't find one's way around, but he assumed he'd learn eventually – then realised he wasn't overly keen on doing so, wasn't sure he was prepared to commit himself to that kind of time or study. The more he thought about it, the more Freddie felt the idea of selling the whole dreadful pile pull at him like a siren song. There was no family attachment to it – Vina's father had bought it and gifted it to his outlier daughter who'd refused a dozen offers of marriage and made it clear she intended to go on in that fashion. The remoteness of the location was as much about keeping her out of the public eye as about giving her the security of a home that was hers alone, Freddie's father had said while refusing to set his youngest son up in a similar manner.

Joke's on you, old man, he thought now.

At last, they broke from the walls of books to a cosy spot by a hearth, a fire burning low there. A green velvet wingback chair, a mahogany side table, and on its top of turtle stone inlay sat a crystal tumbler, matching decanter awash with a golden-brown liquid, a porcelain plate of biscuits and cheese, a leather-bound journal and a rather primitive-looking lamp, unlit. The chair sat in a broad beam of light coming from the French windows. Outside, Freddie could see hills, and grass, glen and more glen. Fielding stood aside to let Freddie get to the chair. As the younger man made himself comfortable, the butler poured a generous measure from the decanter.

'Armagnac,' he explained, 'the mistress's favourite, and she mentioned you were also partial to it.'

'Ah, yes.' Freddie looked around; the solicitor has given him instructions, but he wanted to be sure. 'So, this is it? All I have to do?'

Fielding nodded solemnly. 'The journal is especially for you, she wrote it when she knew her time was coming. I think it one of the great sadnesses of life that we only get to truly know people after they're gone.'

'Quite.'

As if sensing Freddie's urge to simply get it all over and done with, Fielding bowed.

'It's going to get quite dark in here, Fielding.'

The butler nodded toward the beam of sunlight. 'You'll have that for some time, sir, and the lamp gives off a surprising amount of light. It's one your great-aunt specifically said you must use when instructed – and not before.'

'Instructed?'

'In the journal, sir. Everything you need to know is in there. I'll leave you to it. Dinner will be served when you're… done.'

Freddie listened to the man's footsteps fade, then there came the faint sound of a door closing. Perhaps a latch catching – or was it the turning of a key? Freddie almost leapt up to find out, but he didn't trust that he'd be able to find his way to the entrance, or his way back to this chair, and any deviation from Vina's instructions might lose him his windfall. What if… what if there were other staff, if there were one or two of those maids hiding here to watch him? Report on his compliance?

He affixed himself more firmly to the chair, and glanced at the lamp, terracotta, shaped like a supine woman, her arms stretched over her head, hands clasping a wick, the body a reservoir filled with oil, legs the handle. Shifted his gaze to the diary – red leather – and the glass of Armagnac. He reached for the alcohol, stomach growling.

One sip, two, three. A biscuit and sliver of cheese. A grape. Another sip.

C'mon, Freddie. It's just a book. The old girl's last words to you. Just a bit of homework to earn your reward. There you go, pick it up.

He did. The volume felt strangely heavy and he couldn't say why the reluctance had hold of him. It wasn't like he was a huge reader, but it also wasn't as if he were illiterate. He'd read for pleasure now and then – admittedly most of those volumes had more pictures than words – and he'd often read things loaned by Great-Aunt Vina so he could discuss different subjects with her, including the notebook pilfered by her own fine fingers (she'd proudly stated) filled with Schliemann's handwritten notes about his excavation of the Burnt City.

Out loud he repeated 'C'mon, Freddie,' and flipped the cover.

Nothing leapt out. There was just Vina's spidery script, firm and forthright, jagged. Nothing terrifying or designed to test him. Just his great-aunt's voice from beyond the grave. *Steady on, Freddie.*

Another sip, another grape, another sliver of cheese.

Hello, my dear boy.

Well, who'd have thought we'd be at this juncture? I'd certainly have preferred you not be reading this because it means the inevitable — which I've tried my level best to evade — has come to pass. But you are reading this, which means that everything that was mine, is now yours, assets and obligations. Everything I've left behind is now attached to you, lucky lad. This house and the one in London, as are the contents to dispose of as you see fit, and much good may it all do you. There are things I want need you to understand, so I've written this especially for you. There are other volumes on the shelves, filled with my adventures, but I doubt you'll give them anything more than a moment's glance. This one, however, Freddie, is for you and I must insist you read it.

My dear Fielding will have set you up in The Library, in my favourite chair. He will, I suspect, not appeal to you nor your sense of aesthetics, being entirely too old and male, but in his defence, he is an excellent factotum, counsellor and procurer of all manner of things, and he has stood by me when others have not. I have made arrangements for his future, of which he's aware; he will be comfortable in his retirement, and will leave after your inheritance has been passed on. You will have no further need of him.

How nice that she knew him so well! Positively warmed the cockles of his heart. To be known and still loved. It was more than most could hope for in life. God, the brandy was making him maudlin.

Freddie, you are my favourite, by far — perhaps some might say I'm rather like a too-indulgent owner with a vicious pet, but that's over-simplifying things. Your cousins have always been held back in my esteem by their incipient altruism. But you, my boy, there's something to admire about your joie de vivre, your complete lack of care for others. Your utter selfishness. You remind me, my dearest boy, of me. You are the closest thing to my very own child. So perhaps some of this will not come entirely as a shock.

As you know, I was something of an adventurer in my youth — indeed, right up until my mid-fifties when everything became a little too challenging and complicated. So I retired to Tiamat House, tending to my obligations and indulged in my other hobbies, collecting books, reading them — two different activities entirely, but I suspect the distinction shan't bother you — and corresponding with people I'd met in my travels. A letter is a fresh balm for the soul, in my humble opinion, bringing news good or bad, it can change one's entire day.

Just like this journal, which is a letter of sorts and sure to change your day, dear boy.

Where was I?

Oh yes. An adventurer, me. There's something about such an existence that requires a degree of ruthlessness, to go where you want, when you want, get what you want, with no thought for anyone else. It's not a life that thrives on kindness or consideration. A single-minded focus and enormous sense of self (which some might call selfishness), yes.

Kindness, no.

Which you might find hard to believe as I've been very kind to you, over the course of your life. And you have, as I've said many times, always been my favourite. I cannot, however, say I've grown mellow in my old age and I'm proud to say I've never shirked or shied from the things that must be done.

I've always seen something of myself in you ~ that same focus, that drive towards satisfying one's own wants. So, I think you will understand what I am about to tell you, though you might suffer doubts as to its veracity for a while. Do read on, my boy, do.

Freddie paused, reached for the tumbler, took another sip and had to stop himself from gulping the entire contents. It was terribly fine, terribly expensive – but it was his now. For the first time in his life, he wasn't dependent on the charity of others or whatever he could creatively acquire. He could take his leisure; there would be more in the cellar. He was young – ish – he was almost very, very rich. And all thanks to the generosity of dear Great-Aunt Vina. Indulging the wanderings of her fevered mind was the least he could do.

Good old stick.

He took another tiny sip, a soupçon, just a reminder, a promise, of what his life would be like from this point on, forever and always, then set the tumbler down on the little table and returned his attention to the journal. There followed several pages with no text, but lists of names – some he recognised, others remained a mystery written in cyphers he did not know – of goddesses, diagrams that looked like complex compasses and compass points, illustrations, some pornographic, others merely ritualistic. A few pages later, Vina's missive continued, with no explanation for the break – perhaps, he thought, she'd re-used an old one, finding her stash of notebooks run out.

I undertook many trips, collected many items the majority of which you'll see here ~ around the world. But my particular favourite was the Middle East, digging up the bones of Mesopotamia and Babylon and the like. This wasn't my last trip, not by a long shot, but it was certainly the most memorable. Almost a year, across the Mediterranean and the Middle East, archaeological digs aplenty. One never sleeps quite as well as when one's spent a day crouched in a hole in the ground, digging up dead things. Oh, that sounds rather more morbid than I intended ~ disinterring the past, how's that? More noble, less necromantic.

One always hopes to find things ~ plenty of potsherds and the like, the occasional mummified turd

Algernon's voice echoed from somewhere in the Library and Freddie snorted

perhaps an intact goblet or krater, a bronze mirror, figurines, glass beads, jewellery if one's particularly fortunate. Also, a lot of lamps, those shallow little things of cooked earth, to keep the darkness and whatever breathes within it at bay ~ or signal it nearer.

One's never really looking for anything specific on such digs ~ mostly it's random what-have-you unless your leader is guided by some very specific writings and very specific maps, and very specific obsessions. So, I wasn't expecting to find anything much.

But...

I found her.

In the ruins of Nineveh.

The others had given up for the day, gone off to bathe or eat or nap or get drunk, but I kept on digging. Anything else seemed too boring and I just had a feeling about this particular spot in this particular trench. And I kept digging and brushing, brushing and digging until I found a niche and in that niche a statuette, and beside that statuette a lamp.

It was getting dark.

I lit the lamp.

It seemed only reasonable.

There was a great flash of light ~ far greater than it should have been from such a small thing, but later I realised it was her, more than anything, travelling in flame, though it was the tiny spark of a vesta.

She was there, in front of me.

Vicious and famished and ready to feast.

Yet, Freddie, terrified though I was, certain of my own end in those very seconds, I could not and did not look away.

And I must tell you, Freddie, my lad, she was a glory to behold! Terrible as an army with banners, as the good book says. I thought... I thought I might die at the very sight of her, and indeed that may well have been the intent, but something happened. I think she liked the look of me ~ it was only later that I realised she was seeking a factotum of her own. What's a goddess without a high priestess and procurer? But by then, I didn't care.

Still and all, that first night my survival was touch-and-go, my cause aided when one of the other expeditioneers (it's a word if I say it is) came wandering along, looking for me. He was much larger than I, more meat on him. More fit for her particular purpose. And once she was sated, we were able to communicate ~ never let anyone tell you that studying dead languages is a waste of time, my lad, it certainly helped me. A positive babel of ancient Greek, Hebrew, Hurrian, Latin, Akkadian ~ Ancient Egyptian was difficult as no one's spoken it for donkey's ages, but I'm proud to say she taught me over the years and I daresay I could make myself understood by a pharaoh or two. Where was I? Oh, yes. Expeditioneer, eaten. Sebastian Fiennes, if I recall correctly ~ grateful for his however-unwilling sacrifice, and all.

'Christ, Aunty,' Freddie said aloud, and reached for his drink, drained it. He didn't believe it – for the love of God, why would he? – but he'd no idea how badly his aunt's mental health had deteriorated. When had he last seen her? Was it really six months ago? How had she seemed them? He racked his brain but couldn't identify anything that might have been a sign of this... dementia. Hallucination. Madness. Had she been a little distant, perhaps? Quieter at dinner and the theatre? Less enthused about their visit to Madame Eugenia? Nothing. Either there had genuinely been no telltale sign or he was so self-centred – always a possibility – that he'd not have noticed strange behaviour even if she'd stripped off and danced naked on a table.

Freddie refilled his glass, felt the need of it, an unwonted river of guilt gently flowing through him. He really oughtn't have neglected her so. Indeed, she might still have been with—

Then again, no. Then Freddie would still be impecunious, living his life on the sharp edge of poverty his father let him tread – not so poor as to embarrass the family name, but poor enough that one day he might have had to come to heel and be obedient. Take a *job*. He shuddered, looked back at the journal, turned the page.

More of those same scribbles and drawings, praise-names and prayers. It was quite exhausting. But he flicked through, forward, looked at every single page, touched each one and so gave it his attention. Fed each page, every single one. Found the narrative again.

That one single night after she'd fed, oh our night together!

And afterwards, she offered me a deal. Oh, Faustian to be sure, but a deal nonetheless. And I took it. Why wouldn't I?

Because the nights with her! I could never give those up. The things she did to me, dear boy, those things! I'm quite overcome by the memory, but you, I daresay, don't need the details though we've shared some tastes over the years.

I accepted the bargain, sealed it in blood. Brought her home with me. Made this place a shrine to her in all her myriad forms. She has so many names, because they're all one at some point ~ joined at some juncture or other, the same thing flowing between them in the hidden waters of the world. But she's not one thing, never just one simple thing. We give things names, say, "this is this and there's an end to it", because we need to classify and quantify things. Put them on a shelf, in a box, neatly labelled. But she's not so simple. She's not one thing alone, but many. So many. She's rage and appetite, gentleness and death, she gives with one hand and takes with the other. She is birth and demise all in the one breath, fire carried on a feather.

I've called her, mostly, Tiamat. The dragon of the primordial waters, but she's older than that, I think. Older than we can truly understand. Too many things for us to understand, not fully. And so, the bargain, or part of it: twelve lives once a year for as long as I lived. My deal with her ~ never fear, dearest Freddie, I'm not asking you to honour this. Never that. She's not a creature of the day but travels in fire. She lives in the night, born in and borne upon flame. She sleeps most of the year, but for her sacred feast day.

She's very like us, with that tendency towards self, the satisfaction of one's own dreadful wants above all. A sacred mother, a sacred monster ~ what else is a mother who devours children? Just taking it back, really, because children are such dreadful little parasites. So, why shouldn't she? Take it back? That life and power sucked from her by offspring, hers and others, across the millennia?

'Oh, old girl,' Freddie moaned, rubbed his forehead hard. 'Absolutely fucking mad.' Felt his appetite for the alcohol shrink and disappear. Looked up, around the room, thought the shadows were growing but remembered that the lamp was to be lit at Vina's instruction.

As I said, I promised her a harvest, every year of my life and upon my death, my first born. First fruits and all that. And she told me if I failed to fulfil this second part, my soul would be gnawed upon for all eternity ~ Prometheus and his liver would be a whimpering pup compared to my suffering. And even though I didn't have a child and knew I never would, it didn't bother me at the time. Trust me, Freddie, the things you don't believe in in your youth will invariably come to haunt you later in life, as the final darkness grows closer.

She told me, too, six months ago when my last day would be. Knew that tumour was growing inside me. Knew my final darkness was descending.

And this, my dear nephew, is where your part in our play begins.

You'll meet her soon, look! Here she comes!

Freddie looked up and around, almost wrenched his neck. But there was nothing and no one. He glanced back at the page.

Ha ha! Made you look, didn't I? Silly sausage. Always so suggestible, Freddie. Oh, I'm just teasing. But it must be getting dark by now, Freddie. Do light the lamp, don't want you straining your eyes, and my tale is almost done. It's the final request I'll ever make of you, my almost child. The last time I'll trouble you.

Freddie struggled out of the chair – he'd been still too long, felt stiff and old. Took several moments to stretch, warm his backside at the low fire. Took a poker, stirred the embers, added kindling and then larger logs. When it was crackling up at him, he took a burning twig and touched it to the wick of the terracotta lamp.

The light was blinding.

A flare, an apocalypse, a holocaust of white fire.

He thought, for far too many moments, that he'd been blinded.

With time – seconds or minutes, impossible to tell – Freddie could make out shapes and shadows, that gradually resolved themselves into familiar items, the chair, the bookshelves, the turtle stone table; the bottle of Armagnac had fallen and lay smashed on the floor. Had he flailed in his shock, knocked it over? Or was it the force of the flare?

There'd been no sound to it, yet he'd felt entirely deaf. As his sight returned, so too his hearing. The gentle *click-click-click* of heels on the polished floors. Blinking, he turned to where he thought the door might lie, and saw a figure coming towards him. Blinking more, faster. The figure began to resolve itself into a compact body wearing a maid's outfit, he thought, a white frill cap at the crown of her head.

His *company*. Fielding had delivered, the man had not lied.

'Oh, hello,' he called, a little too loudly, and his voice rang in his ears. Shaking his head, he tried a smile. Tried again. 'My, don't you look – lovely?'

The statement turned unintentionally into a question. Freddie blinked again, squinted. Something wasn't right.

It was a woman, yes. Certainly. Or parts of her. But what he'd taken for a dress and apron were in fact swathes of scaled skin. Black and white, leathery wings. Bare breasts. The tapping on the floor came from no boots, no delicate little heels but from the claws front and back on her bird feet. Claws that matched those at the ends of her fingers. The frilled cap, attached to her, not hair but a hood of sorts, cobra-like, moving of its own accord.

He looked down at the book, to Vina's words at the bottom of the page, began to flip desperately – but there were no more pages of drawings and spells and summonings. There was just one final line, the only thing on the next sheet.

My bargain with her was always one of blood, she devours children, and you, dearest boy, wasteful boy, are the closest I've got to a child.

NEXT BIG THING

AMANDA DeBORD

"Hey! Robbie! Good to see you, man!" Dylan's voice cut out at "man," the high pitch and volume too much for my speakers. For a literary agent, he was awfully Hollywood. His white button-up was unbuttoned to his chest, as usual, and though his smiling face took up most of my screen, I was pretty sure I saw a hotel bar in the background. I smoothed down my own shirt, pulling at the hem that kept riding up.

"Hey Dylan. Nice to see you, too. It's been a minute."

"Yeah, what can I say? I'm keeping the road hot. You look healthy! Tara must be feeding you good! She around there somewhere?" He craned his neck, pretending to try to look around me.

"No, no. She's… not. She's—"

"Good, good. Listen, man. You know why I called. They're on my back. When are we going to see that draft?"

"It's coming. I'm almost finished, I think. I heard from some of my beta readers last week, and they think with just a couple more tweaks…"

"Robbie… Robbie. Beta readers and tweaks? We don't have time for tweaks. We need a book. Your contract is up next month. If we don't have something by then, well…"

My T-shirt rode up again. The collar felt tight, and I wanted to tug it away from my throat, but I didn't want him to see. "You can call them,

201

though, right? Get an extension? I've got something special here. I just need a little more time."

"Can I call them?" Dylan chuckled. "We can *always* call them, Robbie. But you've had an extension. You've had two extensions. And after last time… you know they're not feeling exactly generous. Work with me here." *Last time.* My face grew hot. "Last time" meant my most recent book. The sequel. It had flopped like a dead fish, and the publishers had let me know in very few words that I had one more chance before they were cutting me loose.

"Anyway, dude. I know you can get it done. Don't make a liar out of me, right? But in the meantime, come out tomorrow night. You remember Grace? Grace Lynn? We bought her book and she's having her launch party at The Cellar Door. We'll all be there. Bring Tara. It'll be a great time."

"Yeah, sure. I'll come out."

"Great. Great. See you then, man. Until then, don't let us down, you hear?"

◆

I stared at the blank page long after I'd disconnected with Dylan. I stared at it until the power saver came on and the screen went dark again. The glare from the evening sun through my kitchen window was blinding. I was going to need to rearrange things if I was going to write in here. Get the sun out of my face. Just as soon as I write one page. Just one page. I rubbed my eyes.

How hard could it be? I'd written a book before. Two books, to be specific. But one good book. A big good book, my debut novel: a dystopian fantasy that had sold to a big publisher for a big fat check. It went over so well that they'd wanted two more. Gave me an advance, even. Made me think it was OK for me and Tara to buy a big condo with a pool, to make a bigger family.

I fell right into playing the part of the famous writer. The neighborhood was nothing like I'd been told. The neighbors all knew my name. "Hey Rob!" they'd say when they saw me outside. "How's that book coming along?" They'd eye Tara's swelling belly and nod approvingly.

◆

The phone rang. Tara. I fumbled with it, my fingers slow and clumsy. The device felt too small in my hand, like one of Max's toys. When I finally got it facing the right way, I accidentally punched "decline." *Fat fucking fingers.* I tried to call her back, cursing how desperate I felt, but I couldn't get my fingerprint scanner to pick up. My finger was slick and smooth, like I was passing it over ice. I tried and tried. Finally, it rang again.

"Tara?"

"Why'd you hang up on me?"

"I didn't. I tried to call you back."

"Rob? Are you OK?"

"Yeah, I'm just… just tired. Why?"

"Your voice sounds funny. Thick, like you're coming down with something."

I swallowed. The gulp sounded louder than I meant it to.

"Listen, I hate to call about this, but your last payment…"

"I know. I know. I'm sorry. I mixed up the dates for when my check would clear. I'll call the bank and resend it on Monday. I'll send you extra to make up for it."

"It's not the money, Rob. I just hate calling you about it, you know? Hey, hold on…" Her voice brightened. "Max is here. Max? Want to talk to Daddy, honey? Let me switch over to video…"

The screen opened up to my three-year-old's smudgy face. I put on my dad face and smile just in time. "Hey Maxwellington! How's coloring?"

"Dada's face is big!"

<hr />

The sequel hadn't done as well as expected—do they ever?—and we had to cut back. A temporary speed bump in the road to the big time. It wasn't so bad, fewer dinners out, daycare instead of a nanny. Tara's job kept us afloat for a while. Then, after the pandemic, they never called her back to the office. *Indefinite furlough*, they called it. There was nothing indefinite about it. Everything went up except our income— the same story as everyone everywhere. Finally, we had to sell the condo. The morning I went to pick up the moving truck, Tara took Max and went to her mom's instead.

The small apartment hadn't seemed so bad when we signed the lease. Now, without Tara and Max there, it was huge and empty. Tara chose it, enticed by the sunshine-bright colors on every wall. California vibrant, a façade, for sure, but a cheery one. Now, alone, I scowled at the poppy colors. If I had the money, I'd paint it all gray, security deposit be damned. I had to write from the kitchen table, but at least it still had a pool.

The neighbors had eyed me suspiciously as they'd watched me drag my boxes up the stairs alone. Most of those boxes still lined the walls, stacked and unopened. I hated to unpack when I could be writing, but truth be told, I was hardly ever writing.

Now the sun was going down again, and I had nothing. I decided to go for a swim to clear my head. I sat down on the edge of the pool and kicked my legs in the water. The refraction made them look huge, comically so. I laughed and for a couple of minutes I didn't think about my book. I jumped in.

The water felt cool and good, but the dimensions were strange. It was smaller than it looked. Maybe I was reacting to it being so much smaller than our condo pool. Just two strokes and I bumped my head on the concrete side. *This must be what it feels like to be Michael Phelps*, I thought. *Except for the not making any money part. And sitting on your ass all day.*

I felt better after, good enough to venture out to Grace Lynn's launch party. Network more, Dylan always said. Get out and meet people. Writers write, he said, but *authors*, he said, authors shake hands. I squeezed myself into some pants with a waistband (When did I get so fat?) and a button-up shirt that didn't really button like it should and went out to shake hands.

The reading was terrible, as I expected. Grace Lynn was a tiny little woman, and she was so eager, so *proud*. Everyone clapped earnestly for her, gold rings clinking against wine glasses. She reminded me of one of those little yellow butterflies, cheerful and obnoxious and alive for less than a week, flapping their precious seconds away with glee. Dylan was there too, of course. He jumped a little when he saw me. Clapped his hand on my shoulder and said, "Je*sus*, Robbie! You're becoming a mountain! You must be hitting the gym more than you're hitting that keyboard. Ha!"

Ha. Haha. I finished my wine in one gulp. I met the people he introduced me to, laughed at their jokes too, refilled my wine glass at every opportunity. I never did feel drunk, but my cheeks felt hot. My skin felt… tight. Or was it my clothes that were? With every hand I shook, my palm felt wetter, softer. When at last I met Miss Grace Lynn, she was visibly disgusted as she gripped my hand with her tiny fingers.

I mumbled something vaguely congratulatory and pulled out my phone to order my Uber home. *Swipe. Swipe swipe.* Nothing. My phone wouldn't unlock. I shook it, aggravated, then realized people were watching me.

"Alright folks!" I said to no one. "My ride's here!" and slunk out the door. I'd take the Metro.

An hour later, I crawled into bed, feet throbbing, replaying the events of the night and the way people had stared at me on the subway. The way people had looked at me at the reading, stopped talking and shrunk away when I approached. They knew I was snakebit. Three years ago, I'd go to a reading and everyone would want to talk to me, everyone was my friend. Tonight, they acted like I was made of radioactive waste. *Fuck them.* Fuck them and fuck Grace Lynn in particular. If she could write, I could write. I'd do it to spite her and her tiny hands and Dylan and his stupid laugh. I'd start first thing in the morning.

But sleep didn't come. I dozed a little, but mostly I was cold. My feet kept coming uncovered. The sheet was too small, my pillow too thin. My skin itched and pulled uncomfortably across my joints every time I changed position. As soon as I would start to drift off, I'd hear a roaring, like a leaf blower in the next room. It took three times before I realized it was the sound of me snoring.

I was relieved when the sun finally rose.

I ducked into the bathroom, cursing the low doorway. I had to lean down to see myself in the medicine cabinet mirror. Who the hell built this place? Somebody probably wanted an apartment to make them feel tall. Everyone wants to feel good these days. Size 2 jeans the size of bedsheets so fat girls can feel pretty. Thick-soled boots so men can tell themselves they're actually six feet tall. Famous writers endorsing your book because your agent paid them. Good feelings all around, at the expense of reality.

Despite my lack of sleep, I felt pretty good when I sat down to write. I could finally see the natural progression for my plot, the transition from book one. I could tie it up with a shiny red bow and make people forget about that sequel. But it was so hard to write. Literally. My fingers mashed the wrong keys. Every other word was a typo. My wrists throbbed. My eyes stung. I slammed the laptop shut and stalked out into the sunlight for some fresh air.

It was worse outside. The neighbors gave me sidelong glances and shied away. A nice-looking woman by the pool hissed and gathered up her children, shepherding them inside. I walked a few blocks, aiming for the liquor store. My feet ached horribly and sweat dripped down my temples. The sun felt like it was six inches above my head. When I reached the store, I fumbled with the door handle, my hands swollen and clumsy, the doorbells jingling with my efforts. Before I could get it open, the clerk rushed forward and locked it, turning the sign to "Closed" and making weird gestures with his hands. I gave up and sulked back home, knocking my head on the doorframe. Damn this whole town.

I fumed as I lay down on the couch. It wasn't supposed to be like this. You pay your dues first, and everything gets bigger and better from there. Had I run out of all my ideas already? Did I really only have one good book in me? They say to write what you know. What the hell did a thirty-one-year-old white guy from rural Iowa know about dystopian societies? Corn. That's what I knew about. Corn.

The exhaustion caught up to me, and I drifted off into a fitful nap. When I woke, it was late afternoon. The shadows were long from the late-day sun streaming in the windows. Someone was knocking at the door. I was disoriented, forgot I was in my new apartment, alone. The knocking continued, and I heard Tara's voice. A wisp of a white dress billowed on the other side of the frosted glass window, a small shadow next to her.

"Rob? Robbie? Are you in there? Robbie? I've been trying to get ahold of you all day."

"Go away, Tara. I'm sick. I'll call you later."

"Hi Daddy!" Max's small voice cut right through to my heart.

"Hi, Sweetheart! Want to come in and see Daddy's new place?"

"He's not coming in, Rob. I'm only here because Dylan called me." I could tell from the reverberation of her voice that her head was pressed against the door. "He said you weren't looking good last night and asked how you were. I don't think he knows we're split up."

"I'm sure he knows. I'm sure he'd just love to get his hands on you now that you're on the market. Why the hell else would he call you?"

"Max, honey? Go sit down at the bottom of the stairs, OK? Mama will be down in a minute." She paused. I imagined his little feet climbing gingerly down the crumbling concrete steps. I wanted to reach out to him, to tell him to be careful. "Oh fuck you, Rob. Dylan called because he cares about you. We all care about you, if you could pull your head out of that fucking book long enough to pay attention."

"That fucking book? That fucking book is what would have paid for your SUV if you had an ounce of loyalty." I prayed Max couldn't hear me shouting, but I couldn't make myself stop. "Maybe you could have bought Max riding lessons or something bougie like that. Then your friends could all be impressed."

"Why are you being like this?" I could hear the catch in her voice. She was crying. Good. Before I could say anything else, I heard her footsteps running down the concrete stairs. Saying something sharp to Max. Her car starting.

"Tara, wait." I wanted to stop them. Grab them. Pull them both back to me and make everything like it was supposed to be. Without getting up, I reached out to unlock the door and my arm extended the entire length of the living room. My hand was the width of the doorframe, silhouetted in the evening sun. I fainted.

—◆—

I woke again sometime later. My back and neck muscles screamed at me. My head hung over one arm of the couch, my legs draped over the other. I kicked the soles of my feet against the clammy tile floor. I sat up with a start and bumped my head on the ceiling. My heart pounded in my ears. I was *huge*. I couldn't stand upright. I crouched, knees by my face, holding my legs to me and hating the feel of my own smooth skin. My clothes were gone, save for my underwear, which cut into my waist and dug into my balls. I felt like I was made of wet rubber. A muffled sob escaped from my chest, and the sound of my own voice almost made me lose consciousness again.

I tried to stand again, cracking my head a second time and sending plaster raining down on the room. Bits of dust clung to my damp skin. I coughed and tried to slow my breathing. Gradually, I calmed myself enough to look around. If I bent way over, on all fours and walking my fingers along the floor like pale tarantulas, I could almost straighten my legs out. I surveyed my apartment. Everything was indistinct, like clay that had been smoothed over, like I was looking through cellophane. I could barely make out my cell phone on top of the TV stand. There was no hope for me to even get my hand close enough to pick it up. No way my sausage fingers could grasp it.

None of the California bright colors that had previously graced the apartment walls were there anymore. The previously lime green living room was now drab, the floor beige and damp. Against the wall, though, next to the indistinct pile of boxes: a heap of crumpled white fabric. A heap that was impossibly small, but may have been Tara's size, with brown hair spilling out around it, and something red. A smaller crumpled form next to it that I didn't recognize, I couldn't recognize.

But I did. God knows I did. Max. Maxwell. He must be sleeping, I made myself think. They were probably tired, Max and Tara. I'll wake them later, after I get this all figured out. We'll go for ice cream. I just need to help myself right now.

I ducked down as low as I possibly could and tried to squeeze out the front door, but the thought of unfolding myself once I got outside, like one of those inflatable tube people outside the car dealerships... I nearly vomited at the image. I sunk back down onto the floor and tried to stanch the rising panic that threatened to take over again. I was sweating. I laid down on the floor and squeezed my eyes shut to not look at myself, to not see the things in the corner or the way I had to bend my body halfway into the kitchen, halfway into the living room, just to stretch out.

I had to get out. I kicked hard and shattered the back patio door, then I angled myself out over the jagged shards. Nothing cut me. My skin was smooth and so taut, like latex. Tiny pieces of glass stuck to me, but there was no blood. I dragged my body down the iron and concrete steps that led to the pool, my useless feet thumping along behind.

Mercifully, no one was there to see me, but the moon, large and close and mournful. *I'm sorry, Moon,* I thought. *I don't know how I let myself get this way.* I started to cry, and the moon cried with me. He understood what it was like to be big, what it was like to have everyone watching you. What it was like to lose your wife and your house and your son. The rain of the moon's tears fell over me as I lowered myself into the cool, buoyant water. I ripped a cushion off a lounge chair and rested my head on it, putting my feet up on the opposite edge. I closed my eyes and took a deep breath.

It's OK. I'm a fish now, I thought. *A giant fish. A whale. This is my aquarium. This would be a great idea for a book, but whales don't write books. I don't write books.*

I floated.

CORA JARRETT
GETS INTO TROUBLE

JOHNNY MAINS

"If you go home with somebody,
and they don't have books, don't fuck 'em!"

John Waters

The weather is horrible. It hasn't stopped raining for days. It's not that heavy rain that makes everything a nightmare, it's the half-arsed variety. It's slight but it's constant and it soaks you through just the same.

I get off the bus, thanking the driver as I depart. I always thank him. You can never be too kind to people. He never seems to do any other route than this one. The 33. It takes you from Bough Tree, three miles outside of Effingham and into town, then out the other side, all the way to Mercy, then Haven. When he gets there, he turns around and does the same route, but in reverse. He does a twelve-hour shift, which means that he drives that same route five times a day. He seems happy though. I hope he's happy. Is he doing the job for the money, the driving, the people or getting away from his life? I don't know.

The bus pulls in. I get off the bus.

I need to buy books today. Lots of books. But my first port of call is the butchers. I owe the butchers some money. I always pay my debts. Well, I

211

try to settle the ones I remember. Sometimes, someone from a shop will come up to me and say that I owe them this much or that much and I really try to remember, but I forget more often than not. But I try to pay my debts. It got so bad at the bakery that they stopped serving me until I had settled up. I had accrued over three hundred pounds on sausage rolls, pasties, and pastries. I paid my debt when I next went to the bank and got some money out, but it's a bit of a journey now. I don't like taking the bus all the way to Haven. It's a big town and the way that people look at me there, I don't like it. The teenagers that hang out around the bus stop smoking their druggie cigarettes, call me 'smelly' and 'dirty bitch' and 'bag lady'. I wish they hadn't closed the bank in Effingham. I know I can go to the post office and take money from my account there, but I absolutely hate Netty Floyd. She was the one that started the rumour about me all those years ago, and I'm really upset that she hasn't died yet. She's holding on. She's the one that's the dirty bitch, not me.

After the butchers I go to the bakery. I was upset at the butchers. They didn't have what I wanted. I wanted steak. What butcher doesn't have steak? They don't give me a tab anymore, but that's my fault and not theirs. The baker, when I finally paid her what I owed her, said that I wouldn't be allowed to have a tab anymore, and I accepted that, because they are a business, and they would go out of business if everyone did the same and nobody paid them. They have bills to pay as well and I think it would just be like a snake eating its own tail, you'd get to the stage where nobody is paying anything to anyone, and society will crumble, and it all came down to me not paying for three Cornish pasties and a Belgian bun and I can't have that kind of responsibility on my shoulders. I do have enough money in the bank, more than enough, but it's difficult to make the journey to Haven and I'm not smelly. I wash. I shower. My clothes are old, that's all.

This time I do not buy any Cornish pasties as the last lot had too much pepper in them and I couldn't move for a day or two what with the heartburn. On the bad day, the really bad day, the tidal wave of acid that would come out of me would eat away at all of the trees and cars and people just going on with their day-to-day business and...

"I'd like three large sausage rolls and five pink fingers today," and I take out my purse and I remove a twenty-pound note from it.

The young girl behind the counter has pink hair and a piercing through her septum. She has blue eyes and a nice smile. Her tabard is covered in floury hand marks. She doesn't say anything to me. Has she been told not to say anything to me? But she smiles, she always does, she has done every other time I've come into the shop. I suppose she's been told to; she wouldn't have smiled when she thought that her job was at risk because I didn't pay up my bill and I suppose I was the one who threatened her with unemployment so if I was her, I would probably hate me. I better not ask if…

"Do you hate me?" I ask her.

This takes her by surprise and the first sausage roll, grasped firmly in the tongs and about to be put in the paper bag, now hovers at the entrance. She looks at me and her eyes are puzzled, and then full of sympathy.

"No, of course I don't hate you, Cora."

"Please. It's Mrs Jarrett."

"Oh, sorry Mrs Jarrett. It's just that you gave me permission to call you Cora a few months ago."

"That's when I thought that you liked me. But now that I don't think you like me, you can call me Mrs Jarrett."

"I don't hate you, Mrs Jarrett."

The first sausage roll goes into the bag. It is followed by the other. She needs to get a new paper bag for the third sausage roll to go in because the bags are not big enough to house three large sausage rolls.

I do not say anything as she places the two bags on top of the glass counter then opens up a cardboard box and gets a different tong to pick up the pink fingers with. The box isn't big enough for five pink fingers. They are fat and she has to wedge the fifth one in and really push the lid of the box down. This means that the pink finger icing on one of them will be broken and it will take away from the enjoyment of it a little bit, but I do not say this as this has always happened and I do not want to get into a fight today. I am now feeling wrong about my choice of words because the girl with the pink hair and the piercing through the septum says that she does not hate me. I don't think I have ever seen her at Haven bus stop with all of the other teenagers so I don't know if she has ever called me 'smelly' before, but I bet she thinks that when she sees me.

"I *haven't* called you smelly *or* a bitch, *ever*! Why would I? You're a customer. I don't even know you!" Her voice sounds wounded, indignant, and that takes me out of things. I realise that I've been speaking out loud again and my brain is really starting to have fun with me today. I say I am sorry, and I give the young girl with the pink hair the money and I swipe the bags and box from the glass counter and put them into my trolley cart. This time I do not wait for the change. I leave the shop because I don't like it when I make mistakes and say things I am thinking. I wish I had a brolly, but I can't use a brolly and pull my trolley at the same time; it will slow me down too much and make me a target of cars driving past large puddles. I hope that the young girl with the pink hair and the pierced septum isn't talking about me to her boss, the spiteful Sheila, because I know that it might be just a little bit too much for her this time and she might say that I'll never be allowed to go back into the bakery on my next visit and then that will mean I'll have to get my sausage rolls from Iceland which would finish me because the pastry there is too flaky and it goes everywhere and there is no grease and I need the grease as it is comforting.

I walk up Nobody Lane and take the shortcut by the pet store and down the alleyway to the first charity shop. I push the door open with my shoulder – the door is known for sticking in damp weather and this time it is no different, and I open the door and at the same time I make the noise of a bell and the bell above the door rings at the same time. I have always been able to match the ringing of the bell with my making the noise of the bell and it pleases me that I'm able to do this. Someone is looking at jeans and they raise their head at me and look at me when I do this and their nose wrinkles with distaste, but they do not call me a smelly bitch which is a good thing because I really am not. I am clean and I have lots of showers.

"Cora! Hello! How are you, I've not seen you for a while!"

It is Jim. I like Jim. He hasn't been at the shop for a while because he has heart troubles. He once told me that he was sitting in his house watching something thrilling on the television when his heart rate went from seventy beats per minute to two hundred and fifty. He needed to get stents and I think it is because he is generally a lazy person who orders too much from the bakery, but I think that this heart shock has done something to his lifestyle because he is looking healthier than I think I have ever seen him.

"Hello Jim. You have lost a lot of weight."

"Yes, I have, well spotted. I've lost over five stone. Because of the ticker, you know. I suppose there was only so long that I could get away with it. Not like you, I don't know how you manage it. Eating all of that good stuff that you get from the bakery and not putting on a bit of weight! You're like a bird!"

"It's because I'm always on the go. And I have a lot of..." I don't like saying this phrase out loud because it makes my head worry about it more than it should, but I say it anyway because it's the only word that's appropriate for the phrase I'm trying to say "...nervous energy to get rid of."

"Well, we all have our crosses to bear," Jim says. Jim is a Christian. I used to be a Christian when I was younger, but I stopped believing in God after the worst toothache of my life. I was thirteen. I had to have an emergency extraction and the dentist said that one of the nerves in my teeth had simply imploded and I thought *what kind of God would put nerves in somebody's teeth for them to implode on you like that* and it didn't make any sense to me and it was then I didn't believe in God and that caused all sorts of trouble at high school, especially with my religious teacher Mr Stephens. He didn't like me, but he would try to persuade me that there was only one true God and his son Jesus Christ died for our sins. Mr Stephens got into trouble after he left the school. He went to jail because of his fondness of young boys, and I don't know if that is the kind of sin Jesus would have died for as stuff like that is deeply illegal and Mr Stephens had to move town after he was released from jail because this town would never have let him forget it.

Jim is still talking but he will know in a few seconds to stop because I am in the zone. I am by the books. I scan them – there are new ones in, eight new ones, all on the middle shelf. The first book is not for me. It is called *Himalaya* by the Monty Python man even though he is my favourite Monty Python man. I hate the one with the long legs. I am not after any non-fiction books today. I bought fifteen non-fiction books last week and this week I want crime fiction. The book next to it is perfect, it is by Paul Finch. He is a good crime author. It is called *The Killing Club*. I open it up and it is a signed copy. It is signed *"To Parker, a member of our writing/ killing club. Best, Paul Finch."* As far as signatures go, he is not too sloppy a signer. I think that he is right-handed. He could tighten his hand up a little and make his signature much more legible, but I have seen others that are far worse than this. What other books by Paul do I have? I try to think. I go to the next book on the shelf, it is by Marian Keyes, and it is her first book. I have a copy of this at home. I do not want to take the risk. I will go back and have a look at the *Watermelon* I have and if it is a tired copy then I will come back and get this one. But what if this copy is gone by the time I get home and search for it? I won't be coming back into town until tomorrow and the book could have gone and if it is a bad copy that I've got at home then I'll have done myself out of buying a perfectly decent copy. I open it up, but it is not signed. I put the book on top of the Paul Finch. I then look at the next one and I am intrigued. It is called *The Sun Burns* by Mabel North-Jorja. It is an orange and white book. There is a young girl on the front cover and a shadow of an older woman behind her. You cannot really make out either of their details because it is hazy. I turn the book over to read the synopsis on the back:

> *1976. Following the death of her family in a house fire, thirteen-year-old Jessica is sent to stay with her aunt and uncle on Orkney. Far away from anyone she knows and staying with people she believes don't want her there, Jessica discovers 'The Maid Maggie', an embalmed 'witch' who resides in the basement of the Museum of Orcadian Lore. Volunteering there every weekend, Jessica begins to piece together Maggie's sad story. And then, as the once in a generation heatwave begins, so do the dreams. Dreams that seem to slip through*

to Jessica's reality. Dreams where Maggie wants to walk the earth again and Jessica is powerless to stop them and her. The Sun Burns *is a true masterpiece of folk horror and an audacious debut by Mabel North-Jorja.*

I was born in nineteen sixty-nine, so I was seven years old when it was the heatwave of nineteen seventy-six. I remember it as if it was yesterday. This is the kind of book I really want to read. I put it on top of the other two. I feel like I am burning up. I look outside. It is still dark and rainy. I am glad that I am wearing my hood because the worst thing in the world is having wet hair. I wonder how old Mabel North-Jorja was in nineteen seventy-six. I don't know how I will find that out but maybe there is a way. I can go to the library when it opens on Wednesday and ask Thomas who works there to see if he will do an internet search for me, and we can look up Mabel North-Jorja together. I don't like using the internet because it is always too much too fast and when it happens there is no escape from it and it can overtake you too quickly, but Thomas does all of my searching for me when I really need it and he protects me and turns off the computer screen if it gets too much and then, once he does, I can get up and leave the library without any other problems, but I really want to learn more about Mabel North-Jorja. I think she has written my favourite book and I'm sorry to John Kennedy Toole who wrote my all-time favourite book, but you are dead, and I do not think you are going to be bothered that it has been replaced by another book and it has such a lovely orange cover. It's a colour that matches the best sunsets and it reminds me of something, but I don't want to think about that right now. I look at the next book and it is called *The Missing Teeth of Mark Cook* by Charlotte Emily. It is a non-fiction book, and it is a book I bought only last week so I do not want to buy this copy as it is identical to the copy that I bought from this very shop. Why do they have more than one copy?

I pause and take a deep breath. Maybe the house has burned itself down in my absence, and I won't be able to collect books anymore. It would be nice to start over.

"Is this something you have more of out the back?" I hold the book up to Jim and he laughs.

"Yes! You're right, we have another twenty copies. They're from a local journalist. She's self-published this book and she got a lot of stock printed and none of them sold. She told me the sorry story when she came to offload these. She had the nerve to try and sell them to me first, because she had gone to Binky's Books and they didn't want anything at all to do with her, so she tried to sell them to me and I had to remind her that it was a charity shop and she got all huffy, like, and you bought it last week and I don't know if we'll sell any more of them, to be honest."

I feel sad that someone put so much time and energy into something and nobody cares enough. Nobody but me. I don't know where I put the book, but once I go back home, I will read it and I will make sure that I try to find Charlotte Emily and tell her what I thought of the book.

I take my purchases to the counter. Jim makes a big show of looking at them and turning them over in his hands and he asks me if I know that the Paul Finch one is signed and I say that I do and he tells me that I'm not allowed to sell it and make a profit on it but I say how can I, I don't have the internet I don't have a computer I don't even have a smartphone on which to access the internet. I pay one pound for all three books, and I open up my trolley and take out my sausage rolls and cakey pink fingers and a folded plastic bag. I put them all on the counter and I put the books in and place them on the floor of the trolley and once they are flat I put the plastic bag on top of the books and then I place the box of pink fingers and the two bags of sausage rolls on top of the plastic bag so the grease from the sausage rolls doesn't spoil the books because that really would be the worst thing on the planet and it has happened to me several times in the past but I have learned from my mistakes and that's why I don't make that mistake anymore because…

The bell rings on the door and it is the person who was looking at the jeans leaving without buying anything. Someone else comes into the shop as they are leaving and when I see who that person is it makes my heart sink. I have had more than one run-in with Robert Selway. He blames me for killing his dog back when I used to drive. I did not kill his dog; it was someone else. I did not kill it. But no matter how many times I say this to him, he doesn't care, and he always has a go at me. I promise that today will be different, so I barge past him, and my trolley runs over his foot and he yells in pain. I turn to look at him as he hops on one foot, trying to grab the painful foot with his hand but then he falls over and hits the floor of the shop hard. I laugh and I escape into the rain where my laugh is swallowed by the mist and I hear his muffled roar of anger and the door shuts behind me and I run as fast as I can back down the alley and I think that he wouldn't try and chase a woman and scare her, he would want to get me on his own to do that because he is a coward all men are and I need to be seen. The trolley twists in my hand and it sticks in the alley diagonally. I think about leaving it for a second, but I pull and pull and pull and then it is free. I nearly fall over but I do the one thing I need to do when I am like this…

…breathe.

———◆———

I am crossing the biggest street in Effingham. No cars are allowed on the street anymore. There was an accident and a little girl died. Her head burst open like a watermelon and her brains splashed up the car like someone throwing a bucket of soapy water over it. I am going to go to Binky's Books. I do not nearly have enough books to go back home with and I know there will be unpleasantness if I go back to my house and the trolley is not full of books. My breathing is calm now and I am walking. I do not think that I will run into Robert Selway again. If he has really got a sore foot he will probably hobble off home and put his foot up and have a cup of tea and curse me. I will have to watch out for him in the future.

I see a man who looks like William. For a second I think it is William, but William is at home and so it cannot be him. It is quite startling to see how much he does look like William though and I am going to go over to have a closer look at him, but I decide not to just in case it is William and that…

219

There is a woman I do know behind the man who looks like William, and she is now in front of him and takes up all of my view. She is very big. When she walks, she wobbles like jelly. I smile at her and I wonder how her ankles can handle the weight. She must also have to put her feet up for a very long time after a day out. Elephants balancing on marbles.

"Sheena, I thought about you not too long ago when I was reading a book called *Sheena is a Drunk Knocker* by Thom Noosen. His lead character is called Sheena and it reminded me of you so I said that I would tell you the next time I see you."

"It's good to see you too, Cora," Sheena laughs and the wobbles continue. I wonder if she will ever stop wobbling. I think of her in a coffin that has to be made for her and it's the size of a car and as the flames are eating it her skin is burning and she is wobbling and her big skeleton is dancing a jig as the heat gets too much for the bones and they begin to bend.

"Sorry. You know what I'm like," I tell her.

"I do and we love you for it."

"That's nice."

Sheena nods at me and she doesn't say anything else. I really want to go to Binky's Books. I was really upset when the Effingham Dogs Trust run by the Millwards sisters closed down when the sisters died. They had such a good book section. I always used to find antique books there. Well, they killed themselves in a suicide pact because one of them got cancer of the stomach and it was terminal and they couldn't bear to be apart, so they swallowed lots of pills and were found in their separate beds in the same room holding each other's hand. I got really upset when Binky's Books closed in twenty fourteen because I'd thought that it was going to be open forever, but Linwood Brown, the person who had bought it from the famous author Russell Stickles in nineteen ninety, closed it down because an Oxfam bookshop opened and stole all of his trade. But the Oxfam shop closed in twenty-one because of Covid and that…

…that was difficult.

But Linwood Brown opened the shop in the same building as it had been before, and he called it Binky's again. I was very happy when that happened, and Linwood was as well, even though he wasn't working in it as much as he used to. It was just an excuse really to get his son Grover to 'get up off of his lazy arse and do some work'. There is another shop off Roxburgh Street, but I never go to that one because it is named after Primrose Hildebrand, and she was an awful woman who was murdered, and I was very happy the day it happened because it meant that she would never open up that dirty trap mouth of hers and spread tittle-tattle about the people who live in Effingham. I hope the same happens to Netty Floyd. I hope that someone takes offence to her dirty trap mouth and they shove a knife in it and make her swallow the fucking thing till she coughs up blood and then it goes back down her throat and she chokes, the dirty smelly bitch...

Oh no...

...bitch... breathe.

Cora...

...breathe.

I shake my head, but I am far away from Sheena. She has not moved from the spot where I was talking to her, but I have, I have moved further on. I am away from her.

I really need to get some more books. I need to buy more books. William will not be pleased if I do not buy lots of books. I must return with more books.

Oxfam is not there anymore. I remember the day it closed. I went in and bought lots of books. They were all science fiction books. I do not like science fiction books, but they would be welcome at home, and they were all on sale, two for one, and they all had great covers of spaceships, and some had aliens and some had half naked women on them and why are there half naked women in space, it's bloody cold up there they'll freeze their tits off. I managed to get eighty paperbacks crammed into my trolley and it was a nightmare to get it on the bus. The bus driver, I think he has forgotten about it now, but he had to lower the bus down to the level normally used for people in wheelchairs to get on because the trolley was that heavy and there was no way I could lift it on and the driver actually came out from behind his wheel to see if he could help and he looked at me strangely and asked me if I was taking steroids and it was then he lowered the bus down so I could get on and I wheeled the trolley on not a problem and I sat on the seat and was quite happy with my purchases until I got off at the other side and got home and that is always when the problems begin.

The light is on in Binky's Books. I cross the road to it and I smile when I see Linwood is sitting at his desk by the window. He looks out and he sees me, and he smiles a big smile and he puts his book down as he always has a book in his hand, and he gets up from behind his desk and he walks to the door, and I can see all of this because the shop front is all glass and he opens up the door.

"Cora! How are you doing! Sorry that I was closed last week. Grover was in the hospital, did you hear?"

"Hello Mr Linwood Brown sir, I'm very well, thanks, how are you? No, I didn't hear about Grover, is he okay, do you have any good books in for me please?"

I walk through the open door and the shop is warm. It smells of that lovely book smell, all musty and mushroomy and leathery, and I fall in love with the shop again. I fall in love each time I come to it. I don't fall out of love when I leave, but I fall in love more when I come back. The bricks and the shelves and the paint on the walls all sing to me and I sing back in my heart.

"The silly bugger was at an auction getting some books in. He won what he was after and when he was loading everything in the car, he tripped over something or other and banged his head against the bumper and had to go to the hospital. He's got a fractured skull, so I had to go to the hospital to make sure he was okay and get him home. The car was stuck at the auction house, so I had to organise that and get the books back safely, and there are some real gems in there, some that you'll like, I think, but we'll get to that in a moment. Cup of tea or coffee today?"

"I would like a cup of tea. I found a signed book in the charity shop today, would you like to see it?"

"Yes, I would!"

I open my trolley and I take out the two bags of sausage rolls, I pass the bag with one sausage roll over to Linwood. His eyes light up and he breaks out into the biggest smile. He reaches out and takes it with his hand that is covered in brown freckle spots.

"Oh, this is most kind of you to think of me," Linwood tells me, and he tears a bit of the paper bag away revealing the sausage roll and he takes a big bite of it, and he chews away and he is most happy.

I put the bag with the two sausage rolls on the table and I take out the box with the pink fingers and place it next to it. I wipe my fingers on my jacket just in case they've got a little bit of grease on them and I take out the Paul Finch book and I stand next to Linwood and open it up and show him the dedication.

"He must have signed it for another author," Linwood says, peering at it. "Would you like me to go on the computer and find out who it might be? Then we can see if there are any books by that person?"

"No, I just want to look at your new books. I don't have time for internet searches today."

"I can, if you like," Linwood says, and he brushes some sausage roll crumbs off his big blue fisherman's sweater.

"No." I am being contrary.

"Very well, you go over there and look at the new stock on those shelves and I'll make you that cup of tea."

He finishes off his sausage roll, he hoovers it away, he smooshes it all into his mouth and he chews like a cow and it is gone. He goes through to the little kitchen in the back. I have been through there before. It has a rickety table, and it is piled with books that he keeps for himself and takes home for his own collection. People bring books in for him to buy quite a lot of the time. He has only let me through the back once to see it, but I wasn't allowed to buy any of the books that were on the table because they were for him and him only and that made me...

... *frustrated* is a word I can use truthfully here.

The books on the 'new in' shelf are good. They are really, really, really good.

"These books are really, really, really good," I shout.

"I thought you'd like them, Cora," Linwood shouts. He starts to say

223

something else, but it is drowned out as the kettle starts to make its cooking water noise and I cannot hear what he is saying properly anymore. It would help if I took my hat off as it covers my ears a little bit, but my ears are cold, and I would rather be a little bit deaf than have cold ears.

The first book is a Pan Paperback. It is the *30th Pan Book of Horror Stories*.

"This Pan one is a rare one. How much are you asking for it?" I shout to get above the noise of the kettle. Linwood doesn't hear me. I wonder if I can play the game with this book. I pick it up and open it and look at the contents. I look at my open trolley. I could slip it in there. Wouldn't be that bad a thing to do, and it wouldn't be the first time I've played the game with a book in Linwood's shop. No. I have a feeling that this book is a test. That Linwood put it there to make me play the game so he can ask the question: "You wouldn't steal from me now, would you, Cora?"

I leave the book alone, but I am tempted. I am very, very tempted by it. I can imagine it at my house. It would be loved and cherished and devoured.

"Here's your tea," Linwood says. It is a good thing I left the book alone. He would have caught me in the act and that would have brought the rain into the shop.

"Thanks to you," I say, and I take the cup off him. It is yellow and it has little green birds and blue cups on it. The steam floats off the tea like mist on a lake first thing in the morning. I have seen that before when I was on holiday when I was a teenager. It was a magical moment. The rest of the day didn't go so well. There was the 'accident' and then I was coming back home on my own…

"Did you put a sweetener in, I can taste it," and I can. It's tingling on my tongue, and I like it. I like it a lot. I take a big gulp of tea. I don't mind how hot it is.

"Did you see the books on the shelf?"

"Only the *Pan Horror*."

"Eighty pounds for that one. It's a real collectible."

It was a test, a test, a test. I am glad I did not play the game.

"I'm not going to pay that for a paperback."

"You have before."

"But not for that one."

"Fair enough, Cora. Did you see the other ones?"

"No, you brought me the tea."

"Ah, so you were taken by the first book then. You lingered on it."

Linwood is close to figuring out I wanted to play the game.

I drop my cup.

It breaks.

Hot tea goes everywhere but it does not hit any books although that is a risk I am willing to take at this moment.

"Cora!"

"It was an accident."

"I want you to leave, Cora."

"But it was an accident, an accident!"

"You can come back and choose some books another day but not today. I'm going to have to clean this up *and* it was my favourite cup. You just can't do things like this when you think the conversation isn't going your way."

"You can't make me leave."

"I'll close the shop up forever, Cora."

I put everything back in the trolley and I close it up and I hit a pile of books near to the table and I topple them down. Linwood cannot save them as he is by the door holding it open for me. He curses as the books fall but he doesn't say anything else.

I walk and walk. My face is hot with tears. I don't know what I'm going to do.

I'm in trouble. *Real* trouble.

—◆—

I am walking in the heavier rain. My face is wet with rain and tears. I make noises like a cat being strangled.

I hate Linwood Brown. I hate him, *hate him*. He has done this to me. He has got me into so much trouble. If he had let me stay in his shop this would not be happening. *I gave him a sausage roll.*

He is a dirty…

Breathe, Cora.

NO

… He is a dirty bookselling…

BREATHE, CORA.

BOOKSELLING *CUNT.*

I fall onto the ground. It is dirt and pebbles and hate and pain.

I scream.

It stops raining.

I get up.

The sky begins to clear.

I can hear birds sing.

Maybe I'm not in trouble.

Not so much trouble after all.

—◆—

I walk round the long, slow curvy bend and then I get to my house. I am pulling my trolley, but my fingers are cold, and I can't feel it and I have to bend my fingers in and out to try and warm them up, but nothing is really working, and I let go of the trolley more times than I hold onto it.

"Hello house."

"Hello Cora."

"I'm wet and miserable."

"You look cold and bedraggled. Come inside. It's warm."

"Thank you, house. Marshall hasn't bothered you today, has he?"

"No, Marshall has been playing at his own home. I think they had a window open; his laughter was being carried across to me. He's very happy when he laughs."

The door opens before I get to it.

I hear rustling from inside.

I gulp.

The door closes behind me.

—◆—

Onna comes from my room to the left. Her movements are slow and considered. She bumps into a pile of books, and they fall behind her. Onno comes from upstairs. She is fast and her body moves from side to side like an alligator and she is unmindful of the books that she hits on the way down the stairs.

Onna: what did you get us

Onno: i hope itts good

"There's been a bit of a problem," I say as I open up my trolley. My hands are trembling. I pull out the box of pink fingers. The box is damp. The rain has made its way through the trolley. The box falls apart and the pink fingers fall to the floor.

Onna: I love pink fingers

Onno: I love books more what books did you bring lots of books

"I only bought two books today. I'm so sorry. Linwood Brown was..."

Onna: only two fucking books

Onno: twotwotwo this is not good cora

The house is equally unimpressed.

"You've made a mistake, you have to go back and get more books, Cora. This will not do."

"But I can't! Linwood stopped me from buying any!"

"You know the rules, Cora," the house says.

Onna: today of all days Cora

Onno: there better be something fucking magical in that bag

"There is!" I take out the first book, the signed Paul Finch. "It's a signed book, the author wrote his own words amongst his own printed words! I can even go and get the internet tomorrow to find out who the book is signed to if you want. I can go and get it done, please, please don't be angry at me."

Onna: william

Onno: william

"Tomorrow! *Not* William. I *can't* return," I plead.

By the time I get back into town everything will be closed. I'll go tomorrow. I'll go tomorrow.

"*WILLIAM, WAKE UP*," the house yells.

I scream and I run away from Onna and Onno, but it is much more difficult to run away from the house who is omnipresent. I crash against a pile of books, and they all tumble into the living room. It's not really a living room because I don't do any living there, really.

"Cora did *what*?" I hear a booming roar come from the room where I used to work a long time ago. It's the place where William died.

"No, William, it all just got too much today. I'll go back tomorrow, I promise!"

Onna skitters into the room. She lifts the Paul Finch and takes a big bite out of it. Her broken teeth are soon covered in letters.

Onna: book tastes good mind you

"You must be punished, Cora. Punished you must be," William booms. I hear splintering and crackling as William gets up from under the thousands and thousands of books that I put on him to hide him away, but he always comes back. I don't know how he manages it, but he does. The books, the mouldy books, covered in William's burst and long bloomed body, can't hold him down.

Onno: burn a little pile of books

Onna: burn her favourite books just two or three of them

"No, anything but that," I scream. My vocal cords are starting to stretch too much, and they hurt.

"Remember to burn them in the fireplace," the house reminds us all. "Please."

"If you burn books I'll stay here," William yells. "I won't come out to see you. You don't want to see me, you've made that abundantly clear, but if you burn five of your favourite all-time books, then we'll all let you go about your day."

"I can't…"

⋯◈⋯

I *must*.

I have my five favourite books. I cannot read the titles of them or focus too much on the covers because if I do I believe that I won't be able to see anything anymore. William yells from the room and tells me to hurry up.

Onna and Onno are sitting by my side, their imaginative legs all bent and weird. Onno's tongue is trailing along the floor.

Onno: im really excited itts been a long time since we saw fire dance

Onna: william has really hurt her this time she wont go out for a long time after this but that means

My dad bought me my second favourite book. A book of stories by Edgar Allan Poe. A small purple book. Abridged. That goes first. The flames are hungry. They eat and eat. They smoke. I take a puff of my inhaler.

Onno starts to glow with happiness.

William is happy.

"Burn those books!" he roars. I think that the books on top of him all start to jig.

Onna looks concerned. I think she is reading my mind again.

Onna: no dontt do that only do that to the books that you were told to burn

"What's she planning on doing?" the house asks, concerned. "Do I need to turn on the taps?"

I pick up the burning book. It scorches my hand. I look at it and maybe it's time to start collecting something else. I throw the burning book onto the pile to the left of me. They go up very quickly. I try to push myself up, but my hand is too sore. It is blistered and smells of pork chop. I have to move slowly, but the flames move quickly.

Onno: not the books not all the other books shees only gone and done it

Onna: oh fuck weere trapped how the fuck are we going to get out of here cora you mad bastard

I go through to the hallway, and I pick up one of the pink fingers with my good hand and I squish it into my mouth.

Onna and Onno are both covered in flames. They are screaming and they bump into each other and fuse together, then they fall over and a big pile of burning books falls on top of them and there is a wall of flame in the living room.

William screams that he cannot get up. I cannot talk back as my mouth is full of pink finger. The icing makes my teeth hum.

I get out of the house.

<hr>

Marshall holds my hand. My good hand. There's some pink finger icing on that hand but neither of us cares about it. The house is a smouldering ruin. There are fire engines, firemen and policemen. There is an ambulance on the way I am told.

"Onna and Onno are dead," I tell Marshall. I take a puff on my inhaler. My lungs are tight, but bearable. I will need a new apnoea machine.

"That's sad, Mrs Jarrett."

"You've not told your mum and dad about them, have you? Because if you did it would mean that we aren't going to be able to hang out with each other anymore. They think I'm weird enough already."

"No, Mrs Jarrett," Marshall says.

"All those books."

"I have some books you can borrow, Mrs Jarrett, ones that I got from the school library, but I'll need them back."

"We've found something!" a fireman yells from inside the burnt-out wreckage of my house.

"That'll be William," I say to myself.

"Who is William?" Marshall asks.

"Someone who loved *my* books a little *too* much," I reply.

THE WRETCHED TOME

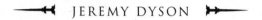

JEREMY DYSON

When two librarians get together, it is perhaps inevitable that their conversation will turn to the matter of books, but what books they speak of, and what specifically they have to say, will very much depend on the temperament of the individual. Whereas I accept that I myself was a man of letters, who enjoyed the life of the mind, and voluntarily turned his head to matters of metaphysics, Ladd, my junior, was of an opposite disposition. A joiner by trade, who prior to that had been invalided out of the East Yorkshire Regiment – he had found his way into our employment as a builder and maintainer of bookcases. He also happened to display a natural ability with matters of organisation and so when a deputy position became available, he was an obvious choice to fill it. He did read, though not voraciously, and the volumes that interested him tended to be of a very earthbound character – technical titles about the railways, or the growing of vegetables, for he kept a small allotment in Holbeck. So, it was a surprise to me when he conveyed the following story to me one moonless October evening, when we had both stayed late in order to work through a backlog of shelving.

It was unusually cold outside, a taste of the winter to come, and the wind drove itself around the smaller rooms of the library, moaning like some lost and miserable animal. After an hour or so's work, Ladd and I sought comfort in the librarian's office, and having stoked what was left of the fire we sat down with a bottle of ale and some cheese and cold meats.

"You know," Ladd said, wafting the warm air from the fire towards himself with his open palms, "on nights like these – I often find myself thinking of a story old McPherson told me, back when I was installing some shelves at the Philosophical Society, in York."

I was taken aback by Ladd's conviviality. He was not normally a garrulous man but something about the night, the cold outside, and the smoky warmth of the room had brought him outside of himself. I was to be even more surprised at the subject of the narrative he was about to share.

He leaned forward, settling himself on the edge of his armchair, and proceeded to begin his tale:

"McPherson told me he had started library work with a posting at Glamis Castle in the employ of the Earl of Strathmore. There was a large collection there and the family took pride in the fact it was properly curated. McPherson was the junior, and when his old superintendent passed away, rather than promoting McPherson, who was only twenty-two at the time, they brought in a man from St Andrews – a university type with letters after his name. This man was a curmudgeon, short tempered, and let's just say he was not troubled by a low opinion of himself, or his abilities. McPherson – gentler in temperament and not as learned – quickly saw the wisest course would be to keep quiet, mind his p's and q's and do as he was asked, as promptly as he could.

"It was only the new man's third day then when he came across the private part of the collection – kept under lock and key, in the basement, not unlike our own." Ladd was referring to the restricted section of our own stock that sat beneath us three floors down. At mention of it, our hearth made an unexpected roar, causing a burst of flame and a loud report which made us both jump. It was, of course, nothing more than a sudden draught down the flue, but it made us both draw a little closer together, as Ladd continued.

"Well, the new man – having gone down there and investigated thoroughly – was annoyed to have come across an uncatalogued casket, bound in black ribbon and an iron chain, all fixed with a rusted old padlock.

"'What the devil's kept in here?' he demanded of McPherson, 'and where's the dashed key? I tried every one on the ring and none would open it.'

"McPherson tried not to tremble before his new superior for he knew exactly what he was looking at. 'If you'll forgive me, sir, the Earl keeps the key for that item separate, because...' he hesitated, knowing this was not going to be well received, 'because of what lies within.'

"'Why? What lies within?' said McPherson, already impatient at this choice of words.

"'A book, sir. A book with a certain reputation.'

"The new man looked at him quizzically as McPherson added, '...a black reputation.'

"'What are you talking about, man – and speak up. I won't have this mumbling in my presence.'

"'Begging your pardon, sir – the book is supposed to be... a magical item.'

"The new man shook his head: 'Magical! This is the nineteenth century! Are we to be bound by children's nursery stories? And pray, what "magic" is it supposed to possess?'

"'Well, sir, according to what I have heard, sir, the end of the book – for it is a book of tales – is always different, in the eyes of whoever reads it.' McPherson continued: 'It writes itself anew, each time it is read.'

"The new man started laughing, allowing his sniggers to continue longer than their natural duration, as if for some unseen audience to whom he wished to communicate his contempt. 'What ludicrous poppycock – you absolute imbecile!' he shouted, as if poor McPherson was the one responsible for this state of affairs.

"'I'm only reporting what's been told to me, begging your pardon again sir.'

"'Where is the key?' said the new man, impatiently.

"'I believe it is kept in the commode over there, sir – the oak one.'

"'Well, my boy – I'll tell you what we're going to do. We, that is you and I, will conduct a little experiment, and together we will put an end to this nonsense once and for all. I will open the casket, read the end of the book, and you will read it after me. We will then independently write down what we have both read, and only then will we compare our versions. I think you will find the book may not be so powerful after all. In fact, I'll wager my first week's salary against yours that what we both write comes out exactly the same.'

"'But sir, if you'll permit me, there is one other thing you must know,' McPherson protested. And now he was ashen faced at the prospect of what was to come. 'The reason the book is locked up like this.' However scared McPherson was to state out loud what he had heard, he was perhaps more afraid of having to take part in the experiment that had just been suggested. 'The reason the ending of the book always changes is because the book is said to be cursed – the work of a diabolist, so they say.'

"'Cursed,' the new man sputtered. 'Cursed! Cursed in what way. For goodness' sake man, what is this babbling?'

"'The legend states, sir, that the reason the ending is different for each person that reads it, is because the book's ending predicts both the manner and the date of the reader's death – and once party to this information, there is no escape from its clutch… according to the legend,' McPherson repeated, to make it clear he was merely reporting what he had heard, rather than claiming to be the source of the story.

"The new man looked at McPherson with a mixture of contempt and disgust. 'You idiot. You medieval simpleton.' He moved closer to McPherson, a wicked look in his eye, 'I will not tolerate this level of ignorance and mindless superstition in any employee of mine. If I am to be cursed – then so are you. And don't think you'll be wriggling out of this. We will *both* read the end of the book as I say. And we will both write down what we find there.' And with that the new man went to the commode, took out the key and finding it was a fit for the black, ugly padlock, he added contemptuously, 'I will be delighted to go first.' And with that he took the whole package to his private room, to begin his experiment.

"Poor McPherson was now in a terrible state. With a young family to feed he needed his job, and was hardly about to hand in his notice. And yet he was so afeared of the curse and the book's reputation that he felt he would not be able to go through with the order he'd just been given.

"Just before the end of the working day, the new man reappeared. McPherson feared he was going to be made to read the book there and then and was so frightened that his stomach was churning as if he had the cholera. But instead, the new man brushed past him, white-faced, as if ill himself. McPherson walked after him to see if he was alright – and also, if truth be told, because he was curious about it, to find out what the man had read. When he put this question – risking its impertinence – he could not help but notice that the new man's eyes were wide with terror.

"'I will not speak of it in darkness,' was all the man said."

Here Ladd paused in his telling – as if this was the end of his tale. I myself was not going to settle for that. Like the new librarian, I needed to know how things concluded.

"Well, what happened in the morning? Were the two endings different?" Again, there was a lacuna, broken only by the cracking of the fire. "Oh, come now," I was compelled to add, "there are no such things. Magic books and curses! This is the modern world. Tell me what happened when they compared notes."

"Well, that's just the thing, you see," said Ladd. "It never got that far. For the new man was in the most terrible accident that night. Knocked down by a coach and horses as he walked back along the Dundee Road." Ladd leaned forward, his eye gleaming in a most uncharacteristic way. "Awful thing," he said, "the fellow's head was clean torn from his body… And that wasn't even the worst thing about it."

"What do you mean," I said, not seeing what could be worse.

"Well," Ladd added, "According to McPherson, the coroner's report remarked that he'd never seen a look on the face of a deceased like it. Normally in those circumstances things move so fast there is no distress evident on the poor, unfortunate party's visage – a fact they use to comfort the bereaved. That wasn't the case here. In this instance there was such a semblance of despair and horror in the man's expression – it was if he knew his head was coming off long before the carriage wheel actually took it." Ladd leaned back and let this information sink in.

"Naturally," he added, "McPherson never opened the damned book for himself after that. It was returned to its casket, rechained and committed once again to the darkness. In fact, I'm pretty sure it remains there to this day." And the coals cracked again in the grate, like some unseen mechanism, twisting inexorably into place.

WRITTEN ON

RAMSEY CAMPBELL

As Ernest let himself into Booked You he heard Quintin say "Is this you in the inscription?"

His customer was stout enough to block the view of the desk beyond the aisle enclosed by books. "Who says it's not?" she demanded.

"Robert sounds like a man."

"You can't tell people what to call themselves." When the bookseller gave this a silence to loiter in she said "If you must know, he's my brother."

"Are you selling this on his behalf?"

"If that's how you need it to be."

"I'm sorry." Quintin barely bothered fitting his tone to the phrase. "I wouldn't feel comfortable buying it," he said.

As the woman snatched the book Ernest reached the desk. "Can I see what it says?"

Quintin folded his wiry arms, which were as decorated as a monastic manuscript, and clenched his small face to condense his habitually dissatisfied look. "It's not signed by the author."

"No, he was my dad." With equal pique the woman said "He's gone and my brother's dead to me as well."

"You know me, Quintin. I think if anybody's written in a book it adds a bit more life."

"You're welcome to this bit," the woman said and thrust the book at him.

The title on the moderately tattered jacket exhorted memory to speak. On the front flyleaf an increasingly tipsy inscription said *For Robert to remind you you've been all a child of mine should be* while it lolled towards a drooping X.

"How much do you want for it?" Ernest said.

"Ask him how much."

For a disconcerted moment Ernest thought she was invoking her father. "I'd have offered fifty," Quintin said, "if I hadn't seen the problem."

"I'll take it," the woman told Ernest, "but you'll need to give me cash."

"I will if you come to the bank. Can we have a bag, Quintin? It was starting to rain."

The bookseller presented him with an unfavourable look in advance of a plastic Booked You carrier. The woman bagged the book as Ernest followed her out of the shop. Under the stained slate of a February sky the street was developing a dark scattered rash. The shower kept rustling the carrier as if its contents had grown wakeful. It brought Ernest's trot close to a jog, five minutes of which took him to the bank. "I'll just get your money," he told the woman, prompting an interested blink from Jane at the welcome desk.

Thin insistent footsteps paced him and the woman to the nearest cash dispenser. Or did they sound more like somebody drumming a pen on a page? They were the plopping of raindrops on the carpet once they'd trickled off the plastic carrier. Ernest felt he was treating his companion like a thief as he blocked her view while he typed his secret number. As soon as she'd exchanged her package for the notes she set about rubbing an inky stain off her hand, then stared at him. "What are you waiting for now?"

He had an odd sense that she was anxious to see the last of him. "I work here."

"I could have charged you more, then." As he gave this a tentative laugh she said "Don't worry, I'm glad to be rid."

As she waddled out of the bank she turned her hand up as though hoping the rain would wash away the ink. He could have fancied she'd used the hand as a blotter. Jane watched him rescue the book from the bag, which he dumped in a bin. At least the bag had protected its contents. In the passage to the staffroom he unburdened himself of his puffy coat and hung it in his locker, where the book joined the one he'd brought to read—a comical Victorian diary inscribed *From a nobody to somebody better than everybody* on the flyleaf. Once he'd stuck his head under the hand dryer in the Gents and combed the unruly result, he took over from Jane at the welcome desk. "I ought to have known what you had to be paying her for," she said.

"I don't know what else you would have thought."

"Maybe wondered if you'd been naughty for a change." When he failed to match her provocative chubby grin she said "It was a lot to spend on nothing but a book."

"Some books are worth it. My friend who sells them told me that one was."

"I'm sure he would when it's his living."

"It's worth that much to me. It's more than what you said. It's a piece of someone's life."

"Books can't really be alive, Ernest. You want to spend more time with people. It's still just a book."

He was poised to argue further when a customer arrived, prompting the standard response Jane would have offered if it hadn't been Ernest's turn. "Do you need any help today?"

The newcomer didn't, making this so plain it was barely polite. Few customers required assistance any more, so that the bank provided just the welcome desk and a token clerk behind the dinky counter in the wall embedded with dispensers, all of which left Ernest feeling like a human component of an automated system, barely necessary or even tolerated. How was he supposed to engage with people like that? Or with his colleagues, when he'd never seen any of them open a book? All they seemed to read were their phones, a process he gathered was meant to be social. As far as he could see it simply yielded power to the electronic medium the bank was part of. He preferred solidity and substance, and few things in his life were more solid than books.

The rain had relented by the time he walked home. Beneath the orange embers of the muted streetlamps the pavements glistened like tar. A bridge swarming with graffiti led to his street near the railway line. His house greeted him with a bookshop's smell. Lorna used to object that the terraced house felt narrowed by its neighbours, but it had all the space he needed, and now he could use it just as he liked.

Besides the thousands on the shelves in the bedrooms and the lounge, every room contained at least one book. Just one would have belonged to Lorna, who had treated books as disposable and couldn't understand why Ernest kept them. She hadn't merely snapped their spines, she'd folded her reading all the way back rather than use any of his bookmarks. The fiercest quarrel had erupted when she'd crippled one of his books. Their separation had felt like reclaiming himself, though he still resented having had to sell books to help buy her share of the house.

He microwaved a supermarket curry and leaned a book against the heavy cruet on the kitchen table to read while he ate—a Dickens dedicated *To Carol, who makes every day Christmas*. In the lounge bereft of its television—he'd encouraged Lorna to take it and its distractions with her—he turned to a Muriel Spark, in which a giver had written *You're always prime to me*. When he used the bathroom a Jerome K. Jerome kept him company, its flyleaf declaring *You're the only man I'll ever need*. The guest room, where he'd slept in the months before Lorna moved away, retained a Jonathan Swift described by a donor as *Some company for you on your travels*. Next door a second Dickens lay on the bed that was wholly his now. *You're so much more than I expected—you're just great*! Why had he never inscribed a book to Lorna? It might even have persuaded her to start taking care of them. He reminded himself how she would grumble when he had the bedside light on, and celebrated his freedom by reading himself to sleep.

He wakened just in time to miss a thought that fled into the dark—some issue with the latest book he'd purchased. He'd read the message on the flyleaf, and that was enough for a while. It was by no means the only unread book he owned, which simply urged him to buy more. In the morning he found it sprawling open on an armchair as though urging him to read the dedication. "I'm not Robert," he reminded it, and made space for the book on a shelf.

Low sunlight through the corridor above the railway made the graffiti look painted afresh. Perhaps some of it was new, but he'd never found it worth deciphering, and could only wonder who the readership was meant to be. At the bank he hung his plump coat in the locker and left the Nabokov on a chair in the staffroom. Today—all day except for breaks—he was behind the counter. He primed an inviting smile whenever a customer approached, but nearly all of them avoided him in favour of the facilities implanted in the wall. Did nobody appreciate contact with a living person any more? By the time Ahmed took over while Ernest went for lunch he was wishing he'd brought his book to the counter, but he doubted the manager would have approved. He bought a sandwich in a plastic wedge to nibble while he headed for the bookshop.

A protracted sound of ripping met him. Quintin was peeling tape off a roll to secure a parcel. "Can't you get enough of us?" he said.

"I hope I'm still welcome."

"Just don't bring your friend or the kind of thing you helped her get rid of."

"I wouldn't call her a friend, even if she's why I'm back. I didn't have a chance to look at your new stock."

"They're still where they were." As Ernest made for the Recent Acquisitions shelves Quintin added "I shouldn't think there's anything for you."

This was just his manner, Ernest reminded himself. You could think Quintin would rather not sell any of his wares or buy any either. Ernest searched the bookcase to prove Quintin's comment wrong and selected a Kingsley Amis novel that seemed to have started to edge off the shelf. When the front board swung open like a lid he felt doubly justified. "So you bought from the family after all."

"I don't believe I know what that's supposed to mean."

Ernest took some pleasure in showing him the flyleaf. Although the inscription was unsteadier than ever, he was sure he recognised the handwriting. *You must think you're the lucky fellow, Bro*, it said before apparently trailing off. The letters inclined progressively towards an X, which appeared to be struggling to stagger upright to minimise the inch that separated it from the final word. "What are you expecting me to see?" Quintin said.

"It's the same chap as the book you wouldn't buy."

"You'd know more about that than I do, but I doubt it. Are you buying that one?"

Ernest had intended just to make his point—he found the dedication unappealingly ambiguous—but now he felt compelled to indulge in his habit. "How much are you asking?"

"From you, call it twenty. It's nothing like a first. Since you want it, there's the deal."

Ernest wasn't sure what kind of special treatment this entailed. Quintin flattened the card receipt between the flyleaf and the front board, then rubbed his finger and thumb together as if he'd encountered a cobweb. The paper bag he wrapped the book in rustled restlessly until Ernest confined it under his arm on his way to the bank. He was storing it in his locker when Jane emerged from the staffroom. "You've never bought another book so soon," she protested. "Don't you ever do anything but read?"

"What else would you like me to do?"

"Be a bit more pleasant for a start."

He didn't think he'd been sufficiently aggressive to warrant the rebuke—certainly not as much as he thought appropriate. He was glad she would be working in the office behind the scenes, which meant they'd be unlikely to encounter each other. He stood unconsulted and unapproached in the cell the counter made until it was time for his afternoon break. He retreated to the staffroom, only to halt in the doorway. The Nabokov was sprawled face down on a chair.

Just the front cover was open, propping up the book as if it had striven to raise itself. As he retrieved the book, sunlight through the window above the staffroom sink caught the flyleaf. For a moment the inscription looked dug into if not out of the page, and he could have fancied someone had added to the ink, emphasising the message. Had the meddler strained the boards or torn the jacket? While Ernest couldn't find any evidence of injury, the possibility infuriated him. He aligned the jacket with the boards as tenderly as he might have handled a lover, and then he marched into the bank. Since there were no customers just now, he declared "I don't mind people looking at my books so long as they take care" loud enough to be heard in the office.

It brought the manager out of his sanctum, sweeping back his hair with one hand as if to highlight his wide frown. "Good grief, what's the commotion? Was that you shouting, Ernest?"

"Just seeing everyone heard what I said, Ralph. Somebody could have damaged my book."

Hearing his first name seemed to deepen Ralph's frown, even though he encouraged the usage. "How?"

"I left in the staffroom, but not in the state I just found it in."

"Then let me suggest you keep your books to yourself in future. And I'd like to be convinced you care at least as much about your job as them."

This sounded like a threat to which Ernest had no response he could risk. He withdrew to the staffroom, only to find the dull weight of his rage hindered his reading so much he was reduced to blundering among the words. Even at home it proved to be a task. He gobbled a microwaved carton of risotto so as to devote more time to concentrating on a book—any book. Recommencing the Dickens didn't help much, not least because the notion of a spectre summoned by thoughtlessness had lost its appeal. He abandoned the book before any further hauntings could appear, and stumbled up to bed.

A solitary footstep wakened him. It was in the bedroom. Pain clutched at the back of his neck as he jerked his head up to peer about for the intruder. Dimness smudged the room so much that he took some seconds, totted up by the thumps of his pulse, to locate the perpetrator. A book had fallen off a shelf, and nobody was visible in the room. Surely lying on the floor wouldn't harm the book, and he felt too exhausted to move more than his head, which subsided onto the pillow and then into sleep.

He was out of bed before dawn, and nearly tripped over the forgotten item. Switching on the light roused him enough to make him wonder what had made the book—a Joseph Conrad—fall. When he inspected it for damage, the inscription on the flyleaf arrested him. The handwriting was so close to supine it looked windblown, but he knew it well enough. *I don't believe you've got a heart, Bro*, it said. At least, Ernest thought so, even if the version of a name was blurred almost beyond recognition. The accompanying X stood practically upright on the far side of not much of a gap. What kind of a dedication was this, especially addressed to a brother? How could Ernest have forgotten such an observation? He pored over the book in the hope of recalling some explanation until he realised he would soon be late for work.

Uncertainty about the inscription burdened him so much as he stood behind the welcome desk that hoisting a smile to greet customers felt like trying to lift a weight off his face. "Do you need any help today?" he made himself keep saying despite a parade of refusals, and eventually blurted "Jesus." He apologised to the newcomer and told her "Just thought what I need to do." He made for Booked You as soon as it was time for lunch.

Quintin turned from adding volumes to the Recent Acquisitions shelves and gave Ernest a look that slumped short of surprise. "We'll be putting in a bed for you at this rate."

"I'm not here to sleep. I'm very much awake." When Quintin renewed his dissatisfaction, perhaps at the fall of his quip, Ernest said "Have you any more books that chap wrote in?"

"Not a ghost of a chance. They'll find no buyer here."

"But you sold me one recently, didn't you?"

"You did your best to make me think I did. I wasn't convinced then, so don't bother trying it now."

"Not yesterday. The last book I bought from you till this week. *Heart of Darkness*. It's another one he'd written in."

"It wasn't when it left my shop."

"I didn't realise either, but we have to be mistaken. He's in there, I promise you. I should have brought it so you could see."

"Don't trouble yourself. I've been meaning to keep any inscribed books for you, since you're so fond of them." Just as reproachfully Quintin said "I know my stock. That's my job."

He must be refusing to acknowledge he'd missed the inscription. "Have you any at the moment?" Ernest said.

"I'd have told you if I had."

Would showing him the Conrad antagonise him? Ernest might have valued someone's interpretation of the message, but he didn't want to make himself unwelcome at the bookshop. He couldn't imagine asking anybody at the bank to read the inscription. He saw Jane start to greet him from the welcome desk until she recognised him, and felt more isolated than ever. He was heading for his locker when Ralph accosted him. "A moment, Ernest."

"More if you like."

The manager lowered his voice and his brows. "We've had a complaint from a customer."

"I'm sorry," Ernest said, only to feel unrequired to be. "Sorry to hear it, I mean. What was the problem?"

"The lady says you swore at her."

"Who?" In the hope of not knowing Ernest added "When?"

"Not long before you made yourself scarce."

"I didn't swear at her. I wouldn't even call it swearing."

"You offended her, and that's good enough for me. With all your books I'd expect you to care more about words."

"You don't seem to. You said offending her was good." Ernest didn't utter this, nor "At least it wasn't the usual crap you make us say to people." Instead he protested "She overheard me when I wasn't meaning anybody to."

"Try confining yourself to the recommended welcome."

"I'll be confined all right," Ernest muttered on the way to his locker.

Having somehow failed to notice the inscription in the book made him wonder what else he might have overlooked, and left him eager if not anxious to be home. "How can I help you today? May I be of some assistance? Do you need me at all?" Varying the salutation didn't quiet his mind, though it brought him more than one spiky look from the manager.

As he hurried across the railway bridge he felt as if the scrawls were multiplying around him, along with the enclosed clangour of his footsteps. The house met him with a mustiness he'd never previously noticed, as though in some fashion the books were going bad. He had little time for dinner, and made do with an apple and a chunk of cheese, both of which he downed almost hastily enough to clog his throat. As soon as he'd ensured his hands were clean enough to handle them he set about inspecting every book.

It was well past midnight when he finished. His eyes felt dusty, and so did his brain, but he hadn't found a single inscription besides the dozens he already knew he had. At least he was already in his bedroom. He lurched not much better than blindly across the room and only just managed to haul the quilt aside before falling into bed.

Knocking wakened him, a solitary knock he might have thought had been performed by a softened hand. The unpleasant fancy meant he hadn't entirely left sleep behind, but something had certainly moved in the room. He clutched at the mattress to raise himself and the ponderous quilt, and made out an object on the carpet—a book. He was tempted to let it and himself lie, but if he'd replaced it so precariously it had toppled off the shelf, might others follow? The possibility sent him out of bed to plod across the room.

Despite the dimness, he recognised the Thackeray, the very last book he'd examined. Torpor rendered his fingers so cumbersome that as he retrieved it he lost his grip. As he barely caught the book with his other clumsy hand, the front board fell open. He peered at the flyleaf and then blundered to switch on the light, to prove he hadn't seen what he imagined he had. But the page was no longer blank.

What you did wasn't fair at all, Bro. While the letters slumped close to horizontal, the X that almost touched the last of them had risen so nearly erect it resembled a rickety cross. Ernest felt as if the dimness were still clinging to his eyes, because the final word was so indistinct it bordered on illegible. If he hadn't seen it elsewhere he mightn't have recognised it at all. He blinked hard in case this cleared his vision while he tried to grasp how he could ever have thought the page was blank, and then his hands jerked, almost dropping the book if not flinging it away. The word was by no means unclear, but his perception had been. It didn't say *Bro*, it said *Ern*.

He staggered downstairs at a run to find the other books that bore the fragment of a word. *You must think you're the lucky fellow, Ern. I don't believe you've got a heart, Ern.* Now that he'd identified the name, it was unmistakable. His bewilderment left no space for thoughts, if indeed he wanted to think. He could only set about scrutinising every book once more in case any of them had acquired an inscription.

He'd found nothing of the kind by the time he needed to leave for work.

He dashed into the bathroom and out of the house as soon as he was dressed. In the midst of a resounding sprint across the bridge he thought the style of some of the graffiti looked unreasonably familiar, but he couldn't loiter to check. He felt a cobweb settling on his face, and before he batted the sensation away he lost sight of the handwriting he'd seemed to glimpse.

Jane was ringing the bell for Ralph to let her into the bank. The sight let Ernest realise he wouldn't be able to cope with unfriendliness on top of his confusion, which felt as if the night had clung to him and massed in his mind. "Hey there, Jane, good morning," he called and strove to be more pleasant still. "How are you today? If you need my help with anything at all, don't be afraid to ask. See, I'm doing what you said I should, being what you said I ought to be, turning over a new leaf, as they used to say. Some of us still do."

He was doing his utmost, but her expression suggested he'd turned over a stone rather than a leaf. Or did she feel confronted by some kind of joke? "I'm dead serious. Deadly serious. Serious, I'm saying," he protested as if he were quoting from three different books. Had he yet to act pleasantly enough? He was rummaging in his cluttered mind for ideas when Ralph unlocked the door. He admitted Jane so speedily he could have been rescuing her from a threat, but only stared at Ernest. "What in the love of heaven is that meant to be?"

Ernest didn't want to think the question summarised him. "What?" he said and felt as brainless as an echo.

"What have you done to your face, for lord's sake? You needn't think you're bringing it in here."

Ernest peered at his blurred reflection in the nearest window of the bank and saw his forehead had acquired a stain like a scribble on a page. "I must have missed it," he tried to believe. "I was in a hurry to get to work."

"Then kindly go and wash it off at once."

Was Ernest sporting the remains of a grubby cobweb from his sprint across the bridge? He hurried to the Gents, where the dryer on the wall greeted his arrival with a feeble rattling gasp. Lurching at the mirror above the sink, he found a scrawl was stretched across his forehead. Surely it couldn't be a word, however much its components resembled letters. The first and the last of them put him in mind of tilted crosses or ironic kisses or both. He supposed that with an effort you could think the stain spelled feint, whatever sense that would make—some kind of pretence or else a mark on a sheet of paper? He was reaching to turn on the tap when he saw he was reading the scribble in reverse. He fumbled for his phone, only to discover he was oddly reluctant to take his own photograph. Once he had he could only laugh, because this image was reversed as well. He fingered the icon that turned it around, and then he almost let the phone drop in the sink. The handwriting was all too familiar, and the word was thief.

The sight left him unable, not to say unwilling, to think. He could only pump the dispenser so hard it rattled against the tiles beneath the mirror and then smear his forehead with soap before dashing water, hot and progressively more scalding, into his face. None of this even started to erase the inscription, and rubbing his forehead with handfuls of paper towel, however ferociously, proved just as ineffectual. At last he took his throbbing brows into the corridor, to find Ralph waiting for him. "I can't seem to shift it," Ernest complained.

"Then go wherever you need to go to get rid of it and don't come back till you have." In a murmur that merely pretended it wasn't meant to be overheard Ralph added "If then."

Ernest knew where he had to go—the only place he could. He blundered through the crowds, avoiding all the eyes that turned to him, and then had to loiter outside the bookshop until Quintin bothered to show up. Well before he reached Ernest, the bookseller's disfavourable look grew masklike. "If that's some sort of crack at me," he said, "don't waste your ink."

"Can't you see who wrote it? You must know you can't do it to yourself. You're a lot more written on than me."

Quintin stared at him to establish if not in the hope that Ernest had finished. "I won't have my customers seeing that," he said and stopped short of unlocking the shop. "It might give them the wrong idea."

"I don't need to come in if you can tell me about the woman who sold me the book you objected to."

"I don't object to books, and I can't tell you a thing."

"I just want to give her brother his book back." When Quintin shrugged and shook his head Ernest pleaded "I don't expect you to know where she lives, but don't you know her name?"

"Neither of those and nothing else either." As Quintin poked the key into the lock he said "Good luck with your hunt."

Ernest heard a dismissal rather than a wish. He trudged away from Booked You, and then a last hope suggested how he might locate the woman. He hastened home to retrieve the book and set about prowling the streets. Surely she had to bear the same description as he did, if not more of one. "Have you seen a woman who looks like me?" he asked everyone he met, tapping his forehead with a fingertip long after both grew bruised. He mustn't expect to find her immediately, and he continued the search, promising himself he'd sleep once he was successful. There were people on the streets all night to ask, and the most he could risk was a doze on the occasional bench. He couldn't let the downpours that drenched him and turned the book into a sodden wad deter him. He kept hoping the rain would wash away his caption—he could describe the woman well enough without it—but whenever he caught sight of his reflection in a window, the word seemed to renew its blackness like a charred brand. The sight made him add denials to the question he addressed to everybody in the streets. "That isn't what I am," he reiterated doggedly, and "This isn't me."

BENEATH THE DIAPHRAGM, THE GUT ITSELF

—◄ ROBERT SHEARMAN ►—

I

There was this boy at my school who gave birth to a novel by Charlotte Brontë. Barry Spitt was his name, he was almost famous for a while. He wasn't a friend of mine or anything – he was in the fifth form, and I was only in the second, this was ages ago – and it wasn't one of the major novels of Charlotte Brontë either, it was *Shirley*. I bet you've never heard of it. I'd never have heard of it myself if the school hadn't made such a fuss. But even a minor novel from a major writer is extremely rare, and there was a lot of excitement about it, and I mean internationally, Barry Spitt kept on having to do interviews about it on the news. And, of course, Barry didn't know anything about the Brontës, it wasn't as if he'd actually written the book, he was just a receptacle, for God's sake – you'd watch him on the telly and he didn't know what to say, his hands in his pockets, all sullen, clenching his teeth over and over, he looked like a cow chewing cud. Not anyone's ideal surrogate for a nineteenth-century novel about industrial depression, and you could tell that the journalists wished for someone a bit more enthused, more aware of the momentous responsibility before him, the *awe*; but that was hardly Barry's fault, was it? The school dined out on it, of course they did – they even made Barry head boy, and gave him a special badge, and after he'd scraped through his exams they packed him off to university. I think he ended up in the civil service, doing a job for which he was fundamentally unsuited. All Barry had wanted to do was play football.

In a way, birthing one of the Brontës ruined Barry's life. Or at any rate changed it so completely you might as well call it ruined – and I suppose what else can you expect, when you're essentially such a small person with something so big inside you?

I read *Shirley*. We all did. The school made it a set text. And I was a bit disappointed, because it was really very boring. But that's the weight of expectation for you, isn't it? *Shirley* may only have just been birthed, but there were already birthed countless academic texts about the Brontë sisters telling us all how important it was and where exactly it fitted into the progress of the social realist novel. Most books aren't like that. Most books come without a fanfare, and get forgotten, they simply get forgotten. We pump them out into the world, and some of them are okay, and most of them are crap, and either way no one much reads them let alone remembers them, and pretty soon they're taken off to landfill. There's something more right about that, I think. Something more beautiful. Books living and then books dying, and we all move on, not like these classics that stagger about for centuries like zombies. A girl in my class gave birth to a tourist guide book to Munich. It was quite old and all the pricing information was out of date, but even so, she cared for that little book of hers more than Barry Spitt ever did his. Why should *Shirley* get the attention instead?

Shirley completed the works of Charlotte Brontë, and it now meant the world had the full set! (If anyone actually wanted them.) And we already had Emily Brontë's only novel, that had been one of the very first classics birthed way back when, we'd had that one since my grandparents. Neither of Anne Brontë's two novels had yet been birthed, however, everyone was now on the lookout for them. And there was a flurry of excitement a year or two later when it was rumoured that a girl in the fourth form was expecting *The Tenant of Wildfell Hall*. Just imagine it – could our school really pull off a Double Brontë? But it was a false reading, or a hoax, or wishful thinking – it was just a book *about The Tenant of Wildfell Hall*, there were tons of those. And everyone calmed down.

I feel sorry for Barry Spitt. Right at the centre of attention, the last place he wanted to be. I even feel a bit sorry for Charlotte Brontë, wherever she is, whoever she was, whatever plane of existence she truly came from. She probably didn't want our entire school reading *Shirley*, and growing to hate her, and drawing obscene graffiti about her in the boys' toilets with *Shirley* shoved up her jacksy. Charlotte Brontë may well have thought that *Shirley* was boring crap as well.

And yet, still – still – in spite of myself, I couldn't help but feel a little pride. In my school, in Barry, in Charlotte Brontë. Watching on television the ceremony when the Scroll was produced, and the birth of the book was recorded for posterity. Every book is recorded in the Scroll, of course, but few get the hoopla of TV coverage, with all the costumes, and all the fireworks! The Scroll upon which is listed every single book the world will ever produce, all the novels that shall ever be, and all the short story collections and poetry pamphlets and the non-fiction books about science and history and art and life and, I don't know, bottle top collecting, yes, even all the books about bottle tops – the Scroll that lists every single scrap of literature the world can ever know. Just waiting for the right child to come along, fall pregnant, and give birth to it. Yes, I watched as the handwritten manuscript of *Shirley* was presented to the official clerk, nice and pristine, with the blood wiped off – because there is always a *little* blood, no matter how hard you train. I watched the clerk flip through *Shirley*, weigh it in his hands. Then turn to the Scroll, find it upon the list, and give it a tick. Of course I felt proud. I even shed a tear. I surprised myself.

II

I was a late developer. Most kids birth when they're fourteen or fifteen years old, though it can happen as young as twelve. By the time I'd turned seventeen everyone else in my class had already produced a book of some sort, and almost everyone in the year below me. It was embarrassing. There was nothing that could be done to hurry the process along – the doctors would tell me I just had to be patient, my book would come when it was good and ready. It made me feel like a baby – my balls had dropped and there was stubble on my chin, but how could I call myself a grown-up until I'd added my little contribution to world literature? Friends at school treated me with growing contempt. Teachers too – Mr Gladstone, who taught P.E., and hated me, one day pushed me up against the lockers in the changing room when no one else was around, and he hissed it straight into my face, and his breath stank of fags: "Let's face it, you're nothing, and if you ever *do* birth a book, it'll just be some self-published small press piece of shit."

Because that's the lie – oh, they tell us that the system is fair, that it's entirely random which books end up inside us. It's the great equaliser, so no one should feel too proud or too ashamed of what their book might be. No status to it – we're all just doing our bit! – but if that's so, why did they put Barry Spitt in the civil service? And why is it always the posh kids who seem to get the postmodern novels and satirical poetry anthologies, while the likes of us get stuck with pushing out celebrity biographies and instruction manuals? Don't tell me it isn't about class. Don't tell me there isn't something going on. I'm not stupid.

"We love you anyway," my parents would tell me, and give me hugs. But I didn't want them to love me because I was different, I just wanted to be *normal*. They were kind people, Mum and Dad, and I don't think I treated them well, not then, and certainly not in the years to come – they were kind, but they were annoying. No one in my family had so much as birthed a single piece of fiction for generations, we were simple stock. My parents had both given birth to maths textbooks for middle schools – one on geometry, one on calculus. You'd have thought there would be a funny story to tell about that. About how, against all the odds, these two shy, lonely people with nothing more in common than maths had gone out into the world and found each other and fallen in love. But there isn't.

I remember them for their patience, for their refusal to show disappointment at every one of my failed pregnancy tests. Even though I was disappointed, I was blazing with it. And that time Grandma came over and just pointed at me

BENEATH THE DIAPHRAGM, THE GUT ITSELF

with such disgust and asked what the hell was wrong with me, was I broken in some way – and it was the only time I ever saw my dad lose his temper, and he ordered his own mother out of the house – and yet the truth is, I thought she was *right*, I sided with *her*, there *was* something wrong with me, I *was* a freak. And when Dad tried to give me a hug and told me she was just a spiteful old woman I pushed him away and ran to my bedroom and refused to come out. And yet it was to my parents I would go each time I thought I had a new symptom, and they would kindly wait with me as I went to the toilet and peed on a pregnancy stick. There were so many symptoms, really, anything could be a symptom – and I'd had them all: tickly cough, nausea, a general sense of ennui. And that night when once again I knocked on my parents' door, and it was three in the morning or something, but they didn't complain – and I said I thought I might be pregnant, because I had this strange tickle behind my eyeball, wasn't that a symptom, a tickle behind the eye? They didn't laugh at me, or tell me to go back to bed and stop wasting their time. And I couldn't really believe it when the stick turned blue – I don't think any of us could – we all just stared at it as I held it out, dripping urine – and then Mum said, "You're going to be an author!" and Dad said, "Congratulations!" and he offered me his hand to shake, it was such a funny formal thing to do, and I shook it, and we laughed, and I know I cried too, none of us could sleep that night we were so excited, and I know I loved them both then, I have never loved anyone more.

—◆—

The next day at school everyone gave me a round of applause, and my teacher looked so pleased, and I don't think anyone was being sarcastic. And then in the afternoon my parents took me to the local library so the doctors could do a scan. It was still too early to determine exactly what the book was going to be, but yes, I was definitely expecting, and there was a ninety-nine per cent chance of the book being fiction – congratulations. And my mum said, "Fiction in our family, I can't believe it!" and Dad said, "Just you wait till my mother knows, that'll wipe the sneer off her face!"

Fiction is the best a baby book can be, so of course I was pleased. But I hadn't even dared dream of that, at this stage I would have been relieved

255

to be birthing a leaflet. And I realised I was scared too. Because everyone knows that fiction is the most difficult pregnancy to go through. For a start, the trimesters tend to last much longer – a standard work of non-fiction can take around three months to gestate, but novels are notoriously more complex and gnarly. There's this one tale of some poor kid who gave birth to an annotated version of *War and Peace* whose pregnancy lasted almost two years! And, of course, with fiction even the physical process is entirely different. With factual material all the work is done in the throat and at the top of the lungs, it hardly uses the intercostal muscles at all. Fiction comes from somewhere much deeper, down in the diaphragm. And for the great classics, of course, it comes deeper still, beneath the diaphragm, the gut itself.

I wasn't sure I wanted anything inside me that would muck about with my diaphragm – that all sounded too committed, and more than that, too intellectual, and more than that, too painful, frankly. I wanted my diaphragm left out of it.

◆

A week later, we were called back to the library. The determination had been made. They'd studied all my X-rays and blood samples and skin scrapings, and consulted the Scroll – and they now knew precisely which book I was going to produce, from its frontispiece down to its ISBN. "Have you ever heard of a writer called J. J. Jacobs?" the doctor asked, and then he chuckled, because he said it was all right, no one ever had. J. J. Jacobs was so obscure that they didn't even know if the Js were for John or for Janet, J. J. Jacobs could have been anyone – this wholly forgotten writer of the late twentieth century. He, or she, had only two books to their name, and neither had been successful, and soon after publication both had fallen out of print.

My book was to be a little collection of short stories called *Ghostings and Hauntings*, and as the doctor told us the title he didn't bother concealing a little smirk – "I doubt it'll be a psychologically penetrating work." Mum and Dad smiled politely, and Dad said that perhaps he wouldn't go bragging to his mother after all. "Ghost stories?" he asked, and the doctor nodded, "Seems certain, I'm afraid – playground stuff. Ghosts, ghouls, things that go bump in the night." I said that I was worried about my diaphragm, and the doctor said the strain wouldn't be a problem, this wasn't *proper* fiction. The book was so slight it'd probably just slip out without my even knowing. And it was going to be such a short pregnancy, just three weeks, that was all. A book like this barely needed time to gestate and we could make an appointment for the procedure at reception on the way out. I didn't quite know what to think, was I happy or not? And the doctor saw my confusion, and he smiled in a way I think was intended to be nice, and he said, "It's another book in the world. That's all that matters. It doesn't have to be a good one. It'll all be over soon, and you'll have done your biological and literary duty, and you'll be free to get on living your life." I nodded, and I said, yes, yes, that's exactly what I wanted – have it all done with, find a life and get on with it – and I don't know, I may even have meant it.

Mother asked if there was anything at all we could do in preparation – vitamins, push-ups, reading classes? The doctor shook his head. We couldn't even read J. J. Jacobs' other book to get a taster, as it hadn't yet been birthed either. "And even if it had, there's an X-notice on it, it wouldn't have been archived. The Scroll says it's worthless, and of no value for posterity." And he put his hand upon my shoulder, and gave me a wink. "Just like your book, son. We'll whip it out of you, then take it straight off to be pulped. You don't have to worry about that."

When we got back home Dad said, "Well, that went well, I think!" and Mum said, "Shall I put the kettle on?" And I burst into tears. And Mum gave me a hug, and Dad said that my hormones were probably just playing up.

III

Nowadays birthing centres are state of the art, and come with all the mod cons. Private wards, pumped full of floral scent and ambient music. Ergonomic chairs, with soft armrests for aching wrists. Even an entertainment system to distract the authors in case the book they are writing is particularly tedious. It wasn't like that in my day. I was led into a vast room, segregated into little cubicles draped all around with curtains. A table and a hard chair – you were advised to bring your own cushion if required. On the table, a pot of black coffee, a pack of cigarettes – stimulants or relaxants, whichever you preferred. A couple of pens, of course, and paper. Lots and lots of paper.

Every book is different, and so every birthing is different, but even so, the night before, my parents had offered me advice. Dad said, "Grit your teeth and don't think about all the words pouring out of you, it'll only make you feel sick." And Mum, wistfully, "I found mine rather relaxing, I just sat back and let all the isosceles triangles flow." I signed all the forms they put in front of me – name, date of birth, title of book I'd be birthing, A personal injury waiver form, and a form accepting my book had been categorised as X-notice, that it would be requisitioned and disposed of. The nurse showed me everything I needed to do, and she was brusque, but not unkind.

"Now, when you're ready, you can pick up the pen, and just play with it on the paper. Allow your body a chance to adjust to the task ahead. You can draw figures of eight, if you like – we recommend figures of eight. Glide your pen across the page, and think *of* it but don't think *at* it – and your book will come when it's ready." She made to leave, and I said, "But what if I need anything?" And she blinked at me, and looked surprised, and said more softly, "Dear, producing a book is the most natural thing in the world. It's what your body and brain have been designed for, and at last they're going to work together for what they've always been intended, in perfect purest harmony. Why should you need anything?"

I sat back, breathed deep. Picked up a pen, held it loose between my fingers the way we'd been taught. I drew a figure of eight on the paper in front of me, and another figure of eight. Letting the pen do all the work – a flow of the wrist, that was all, and look, the empty white is being filled. Filled with figures of eight. The paper was nothing but a scrawl now, my doodles overlapping and obliterating each other, I thought I had better turn the page – lifting my hand up off the table, and my wrist still swirling and twisting, the pen making figures of eight dance pointlessly in the air – then back to fresh paper, all new white to destroy. Figures of eight. And it did seem to me that I was wasting a lot of paper with my figures of eight. I wondered whether they'd get angry with me if that was all I could produce, just these useless squiggles, but it was a distant wonder, I didn't worry about it, figures of eight, another page, figures of eight, and now I wondered whether this really was my due date at all, perhaps no book was ever coming out – or, no, perhaps this was my book, just this, a series of figures of eight? Odd sort of a book – I thought I was writing a bunch of ghost stories – should I be feeling something? All these words inside me, and I knew they were waiting to come out, so why did I now feel so empty? Like I'd been hollowed out, guts and all – or is this what writing is like, the dread that actually you have nothing to say, the emptiest feeling in the world?

And then – yes – yes, I was feeling… Yes, the tickle was back. That tickle behind the eyeball. I hadn't felt it since that night I took the pregnancy test, but here it was, back again, itching away somewhere my nails couldn't reach to scratch. Warm, even burning, but not painful, nothing like that – and I looked down at the paper and I saw my figures of eight were beginning to flatten out, the marks on the page were getting smaller and tighter and starting to twitch, and my fingers were twitching too, everything was a-twitch. I was calm. I took hold of a new sheet of paper. I began to write my book.

Some people say writing a book is like walking a tightrope. Let your instincts take over, and don't look down. Don't think, or you'll become so amazed by the sheer magic of creation, that you're breaking all the laws of science and creating matter that didn't exist, that the impossible will stop becoming possible after all. And that's how it began, I promise you – I let my fingers glide over the page, and didn't let my brain get in the way.

I looked down. And just to admire the handwriting – that confident lettering, so much more grown-up than my own, properly adult – and I didn't look at the words, I tried to look *through* them.

But what can I say? I was a child. The balls dropping, the stubble, it didn't matter – I was a kid. And I got bored, and I wanted something to do. I didn't like coffee, and I didn't want to smoke. So, without even much curiosity, I started to read.

The first thing that was clear was this – that the prose style of J. J. Jacobs in no way measured up to the quality of his handwriting. The ink on the page looked steadfast and true – the actual words wandered about awkwardly without point. Sometimes Jacobs would take several entire paragraphs to extract some laborious simile or another – they seemed desperate to describe something or another to me, but without knowing the right words, either for the object they were describing or the object to which it was being compared – it was like watching someone try to navigate without using a map, or instinct, or even, at times, actual bloody eyesight. I read, always making allowances – trying to provide the similes for myself, or the words they were probably aiming for, guessing at what sense they were struggling to find. At one point I remember thinking I was starting to enjoy a story, only to realise it was a story I was entirely inventing for myself in lieu of anything better on the page. And just as I'd find myself adjusting to the bizarre wayward grammar of it all, just as I thought I'd found a way to interpret it, up it would buck like a bronco and throw me off the saddle again, suddenly speeding up, leaping ahead in the narrative without explanation, and leaving me trying to keep up as the words ran off into the distance.

Yet the biggest problem was the stories themselves which, for all their overcomplicated verbosity, were exasperatingly obvious. They were ghost stories, yes, but without any chill to them. For all the horror of their actual prose, Jacobs seemed unable to rustle up a single frisson of unease. There was the story Jacobs entitled 'The Phantom in the Library'; the only twist to the tale being that there was, indeed, a library, and that there was a phantom in it. 'The Haunted Mansion' offered no surprises either, presenting me with a mansion that was haunted. 'The Ghost in the Garden' not only didn't bother with surprises, it also disdained plot, character and point. 'The Spook in the Cellar' began more promisingly, but when at the end of the tale it turned out the whole thing had been just a dream it was all I could do not to throw away my own pen in disgust.

I realised I felt jealous of Barry Spitt. At least his book meant something – if not to Barry, and if not to me, then someone, surely, to all the academics who studied it and to the particular Brontë sibling who had conceived it. It had had purpose. J. J. Jacobs had lived in a world in which books could actually be *created*, as works of actual *imagination*, where your own thoughts and beliefs were responsible for dragging into being fictions that had no earthly right to exist. Something magical. Incredible. Did Jacobs never marvel at the extraordinary miracle that was? – at the extraordinary privilege they had? And yet they had taken that miracle and torn off its wings and stomped it into the ground. When there were so many other books in the world, jostling for a bit of air, fighting for attention, how dare Jacobs add more to the heap? When there is so much to be read, and which deserves to be read, and which still will *never* be read. What arrogance. Worse, what *cruelty*.

I felt such rage. And I don't think I'd ever felt *rage* before, I don't think I had ever felt *anything* before, not really, not in comparison – was this being a grown-up at last? If I had seen J. J. Jacobs, in that moment, I think I would have killed them. And yet, still, my hand gliding over the paper, and the words pouring out nice and smoothly, not betraying my fury in any way at all.

I started to write the final ghost story. It was called 'The Cursed Book'. I didn't have high hopes for it.

It's hard for me even now to describe what was so unsettling about 'The Cursed Book'. I've had a lifetime of trying to do exactly that – if not to anyone else, at least to myself. The sleepless nights I have spent going over it in my head – and the dreams it has given me, all the bad dreams. And in my waking hours, too, it has never felt far away – even as I walk and talk and eat and drink like people are supposed to do – even as I smile and laugh and pretend to idiots that I am happy – the story is still there, somehow, just out of reach. A tickle under my eyeball.

—◆—

'The Cursed Book' begins like every other story by J. J. Jacobs, in a fit of long paragraphs and confused syntax. And then at some point, I suppose, it changes. I can't work out at what point it changes. But, bit by bit the prose becomes more sparse. Colder, somehow – with all the excess fallen away,

261

and each word carrying its own dreadful weight. Reading it upon the page, the first person to do so – the only person, at least, in this world – it was as if everything that I thought I understood was cracking apart, and for all the fact that it was my hand on the page causing those cracks to appear there was nothing I could do to stop it.

Understand – it's not the plot. It's not the plot. And yet, maybe it is? A bit? Maybe the plot is the key to it all. I shall describe the plot, best as I remember it.

A man arrives at a hotel. He takes a room. (The man is given no name.)

He is in a foreign city. (The city, too, left nameless.)

The purpose of his visit to the unnamed city is never made clear, but we can presume it is some kind of a holiday.

The man inspects the room. Doing so, he finds a book inside his bedside cabinet. It is written in English. Idly, the man begins to read it.

At length, the man puts aside the book, and gets dressed for dinner.

He goes down to eat.

When he returns to his room, he gets undressed, and climbs into bed. He picks up the book once more. Reads from it until he tires. Goes to sleep.

The next morning, refreshed, he wakes, and goes down to breakfast.

He eats his breakfast. Calm, unhurried.

He returns to his room, gets dressed for the day. He picks up the book, reads a little from it, then puts it down, and leaves the hotel.

He explores the city. Visits, I think, a cathedral. Or perhaps a church.

At no point is any description given to what the man thinks of the city. Or of the cathedral. Or, indeed, of his breakfast. Or, indeed, of the book.

And at all times, still, the man is calm and unhurried. That is important. That is one of the things that feel wrong.

All these words on the paper, all from my body.

The man returns to the hotel. The man returns to the room. He returns to the book, reads some more from it.

He dresses for dinner, goes down to eat.

He returns to his room. Picks up the book and reads.

And we still don't even know what it is he is reading. We are excluded from that. We feel, very much, excluded. We are deliberately left out in the cold. And we don't know what the man is thinking. We feel excluded from that as well.

He reads late into the night. Every other paragraph or so he turns a page. At last he tires, and puts down the book, and sleeps.

In the morning he wakes and goes down to breakfast. This time he eats only a part of his breakfast, then pushes the plate away. With no irritation, or impatience. He has had enough.

He returns to the room. He picks up the book. He reads.

At one point he gets dressed to go out, once again to explore the city. But having dressed, he doesn't leave the room. He sits back down and reads.

We become aware that the book is no longer in English, but some foreign language. Still, he reads.

We become aware that the book no longer uses an alphabet we recognise. Still, he reads.

There is a knock at his door, The man ignores it.

The man dresses for dinner, but does not go down for dinner. The man undresses for bed, but does not go to bed. Still, he reads.

There is a knock at the door. The man ignores it.

Still, he reads.

There is some vague sense that the room may be getting smaller? But this may be some stylistic device of Jacobs's, it may not really be happening. But it is a possibility.

There is a knock at the door. The man ignores it, but his ignoring it now seems deliberate and hostile. And still he reads. And outside the door a howl, maybe from an animal?

Still, he reads.

Still, he reads.

He reads.

The howls outside the door are getting louder – and no, not from an animal – and the knocking is more insistent, but not, perhaps, human? Still, he reads.

The book no longer uses an alphabet. It is not an alphabet, and these are not words, and this is not language, and there is no meaning here or life or sense. And still, still he reads. Calm. Unhurried.

The door bursts open. And the man at last looks up.

All these words filling the paper, the pages thick with ink, the pages thick with words, my body thick, the words making my body thick. My hand moving, but everything else so heavy, will I ever be able to use my body again? And are these really words? (And is this my hand?)

There is pain in the pit of my chest, and I think vaguely, oh, that'll be my diaphragm, and I wonder whether my diaphragm has just cracked open.

I'm screaming by the time the nurse comes to get me. I'm screaming as the book crashes to a halt with its stupid, mocking, final words – 'To Be Continued'.

"It's all over now, well done," says the nurse, and my parents are there with her, when did they fetch my parents, I don't want my parents there – "Well done, we're so proud of you!" – and the nurse is taking the manuscript from my hands, and my wrist is bleeding, there's always blood on the manuscript no matter how hard you train. I tell them I want my book back, but they tell me it's all over, it's X-noticed, I signed the form, it's being taken out to the fire – and I scream that I want my book back, it's mine, it's mine, it's mine, give me back my child – and I think that's when I was sedated.

IV

This is when my parents started lying to me. Over the months that followed, that I was getting better, that everything was going to be all right. That this was *normal* – when there was nothing normal about it, all the visits to the hospital, the doctors with their fixed expressions of dispassion injecting things with one needle and extracting things with another. I don't know how long I was kept in isolation after the birthing; my parents said it hadn't been too bad, just a week or two, but how could I believe a word they said? When they kept up their pretence that they weren't ashamed of me, that they even felt pride.

It isn't unknown for a surrogate to feel an attachment to the text they have birthed. But it's usually expressed as a sense of exhilaration; a joy that you have participated in the quests of Middle Earth, or the investigation into the Roger Ackroyd murder, or even the journey through an infant's A B C. Empathy with your text is never encouraged – I think most normal healthy people feel it smacks of self-indulgence – but it is at least understood. I heard a nurse one day mutter, as I had my sleeve rolled up for another jab, "All this fuss for a worthless potboiler." And I knew she meant me, that I was worthless, that I had no point at all.

They told me I was having nightmares. How could I make them realise, they weren't nightmares? Yes, the story flooded my dreams, and some nights I know I screamed so loud that my parents would be forced to sit beside my bed and hold my hand and try to hurry away the darkness – but it was *always* there, waking or sleeping, in my mind's eye and beyond it, every part of me, everywhere. "But what is it you *see*?" a doctor might ask, and I did try to explain, I didn't *see* anything, or rather I did, but it was always vague, just out of view: it wasn't what I *saw*, it was in what I smelled, and tasted, and touched. And it wasn't that a story hadn't ended, it was also that a story hadn't yet begun – and it wasn't that it was one book, it was that it was every book, that the world was stuffed with so many words, and sentences that led nowhere, and tales that were indistinct and unresolved, that any road taken was a story and every road not taken was a story too, it was a wonder we didn't all drown in them.

"We love you, it'll be all right, we love you." My mum held on to me with tears streaming down her face, with all her promises she had no bloody right to make, and my dad stood in the doorway, ashen face, hushed voice, watching on. Liars, both of them.

Until one day I said it was all over. "The story's gone," I said. "Like a miracle." The doctors checked my blood pressure, my cortisol levels, said that all the readings were back to normal. My parents beamed with relief, and I smiled too, I smiled deliberately, I gave the world a smile wide enough to choke on. Because if they were all going to lie, then I would lie too. It wasn't gone, of course it wasn't gone, where could it go? But that didn't matter any longer. I knew what I wanted to do with my life. At last I had a purpose.

V

It was the 'To Be Continued' that undid me. I think I could have adjusted without that. Our unnamed hero in his room, reading his book, and then the door bursting open – some rescue from the outside world, perhaps? I could have accepted that. Even an ending of unsatisfactory ambiguity is an ending, of sorts. I could have moved on – but no, 'To Be Continued' – was that a promise, or a threat?

I had to find out what that ending was.

The positives, first, then. (There weren't many.) The book that continued the story hadn't yet been birthed. Better that it didn't exist yet, than it had once existed, only to have been rejected by the archives then destroyed. And I had no doubt that was its fate. I had to get to it before it was put out of print forever.

The negatives? Well, everything else.

To start just with the statistics. The world birth rate is staggering, and only rises exponentially. Right now there are a quarter of a million books being birthed, somewhere around the globe, every single day. That's more than ten thousand books an hour, a hundred and fifty a minute, a new book born to potential readership every three seconds. Trying to anticipate the birth of one specific book is not just like finding a needle in a haystack, it's trying to find one particular needle with the name J. J. Jacobs engraved upon it.

Then there was the matter of confidentiality. The sensors of the Scroll are carefully set so that if a very important novel comes out an alarm is triggered – a Brontë, a Dickens, that final book in the Game of Thrones series. But otherwise the books are very much the products of real children with real families, protected by very real privacy laws.

That was the frustration. The knowledge that at some point the ending to 'The Cursed Book' would certainly be released into the world, but I would never know, could never know, and even if I could find some way to know it would be turned to landfill before I could get to it.

I was back at school, and the teachers were being very gentle with me. No doubt that was why they were so indulgent when I began to ask difficult questions. How could I get a job working with the Scroll? Well, you'd have to be in the Government, I expect. And how could I be in the Government? You'd probably need to go to the right university. And how would I...? Look, you'd need to study really hard, but with your grades we don't think that's very... "Show me what I need to learn," I said. "Show me right away."

—◆—

At university I met a girl named Sarah who had given birth to an Enid Blyton book about fairies and who had a face like a horse, and at a drunken party she let slip that her Daddy worked in the Ministry of Literature, and so I started sleeping with Sarah and once I'd got her pregnant her Daddy said we could get married and that he'd find me a job. And once I got my job I soon realised that my boss could promote me to a better department, so I slept with him too.

"We're so proud of you." I'd hear from Mum on the answering machine. "We don't see you any more," said Dad. Of course I didn't see them. I know it's supposed to be the great equaliser, but I didn't feel comfortable associating with people who'd birthed non-fiction.

I watched as Sarah's tummy grew rounder, and I marvelled at how every single human baby gets nine months to grow. The same nine months, no matter whether the kid turns out smart or stupid or kind or mean or important or so, so useless, whether they'll end up with a job in the Government or a job working with landfill – and I thought, what a ridiculous system.

VI

At some point Sarah and I got divorced, and I don't get to see Ben any more, or little Amy, but I suppose that's the way I want it. And then later Janet and I got divorced too. Mum died, and then Dad, or it may have been the other way around. Oh, I had my companions along the way, but my only true constant was the story of 'The Cursed Book', and sometimes it would sit heavy and make my head ache, but most of the time it soothed and made the world feel better.

Being a department head came with certain privileges, so long as I was discreet. And every morning I would lock myself in my office and widen the Scroll's search parameters to scan for J. J. Jacobs. I had, years ago, accepted I would never find a positive result, that the odds of finding his final book were truly astronomical. And I was no longer even sure that I *needed* to find it: maybe the fragment I'd been gifted was enough, maybe I could even pretend that the fragment was the whole *point*, that stories can only ever be unresolved, that no matter what the author shares there are always gaps and absences and missing details. That the purpose of a story may not be in what is presented on the page, but in what is left out. That was my life, wasn't it? Years of absences and missing details and opportunities still unconsidered, and I did wonder increasingly whether one day soon I would simply stop searching for J. J. Jacobs after all, and if I did that, I wouldn't ever need to come to the office either, I could do whatever I wanted, for the rest of my life I'd be truly free. And so that morning when once again I set my search going, and at last the screen lit up positive – here was the birther's name, and here was her address – a part of me said, *let it go. Turn off the computer, walk away, and let it go.* And I nearly did.

What stopped me was the information at the bottom of the report, written in an inconspicuous small font. That the birther was a little girl who was nine years old – and that was ridiculous, no one had ever birthed that young before. And that the pregnancy period was only thirty-six hours – and that was impossible, completely impossible. If I had ever found a positive result for the book, I'd expected it to be my little secret. In one moment I could see my personal quiet triumph taken away from me. This would get attention, this would be on the news. This was history! And as I stared at the screen, I realised a countdown was already ticking away – only a day and a half before the book was birthed, and God knows how long until the world took an interest in it. The longer I hesitated, second by second, the greater the certainty that after all these years of waiting I would lose my story forever.

And, of course, I had no plan. I'd always assumed I'd have the luxury of time to devise one: even the hasty three weeks of my own pregnancy would have been sufficient. I checked the girl's address. In this country – good – a fifteen-hour drive, but that was still possible, agonisingly possible. And wouldn't it have been better if she'd lived overseas, wouldn't it have been better if I'd already lost? But no, I would have to leave *now*. I should be on the road *now*. And still I stood frozen to the spot. With every second wasting – think, *think*. I phoned my secretary, and told her that I felt ill and was going home. Already that felt like a mistake, I never fell ill, I never left the office early, was that suspicious? And was my voice wavering? I was trying so hard to keep it under control. Too late, go, go. I walked out of my office, I wanted to run, but I mustn't be seen running, and I walked past my colleagues trying not to catch their eye, and wondering whether I'd ever see them again – I supposed not. I kept my face composed and my breathing under control as I strode past reception and out to my car, and then I let the panic out in a whoosh that took me down the motorway as fast as I could go.

Fifteen hours' drive ahead of me, and I knew I'd think of a plan along the way. But I didn't. And now it was two o'clock in the morning, and I was sitting in my car, parked outside the girl's house. Should I just wait here, and make sure no one else came to take my story away? But what could I do if they tried? The only advantage I had was that I was here first, and I had to act now. And so that's why I found myself getting out of the car, and walking up the path to a stranger's house in the middle of the night. Was I just going to take the girl? Yes. Yes, I was just going to take the girl. And what about her parents? What if they tried to stop me? Of course they would try to stop me. Would I have to hurt them? How much?

And now there was no more path to walk, I was outside the front door.

Taking deep breaths. Feeling woozy with the adrenalin, and the long drive, I was so tired. I could just give up, couldn't I? Even now I could just turn around and go home. Even now it wasn't too late – and the relief broke over me and it felt so good, *of course* I wasn't really going to do this. I let myself believe that for a few wonderful happy seconds.

I'd knock at the door. And when the door was opened, I'd fight my way in, I'd hit them quick before they had a chance to react. What could I hit them with? I looked around, it was too dark, a fist, I'd just have to use a fist. Had I ever hit anything with a fist before? So I put my fist up to the door – and saw that it was already ajar. Slowly, carefully, I pushed it open. Peered into the dark house inside.

Two bodies lying side by side on the floor. Standing behind them was a little girl. She had her coat on, standing ready.

All these years I'd been waiting for the story – and with a shudder, I now knew it had been waiting for me.

"They're safe, they'll sleep for hours," said the girl. "But I think we'd best be on our way."

VII

We drove on into the darkness, I don't know for how long. "Do you know where you're taking me?" the girl asked, but it wasn't accusing, and I admitted that I didn't. "Follow this way, and at last we'll come to the forest. It's deep and dark in the forest, no one will find us there. And forests are a good place for stories."

The girl dozed for a while, and I feel I dozed too, but that can't be, because I was driving. I do know I felt at peace, for the first time in many, many years.

Dawn was breaking, light was breaking across the sky. It was easy to find the path to the forest, I just kept driving towards the dark.

And the road became a track of loose stone, and then a path of the richest, greenest grass, and we were surrounded by trees on all sides. "This will do," said the girl, and that felt right, because the car couldn't go any further.

271

Here at the centre of a ring of trees was a perfect patch of grass, gleaming silver with dew; I laid my jacket upon it as a blanket. The girl sat down upon it, I put the paper all around her. No table, no ergonomic chair, but the girl didn't seem to mind, and she looked up at me and smiled. "I have no coffee for you," I said. "I don't need coffee," she said. "I don't have any cigarettes either." "I don't need cigarettes." I began to explain to her how she should just let the pen glide across the paper, she should draw figures of eight – "I think you'll find," she said, "I know exactly what I'm doing," and she drew for me a figure of eight that was so neat and perfectly proportioned it looked almost ironic. "Is there anything I can do for you at all?" I asked, but she was no longer listening to me; she let her fingers dance in the air for a few seconds, like a conductor weighing her baton, and then set the pen to the paper and began to write.

I recognised the same handwriting I had once used – but the strokes of her pen were more direct, more decisive, and they scratched across the paper like they were scolding it.

There was no preamble from J. J. Jacobs this time – it was straight into 'The Cursed Book'.

And for a while I thought this story was merely an exact copy of the version I had birthed. The unnamed man in the unnamed city. Arriving at his hotel room. Finding his strange book. Beginning to read.

I felt sick as I watched the same words pour out, the fog of long-dreamed nightmares cleared and here it was, stark and real in front of me – and I couldn't look away.

The man reads, and eats, and sleeps. He loses interest in the eating. He abandons his sleep. Until only the book is left, and then he read, and only reads, with greater speed than I remember, but no greater enthusiasm, always with the same disturbing dispassion.

And yet this time it seems that every little often the man will look up from his book. Stealing a glance outside it, coming up for air. Just for a second, he looks out from his own story, and out to the reader.

The girl scribbling away so fast, but never frantic, her face still a mask of calm. Even though telltale sweat is starting to run down her forehead.

There is a knock at the door. The man ignores it.

Still, he reads.

There is some vague sense that the room is getting smaller. There is some sense that the forest is getting tighter, that the trees are creeping in.

There is another knock at the door. The man ignores it. But he lifts his head off the page again, and looks out, and this time it isn't a glance, it's bolder – he looks out at me.

The little girl, dripping with sweat, and she moans quietly, and I don't think she knows she's doing it.

Still, he reads. Still, the knock at the door, and there is some sort of distant howl, and the man ignores it – he refuses to be distracted by the sound outside his own room, but nevertheless he is distracted, his eyes raised off the page more and more, distracted by my eyes upon him, and for just a moment our eyes seem to lock.

The man reads. The words are in English, and then another language, and then another alphabet, and then something else entirely. The girl cries out now, she can't help it, she keeps her face deadpan and focused, but the pain is too much – and I want to help her, and I want to pull her away from the book she is writing, and I want to urge her to carry on, never mind the agony of it, let the book break your wrists if it has to, don't stop now, don't you dare stop now. She grits her teeth, the story pulling deep at her diaphragm.

The door bursts open. And this is it, this is the point where my story ended.

And the man in the room stops reading. At last he lays down his book. He looks only at me. He stares.

And the girl lays down her pen, in mid-sentence, at this very stare, and she turns to me, and her face is now dripping with sweat, and there is blood too, and yet she keeps her voice steady, and she stares at me too, she takes that stare off the page and flings it straight at me. "You really want me to continue?" she says to me, gently.

Yes, I say. Yes, go on. Tell me what happens next.

So, she goes on.

In the bedroom the man is surrounded on all sides. They seem to be staff from the hotel. There's a manager, there's a bellhop, the waiter from the restaurant. But who are all the people at the back, and why are their faces so shadowed and blurred?

The man looks at them without fear.

They take his book from him. He lets it go without protest. And they give him another book. He opens it. The pages are blank.

And they say,

This is the book you are to write.

And they say,

This is your last book.

And the man says he does not know how to write a book. And they say,

Time with a book is never passive. You take from it, and it takes from you, too.

And they say,

One cannot merely consume, one has to produce. You can eat and eat and eat and eat and eat, but sooner or later, you're going to have to shit something out.

And they say,

Did you really think there would never be a reckoning?

And so, the man begins to write. He doesn't have a pen. So he has to scratch at the paper with his fingernails.

They all stand about and watch, and when he finishes his first page, they give him a brief and unfeeling round of applause.

The man writes.

He writes in English, and when he runs out of English words, he has to use another language.

His fingernails break, and his fingers bleed. And when he runs out of foreign words, he has to find a new alphabet.

Still, he writes.

Faster and faster, and the applause is constant, it's a metronome keeping his rhythm true, and the blood is flowing, his fingers broken down to stumps, and he's smearing on to the paper symbols he cannot understand with those bloodied aching stumps.

The man writes, and the girl writes, and there is blood on my jacket, and blood on the grass all around, it gleams like the dew, and the paper is spattered with blood – from the girl's wrists? Maybe? Or elsewhere?

I know I must get her to stop, but I will not get her to stop.

The man writing still but not daring to look down at the terrors he is creating and he is looking straight at me, and his mouth is set tight and his teeth are clenched fast and yet somehow he is screaming.

The girl writing still but it's not from her diaphragm any longer, it's beneath the diaphragm, from the gut itself.

"Stop," I say, but I only dare whisper it. "Please stop."

She turns to me, and for all the pain, she gives me a smile.

"Make me," she says.

And I snatch the pen from her hands, and I pick up the bloodied pages, and I tear them into pieces, I tear them until I'm sure they are all destroyed.

VIII

For the longest few seconds there was silence. And the little girl was a tight ball, all hunched over.

I reached out and touched her shoulder. I thought maybe she would be angry. But when she turned to look at me, her eyes seemed to gleam.

She reached for her pen, and a new sheet of paper.

"No," I said, "don't." But she took no notice.

She began to write. It was hard to read it. It was the scrawl of a little girl. She was telling a story of her very own. "No, you can't," I said.

276

"Can't? Because it's impossible, or it's not allowed?"

She resumed her story, and said to me, "You can't just eat forever. Sooner or later, you have to shit your own stuff out."

IX

She wrote for about an hour or so. It wasn't frenzied. She seemed to enjoy it. At the end she gave me this brand-new story, and I read it.

"It isn't very good," I told her.

"What do you expect? I'm only nine years old." She took back the story, looked it through critically, gave a sniff. "I suppose I'll get better."

X

We found our way back to the car, but when I turned the ignition the engine wouldn't catch, and when we tried to push it the tyres kept sliding back into the mud. "We don't need it anymore," said the girl, "we can walk." And we did.

Though the forest was deep and dark there was an end to it, and one day we came out and there before us was a village. We knocked on the door of every house but no one was home. We chose a house that looked warm, and which had wood in the fireplace and chickens in the yard. The girl picked one of the chickens, thanked it kindly for its sacrifice, and wrung its neck. And that night we ate our fill, because we were very hungry.

The house gave us everything we could want – soft beds and good food and shelter from the elements. But there were no books, nor any shelves to keep them.

I wondered whether the world had changed, or whether we had – and the girl shrugged, and asked why it had to be one or the other.

And during the day I would go to the forest for wood, and the girl would pluck a chicken for the pot, and in the evening, we would sit by the fire and she would write another of her stories.

Then I would read her story, and I'd tell her they were getting better, this latest was the best yet, and she would either smile or shake her head. And she would put the story on to the fire. "One day," she'd say, "there'll be one worth keeping."

She urged me to write a story of my own. She told me at first it would amuse me, and help me fill the long empty hours. I told her that I took pleasure enough in reading hers. Then she told me she wanted something of her own to read. I'd say that my stories wouldn't be worth her reading, and that she could find better amusement than that. And then she told me that if this new world needed to be filled with stories, the burden was too great. "Please," she said. "I can't do it on my own." Still I refused.

◆

When I woke up this morning I knew at once the house was empty. There was something colder in the air. And I checked her bedroom, and then I checked all the other rooms, and then I checked every other house in the village. But she had gone.

I began to write this story, because I knew it was the only thing that might make her return.

I wrote all the day, and all the night too, and I couldn't go to the forest for wood so now the hearth is cold, and there's no chicken in the pot so I'm hungry too. But I have reached the end, and it is a tale, of sorts, and I would like to share it with her.

I shall go to bed soon, and I shall leave it upon the table, and I hope it may bring her back by morning. And if she isn't here, then it just means my story isn't good enough, so I shall have to write another. I shall keep writing for her. I think I can do it. I have some ideas. And I can feel something I thought I had long lost – a slight twitch behind the eyeball. It's very faint, but it's there.

This being a true and honest account of my life so far, and all my feelings, and all my betrayings, and all my hopes and dreams as well. With the promise that my next story will be better.

BIBLIETTE

GUY ADAMS

Look at the state of him. Blotched with foxing, spine bent, reeking of years kept in smoke and damp. Shop bell rings; 'bring out your dead'.

"Hello…" This is not a man who often speaks aloud.

There's nobody about so he flounders into silence, gazing at a mille-feuille of cookery books. He strokes them, on the hunt for grease ghosts.

Shop shadows flex at the few spoons of sunshine that are flung over the threshold, afraid the air might curdle. The door closes. The world settles.

He moves further in, gaberdine dust jacket crumpling and creasing as he navigates between waist-high stacks. This is not a two-way process; books are designed to enter but not leave. Arrogant that he can buck the trend, he looks for stars to navigate by. Menthol green signs promise HERALDRY, TRAVEL and WAR. He risks a deeper look. Nausea-yellow strip lights jut from the ceiling like a smoker's teeth, pouring their urine-sample light onto the shelves. He has to turn side-on, shimmying between books and hoping nothing will give way, especially his nerves.

Shouldn't there be someone to hand? Perhaps they're as lost as he soon will be.

He's in the market for books on cinema. He's aware of the absurdity, forcing one medium into the killing jar of another, but it's what he loves. Biographies of snuffed-out stars; gruelling guides to technique; director studies; genres dissected. It's all nourishment. In his bag right now, Josef von Sternberg is having *Fun in a Chinese Laundry* while Ray Milland is *Wide-Eyed in Babylon*. There's room for more and if this place turns its attention to the silver screen then surely there must be something? This is not a shop with a circumspect attitude towards stock. This is an attempt to gather everything that ever was. A few more books and there'll be enough critical mass to tear the English language free from our tongues.

He wants to call out, but the silence is too deep. Drawing attention to himself feels like the last thing he should do.

Where is he now? The verdant green can only mean Penguin Crime. Erle Stanley Gardner has *Murder Up His Sleeve*. Blood and ink spilled. He stumbles, tumbling over Simenon and coming face down into a musty nest of Allingham. Surely the racket will have alerted whoever owns this place? Any minute now they'll come.

He gets his bearings, awash in arsenic poisoning and candlestick blunt trauma. A beam of light is reaching for a set of Christies, goddess Agatha, haloed and holy.

He gets to his feet and tries to sort the paperbacks so he'll look responsible once the owner arrives.

The owner doesn't arrive.

He doglegs into MUSIC. Eye to eye with a Buddy Rich biography, he finds himself trapped in a shelf-edge paradiddle. He must stop catching himself on these thoughts, wool on the barbed-wire fence, wind-wafted and vacant.

He circumnavigates a twisted column of dead composers, faces made for clay, reaching for the freedom of the Manchester scene. Fingers on a nicotine-blushed history of the Haçienda he grounds himself, reversing into a corner devoted to West End musicals. Surely this is time for a break? He'll never get through this without pacing himself. He takes time out – finger click metronome tick – in the company of Sondheim and Bernstein. Then wonders when he might meet someone simpler than paper and ideas. Not that he ever hankers for skin and bone, huffing its meat-stained air all over you and expecting tit for tat. Fuck that. What a headache. Still, it was usual.

He's turned around now and not even a catcher's mitt curl of Ordnance

Survey maps could guide him back to the front door. He uses them to waft imagined Pennine air onto his hot face.

How long has he been here? It's all got slippery. Did he just come in? If so why's he so tired? Is he always this absurdly tired?

Where next? He shares a conspiratorial nod with the ghost of John Lennon then regrets it as he finds himself imagining crosshairs on his back. Wasn't he anxious enough without ruminating on brass chipping bone? The air whistles with the one bullet that got away.

By the time he has his hands around the corner of a bookshelf, pulling himself from one world to another, he's distinctly breathless. He tilts his head up towards the ceiling, hoping to catch a breath as his cheeks crinkle plastic-covered spines of MODERN FIRSTS. Cellophane body-bags. Corpses of commercial fiction. They're cool on his face, and he chances a quick lick of slippery comfort, the embossing bumping and grinding on his tongue.

Tiredness taking over, he curls up beneath a row of Le Carré and tries to distract himself from a lower belly stirring of arousal by listing the dead man's catalogue. He's barely brushed past *A Naïve and Sentimental Lover* before he's unconscious.

He wakes delirious, spine bent back, flopped out on the piebald carpet. Surely one shouldn't sleep in shops? Did other customers chance upon him while he snored? Such behaviour wasn't to be tolerated.

He checks the screen of his phone to see what the time might be. It's dead. It was old enough.

He tries to stretch life into legs that have twisted and contorted amongst Richard Osman's *Thursday Murder Club*. Spooning sleuths.

Surely this state of affairs shouldn't be allowed to continue? There must be laws, prison sentences applied to folk who do this sort of thing.

It's hard to walk with decorum, cramped muscles have too much taste in comedy. He has Elvis Presley thighs as he peers around.

His skin feels dry, and scratching it sounds like a thumb trying to find its page. This place isn't great for his health. Let's hope he can find something he loves, and then the front door. He won't be distracted. Head down, march on.

He's sure hours pass as he pushes forward. Impossible but there we are, the signs all confirm it: his legs weaken, his stomach rumbles, the strip light seems to revolve above him, rising to the left and sinking to the right.

His determination to keep straight wanes and he cuts into poetry. He needs to get some perspective and all he can think to do is head upwards. Careful does it, toe to Larkin, nose to Coleridge he starts to climb. He's a slender volume so hopefully the shelves can bear him.

The shelves are unhelpfully duplicating the higher he gets. He gives up counting at twenty, nobody can stack that high and he refuses to endorse the madness. Either the shelf is crazy or he is.

One of them gives up their nonsense and the ceiling settles into reach. Thick, whipped plaster, a trifle top turned sour, touching it is all about slime and dead skin and he can't bear to do it twice.

Can he get his bearings? A sense of the world he's in? Clouds have begun to form around Folio Society slipcases, and he accepts that he's going to need considerable rest before attempting to climb down.

The top of the bookshelf is as greasy as the ceiling but what choice does he have? Someone's been here before, a florid finger having cleared a path through the dust, a crop circle of swirls. He lies back and wonders on the nonsense of it all. He tries to remember what this place looked like from the street, anything will do, a name, a paint colour, an A4 poster for a local theatre production, something to hang on to. It's all slipped away.

He's exhausted again but hunger is keeping him awake. He reaches over the lip of the bookshelf to grab something from below, doesn't care what. He finds a copy of Kingsley Amis's poems. 'Something Nasty in the Bookshop', indeed. He tears out a couple of pages and tries them on the tongue.

It's almost more than his palate can take, every word a flavour... ideas are so damned dense. Thank God he hadn't tried to chow down on Rosetti.

A delirium of over-stimulation and he wonders if Amis truly has gone toxic over the years. His vision blurs and he writhes up there at the summit, aching and alone until finally he's still.

Darkness kicks in. He wakes feeling wild. What dream has he woken from that's stiffened him so? He's thicker than *Ulysses*. Sure he can't be seen, he finds himself a welcoming Whitman. Unbuckling, he inserts himself into *Leaves of Grass*. It's unusual how little flexing is needed before the body electric gets its fill. Folding over the covers, sticky pressed flower, he slides the book along the top of the shelf, relieved that anyone who comes across it will be in the same state as him.

He sleeps again.

Later, something is moving amongst the bookshelves. As far as he can tell it has far too many legs.

Morning brings the sudden and hot burning of fluorescent tubes, and he begins the climb back down to avoid them. It's hard to move, his body stiffer than ever, his back crumbling and itchy. He's unsure whether the words that appear on his exposed skin are his thoughts or not, they disappear too quickly for him to catch them. Flighty.

The ground is taking longer to get to than it did to leave. Perhaps more books have been added while he slept. It soon becomes clear he's unlikely to reach it.

Legs shaking, skin drying, he folds himself between a pair of Muriel Sparks, squeezed tight, a willing victim.

Maybe he'll try to move again soon. Maybe. Chances are it's time someone else put the effort in. He can feel his legs flattening out into pages, the only place they'll carry him is into someone's imagination.

"Goodbye," he says, more to graze the air one last time than anything else.

It's a relief to be still rather than still be.

NEAR ZENNOR

ELIZABETH HAND

He found the letters inside a round metal candy tin, at the bottom of a plastic storage box in the garage, alongside strings of outdoor Christmas lights and various oddments his wife had saved for the yard sale she'd never managed to organise in almost thirty years of marriage. She'd died suddenly, shockingly, of a brain aneurysm, while planting daffodil bulbs the previous September.

Now everything was going to Goodwill. The house in New Canaan had been listed with a realtor; despite the terrible market, she'd reassured Jeffrey that it should sell relatively quickly, and for something close to his asking price.

"It's a beautiful house, Jeffrey," she said, "not that I'm surprised." Jeffrey was a noted architect: she glanced at him as she stepped carefully along a flagstone path in her Louboutin heels. "And these gardens are incredible."

"That was all Anthea." He paused beside a stone wall, surveying an emerald swathe of new grass, small exposed hillocks of black earth, piles of neatly-raked leaves left by the crew he'd hired to do the work that Anthea had always done on her own. In the distance, birch trees glowed spectral white against a leaden February sky that gave a twilit cast to midday. "She always said that if I'd had to pay her for all this, I wouldn't have been able to afford her. She was right."

He signed off on the final sheaf of contracts and returned them to the realtor. "You're in Brooklyn now?" she asked, turning back toward the house.

"Yes. Green Park. A colleague of mine is in Singapore for a few months, he's letting me stay there till I get my bearings."

"Well, good luck. I'll be in touch soon." She opened the door of her Prius and hesitated. "I know how hard this is for you. I lost my father two years ago. Nothing helps, really."

Jeffrey nodded. "Thanks. I know."

He'd spent the last five months cycling through wordless, imageless night terrors from which he awoke gasping; dreams in which Anthea lay beside him, breathing softly then smiling as he touched her face; nightmares in which the neuroelectrical storm that had killed her raged inside his own head, a flaring nova that engulfed the world around him and left him floating in an endless black space, the stars expiring one by one as he drifted past them.

He knew that grief had no target demographic, that all around him versions of this cosmic reshuffling took place every day. He and Anthea had their own shared experience years before, when they had lost their first and only daughter to sudden infant death syndrome. They were both in their late thirties at the time. They never tried to have another child, on their own or through adoption. It was as though some psychic house fire had consumed them both: it was a year before Jeffrey could enter the room that had been Julia's, and for months after her death neither he nor Anthea could bear to sit at the dining table and finish a meal together, or sleep in the same bed. The thought of being that close to another human being, of having one's hand or foot graze another's and wake however fleetingly to the realisation that this too could be lost – it left both of them with a terror that they had never been able to articulate, even to each other.

Now as then, he kept busy with work at his office in the city, and dutifully accepted invitations for lunch and dinner there and in New Canaan. Nights were a prolonged torment: he was haunted by the realisation that Anthea been extinguished, a spent match pinched between one's fingers. He thought of Houdini, arch-rationalist of another century who desired proof of a spirit world he desperately wanted to believe in. Jeffrey believed in nothing, yet if there had been a drug to twist his neurons into some synaptic impersonation of faith, he would have taken it.

For the past month he'd devoted most of his time to packing up the house, donating Anthea's clothes to various charity shops, deciding what to store and what to sell, what to divvy up among nieces and nephews, Anthea's sister, a few close friends. Throughout he experienced grief as a sort of low-grade flu, a persistent, inescapable ache that suffused not just his thoughts but his bones and tendons: a throbbing in his temples, black sparks that distorted his vision; an acrid chemical taste in the back of his throat, as though he'd bitten into one of the pills his doctor had given him to help him sleep.

He watched as the realtor drove off soundlessly, returned to the garage and transferred the plastic bin of Christmas lights into his own car, to drop off at a neighbour's the following weekend. He put the tin box with the letters on the seat beside him. As he pulled out of the driveway, it began to snow.

——◆——

That night, he sat at the dining table in the Brooklyn loft and opened the candy tin. Inside were five letters, each bearing the same stamp: RETURN TO SENDER. At the bottom of the box was a locket on a chain, cheap gold-coloured metal and chipped red enamel circled by tiny fake pearls. He opened it: it was empty. He examined it for an engraved inscription, initials, a name, but there was nothing. He set it aside and turned to the letters.

All were postmarked 1971 – February, March, April, July, end of August – all addressed to the same person at the same address, carefully spelled out in Anthea's swooping, schoolgirl's hand.

> Mr. Robert Bennington,
> Trawraethun Farm,
> Padwithiel,
> Cornwall.

Love letters? He didn't recognise the name. Anthea would have been thirteen in February; her birthday was in May. He moved the envelopes across the table, as though performing a card trick. His heart pounded, which was ridiculous. He and Anthea had told each other about everything – three-ways at university, coke-fuelled orgies during the 1980s, affairs and flirtations throughout their marriage.

None of that mattered now; little of it had mattered then. Still, his hands shook as he opened the first envelope. A single sheet of onionskin was inside. He unfolded it gingerly and smoothed it on the table.

His wife's handwriting hadn't changed much in forty years. The same cramped cursive, each *i* so heavily dotted in black ink that the pen had almost poked through the thin paper. Anthea had been English, born and raised in North London. They'd met at the University of London, where they were both studying, and moved to New Canaan after they'd married. It was an area that Sarah had often said reminded her of the English countryside, though Jeffrey had never ventured outside London, other than a few excursions to Kent and Brighton. Where was Padwithiel?

21 February, 1971

Dear Mr. Bennington,

My name is Anthea Ryson...

And would a thirteen-year-old girl address her boyfriend as 'Mr.,' even forty years ago?

...I am thirteen years old and live in London. Last year my friend Evelyn let me read Still the Seasons for the first time and since then I have read it two more times, also Black Clouds Over Bragmoor and The Second Sun. They are my favourite books! I

keep looking for more but the library here doesn't have them. I have asked and they said I should try the shops but that is expensive. My teacher said that sometimes you come to schools and speak, I hope some day you'll come to Islington Day School. Are you writing more books about Tisha and the great Battle? #

I hope so, please write back! My address is 42 Highbury fields, London NW1.

*Very truly yours,
Anthea Ryson*

Jeffrey set aside the letter and gazed at the remaining four envelopes. *What a prick*, he thought. He never even wrote her back. He turned to his laptop and googled Robert Bennington.

Robert Bennington (1932–), British author of a popular series of children's fantasy novels published during the 1960s known as 'The Sun Battles'. Bennington's books rode the literary tidal wave generated by J.R.R. Tolkien's work, but his commercial and critical standing were irrevocably shaken in the late 1990s, when he became the centre of a drawn-out court case involving charges of paedophilia and sexual assault, with accusations lodged against him by several girl fans, now adults. One of the alleged victims later changed her account, and the case was eventually dismissed amidst much controversy by child advocates and women's rights groups. Bennington's reputation never recovered: school libraries refused to keep his books on their shelves. All of his novels are now out of print, although digital editions (illegal) can be found, along with used copies of the four books in the 'Battles' sequence...

Jeffrey's neck prickled. The court case didn't ring a bell, but the books did. Anthea had thrust one upon him shortly after they first met.

"These were my *favourites*." She rolled over in bed and pulled a yellowed paperback from a shelf crowded with textbooks and Penguin editions of the mystery novels she loved. "I must have read this twenty times."

"Twenty?" Jeffrey raised an eyebrow.

"Well, maybe seven. A *lot*. Did you ever read them?"

"I never even heard of them."

"You have to read it. Right now." She nudged him with her bare foot. "You can't leave here till you do."

"Who says I want to leave?" He tried to kiss her but she pushed him away.

"Uh uh. Not till you read it. I'm serious!"

So he'd read it, staying up till 3:00 a.m., intermittently dozing off before waking with a start to pick up the book again.

"It gave me bad dreams," he said as grey morning light leaked through the narrow window of Anthea's flat. "I don't like it."

"I know." Anthea laughed. "That's what I liked about them – they always made me feel sort of sick."

Jeffrey shook his head adamantly. "I don't like it," he repeated.

Anthea frowned, finally shrugged, picked up the book and dropped it onto the floor. "Well, nobody's perfect," she said, and rolled on top of him.

A year or so later he did read *Still the Seasons*, when a virus kept him in bed for several days and Anthea was caught up with research at the British Library. The book unsettled him deeply. There were no monsters *per se*, no dragons or Nazgûl or witches. Just two sets of cousins, two boys and two girls, trapped in a portal between one of those grim post-war English cities, Manchester or Birmingham, and a magical land that wasn't really magical at all but even bleaker and more threatening than the council flats where the children lived.

Jeffrey remembered unseen hands tapping at a window, and one of the boys fighting off something invisible that crawled under the bedcovers and attacked in a flapping wave of sheets and blankets. Worst of all was the last chapter, which he read late one night and could never recall clearly, save for the vague, enveloping dread it engendered, something he had never encountered before or since.

Anthea had been right – the book had a weirdly visceral power, more like the effect of a low-budget, black-and-white horror movie than a children's fantasy novel. How many of those grown-up kids now knew their hero had been a paedophile?

Jeffrey spent a half-hour scanning articles on Bennington's trial, none of them very informative. It had happened over a decade ago; since then there'd been a few dozen blog posts, pretty equally divided between *Whatever happened to...?* and excoriations by women who themselves had been sexually abused, though not by Bennington.

He couldn't imagine that had happened to Anthea. She'd certainly never mentioned it, and she'd always been dismissive, even slightly callous, about friends who underwent counselling or psychotherapy for childhood traumas. As for the books themselves, he didn't recall seeing them when he'd sorted through their shelves to pack everything up. Probably they'd been donated to a library book sale years ago, if they'd even made the crossing from London.

He picked up the second envelope. It was postmarked 'March 18, 1971'. He opened it and withdrew a sheet of lined paper torn from a school notebook.

> Dear Rob,
>
> Well, we all got back on the train, Evelyn was in a lot of trouble for being out all night and of course we couldn't tell her aunt why, her mother said she can't talk to me on the phone but I see her at school anyway so it doesn't matter. I still can't believe it all happened. Evelyn's mother said she was going to call my mother and Moira's but so far she didn't. Thank you so much for talking to us. You signed Evelyn's book but you forgot to sign mine. Next time!!!
>
> Yours sincerely your friend,
> Anthea

Jeffrey felt a flash of cold through his chest. *Dear Rob, I still can't believe it all happened.* He quickly opened the remaining envelopes, read first one then the next and finally the last.

12 April, 1971

Dear Rob,

Maybe I wrote down your address wrong because the last letter I sent was returned. But I asked Moira and she had the same address and she said her letter wasn't returned. Evelyn didn't write yet but says she will. It was such a really, really great time to see you! Thank you again for the books, I thanked you in the last letter but thank you again. I hope you'll write back this time, we still want to come back on holiday in July! I can't believe it was exactly one month ago we were there.

Your friend,
Anthea Ryson

July 20, 1971

Dear Rob,

Well I still haven't heard from you so I guess you're mad maybe or just forgot about me, ha ha. School is out now and I was wondering if you still wanted us to come and stay? Evelyn says we never could and her aunt would tell her mother but we could hitch-hike, also Evelyn's brother Martin has a caravan and he and his girlfriend are going to Wales for a festival and we thought they might give us a ride partway, he said maybe they would. Then we could hitch-hike the rest. The big news is Moira ran away from home and they called the POLICE. Evelyn said she went without us to see you and she's really mad. Moira's boyfriend Peter is mad too.

If she is there with you is it okay if I come too? I could come alone without Evelyn, her mother is a BITCH.

Please please write!
Anthea (Ryson)

Dear Rob,

I hate you. I wrote FIVE LETTERS including this one and I know it is the RIGHT address. I think Moira went to your house without us. FUCK YOU Tell her I hate her too and so does Evelyn. We never told anyone if she says we did she is a LIAR.

FUCK YOU FUCK YOU FUCK YOU

Where a signature should have been, the page was ripped and blotched with blue ink – Anthea had scribbled something so many times the pen tore through the lined paper. Unlike the other four, this sheet was badly crumpled, as though she'd thrown it away then retrieved it. Jeffrey glanced at the envelope. The postmark read 'August 28'. She'd gone back to school for the fall term, and presumably that had been the end of it.

Except, perhaps, for Moira, whoever she was. Evelyn would be Evelyn Thurlow, Anthea's closest friend from her school days in Islington. Jeffrey had met her several times while at university, and Evelyn had stayed with them for a weekend in the early 1990s, when she was attending a conference in Manhattan. She was a flight-test engineer for a British defence contractor, living outside Cheltenham; she and Anthea would have hour-long conversations on their birthdays, for several years planning a dream vacation together to someplace warm – Greece or Turkey or the Caribbean.

Jeffrey had emailed her about Anthea's death, and they had spoken on the phone – Evelyn wanted to fly over for the funeral but was on deadline for a major government contract and couldn't take the time off.

"I so wish I could be there," she'd said, her voice breaking. "Everything's just so crazed at the moment. I hope you understand…"

"It's okay. She knew how much you loved her. She was always so happy to hear from you."

"I know," Evelyn choked. "I just wish – I just wish I'd been able to see her again."

Now he sat and stared at the five letters. The sight made him feel lightheaded and slightly queasy: as though he'd opened his closet door and found himself at the edge of a precipice, gazing down some impossible distance to a world made tiny and unreal. Why had she never mentioned any of this? Had she hidden the letters for all these years, or simply forgotten she had them? He knew it wasn't rational; knew his response derived from his compulsive sense of order, what Anthea had always called his architect's left brain.

"Jeffrey would never even try to put a square peg into a round hole," she'd said once at a dinner party. "He'd just design a new hole to fit it."

He could think of no place he could fit the five letters written to Robert Bennington. After a few minutes, he replaced each in its proper envelope and stacked them atop each other. Then he turned back to his laptop, and wrote an email to Evelyn.

—◆—

He arrived in Cheltenham two weeks later. Evelyn picked him up at the train station early Monday afternoon. He'd told her he was in London on business, spent the preceding weekend at a hotel in Bloomsbury and wandered the city, walking past the building where he and Anthea had lived right after university, before they moved to the US.

It was a relief to board the train and stare out the window at an unfamiliar landscape, suburbs giving way to farms and the gently rolling outskirts of the Cotswolds.

Evelyn's husband, Chris, worked for one of the high-tech corporations in Cheltenham; their house was a rambling, expensively renovated cottage twenty minutes from the congested city centre.

"Anthea would have loved these gardens," Jeffrey said, surveying swathes of narcissus already in bloom, alongside yellow primroses and a carpet of bluebells beneath an ancient beech. "Everything at home is still brown. We had snow a few weeks ago."

"It must be very hard, giving up the house." Evelyn poured him a glass of Medoc and sat across from him in the slate-floored sunroom.

"Not as hard as staying would have been," Jeffrey raised his glass. "To old friends and old times."

"To Anthea," said Evelyn.

They talked into the evening, polishing off the Medoc and starting on a second bottle long before Chris arrived home from work. Evelyn was florid and heavy-set, her unruly raven hair long as ever and braided into a single plait, thick and grey-streaked. She'd met her contract deadline just days ago, and her dark eyes still looked hollowed from lack of sleep. Chris prepared dinner, lamb with fresh mint and new peas; their children were both off at university, so Jeffrey and Chris and Evelyn lingered over the table until almost midnight.

"Leave the dishes," Chris said, rising. "I'll get them in the morning." He bent to kiss the top of his wife's head, then nodded at Jeffrey. "Good to see you, Jeffrey."

"Come on." Evelyn grabbed a bottle of Armagnac and headed for the sunroom. "Get those glasses, Jeffrey. I'm not going in till noon. Project's done, and the mice will play."

Jeffrey followed her, settling onto the worn sofa and placing two glasses on the side-table. Evelyn filled both, flopped into an armchair and smiled. "It *is* good to see you."

"And you."

He sipped his Armagnac. For several minutes they sat in silence, staring out the window at the garden, narcissus and primroses faint gleams in the darkness. Jeffrey finished his glass, poured another, and asked, "Do you remember someone named Robert Bennington?"

Evelyn cradled her glass against her chest. She gazed at Jeffrey for a long moment before answering. "The writer? Yes. I read his books when I was a girl. Both of us did – me and Anthea."

"But – you knew him. You met him, when you were thirteen. On vacation or something."

Evelyn turned, her profile silhouetted against the window. "We did," she said at last, and turned back to him. "Why are you asking?"

"I found some letters that Anthea wrote to him. Back in 1971, after you and her and a girl named Moira saw him in Cornwall. Did you know he was a paedophile? He was arrested about fifteen years ago."

"Yes, I read about that. It was a big scandal." Evelyn finished her Armagnac and set her glass on the table. "Well, a medium-sized scandal. I don't think many people even remembered who he was by then. He was a cult writer, really. The books were rather dark for children's books."

She hesitated. "Anthea wasn't molested by him, if that's what you're asking about. None of us were. He invited us to tea – we invited ourselves, actually, he was very nice and let us come in and gave us Nutella sandwiches and tangerines."

"Three little teenyboppers show up at his door, I bet he was very nice," said Jeffrey. "What about Moira? What happened to her?"

"I don't know." Evelyn sighed. "No one ever knew. She ran away from home that summer. We never heard from her again."

"Did they question him? Was he even taken into custody?"

"Of course they did!" Evelyn said, exasperated. "I mean, I don't know for sure, but I'm certain they did. Moira had a difficult home life, her parents were Irish and the father drank. And a lot of kids ran away back then, you know that – all us little hippies. What did the letters say, Jeffrey?"

He removed then from his pocket and handed them to her. "You can read them. He never did – they all came back to Anthea. Where's Padwithiel?"

"Near Zennor. My aunt and uncle lived there, we went and stayed with them during our school holidays one spring." She sorted through the envelopes, pulled out one and opened it, unfolding the letter with care. "February twenty-first. This was right before we knew we'd be going there for the holidays. It was my idea. I remember when she wrote this – she got the address somehow, and that's how we realised he lived near my uncle's farm. Padwithiel."

She leaned into the lamp and read the first letter, set it down and continued to read each of the others. When she was finished, she placed the last one on the table, sank back into her chair and gazed at Jeffrey.

"She never told you about what happened."

"You just said that nothing happened."

"I don't mean with Robert. She called me every year on the anniversary. March 12." She looked away. "Next week, that is. I never told Chris. It wasn't a secret, we just – well, I'll just tell you.

"We went to school together, the three of us, and after Anthea sent that letter to Robert Bennington, she and I cooked up the idea of going to see him. Moira never read his books – she wasn't much of a reader. But she heard us talking about his books all the time, and we'd all play these games where we'd be the ones who fought the Sun Battles. She just did whatever we told her to, though for some reason she always wanted prisoners to be boiled in oil. She must've seen it in a movie.

"Even though we were older now, we still wanted to believe that magic could happen like in those books – probably we wanted to believe it even more. And all that New Agey, hippie stuff, Tarot cards and Biba and 'Ride a White Swan' – it all just seemed like it could be real. My aunt and uncle had a farm near Zennor, my mother asked if we three could stay there for the holidays and Aunt Becca said that would be fine. My cousins are older, and they were already off at university. So we took the train and Aunt Becca got us in Penzance.

"They were turning one of the outbuildings into a pottery studio for her, and that's where we stayed. There was no electricity yet, but we had a kerosene heater and we could stay up as late as we wanted. I think we got maybe five hours sleep the whole time we were there." She laughed. "We'd be up all night, but then Uncle Ray would start in with the tractors at dawn. We'd end up going into the house and napping in one of my cousin's beds for half the afternoon whenever we could. We were very grumpy houseguests.

"It rained the first few days we were there, just pissing down. Finally one morning we got up and the sun was shining. It was cold, but we didn't care – we were just so happy we could get outside for a while. At first we just walked along the road, but it was so muddy from all the rain that we ended up heading across the moor. Technically it's not really open moorland – there are old stone walls criss-crossing everything, ancient field systems. Some of them are thousands of years old, and farmers still keep them up and use them. These had not been kept up. The land was completely overgrown, though you could still see the walls and climb them. Which is what we did.

"We weren't that far from the house – we could still see it, and I'm pretty sure we were still on my uncle's land. We found a place where the walls were higher than elsewhere, more like proper hedgerows. There was no break in the wall like there usually is, no gate or old entryway. So we found a spot that was relatively untangled and we all climbed up and then jumped to the other side. The walls were completely overgrown with blackthorn and all these viney things. It was like Sleeping Beauty's castle – the thorns hurt like shit. I remember I was wearing new boots and they got ruined, just scratched everywhere. And Moira tore her jacket and we knew she'd catch grief for that. But we thought there must be something wonderful on the other side – that was the game we were playing, that we'd find some amazing place. Do you know *The Secret Garden*? We thought it might be like that. At least I did."

"And was it?"

Evelyn shook her head. "It wasn't a garden. It was just this big overgrown field. Dead grass and stones. But it was rather beautiful in a bleak way. Ant laughed and started yelling 'Heathcliff, Heathcliff!' And it was warmer – the walls were high enough to keep out the wind, and there were some trees that had grown up on top of the walls as well. They weren't in leaf yet, but they formed a bit of a windbreak.

"We ended up staying there all day. Completely lost track of the time. I thought only an hour had gone by, but Ant had a watch, at one point she said it was past three and I was shocked – I mean, really shocked. It was like we'd gone to sleep and woken up, only we weren't asleep at all."

"What were you doing?"

Evelyn shrugged. "Playing. The sort of let's-pretend game we always did when we were younger and hadn't done for a while. Moira had a boyfriend, Ant and I really *wanted* boyfriends – mostly that's what we talked about whenever we got together. But for some reason, that day Ant said 'Let's do Sun Battles,' and we all agreed. So that's what we did. Now of course I can see why – I've seen it with my own kids when they were that age, you're on the cusp of everything, and you just want to hold on to being young for as long as you can.

"I don't remember much of what we did that day, except how strange it all felt. As though something was about to happen. I felt like that a lot, it was all tied in with being a teenager; but this was different. It was like being high, or tripping, only none of us had ever done any drugs at that stage. And we were stone-cold sober. Really all we did was wander around the moor and clamber up and down the walls and hedgerows and among the trees, pretending we were in Gearnzath. That was the world in *The Sun Battles* – like Narnia, only much scarier. We were mostly just wandering around and making things up, until Ant told us it was after three o'clock.

"I think it was her idea that we should do some kind of ritual. I know it wouldn't have been Moira's, and I don't think it was mine. But I knew there was going to be a full moon that night – I'd heard my uncle mention it – and so we decided that we would each sacrifice a sacred thing, and then retrieved them all before moonrise. We turned our pockets inside-out looking for what we could use. I had a comb, so that was mine – just a red plastic thing, I think it cost ten pence. Ant had a locket on a chain from Woolworths, cheap but the locket part opened.

"And Moira had a pencil. It said RAVENWOOD on the side, so we called the field Ravenwood. We climbed up on the wall and stood facing the sun, and made up some sort of chant. I don't remember what we said. Then we tossed our things onto the moor. None of us threw them far, and Ant barely tossed hers – she didn't want to lose the locket. I didn't care about the comb, but it was so light it just fell a few yards from where we stood. Same with the pencil. We all marked where they fell – I remember mine very clearly, it came down right on top of this big flat stone.

"Then we just left. It was getting late, and cold, and we were all starving – we'd had nothing to eat since breakfast. We went back to the house and hung out in the barn for a while, and then we had dinner. We didn't talk much. Moira hid her jacket so they couldn't see she'd torn it, and I took my boots off so no one would see how I'd got them all mauled by the thorns. I remember my aunt wondering if we were up to something, and my uncle saying what the hell could we possibly be up to in Zennor? After dinner we sat in the living room and waited for the sun to go down, and when we saw the moon start to rise above the hills, we went back outside.

"It was bright enough that we could find our way without a torch – a flashlight. I think that must have been one of the rules, that we had to retrieve our things by moonlight. It was cold out, and none of us had dressed very warmly, so we ran. It didn't take long. We climbed back over the wall and then down onto the field, at the exact spot where we'd thrown our things.

"They weren't there. I knew exactly where the rock was where my comb had landed – the rock was there, but not the comb. Ant's locket had landed only a few feet past it, and it wasn't there either. And Moira's pencil was gone, too."

"The wind could have moved them," said Jeffrey. "Or an animal."

"Maybe the wind," said Evelyn. "Though the whole reason we'd stayed there all day was that there was no wind – it was protected, and warm."

"Maybe a bird took it? Don't some birds like shiny things?"

"What would a bird do with a pencil? Or a plastic comb?"

Jeffrey made a face. "Probably you just didn't see where they fell. You thought you did, in daylight, but everything looks different at night. Especially in moonlight."

"I knew where they were." Evelyn shook her head and reached for the bottle of Armagnac. "Especially my comb. I have that engineer's eye, I can look at things and keep a very precise picture in my mind. The comb wasn't where it should have been. And there was no reason for it to be gone, unless…"

"Unless some other kids had seen you and found everything after you left," said Jeffrey.

"No." Evelyn sipped her drink. "We started looking. The moon was coming up – it rose above the hill, and it was very bright. Because it was so cold there was hoarfrost on the grass, and ice in places where the rain had frozen. So all that reflected the moonlight. Everything glittered. It was beautiful, but it was no longer fun – it was scary. None of us was even talking; we just split up and criss-crossed the field, looking for our things.

"And then Moira said, 'There's someone there,' and pointed. I thought it was someone on the track that led back to the farmhouse – it's not a proper road, just a rutted path that runs alongside one edge of that old field system. I looked up and yes, there were three people there – three torches, anyway. Flashlights. You couldn't see who was carrying them, but they were walking slowly along the path. I thought maybe it was my uncle and two of the men who worked with him, coming to tell us it was time to go home. They were walking from the wrong direction, across the moor, but I thought maybe they'd gone out to work on something. So I ran to the left edge of the field and climbed up on the wall."

She stopped, glancing out the window at the black garden, and finally turned back. "I could see the three lights from there," she said. "But the angle was all wrong. They weren't on the road at all – they were in the next field, up above Ravenwood. And they weren't flashlights. They were high up in the air, like this—"

She set down her glass and got to her feet, a bit unsteadily, extended both her arms and mimed holding something in her hands. "Like someone was carrying a pole eight or ten feet high, and there was a light on top of it. Not a flame. Like a ball of light…"

She cupped her hands around an invisible globe the size of a soccer ball. "Like that. White light, sort of foggy. The lights bobbed as they were walking."

"Did you see who it was?"

"No. We couldn't see anything. And, this is the part that I can't explain – it just felt bad. Like, horrible. Terrifying."

"You thought you'd summoned up whatever it was you'd been playing at." Jeffrey nodded sympathetically and finished his drink. "It was just marsh gas, Ev. You know that. Will o' the wisp, or whatever you call it here. They must get it all the time out there in the country. Or fog. Or someone just out walking in the moonlight."

Evelyn settled back into her armchair. "It wasn't," she said. "I've seen marsh gas. There was no fog. The moon was so bright you could see every single rock in that field. Whatever it was, we all saw it. And you couldn't hear anything – there were no voices, no footsteps, nothing. They were just there, moving closer to us – slowly," she repeated, and moved her hand up and down, as though calming a cranky child. "That was the creepiest thing, how slowly they just kept coming."

"Why didn't you just run?"

"Because we couldn't. You know how kids will all know about something horrible, but they'll never tell a grown-up? It was like that. We knew we had to find our things before we could go.

"I found my comb first. It was way over – maybe twenty feet from where I'd seen it fall. I grabbed it and began to run across the turf, looking for the locket and Moira's pencil. The whole time the moon was rising, and that was horrible too – it was a beautiful clear night, no clouds at all. And the moon was so beautiful, but it just terrified me. I can't explain it."

Jeffrey smiled wryly. "Yeah? How about this: three thirteen-year-old girls in the dark under a full moon, with a very active imagination?"

"Hush. A few minutes later Moira yelled: she'd found her pencil. She turned and started running back toward the wall, I screamed after her that she had to help us find the locket. She wouldn't come back. She didn't go over the wall without us, but she wouldn't help. I ran over to Ant but she yelled at me to keep searching where I was. I did, I even started heading for the far end of the field, toward the other wall – where the lights were.

"They were very close now, close to the far wall I mean. You could see how high up they were, taller than a person. I could hear Moira crying, I looked back and suddenly I saw Ant dive to the ground. She screamed 'I found it!' and I could see the chain shining in her hand.

"And we just turned and hightailed it. I've never run so fast in my life. I grabbed Ant's arm, by the time we got to the wall Moira was already on top and jumping down the other side. I fell and Ant had to help me up, Moira grabbed her and we ran all the way back to the farm and locked the door when we got inside.

"We looked out the window and the lights were still there. They were there for hours. My uncle had a Border Collie, we cracked the door to see if she'd hear something and bark but she didn't. She wouldn't go outside, though – we tried to get her to look and she wouldn't budge."

"Did you tell your aunt and uncle?"

Evelyn shook her head. "No. We stayed in the house that night, in my cousin's room. It overlooked the moor, so we could watch the lights. After about two hours they began to move back the way they'd come – slowly, it was about another hour before they were gone completely. We went out next morning to see if there was anything there – we took the dog to protect us."

"And?"

"There was nothing. The grass was all beat down, as though someone had been walking over it, but probably that was just us."

She fell silent. "Well," Jeffrey said after a long moment. "It's certainly a good story."

"It's a true story. Here, wait."

She stood and went into the other room, and Jeffrey heard her go upstairs. He crossed to the window and stared out into the night, the dark garden occluded by shadow and runnels of mist, blueish in the dim light cast from the solarium.

"Look. I still have it."

He turned to see Evelyn holding a small round tin box. She withdrew a small object and stared at it, placed it back inside and handed the box to him. "My comb. There's some pictures here too."

"That box." He stared at the lid, blue enamel with the words ST. AUSTELL CANDIES: FUDGE FROM REAL CORNISH CREAM stamped in gold above the silhouette of what looked like a lighthouse beacon. "It's just like the one I found, with Anthea's letters in it."

Evelyn nodded. "That's right. Becca gave one to each of us the day we arrived. The fudge was supposed to last the entire two weeks, and I think we ate it all that first night."

He opened the box and gazed at a bright-red plastic comb sitting atop several snapshots; dug into his pocket and pulled out Anthea's locket.

"There it is," said Evelyn wonderingly. She took the locket and dangled it in front of her, clicked it open and shut then returned it to Jeffrey. "She never had anything in it that I knew. Here, look at these."

She took back the tin box. He sat, waiting as she sorted through the snapshots then passed him six small black-and-white photos, each time-stamped OCTOBER 1971.

"That was my camera. A Brownie." Evelyn sank back into the armchair. "I didn't finish shooting the roll till we went back to school."

There were two girls in most of the photos. One was Anthea, apple-cheeked, her face still rounded with puppy fat and her brown hair longer than he'd ever seen it; eyebrows unplucked, wearing baggy bell-bottom jeans and a white peasant shirt. The other girl was taller, sturdy but long-limbed, with long straight blonde hair and a broad smooth forehead, elongated eyes and a wide mouth bared in a grin.

"That's Moira," said Evelyn.

"She's beautiful."

"She was. We were the ugly ducklings, Ant and me. Fortunately I was taking most of the photos, so you don't see me except in the ones Aunt Becca took."

"You were adorable." Jeffrey flipped to a photo of all three girls laughing and feeding each other something with their hands, Evelyn still in braces, her hair cut in a severe black bob. "You were all adorable. She's just—"

He scrutinised a photo of Moira by herself, slightly out of focus so all you saw was a blurred wave of blonde hair and her smile, a flash of narrowed eyes. "She's beautiful. Photogenic."

Evelyn laughed. "Is that what you call it? No, Moira was very pretty, all the boys liked her. But she was a tomboy like us. Ant was the one who was boy-crazy. Me and Moira, not so much."

"What about when you saw Robert Bennington? When was that?"

"The next day. Nothing happened – I mean, he was very nice, but there was nothing strange like that night. Nothing *untoward*," she added, lips pursed. "My aunt knew who he was – she didn't know him except to say hello to at the post office, and she'd never read his books. But she knew he was the children's writer, and she knew which house was supposed to be his. We told her we were going to see him, she told us to be polite and not be a nuisance and not stay long.

"So we were polite and not nuisances, and we stayed for two hours. Maybe three. We trekked over to his house, and that took almost an hour. A big old stone house. There was a standing stone and an old barrow nearby, it looked like a hayrick. A fogou. He was very proud that there was a fogou on his land – like a cave, but man-made. He said it was three thousand years old. He took us out to see it, and then we walked back to his house and he made us Nutella sandwiches and tangerines and orange squash. We just walked up to his door and knocked – *I* knocked, Ant was too nervous and Moira was just embarrassed. Ant and I had our copies of *The Second Sun*, and he was very sweet and invited us in and said he'd sign them before we left."

"Oh, sure – 'Come up and see my fogou, girls'."

"No – he wanted us to see it because it gave him an idea for his book. It was like a portal, he said. He wasn't a dirty old man, Jeffrey! He wasn't even that old – maybe forty? He had long hair, longish, anyway – to his shoulders – and he had cool clothes, an embroidered shirt and corduroy flares. And pointy-toed boots – blue boot, bright sky-blue, very pointy toes. That was the only thing about him I thought was odd. I wondered how his toes fit into them – if he had long pointy toes to go along with the shoes." She laughed. "Really, he was very charming, talked to us about the books but wouldn't reveal any secrets – he said there would be another in the series but it never appeared. He signed our books – well, he signed mine, Moira didn't have one and for some reason he forgot Ant's. And eventually we left."

"Did you tell him about the lights?"

"We did. He said he'd heard of things like that happening before. That part of Cornwall is ancient, there are all kinds of stone circles and menhirs, cromlechs, things like that."

"What's a cromlech?"

"You know – a dolmen." At Jeffrey's frown she picked up several of the snapshots and arranged them on the side table, a simple house of cards: three photos supporting a fourth laid atop them. "Like that. It's a kind of prehistoric grave, made of big flat stones. Stonehenge, only small. The fogou was a bit like that. They're all over West Penwith – that's where Zennor is. Alaister Crowley lived there, and D.H. Lawrence and his wife. That was years before Robert's time, but he said there were always stories about odd things happening. I don't know what kind of things – it was always pretty boring when I visited as a girl, except for that one time."

Jeffrey made a face. "He was out there with a flashlight, Ev, leading you girls on."

"He didn't even know we were there!" protested Evelyn, so vehemently that the makeshift house of photos collapsed. "He looked genuinely startled when we knocked on his door – I was afraid he'd yell at us to leave. Or, I don't know, have us arrested. He said that field had a name. It was a funny word, Cornish. It meant something, though of course I don't remember what. A lake, maybe, though there was no lake there, no water at all."

She stopped and leaned toward Jeffrey. "Why do you care about this, Jeffrey? *Did* Anthea say something?"

"No. I just found those letters, and…"

He lay his hands atop his knees, turned to stare past Evelyn into the darkness, so that she wouldn't see his eyes welling. "I just wanted to know. And I can't ask her."

Evelyn sighed. "Well, there's nothing to know, except what I told you. We went back once more – we took torches this time, and walking sticks and the dog. We stayed out till 3:00 a.m. Nothing happened except we caught hell from my aunt and uncle because they heard the dog barking and looked in the barn and we were gone.

"And that was the end of it. I still have the book he signed for me. Ant must have kept her copy – she was always mad he didn't sign it."

"I don't know. Maybe. I couldn't find it. Your friend Moira, you're not in touch with her?"

Evelyn shook her head. "I told you, she disappeared – she ran away that summer. There were problems at home, the father was a drunk and maybe the mother, too. We never went over there – it wasn't a welcoming place. She had an older sister but I never knew her. Look, if you're thinking Robert Bennington killed her, that's ridiculous. I'm sure her name came up during the trial, if anything had happened we would have heard about it. An investigation."

"Did you tell them about Moira?"

"Of course not. Look, Jeffrey – I think you should forget about all that. It's nothing to do with you, and it was all a long time ago. Ant never cared about it – I told her about the trial, I'd read about it in *The Guardian*, but she was even less curious about it than I was. I don't even know if Robert Bennington is still alive. He'd be an old man now."

She leaned over to take his hand. "I can see you're tired, Jeffrey. This has all been so awful for you, you must be totally exhausted. Do you want to just stay here for a few days? Or come back after your meeting in London?"

"No – I mean, probably not. Probably I need to get back to Brooklyn. I have some projects I backburnered, I need to get to them in the next few weeks. I'm sorry, Ev."

He rubbed his eyes and stood. "I didn't mean to hammer you about this stuff. You're right – I'm just beat. All this—" He sorted the snapshots into a small stack, and asked, "Could I have one of these? It doesn't matter which one."

"Of course. Whichever, take your pick."

He chose a photo of the three girls, Moira and Evelyn doubled over laughing as Anthea stared at them, smiling and slightly puzzled.

"Thank you, Ev," he said. He replaced each of Anthea's letters into its envelope, slid the photo into the last one, then stared at the sheaf in his hand, as though wondering how it got there. "It's just, I dunno. Meaningless, I guess; but I want it to mean something. I want *something* to mean something."

"Anthea meant something." Evelyn stood and put her arms around him. "Your life together meant something. And your life now means something."

"I know." He kissed the top of her head. "I keep telling myself that."

—◆—

Evelyn dropped him off at the station next morning. He felt guilty, lying that he had meetings back in London, but he sensed both her relief and regret that he was leaving.

"I'm sorry about last night," he said as Evelyn turned into the parking lot. "I feel like the Bad Fairy at the christening, bringing up all that stuff."

"No, it was interesting." Evelyn squinted into the sun. "I hadn't thought about any of that for a while. Not since Ant called me last March."

Jeffrey hesitated, then asked, "What do you think happened? I mean, you're the one with the advanced degree in structural engineering."

Evelyn laughed. "Yeah. And see where it's got me. I have no idea, Jeffrey. If you ask me, logically, what do I think? Well, I think it's just one of those things that we'll never know what happened. Maybe two different dimensions overlapped – in superstring theory, something like that is theoretically possible, a sort of duality."

She shook her head. "I know it's crazy. Probably it's just one of those things that don't make any sense and never will. Like how did Bush stay in office for so long?"

"That I could explain." Jeffrey smiled. "But it's depressing and would take too long. Thanks again, Ev."

They hopped out of the car and hugged on the kerb. "You should come back soon," said Ev, wiping her eyes. "This is stupid, that it took so long for us all to get together again."

"I know. I will – soon, I promise. And you and Chris, come to New York. Once I have a place, it would be great."

He watched her drive off, waving as she turned back onto the main road; went into the station and walked to a ticket window.

"Can I get to Penzance from here?"

"What time?"

"Now."

The station agent looked at her computer. "There's a train in about half an hour. Change trains in Plymouth, arrive at Penzance a little before four."

He bought a first-class, one-way ticket to Penzance, found a seat in the waiting area, took out his phone and looked online for a place to stay near Zennor. There wasn't much – a few farmhouses designed for summer rentals, all still closed for the winter. An inn that had in recent years been turned into a popular gastropub was open; but even now, the first week of March, they were fully booked. Finally he came upon a B&B called Cliff Cottage in a neighbouring village just two miles away. There were only two rooms, and the official opening date was not until the following weekend, but he called anyway.

"A room?" The woman who answered sounded tired but friendly. "We're not really ready yet, we've been doing some renovations and—"

"All I need is a bed," Jeffrey broke in. He took a deep breath. "The truth is, my wife died recently. I just need some time to be away from the rest of the world and…"

His voice trailed off. He felt a pang of self-loathing, playing the pity card; listened to a long silence on the line before the woman said, "Oh, dear, I'm so sorry. Well, yes, if you don't mind that we're really not up and running. The grout's not even dry yet in the new bath. Do you have a good head for heights?"

"Heights?"

"Yes. Vertigo? Some people have a very hard time with the driveway. There's a two night minimum for a stay."

Jeffrey assured her he'd never had any issues with vertigo. He gave her his credit card info, rang off and called to reserve a car in Penzance.

He slept most of the way to Plymouth, exhausted and faintly hungover. The train from Plymouth to Penzance was nearly empty. He bought a beer and a sandwich in the buffet car, and went to his seat. He'd bought a novel in London at Waterstones, but instead of reading gazed out at a landscape that was a dream of books he'd read as a child – granite farmhouses, woolly-coated ponies in stone paddocks; fields improbably green against lowering grey sky, graphite clouds broken by blades of golden sun, a rainbow that pierced a thunderhead then faded as though erased by some unseen hand. Ringnecked pheasants, a running fox. More fields planted with something that shone a startling goldfinch-yellow. A silvery coastline hemmed by arches of russet stone. Children wrestling in the middle of an empty road. A woman walking with head bowed against the wind, hands extended before her like a diviner.

Abandoned mineshafts and slagheaps; ruins glimpsed in an eyeflash before the train dove into a tunnel; black birds wheeling above a dun-coloured tor surrounded by scorched heath.

And, again and again, groves of gnarled oaks that underscored the absence of great forests in a landscape that had been scoured of trees thousands of years ago. It was beautiful yet also slightly disturbing, like watching an underpopulated, narratively fractured silent movie that played across the train window.

The trees were what most unsettled Jeffrey: the thought that men had so thoroughly occupied this countryside for so long that they had flensed it of everything – rocks, trees, shrubs, all put to some human use so that only the abraded land remained. He felt relieved when the train at last reached Penzance, with the beachfront promenade to one side, glassy waves breaking on the sand and the dark towers of St. Michael's Mount suspended between aquamarine water and pearly sky.

He grabbed his bag and walked through the station, outside to where people waited on the kerb with luggage or headed to the parking lot. The clouds had lifted: a chill steady wind blew from off the water, bringing the smell of salt and sea wrack. He shivered and pulled on his wool overcoat, looking around for the vehicle from the rental car company that was supposed to meet him.

He finally spotted it, a small white sedan parked along the sidewalk. A man in a dark blazer leaned against the car, smoking and talking to a teenage boy with dreadlocks and rainbow-knit cap and a somewhat older woman with matted dark-blonde hair.

"You my ride?" Jeffrey said, smiling.

The man took a drag from his cigarette and passed it to the woman. She was older than Jeffrey had first thought, in her early thirties, face seamed and sun-weathered and her eyes bloodshot. She wore tight flared jeans and a fuzzy sky-blue sweater beneath a stained Arsenal windbreaker.

"Spare anything?" she said as he stopped alongside the car. She reeked of sweat and marijuana smoke.

"Go on now, Erthy," the man said, scowling. He turned to Jeffrey. "Mr. Kearin?"

"That's me," said Jeffrey.

"Gotta 'nother rollie, Evan?" the woman prodded.

"Come on, Erthy," said the rainbow-hatted boy. He spun and began walking toward the station. "Peace, Evan."

"I apologise for that," Evan said as he opened the passenger door for Jeffrey. "I know the boy, his family's neighbours of my sister's."

"Bit old for him, isn't she?" Jeffrey glanced to where the two huddled against the station wall, smoke welling from their cupped hands.

"Yeah, Erthy's a tough nut. She used to sleep rough by the St. Erth train station. Only this last winter she's taken up in Penzance. Every summer we get the smackhead hippies here, there's always some poor souls who stay and take up on the street. Not that you want to hear about that," he added, laughing as he swung into the driver's seat. "On vacation?"

Jeffrey nodded. "Just a few days."

"Staying here in Penzance?"

"Cardu. Near Zennor."

"Might see some sun, but probably not till the weekend."

———◆———

He ended up with the same small white sedan. "Only one we have, this last minute," Evan said, tapping at the computer in the rental office. "But it's better really for driving out there in the countryside. Roads are extremely narrow. Have you driven around here before? No? I would strongly recommend the extra damages policy ..."

It had been decades since Jeffrey had been behind the wheel of a car in the UK. He began to sweat as soon as he left the rental car lot, eyes darting between the map Evan had given him and the GPS on his iPhone. In minutes the busy roundabout was behind him; the car crept up a narrow, winding hillside, with high stone walls to either side that swiftly gave way to hedgerows bordering open farmland. A brilliant yellow field proved to be planted with daffodils, their constricted yellow throats not yet in bloom. After several more minutes, he came to a crossroads.

Almost immediately he got lost. The distances between villages and roads were deceptive: what appeared on the map to be a mile or more instead contracted into a few hundred yards, or else expanded into a series of zigzags and switchbacks that appeared to point him back toward Penzance. The GPS directions made no sense, advising him to turn directly into stone walls or gated driveways or fields where cows grazed on young spring grass. The roads were only wide enough for one car to pass, with tiny turnouts every fifty feet or so where one could pull over, but the high hedgerows and labyrinthine turns made it difficult to spot oncoming vehicles.

His destination, a village called Cardu, was roughly seven miles from Penzance; after half an hour, the odometer registered that he'd gone fifteen miles, and he had no idea where he was. There was no cell phone reception. The sun dangled a hand's-span above the western horizon, staining ragged stone outcroppings and a bleak expanse of moor an ominous reddish-bronze, and throwing the black fretwork of stone walls into stark relief. He finally parked in one of the narrow turnouts, sat for a few minutes staring into the sullen blood-red eye of the sun, and at last got out.

The hedgerows offered little protection from the harsh wind that raked across the moor. Jeffrey pulled at the collar of his wool coat, turning his back to the wind, and noticed a small sign that read PUBLIC FOOTPATH. He walked over and saw a narrow gap in the hedgerow, three steps formed of wide flat stones. He took the three in one long stride and found himself at the edge of an overgrown field, similar to what Evelyn had described in her account of the lights near Zennor. An ancient-looking stone wall bounded the far edge of the field, with a wider gap that opened to the next field and what looked like another sign. He squinted, but couldn't make out what it read, and began to pick his way across the turf.

It was treacherous going – the countless hummocks hid deep holes, and more than once he barely kept himself from wrenching his ankle. The air smelled strongly of raw earth and cow manure. As the sun dipped lower, a wedge of shadow was driven between him and the swiftly darkening sky, making it still more difficult to see his way. But after a few minutes he reached the far wall, and bent to read the sign beside the gap into the next field.

CAS CIRCLE

He glanced back, saw a glint of white where the rental car was parked, straightened and walked on.

There was a footpath here. Hardly a path, really; just a trail where turf and bracken had been flattened by the passage of not-many feet. He followed it, stopping when he came to a large upright stone that came up his waist. He looked to one side then the other and saw more stones, forming a group more ovoid than circular, perhaps thirty feet in diameter. He ran his hand across the first stone – rough granite, ridged with lichen and friable bits of moss that crumbled at his touch.

The reek of manure was fainter here: he could smell something fresh and sweet, like rain, and when he looked down saw a silvery gleam at the base of the rock. He crouched and dipped his fingers into a tiny pool, no bigger than his shoe. The water was icy cold, and even after he withdrew his hand, the surface trembled.

A spring. He dipped his cupped palm into it and sniffed warily, expecting a foetid whiff of cow muck.

But the water smelled clean, of rock and rain. Without thinking he drew his hand to his mouth and sipped, immediately flicked his fingers to send glinting droplets into the night.

That was stupid, he thought, hastily wiping his hand on his trousers. *Now I'll get dysentery. Or whatever one gets from cows.*

He stood there for another minute, then turned and retraced his steps to the rental car. He saw a pair of headlights approaching and flagged down a white delivery van.

"I'm lost," he said, and showed the driver the map that Evan had given him.

"Not too lost." The driver perused the map, then gave him directions. "Once you see the inn you're almost there."

Jeffrey thanked him, got back into the car and started to drive. In ten minutes he reached the inn, a rambling stucco structure with a half-dozen cars out front. There was no sign identifying Cardu, and no indication that there was anything more to the village than the inn and a deeply rutted road flanked by a handful of granite cottages in varying states of disrepair. He eased the rental car by the mottled grey buildings, to where what passed for a road ended; bore right and headed down a cobblestoned, hairpin drive that zigzagged along the cliff edge.

He could hear but could not see the ocean, waves crashing against rocks hundreds of feet below. Now and then he got a skin-crawling glimpse of immense cliffs like congealed flames – ruddy stone, apricot-yellow gorse, lurid flares of orange lichen all burned to ash as afterglow faded from the western sky.

He wrenched his gaze back to the narrow strip of road immediately in front of him. Gorse and brambles tore at the doors; once he bottomed out, then nosed the car across a water-filled gulley that widened into a stream that cascaded down the cliff to the sea below.

"Holy fucking Christ," he said, and kept the car in first gear. In another five minutes he was safely parked beside the cottage, alongside a small sedan.

"We thought maybe you weren't coming," someone called as Jeffrey stepped shakily out onto a cobblestone drive. Straggly rosebushes grew between a row of granite slabs that resembled headstones. These were presumably to keep cars from veering down an incline that led to a ruined outbuilding, a few faint stars already framed in its gaping windows. "Some people, they start down here and just give up and turn back."

Jeffrey looked around, finally spotted a slight man in his early sixties standing in the doorway of a grey stone cottage tucked into the lee of the cliff. "Oh, hi. No, I made it."

Jeffrey ducked back into the car, grabbed his bag and headed for the cottage.

"Harry," the man said, and held the door for him.

"Jeffrey. I spoke to your wife this afternoon."

The man's brow furrowed. "Wife?" He was a head shorter than Jeffrey, clean-shaven, with a sun-weathered face and sleek grey-flecked dark brown hair to his shoulders. A ropey old cable knit sweater hung from his lank frame.

"Well, someone. A woman."

"Oh. That was Thomsa. My sister." The man nodded, as though this confusion had never occurred before. "We're still trying to get unpacked. We don't really open till this weekend, but…"

He held the door so Jeffrey could pass inside. "Thomsa told me of your loss. My condolences."

Inside was a small room with slate floors and plastered walls, sparely furnished with a plain deal table and four chairs intricately carved with Celtic knots; a sideboard holding books and maps and artfully mismatched crockery; large gas cooking stove and a side table covered with notepads and pens, unopened bills, and a laptop. A modern cast-iron wood-stove had been fitted into a wide, old-fashioned hearth. The stove radiated warmth and an acrid, not unpleasant scent, redolent of coal-smoke and burning sage. Peat, Jeffrey realised with surprise. There was a closed door on the other side of the room, and from behind this came the sound of a television. Harry looked at Jeffrey, cocking an eyebrow.

"It's beautiful," said Jeffrey.

Harry nodded. "I'll take you to your room," he said.

Jeffrey followed him up a narrow stair beneath the eaves, into a short hallway flanked by two doors. "Your room's here. Bath's down there, you'll have it all to yourself. What time would you like breakfast?"

"Seven, maybe?"

"How about seven-thirty?"

Jeffrey smiled wanly. "Sure."

The room was small, white plaster walls and a window-seat overlooking the sea, a big bed heaped with a white duvet and myriad pillows, corner wardrobe carved with the same Celtic knots as the chairs below. No TV or radio or telephone, not even a clock. Jeffrey unpacked his bag and checked his phone for service: none.

315

He closed the wardrobe, looked in his backpack and swore. He'd left his book on the train. He ran a hand through his hair, stepped to the window-seat and stared out.

It was too dark now to see much, though light from windows on the floor below illuminated a small, winding patch of garden, bound at the cliff-side by a stone wall. Beyond that there was only rock and, far below, the sea. Waves thundered against the unseen shore, a muted roar like a jet turbine. He could feel the house around him shake.

And not just the house, he thought; it felt as though the ground and everything around him trembled without ceasing. He paced to the other window, overlooking the drive, and stared at his rental car and the sedan beside it through a freize of branches, a tree so contorted by wind and salt that the limbs only grew in one direction. He turned off the room's single light, waited for his eyes to adjust; stared back out through one window, and then the other.

For as far as he could see, there was only night. Ghostly light seeped from a room downstairs onto the sliver of lawn. Starlight touched on the endless sweep of moor, like another sea unrolling from the line of cliffs brooding above black waves and distant headlands. There was no sign of human habitation: no distant lights, no street-lamps, no cars, no ships or lighthouse beacons: nothing.

He sank onto the window seat, dread knotting his chest. He had never seen anything like this – even hiking in the Mojave Desert with Anthea ten years earlier, there had been a scattering of lights sifted across the horizon and satellites moving slowly through the constellations. He grabbed his phone, fighting a cold black solitary horror. There was still no reception.

He put the phone aside and stared at a framed sepia-tinted photograph on the wall: a three-masted schooner wrecked on the rocks beneath a cliff he suspected was the same one where the cottage stood. Why was he even here? He felt as he had once in college, waking in a strange room after a night of heavy drinking, surrounded by people he didn't know in a squalid flat used as a shooting gallery. The same sense that he'd been engaged in some kind of psychic somnambulism, walking perilously close to a precipice.

Here, of course he actually *was* perched on the edge of a precipice. He stood and went into the hall, switching on the light; walked into the bathroom and turned on all the lights there as well.

It was almost as large as his bedroom, cheerfully appointed with yellow and blue towels piled atop a wooden chair, a massive porcelain tub, hand-woven yellow rugs and a fistful of daffodils in a cobalt glass vase on a wide windowsill. He moved the towels and sat on the chair for a few minutes, then crossed to pick up the vase and drew it to his face.

The daffodils smelled sweetly, of overturned earth warming in the sunlight. Anthea had loved daffodils, planting a hundred new bulbs every autumn; daffodils and jonquil and narcissus and crocuses, all the harbingers of spring. He inhaled again, deeply, and replaced the flowers on the sill. He left a light on beside the sink, returned to his room and went to bed.

——◆——

He woke before 7:00. Thin sunlight filtered through the white curtains he'd drawn the night before, and for several minutes he lay in bed, listening to the rhythmic boom of surf on the rocks. He finally got up, pulled aside the curtain and looked out.

A line of clouds hung above the western horizon, but over the headland the sky was pale blue, shot with gold where the sun rose above the moor. Hundreds of feet below Jeffrey's bedroom, aquamarine swells crashed against the base of the cliffs and swirled around ragged granite pinnacles that rose from the sea, surrounded by clouds of white seabirds. There was a crescent of white sand, and a black cavern-mouth gouged into one of the cliffs where a vortex rose and subsided with the waves.

The memory of last night's horror faded: sunlight and wheeling birds, the vast expanse of air and sea and all but treeless moor made him feel exhilarated. For the first time since Anthea's death, he had a premonition not of dread but of the sort of exultation he felt as a teenager, waking in his boyhood room in early spring.

He dressed and shaved – there was no shower, only that dinghy-sized

317

tub, so he'd forgo bathing till later. He waited until he was certain he heard movement in the kitchen, and went downstairs.

"Good morning." A woman who might have been Harry's twin leaned against the slate sink. Slender, small-boned, with straight dark hair held back with two combs from a narrow face, brown-eyed and weathered as her brother's. "I'm Thomsa."

He shook her hand, glanced around for signs of coffee then peered out the window. "This is an amazing place."

"Yes, it is," Thomsa said evenly. She spooned coffee into a glass cafetière, picked up a steaming kettle and poured hot water over the grounds. "Coffee, right? I have tea if you prefer. Would you like eggs? Some people have all sorts of food allergies. Vegans, how do you feed them?" She stared at him in consternation, turned back to the sink, glancing at a bowl of eggs. "How many?"

The cottage was silent, save for the drone of a television behind the closed door and the thunder of waves beating against the cliffs. Jeffrey sat at a table set for one, poured himself coffee and stared out to where the moor rose behind them. "Does the sound of the ocean ever bother you?" he asked.

Thomsa laughed. "No. We've been here thirty-five years, we're used to that. But we're building a house in Greece, in Hydra, that's where we just returned from. There's a church in the village and every afternoon the bells ring, I don't know why. At first I thought, isn't that lovely, church bells! Now I'm sick of them, just wish they'd just shut up."

She set a plate of fried eggs and thick-cut bacon in front of him, along with slabs of toasted brown bread and glass bowls of preserves, picked up a mug and settled at the table. "So are you here on holiday?"

"Mmm, yes." Jeffrey nodded, his mouth full. "My wife died last fall. I just needed to get away for a bit."

"Yes, of course. I'm very sorry."

"She visited here once when she was a girl – not here, but at a farm nearby, in Zennor. I don't know the last name of the family, but the woman was named Becca."

"Becca? Mmmm, no, I don't think so. Maybe Harry will know."

"This would have been 1971."

"Ah – no, we didn't move here till '75. Summer, us and all the other hippie types from back then." She sipped her tea. "No tourists around this time of year. Usually we don't open till the second week in March. But we don't have anyone scheduled yet, so." She shrugged, pushing back a wisp of dark hair. "It's quiet this time of year. No German tour buses. Do you paint?"

"Paint?" Jeffrey blinked. "No. I'm an architect, so I draw, but mostly just for work. I sketch sometimes."

"We get a lot of artists. There's the Tate in St. Ives, if you like modern architecture. And of course there are all the prehistoric ruins – standing stones, and Zennor Quoit. There are all sorts of legends about them, fairy tales. People disappearing. They're very interesting if you don't mind the walk."

"Are there places to eat?"

"The inn here, though you might want to stop in and make a booking. There's the pub in Zennor, and St. Ives of course, though it can be hard to park. And Penzance."

Jeffrey winced. "Not sure I want to get back on the road again immediately."

"Yes, the drive here's a bit tricky, isn't it? But Zennor's only two miles, if you don't mind walking – lots of people do, we get hikers from all over on the coastal footpath. And Harry might be going out later, he could drop you off in Zennor if you like."

"Thanks. Not sure what I'll do yet. But thank you."

He ate his breakfast, making small talk with Thomsa and nodding at Harry when he emerged and darted through the kitchen, raising a hand as he slipped outside. Minutes later, Jeffrey glimpsed him pushing a wheelbarrow full of gardening equipment.

"I think the rain's supposed to hold off," Thomsa said, staring out the window. "I hope so. We want to finish that wall. Would you like me to make more coffee?"

"If you don't mind."

Jeffrey dabbed a crust into the blackcurrant preserves. He wanted to ask if Thomsa or her brother knew Robert Bennington, but was afraid he might be stirring up memories of some local scandal, or that he'd be taken for a journalist or some other busybody. He finished the toast, thanked Thomsa when she poured him more coffee, then reached for one of the brochures on the sideboard.

"So does this show where those ruins are?"

"Yes. You'll want the Ordnance map. Here—"

She cleared the dishes, gathered a map and unfolded it. She tapped the outline of a tiny cove between two spurs of land. "We're here."

She traced one of the spurs, lifted her head to stare out the window to a grey-green spine of rock stretching directly to the south. "That's Gurnard's Head. And there's Zennor Head—"

She turned and pointed in the opposite direction, to a looming promontory a few miles distant, and looked back down at the map. "You can see where everything's marked."

Jeffrey squinted to make out words printed in a tiny, Gothic font. TUMULI, STANDING STONE, HUT CIRCLE, CAIRN. "Is there a fogou around here?"

"A fogou?" She frowned slightly. "Yes, there is – out toward Zennor, across the moor. It's a bit of a walk."

"Could you give me directions? Just sort of point the way? I might try and find it – give me something to do."

Thomsa stepped to the window. "The coastal path is there – see? If you follow it up to the ridge, you'll see a trail veer off. There's an old road there, the farmers use it sometimes. All those old fields run alongside it. The fogou's on the Golovenna Farm, I don't know how many fields back that is. It would be faster if you drove toward Zennor then hiked over the moor, but you could probably do it from here. You'll have to find an opening in the stone walls or climb over – do you have hiking shoes?" She looked dubiously at his sneakers. "Well, they'll probably be all right."

"I'll give it a shot. Can I take that map?"

"Yes, of course. It's not the best map – the Ordnance Survey has a more detailed one, I think."

He thanked her and downed the rest of his coffee, went upstairs and pulled a heavy woollen sweater over his flannel shirt, grabbed his cell phone and returned downstairs. He retrieved the map and stuck it in his coat pocket, said goodbye to Thomsa rinsing dishes in the sink, and walked outside.

The air was warmer, almost balmy despite a stiff wind that had torn the line of clouds into grey shreds. Harry knelt beside a stone wall, poking at the ground with a small spade. Jeffrey paused to watch him, then turned to survey clusters of daffodils and jonquils, scores of them scattered across the terraced slopes among rocks and apple trees. The flowers were not yet in bloom, but he could glimpse sunlit yellow and orange and saffron petals swelling within the green buds atop each slender stalk.

"Going out?" Harry called.

"Yes." Jeffrey stooped to brush his fingers across one of the flowers. "My wife loved daffodils. She must have planted thousands of them."

Harry nodded. "Should open in the next few days. If we get some sun."

Jeffrey waved farewell and turned to walk up the drive.

In a few minutes, the cottage was lost to sight. The cobblestones briefly gave way to cracked concrete, then a deep rut that marked a makeshift path that led uphill, toward the half-dozen buildings that made up the village. He stayed on the driveway, and after another hundred feet reached a spot where a narrow footpath meandered off to the left, marked by a sign. This would be the path that Thomsa had pointed out.

He shaded his eyes and looked back. He could just make out Cliff Cottage, its windows a flare of gold in the sun. He stepped onto the trail, walking with care across loose stones and channels where water raced downhill, fed by the early spring rains. To one side, the land sheared away to cliffs and crashing waves; he could see where the coastal path wound along the headland, fading into the emerald crown of Zennor Head. Above him, the ground rose steeply, overgrown with coiled ferns, newly sprung grass, thickets of gorse in brilliant sun-yellow bloom where bees and tiny orange butterflies fed. At the top of the incline, he could see the dark rim of a line of stone walls. He stayed on the footpath until it began to bear toward the cliffs, then looked for a place where he could break away and make for the ancient fields. He saw what looked like a path left by some

321

kind of animal and scrambled up, dodging gorse, his sneakers sliding on loose scree, until he reached the top of the headland.

The wind here was so strong he nearly lost his balance as he hopped down into a grassy lane. The lane ran parallel to a long ridge of stone walls perhaps four feet high, braided with strands of rusted barbed wire. On the other side, endless intersections of yet more walls divided the moor into a dizzyingly ragged patchwork: jade-green, beryl, creamy yellow; ochre and golden amber. Here and there, twisted trees grew within sheltered corners, or rose from atop the walls themselves, gnarled branches scraping at the sky. High overhead, a bird arrowed toward the sea, and its plaintive cry rose above the roar of wind in his ears.

He pulled out the map, struggling to open it in the wind, finally gave up and shoved it back into his pocket. He tried to count back four fields, but it was hopeless – he couldn't make out where one field ended and another began.

And he had no idea what field to start with. He walked alongside the lane, away from the cottage and the village of Cardu, hoping he might find a gate or opening. He finally settled on a spot where the barbed wire had become engulfed by a protective thatch of dead vegetation. He clambered over the rocks, clutching desperately at dried leaves as the wall gave way beneath his feet and nearly falling onto a lethal-looking knot of barbed wire. Gasping, he reached the top of the wall, flailed as wind buffeted him then crouched until he could catch his breath.

The top of the wall was covered with vines, grey and leafless, as thick as his fingers and unpleasantly reminiscent of veins and arteries. This serpentine mass seemed to hold the stones together, though when he tried to step down the other side, the rocks once again gave way and he fell into a patch of whip-like vines studded with thorns the length of his thumbnail. Cursing, he extricated himself, his chinos torn and hands gouged and bloody, and staggered into the field.

Here at least there was some protection from the wind. The field sloped slightly uphill, to the next wall. There was so sign of a gate or breach. He shoved his hands into his pockets and strode through knee-high grass, pale green and starred with minute yellow flowers. He reached the wall and walked alongside it. In one corner several large rocks had fallen. He hoisted himself up until he could see into the next field. It was no different from the one he'd just traversed, save for a single massive evergreen in its centre.

Other than the tree, the field seemed devoid of any vegetation larger than a tussock. He tried to peer into the field beyond, and the ones after that, but the countryside dissolved into a glitter of green and topaz beneath the morning sun, with a few stone pinnacles stark against the horizon where moor gave way to sky.

He turned and walked back, head down against the wind; climbed into the first field and crossed it, searching until he spied what looked like a safe place to gain access to the lane once more. Another tangle of blackthorn snagged him as he jumped down and landed hard, grimacing as a thorn tore at his neck. He glared at the wall, then headed back to the cottage, picking thorns from his overcoat and jeans.

He was starving by the time he arrived at the cottage, also filthy. It had grown too warm for his coat; he slung it over his shoulder, wiping sweat from his cheeks. Thomsa was outside, removing a shovel from the trunk of the sedan.

"Oh, hello! You're back quickly!"

He stopped, grateful for the wind on his overheated face. "Quickly?"

"I thought you'd be off till lunchtime. A few hours, anyway?"

"I thought it *was* lunchtime." He looked at his watch and frowned. "That can't be right. It's not even ten."

Thomsa nodded, setting the shovel beside the car. "I thought maybe you forgot something." She glanced at him, startled. "Oh my. You're bleeding – did you fall?"

He shook his head. "No, well, yes," he said sheepishly. "I tried to find that fogou. Didn't get very far. Are you sure it's just ten? I thought I was out there for hours – I figured it must be noon, at least. What time did I leave?"

"Half-past nine, I think."

He started to argue, instead shrugged. "I might try again. You said there's a better map from the Ordnance Survey? Something with more details?"

"Yes. You could probably get it in Penzance – call the bookstore there if you like, phone book's on the table."

He found the phone book in the kitchen and rang the bookshop. They had a copy of the Ordnance map and would hold it for him. He rummaged on the table for a brochure with a map of Penzance, went upstairs to spend a few minutes washing up from his trek, and hurried outside. Thomsa and Harry were lugging stones across the grass to repair the wall. Jeffrey waved, ducked into the rental car and crept back up the drive toward Cardu.

In broad daylight it still took almost ten minutes. He glanced out to where the coastal footpath wound across the top of the cliffs, could barely discern a darker trail leading to the old field systems, and, beyond that, the erratic cross-stitch of stone walls fading into the eastern sky. Even if he'd only gone as far as the second field, it seemed impossible that he could have hiked all the way there and back to the cottage in half an hour.

The drive to Penzance took less time than that; barely long enough for Jeffrey to reflect how unusual it was for him to act like this, impulsively, without a plan. Everything an architect did was according to plan. Out on the moor and gorse-grown cliffs, the strangeness of the immense, dour landscape had temporarily banished the near-constant presence of his dead wife. Now, in the confines of the cramped rental car, images of other vehicles and other trips returned, all with Anthea beside him. He pushed them away, tried to focus on the fact that here at last was a place where he'd managed to escape her; and remembered that was not true at all.

Anthea had been here, too. Not the Anthea he had loved but her mayfly self, the girl he'd never known; the Anthea who'd contained an entire secret world he'd never known existed. It seemed absurd, but he desperately wished she had confided in him about her visit to Bennington's house, and the strange night that had preceded it. Evelyn's talk of superstring theory was silly – he found himself sympathising with Moira, content to let someone else read the creepy books and tell her what to do. He believed in none of it, of course. Yet it didn't matter what he believed, but whether Anthea had, and why.

Penzance was surprisingly crowded for a weekday morning in early March. He circled the town's winding streets twice before he found a parking space, several blocks from the bookstore. He walked past shops and restaurants featuring variations on themes involving pirates, fish, pixies, sailing ships. As he passed a tattoo parlour, he glanced into the adjoining alley and saw the same rainbow-hatted boy from the train station, holding a skateboard and standing with several other teenagers who were passing around a joint. The boy looked up, saw Jeffrey and smiled. Jeffrey lifted his hand and smiled back. The boy called out to him, his words garbled by the wind, put down his skateboard and did a headstand alongside it. Jeffrey laughed and kept going.

There was only one other customer in the shop when he arrived, a man in a business suit talking to two women behind the register.

"Can I help you?" The older of the two women smiled. She had close-cropped red hair and fashionable eyeglasses, and set aside an iPad as Jeffrey approached.

"I called about an Ordnance map?"

"Yes. It's right here."

She handed it to him, and he unfolded it enough to see that it showed the same area of West Penwith as the other map, enlarged and far more detailed.

The woman with the glasses cocked her head. "Shall I ring that up?"

Jeffrey closed the map and set it onto the counter. "Sure, in a minute. I'm going to look around a bit first."

She returned to chatting. Jeffrey wandered the shop. It was small but crowded with neatly stacked shelves and tables, racks of maps and postcards, with an extensive section of books about Cornwall – guidebooks, tributes to Daphne du Maurier and Barbara Hepworth, DVDs of *The Pirates of Penzance* and *Rebecca*, histories of the mines and glossy photo volumes about surfing Newquay. He spent a few minutes flipping through one of these, and continued to the back of the store. There was an entire wall of children's books, picture books near the floor, chapter books for older children arranged alphabetically above them. He scanned the Bs, and looked aside as the younger woman approached, carrying an armful of calendars.

"Are you looking for something in particular?"

He glanced back at the shelves. "Do you have anything by Robert Bennington?"

The young woman set the calendars down, ran a hand along the shelf housing the Bs; frowned and looked back to the counter. "Rose, do we have anything by Robert Bennington? It rings a bell but I don't see anything here. Children's writer, is he?" she added, turning to Jeffrey.

"Yes. *The Sun Battles*, I think that's one of them."

The other customer nodded goodbye as Rose joined the others in the back.

"Robert Bennington?" She halted, straightening a stack of coffee table books, tapped her lower lip then quickly nodded. "Oh yes! The fantasy writer. We did have his books – he's fallen out of favour." She cast a knowing look at the younger clerk. "He was the child molester."

"Oh, right." The younger woman made a face. "I don't think his books are even in print now, are they?"

"I don't think so," said Rose. "I'll check. We could order something for you, if they are."

"That's okay – I'm only here for a few days."

Jeffrey followed her to the counter and waited as she searched online.

"No, nothing's available." Rose shook her head. "Sad bit of business, wasn't it? I heard something recently, he had a stroke I think. He might even have died, I can't recall now who told me. He must be quite elderly, if he's still alive."

"He lived around here, didn't he?" said Jeffrey.

"Out near Zennor, I think. He bought the old Golovenna Farm, years ago. We used to sell quite a lot of his books – he was very popular. Like the *Harry Potter* books now. Well, not that popular." She smiled. "But he did very well. He came in here once or twice, it must be twenty years at least. A very handsome man. Theatrical. He wore a long scarf, like Doctor Who. I'm sure you could find used copies online, or there's a second-hand bookstore just round the corner – they might well have something."

"That's all right. But thank you for checking."

He paid for the map and went back out onto the sidewalk. It was getting on to noon. He wandered the streets for several minutes looking for a place to eat, settled on a small, airy Italian restaurant where he had grilled sardines and spaghetti and a glass of wine. Not very Cornish, perhaps, but he promised himself to check on the pub in Zennor later.

The Ordnance map was too large and unwieldy to open at his little table, so he stared out the window, watching tourists and women with small children in tow as they popped in and out of the shops across the street. The rainbow-hatted boy and his cronies loped by, skateboards in hand. Dropouts or burnouts, Jeffrey thought; the local constabulary must spend half its time chasing them from place to place. He finished his wine and ordered a cup of coffee, gulped it down, paid the check, and left.

A few high white clouds scudded high overhead, borne on a steady wind that sent up flurries of grit and petals blown from ornamental cherry trees. Here in the heart of Penzance, the midday sun was almost hot: Jeffrey hooked his coat over his shoulder and ambled back to his car. He paused to glance at postcards and souvenirs in a shop window, but could think of no one to send a card to. Evelyn? She'd rather have something from Zennor, another reason to visit the pub.

He turned the corner, had almost reached the tattoo parlour when a plaintive cry rang out.

"*Have you seen him?*"

Jeffrey halted. In the same alley where he'd glimpsed the boys earlier, a forlorn figure sat on the broken asphalt, twitchy fingers toying with an unlit cigarette. Erthy, the woman who'd been at the station the day before. As Jeffrey hesitated she lifted her head, swiped a fringe of dirty hair from her eyes and stumbled to her feet. His heart sank as she hurried toward him, but before he could flee she was already in his face, her breath warm and beery. "Gotta light?"

"No, sorry," he said, and began to step away.

"Wait – you're London, right?"

"No, I'm just visiting."

"No – I saw you."

He paused, thrown off-balance by a ridiculous jolt of unease. Her eyes were bloodshot, the irises a peculiar marbled blue like flawed bottle-glass, and there was a vivid crimson splotch in one eye, as though a capillary had burst. It made it seem as though she looked at him sideways, even though she was staring at him straight on.

"You're on the London train!" She nodded in excitement. "I need to get back."

"I'm sorry." He spun and walked off as quickly as he could without breaking into a run. Behind him he heard footsteps, and again the same wrenching cry.

"*Have you seen him?*"

He did run then, as the woman screamed expletives and a shower of gravel pelted his back.

He reached his rental car, his heart pounding. He looked over his shoulder, jumped inside and locked the doors before pulling out into the street. As he drove off, he caught a flash in the rear-view mirror of the woman sidling in the other direction, unlit cigarette still twitching between her fingers.

—◦—

When he arrived back at the cottage, he found Thomsa and Harry sitting at the kitchen table, surrounded by the remains of lunch, sandwich crusts and apple cores.

"Oh, hello." Thomsa looked up, smiling, and patted the chair beside her. "Did you go to The Tinners for lunch?"

"Penzance." Jeffrey sat and dropped his map onto the table. "I think I'll head out again, then maybe have dinner at the pub."

"He wants to see the fogou," said Thomsa. "He went earlier but couldn't find it. There is a fogou, isn't there, Harry? Out by Zennor Hill?"

Jeffrey hesitated, then said, "A friend of mine told me about it – she and my wife saw it when they were girls."

"Yes," said Harry after a moment. "Where the children's writer lived. Some sort of ruins there, anyway."

Jeffrey kept his tone casual. "A writer?"

"I believe so," said Thomsa. "We didn't know him. Someone who stayed here once went looking for him, but he wasn't home – this was years ago. The old Golovenna Farm."

Jeffrey pointed to the seemingly random network of lines that covered the map, like crazing on a piece of old pottery. "What's all this mean?"

Harry pulled his chair closer and traced the boundaries of Cardu with a dirt-stained finger. "Those are the field systems – the stone walls."

"You're kidding." Jeffrey laughed. "That must've driven someone nuts, getting all that down."

"Oh, it's all GPS and satellite photos now," said Thomsa. "I'm sorry I didn't have this map earlier, before you went for your walk."

"It'll be on this survey." Harry angled the map so the sunlight illuminated the area surrounding Cardu. "This is our cove, here…"

They pored over the Ordnance survey. Jeffrey pointed at markers for hut circles and cairns, standing stones and tumuli, all within a hand's-span of Cardu, as Harry continued to shake his head.

"It's this one, I think," Harry said at last, and glanced at his sister. He scored a square half-inch of the page with a blackened fingernail, minute Gothic letters trapped within the web of field systems.

CHAMBERED CAIRN

"That looks right," said Thomsa. "But it's a ways off the road. I'm not certain where the house is – the woman who went looking for it said she roamed the moor for hours before she came on it."

Jeffrey ran his finger along the line marking the main road. "It looks like I can drive to here. If there's a place to park, I can just hike in. It doesn't look that far. As long as I don't get towed."

"You shouldn't get towed," said Thomsa. "All that land's part of Golovenna, and no one's there. He never farmed it, just let it all go back to the moor. You'd only be a mile or so from Zennor if you left your car. They have musicians on Thursday nights, some of the locals come in and play after dinner."

Jeffrey refolded the map. When he looked up, Harry was gone. Thomsa handed him an apple.

"Watch for the bogs," she said. "Marsh grass, it looks sturdy but when you put your foot down it gives way and you can sink under. Like quicksand. They found a girl's body ten years back. Horses and sheep, too." Jeffrey grimaced and she laughed. "You'll be all right – just stay on the footpaths."

He thanked her, went upstairs to exchange his overcoat for a windbreaker, and returned to his car. The clouds were gone: the sun shone high in a sky the summer blue of gentians. He felt the same surge of exultation he'd experienced that morning, the sea-fresh wind tangling the stems of daffodils and iris, white gulls crying overhead. He kept the window down as he drove up the twisting way to Cardu, and the honeyed scent of gorse filled the car.

The road to Zennor coiled between hedgerows misted green with new growth and emerald fields where brown-and-white cattle grazed. In the distance a single tractor moved so slowly across a black furrow that Jeffrey could track its progress only by the skein of crows that followed it, the birds dipping then rising like a black thread drawn through blue cloth.

Twice he pulled over to consult the map. His phone didn't work here – he couldn't even get the time, let alone directions. The car's clock read 14:21. He saw no other roads, only deeply rutted tracks protected by stiles, some metal, most of weathered wood. He tried counting stone walls to determine which marked the fields Harry had said belonged to Golovenna Farm, and stopped a third time before deciding the map was all but useless. He drove another hundred feet, until he found a swathe of gravel between two tumbledown stone walls, a rusted gate sagging between them. Beyond it stretched an overgrown field bisected by a stone-strewn path.

He was less than a mile from Zennor. He folded the map and jammed it into his windbreaker pocket along with the apple, and stepped out of the car.

The dark height before him would be Zennor Hill. Golovenna Farm was somewhere between there and where he stood. He turned slowly, scanning everything around him to fix it in his memory: the winding road, intermittently visible between walls and hedgerows; the ridge of cliffs falling down to the sea, book-ended by the dark bulk of Gurnards Head in the south-west and Zennor Head to the north-east. On the horizon were scattered outcroppings that might have been tors or ruins or even buildings.

He locked the car, checked that he had his phone, climbed over the metal gate and began to walk.

The afternoon sun beat down fiercely. He wished he'd brought a hat, or sunglasses. He crossed the first field in a few minutes, and was relieved to find a break in the next wall, an opening formed by a pair of tall, broad stones. The path narrowed here, but was still clearly discernible where it bore straight in front of him, an arrow of new green grass flashing through ankle-high turf overgrown with daisies and fronds of young bracken.

The ground felt springy beneath his feet. He remembered Thomsa's warning about the bogs, and glanced around for something he might use as a walking stick. There were no trees in sight, only wicked-looking thickets of blackthorn clustered along the perimeter of the field.

He found another gap in the next wall, guarded like the first by two broad stones nearly as tall as he was. He clambered onto the wall, fighting to open his map in the brisk wind, and examined the survey, trying to find some affinity between the fields around him and the crazed pattern on the page. At last he shoved the map back into his pocket, set his back to the wind and shaded his eyes with his hand.

It was hard to see – he was staring due west, into the sun – but he thought he glimpsed a black bulge some three or four fields off, a dark blister within the haze of green and yellow. It might be a ruin, or just as likely a farm or outbuildings. He clambered down into the next field, crushing dead bracken and shoots of heather; picked his way through a breach where stones had fallen and hurried until he reached yet another wall.

There were the remnants of a gate here, a rusted latch and iron pins protruding from the granite. Jeffrey crouched beside the wall to catch his breath. After a few minutes he scrambled to his feet and walked through the gap, letting one hand rest for an instant upon the stone. Despite the hot afternoon sun it felt cold beneath his palm, more like metal than granite. He glanced aside to make sure he hadn't touched a bit of rusted hardware, but saw only a boulder seamed with moss.

The fields he'd already passed through had seemed rank and overgrown, as though claimed by the wilderness decades ago. Yet there was no mistaking what stretched before him as anything but open moor. Clumps of gorse sprang everywhere, starbursts of yellow blossom shadowing pale-green ferns and tufts of dogtooth violets. He walked cautiously – he couldn't see the earth underfoot for all the new growth – but the ground felt solid beneath mats of dead bracken that gave off a spicy October scent. He was so intent on watching his step that he nearly walked into a standing stone.

He sucked his breath in sharply and stumbled backward. For a fraction of a second he'd perceived a figure there, but it was only a stone, twice his height and leaning at a forty-five degree angle, so that it pointed toward the sea. He circled it, then ran his hand across its granite flank, sun-warmed and furred with lichen and dried moss. He kicked at the thatch of ferns and ivy that surrounded its base, stooped and dug his hand through the vegetation, until his fingers dug into raw earth.

He withdrew his hand and backed away, staring at the ancient monument, at once minatory and banal. He could recall no indication of a standing stone between Cardu and Zennor, and when he checked the map he saw nothing there.

But something else loomed up from the moor a short distance away – a house. He headed toward it, slowing his steps in case someone saw him, so that they might have time to come outside.

No one appeared. After five minutes he stood in a rutted drive beside a long, one-storey building of grey stone similar to those he'd passed on the main road; slate-roofed, with deep small windows and a wizened tree beside the door, its branches rattling in the wind. A worn hand-lettered sign hung beneath the low eaves: GOLOVENNA FARM.

Jeffrey looked around. He saw no car, only a large plastic trash bin that had blown over. He rapped at the door, waited then knocked again, calling out a greeting. When no one answered he tried the knob, but the door was locked.

He stepped away to peer in through the window. There were no curtains. Inside looked dark and empty, no furniture or signs that someone lived here, or indeed if anyone had for years. He walked round the house, stopping to look inside each window and half-heartedly trying to open them, without success. When he'd completed this circuit, he wandered over to the trash bin and looked inside. It too was empty.

He righted it, then stood and surveyed the land around him. The rutted path joined a narrow, rock-strewn drive that led off into the moor to the west. He saw what looked like another structure not far from where the two tracks joined, a collapsed building of some sort.

He headed towards it. A flock of little birds flittered from a gorse bush, making a sweet high-pitched song as they soared past him, close enough that he could see their rosy breasts and hear their wings beat against the wind. They settled on the ruined building, twittering companionably as he approached, then took flight once more.

It wasn't a building but a mound. Roughly rectangular but with rounded corners, maybe twenty feet long and half again as wide; as tall as he was, and so overgrown with ferns and blackthorn that he might have mistaken it for a hillock. He kicked through brambles and clinging thorns until he reached one end, where the mound's curve had been sheared off.

Erosion, he thought at first; then realised that he was gazing into an entryway. He glanced behind him before drawing closer, until he stood knee-deep in dried bracken and whip-like blackthorn.

In front of him was a simple doorway of upright stones, man-high, with a larger stone laid across the tops to form a lintel. Three more stones were set into the ground as steps, descending to a passage choked with young ferns and ivy mottled black and green as malachite.

Jeffrey ducked his head beneath the lintel and peered down into the tunnel. He could see nothing but vague outlines of more stones and straggling vines. He reached to thump the ceiling to see if anything moved.

Nothing did. He checked his phone – still no signal – turned to stare up into the sky, trying to guess what time it was. He'd left the car around 2:30, and he couldn't have been walking for more than an hour. Say it was four o'clock, to be safe. He still had a good hour and a half to get back to the road before dark.

He took out the apple Thomsa had given him and ate it, dropped the core beside the top step; zipped his windbreaker and descended into the passage.

He couldn't see how long it was, but he counted thirty paces, pausing every few steps to look back at the entrance, before the light faded enough that he needed to use his cell phone for illumination. The walls glittered faintly where broken crystals were embedded in the granite, and there was a moist, earthy smell, like a damp cellar. He could stand upright with his arms outstretched, his fingertips grazing the walls to either side. The vegetation disappeared after the first ten paces, except for moss, and after a few more steps there was nothing beneath his feet but bare earth. The walls were of stone, dirt packed between them and hardened by the centuries so that it was almost indistinguishable from the granite.

He kept going, glancing back as the entryway diminished to a bright mouth, then a glowing eye, and finally a hole no larger than that left by a finger thrust through a piece of black cloth.

A few steps more and even that was gone. He stopped, his breath coming faster, then walked another five paces, the glow from his cell phone a blue moth flickering in his hand. Once again he stopped to look back.

He could see nothing behind him. He shut off the cell phone's light, experimentally moved his hand swiftly up and down before his face; closed his eyes then opened them. There was no difference.

His mouth went dry. He turned his phone on, took a few more steps deeper into the passage before halting again. The phone's periwinkle glow was insubstantial as a breath of vapour: he could see neither the ground beneath him nor the walls to either side. He raised his arms and extended them, expecting to feel cold stone beneath his fingertips.

The walls were gone. He stepped backward, counting five paces, and again extended his arms. Still nothing. He dropped his hands and began to walk forward, counting each step – five, six, seven, ten, thirteen – stopped and slowly turned in a circle, holding the phone at arm's length as he strove to discern some feature in the encroaching darkness. The pallid blue gleam flared then went out.

He swore furiously, fighting panic. He turned the phone on and off, to no avail; finally shoved it into his pocket and stood, trying to calm himself.

It was impossible that he could be lost. The mound above him wasn't that large, and even if the fogou's passage continued for some distance underground, he would eventually reach the end, at which point he could turn around and painstakingly wend his way back out again. He tried to recall something he'd read once, about navigating the maze at Hampton Court – always keep your hand on the left-hand side of the hedge. All he had to do was locate a wall, and walk back into daylight.

He was fairly certain that he was still facing the same way as when he had first entered. He turned, so that he was now facing where the doorway should be, and walked, counting aloud as he did. When he reached one hundred he stopped.

There was no way he had walked more than a hundred paces into the tunnel. Somehow, he had gotten turned around. He wiped his face, slick and chill with sweat, and breathed deeply, trying to slow his racing heart. He heard nothing, saw nothing save that impenetrable darkness. Everything he had ever read about getting lost advised staying put and waiting for help; but that involved being lost above ground, where someone would eventually find you. At some point Thomsa and Harry would notice he hadn't returned, but that might not be till morning.

And who knew how long it might be before they located him? The thought of spending another twelve hours or more here, motionless, unable to see or hear, or touch anything save the ground beneath his feet, filled Jeffrey with such overwhelming horror that he felt dizzy.

And that was worst of all: if he fell, would he even touch the ground? He crouched, felt an absurd wash of relief as he pressed his palms against the floor. He straightened, took another deep breath and began to walk.

He tried counting his steps, as a means to keep track of time, but before long a preternatural stillness came over him, a sense that he was no longer awake but dreaming. He pinched the back of his hand, hard enough that he gasped. Yet still the feeling remained, that he'd somehow fallen into a recurring dream, the horror deadened somewhat by a strange familiarity. As though he'd stepped into an icy pool, he stopped, shivering, and realised the source of his apprehension.

It had been in the last chapter of Robert Bennington's book, *The Sun Battles*; the chapter that he'd never been able to recall clearly. Even now it was like remembering something that had happened *to* him, not something he'd read: the last of the novel's four children passing through a portal between one world and another, surrounded by utter darkness and the growing realisation that with each step the world around her was disintegrating and that she herself was disintegrating as well, until the book ended with her isolated consciousness fragmented into incalculable motes within an endless, starless void.

The terror of that memory jarred him. He jammed his hands into his pockets and felt his cell phone and the map, his car keys, some change. He walked more quickly, gazing straight ahead, focused on finding the spark within the passage that would resolve into the entrance.

After some time his heart jumped – it was there, so small he might have imagined it, a wink of light faint as a clouded star.

But when he ran a few paces he realised it was his mind playing tricks on him. A phantom light floated in the air, like the luminous blobs behind one's knuckled eyelids. He blinked and rubbed his eyes: the light remained.

"Hello?" he called, hesitating. There was no reply.

He started to walk, but slowly, calling out several times into the silence. The light gradually grew brighter. A few more minutes and a second light appeared, and then a third. They cast no glow upon the tunnel, nor shadows: he could see neither walls nor ceiling, nor any sign of those who carried the lights. All three seemed suspended in the air, perhaps ten feet above the floor, and all bobbed slowly up and down, as though each was borne upon a pole.

Jeffrey froze. The lights were closer now, perhaps thirty feet from where he stood.

"Who is it?" he whispered.

He heard the slightest of sounds, a susurrus as of escaping air. With a cry he turned and fled, his footsteps echoing through the passage. He heard no sounds of pursuit, but when he looked back, the lights were still there, moving slowly toward him. With a gasp he ran harder, his chest aching, until one foot skidded on something and he fell. As he scrambled back up, his hand touched a flat smooth object; he grabbed it and without thinking jammed it into his pocket, and raced on down the tunnel.

And now, impossibly, in the vast darkness before him he saw a jot of light that might have been reflected from a spider's eye. He kept going. Whenever he glanced back, he saw the trio of lights behind him.

They seemed to be more distant now. And there was no doubt that the light in front of him spilled from the fogou's entrance – he could see the outlines of the doorway, and the dim glister of quartz and mica in the walls to either side. With a gasp he reached the steps, stumbled up them and back out into the blinding light of afternoon. He stopped, coughing and covering his eyes until he could see, then staggered back across first one field and then the next, hoisting himself over rocks heedless of blackthorns tearing his palms and clothing, until at last he reached the final overgrown tract of heather and bracken, and saw the white roof of his rental car shining in the sun.

He ran up to it, jammed the key into the lock and with a gasp fell into the driver's seat. He locked the doors, flinching as another car drove past, and finally looked out the window.

To one side was the gate he'd scaled, with field after field beyond; to the other side the silhouettes of Gurnard's Head and its sister promontory. Beyond the fields, the sun hung well above the lowering mass of Zennor Hill. The car's clock read 15:23.

He shook his head in disbelief: it was impossible he'd been gone for scarcely an hour. He reached for his cell phone and felt something in the pocket beside it – the object he'd skidded on inside the fogou.

He pulled it out. A blue metal disc, slightly flattened where he'd stepped on it, with gold-stamped words above a beacon.

ST. AUSTELL CANDIES: FUDGE FROM REAL CORNISH CREAM
He turned it over in his hands and ran a finger across the raised lettering.

Becca gave one to each of us the day we arrived. The fudge was supposed to last the entire two weeks, and I think we ate it all that first night.

The same kind of candy tin where Evelyn had kept her comb and Anthea her locket and chain. He stared at it, the tin bright and enamel glossy-blue as though it had been painted yesterday. Anyone could have a candy tin, especially one from a local company that catered to tourists.

After a minute he set it down, took out his wallet and removed the photo Evelyn had given him: Evelyn and Moira doubled-up with laughter as Anthea stared at them, slightly puzzled, a half-smile on her face as though trying to determine if they were laughing at her.

He gazed at the photo for a long time, returned it to his wallet, then slid the candy lid back into his pocket. He still had no service on his phone

——◆——

He drove very slowly back to Cardu, nauseated from sunstroke and his terror at being underground. He knew he'd never been seriously lost – a backwards glance as he fled the mound reassured him that it hadn't been large enough for that.

Yet he was profoundly unnerved by his reaction to the darkness, the way his sight had betrayed him and his imagination reflexively dredged up the images from Evelyn's story. He was purged of any desire to remain another night at the cottage, or even in England, and considered checking to see if there was an evening train back to London.

But by the time he edged the car down the long drive to the cottage, his disquiet had ebbed somewhat. Thomsa and Harry's car was gone. A stretch of wall had been newly repaired, and many more daffodils and narcissus had opened, their sweet fragrance following him as he trudged to the front door.

Inside he found a plate with a loaf of freshly baked bread and some local blue cheese, beside it several pamphlets with a yellow Sticky note.

Jeffrey

Gone to see a play in Penzance. Please turn off lights downstairs. I found these books today and thought you might be interested in them.

Thomsa

He glanced at the pamphlets – another map, a flyer about a music night at the pub in Zennor, a small paperback with a green cover – crossed to the refrigerator and foraged until he found two bottles of ale. Probably not proper B&B etiquette, but he'd apologise in the morning.

He grabbed the plate and book and went upstairs to his room. He kicked off his shoes, groaning with exhaustion, removed his torn windbreaker and regarded himself in the mirror, his face scratched and flecked with bits of greenery.

"What a mess," he murmured, and collapsed onto the bed.

He downed one of the bottles of ale and most of the bread and cheese. Outside, light leaked from a sky deepening to ultramarine. He heard the boom and sigh of waves, and for a long while he reclined in the window-seat and stared out at the cliffs, watching as shadows slipped down them like black paint. At last he stood and got some clean clothes from his bag. He hooked a finger around the remaining bottle of ale, picked up the book Thomsa had left for him, and retired to the bathroom.

The immense tub took ages to fill, but there seemed to be unlimited hot water. He put all the lights on and undressed, sank into the tub and gave himself over to the mindless luxury of hot water and steam and the scent of daffodils on the windowsill.

Finally he turned the water off. He reached for the bottle he'd set on the floor and opened it, dried his hands and picked up the book. A worn paperback, its creased cover showing a sweep of green hills topped by a massive tor, with a glimpse of sea in the distance.

OLD TALES FOR NEW DAYS
BY ROBERT BENNINGTON

Jeffrey whistled softly, took a long swallow of ale and opened the book. It was not a novel but a collection of stories, published in 1970 – Cornish folk tales, according to a brief preface, 'told anew for today's generation'. He scanned the table of contents – 'Pisky-Led', 'Tregeagle and the Devil', 'Jack the Giant Killer' – then sat up quickly in the tub, spilling water as he gazed at a title underlined with red ink: 'Cherry of Zennor'. He flipped through the pages until he found it.

Sixteen-year-old Cherry was the prettiest girl in Zennor, not that she knew it. One day while walking on the moor she met a young man as handsome as she was lovely.

"Will you come with me?" he asked, and held out a beautiful lace handkerchief to entice her. "I'm a widower with an infant son who needs tending. I'll pay you better wages than any man or woman earns from here to Kenidjack Castle, and give your dresses that will be the envy of every girl at Morvah Fair."

Now, Cherry had never had a penny in her pocket in her entire young life, so she let the young man take her arm and lead her across the moor...

There were no echoes here of *The Sun Battles*, no vertiginous terrors of darkness and the abyss; just a folk tale that reminded Jeffrey a bit of 'Rip Van Winkle', with Cherry caring for the young son and, as the weeks passed, falling in love with the mysterious man.

Each day she put ointment on the boy's eyes, warned by his father never to let a drop fall upon her own. Until of course one day she couldn't resist doing so, and saw an entire host of gorgeously dressed men and women moving through the house around her, including her mysterious employer and a beautiful woman who was obviously his wife. Betrayed and betrayed, Cherry fled; her lover caught up with her on the moor and pressed some coins into her hand.

"You must go now and forget what you have seen," he said sadly, and touched the corner of her eye. When she returned home she found her parents dead and gone, along with everyone she knew, and her cottage a ruin open to the sky. Some say it is still a good idea to avoid the moors near Zennor.

Jeffrey closed the book and dropped it on the floor beside the tub. When he at last headed back down the corridor, he heard voices from the kitchen, and Thomsa's voice raised in laughter. He didn't go downstairs; only returned to his room and locked the door behind him.

He left early the next morning, after sharing breakfast with Thomsa at the kitchen table.

"Harry's had to go to St. Ives to pick up some tools he had repaired." She poured Jeffrey some more coffee and pushed the cream across the table toward him. "Did you have a nice ramble yesterday and go to The Tinners?"

Jeffrey smiled but said nothing. He was halfway up the winding driveway back to Cardu before he realised he'd forgotten to mention the two bottles of ale.

He returned the rental car then got a ride to the station from Evan, the same man who'd picked him up two days earlier.

"Have a good time in Zennor?"

"Very nice," said Jeffrey.

"Quiet this time of year." Evan pulled the car to the kerb. "Looks like your train's here already."

Jeffrey got out, slung his bag over his shoulder and started for the station entrance. His heart sank when he saw two figures arguing on the sidewalk a few yards away, one a policeman.

"Come on now, Erthy," he said, glancing as Jeffrey drew closer. "You know better than this."

"Fuck you!" she shouted, and kicked at him. "Not my fucking name!"

"That's it."

The policeman grabbed her wrist and bent his head to speak into a walkie-talkie. Jeffrey began to hurry past. The woman screamed after him, shaking her clenched fist. Her eye with its bloody starburst glowed crimson in the morning sun.

"London!" Her voice rose desperately as she fought to pull away from the cop. "London, please, take me—"

Jeffrey shook his head. As he did, the woman raised her fist and

341

flung something at him. He gasped as it stung his cheek, clapping a hand to his face as the policeman shouted and began to drag the woman away from the station.

"London! *London!*"

As her shrieks echoed across the plaza, Jeffrey stared at a speck of blood on his finger. Then he stooped to pick up what she'd thrown at him: a yellow pencil worn with toothmarks, its graphite tip blunted but the tiny, embossed black letters still clearly readable above the ferrule.

RAVENWOOD.

PENDING LICENSOR
APPROVAL

 ADAM CESARE

"You're a writer?" the bartender asks. "That's cool."

That's cool.

I think she means it.

She isn't blowing me off.

Which is bad.

This should be my final round.

If I stay, she might start asking follow-up questions.

I watch as the bartender steps a few feet away, works the soda gun, mixing a drink for another patron.

There's four other men in the bar.

A sad-looking guy four stools over, who just ordered another vodka soda; two weekend warriors in the corner playing the quietest game of pool I've ever heard; and a man standing at a high top near the door, rubbing his eyes against the glare of his phone screen, probably ruining his vision.

The place isn't empty. But it's empty *enough* that the bartender might not wait for me to need another drink. She might mosey back here to continue our conversation after she's done delivering the vodka soda.

Fuck.

Here she comes.

Fuck.

Yes, I'm exhausted and stressed. But it's more than that.

I don't want to discuss writing.

My profession embarrasses me.

Even on a good day, I hate talking about it.

Don't get me wrong. I *am* a writer. Not a hobbyist or a dilettante.

I've been publishing for twenty years now.

Professionally.

Meaning I get paid for my work.

Really paid. Not 'one grocery bill a month from Kindle royalties' fun-money. Checks big enough I can live on them.

Well. Live *modestly*. Most months of the year. As long as publishers pay on time. Which they rarely do.

But still.

Tonight I should have said I was an UberEats driver.

Or an accountant. Or a brain surgeon.

Tonight, of all nights, I should have lied.

You see, I've just handed in a book.

It's why I'm here. It was a tight deadline. An interesting project. Well, interesting, in scare quotes.

But this isn't a celebration.

It's a wake.

I want to drink myself some distance from the manuscript I've just delivered.

Not that I'm one of *those* writers, the drinking kind, I—

"Anything I've heard of?" the bartender asks.

I play dumb to get myself an extra nanosecond to think.

"Huh?"

"You said you're a writer. Have you *written* anything I've heard of?"

Is she genuinely interested? Is she flirting? More likely she's acting like she's both to inflate her tip.

But I can't be sure.

This is my third round and I'm only here, drinking in public, because yesterday, in the buildup to hitting 'send' to email my manuscript to my editor, I drank everything in my apartment.

Today's Sunday and the city has weird blue laws.

So I can't tell what the woman in front of me wants.

I'm buzzed, exhausted, and stressed beyond libido or the capacity to judge social cues.

Not that it matters if I find the—what? Goth? Alternative?—woman in front of me attractive.

Nothing I can say would change the outcome here.

I've had conversations like this before. With women.

I know where they lead.

It's never to success.

And the failures are always depressing.

"No. Probably nothing you've heard of."

"You'd be surprised," she says. "I watch a lot of Netflix."

She leans forward. Filling a highball glass with ice.

She has a bat, its wings outstretched, tattooed across her cleavage.

"Oh. No Netflix for me," I say. "I'm not a screenwriter. Books. I write books. And short stories. But mostly books."

She turns her eyes up. Catches me staring at the bat. And instead of every other time this exact thing has happened to me—from age twelve onward—she smiles.

"Oh. A *real* fucking writer," she says, then fills the glass with cola, tosses in a straw and takes a sip.

The bartender has made a drink for herself.

Is planning to stay here, parked in front of my barstool, for a while.

Something stirs in me.

Maybe I'm not too drunk.

Maybe not too tired.

Maybe I'm suddenly stressed in a different, more pleasant way.

Because I have hope. A chance with this woman.

"What are your books about?" she asks.

How do I navigate that question without the bat on her chest shriveling up, its wings breaking to dust as it tries to fly away?

I don't tell her how my career started with homebrew Dungeons & Dragons modules. Little chapbooks, run off the middle school photocopier and stapled once in the center.

Not only does it sound nerdy, but it would age me, too.

Guy in his forties, talking to this... I don't know. Could be later-twenties, could be thirties. Younger than me, but still a real woman.

I chance a peek at the rest of her tattoos.

There's a cartoon ghost on her left shoulder.

The back of her right hand is inked with a photorealistic representation of the bones underneath.

I could tell her how I've written a few backup stories for Marvel comics, but I doubt that will impress her. I never got to write any of the scary, cool characters. No Ghost Rider or Blade or Man-Thing for me.

And I certainly can't tell her about the big one, my magnum opus. The ElsePlanes series. My contemporary fantasy quartet. Hopefully more than a quartet, if I ever get back to it.

Even if this bartender had a Harry Potter phase as a kid, I can see that she's grown out of it now. She'll think my doorstop novels about dreamweaving wizards are lame. They're too light. Too bright. Too hopeful. Too many dragons, to woo her.

"Come on," she says, biting the straw. I don't think she has fangs. I think those are just normal canine teeth. Wishful thinking on my part. "Tell me about them."

That's when I see the tattoo on her throat.

I mistook it as a necklace, a choker, at first glance.

The bartender has a dotted line inked across her neck.

Under the line, the words 'Cut Here' are tattooed in Courier font.

Yes.

No.

I can't tell her.

But I have to.

There's only *one* book I've written that'll interest the bartender.

Only one that can help me out here, help me search for more tattoos.

I have no choice but to share with her what I've just delivered.

The reason I'm drinking.

The *horror* book.

"I'm working on something now," I say. "You ever hear of, well, they're Japanese, but you ever hear of the Angel Wings movies?"

At first I think I'm getting a blank stare back.

But I'm not.

The glass of Coke—Diet Coke?—starts to slip out of her grip, but she catches it before it crashes to the floor.

"Are you..." Even in the low light of the bar, I can see the fannish blush—the *squee*—rising in her cheeks.

The bartender sets down the glass.

"Are you kidding me?"

I blink.

"Wait. You know them?" I say, even though she clearly does.

"Know them! *Guts of the Maiden? Fish Hooks in the Flesh of the Valkyrie? Black Blood Drowning Ghost?* Oh my god I *love* those fucking things."

My stomach gives a little twinge, hearing the titles of those sequels spoken aloud.

"Really?" I ask. "You *love* them?"

"Yes," she says, then she screws up her face, scrunching her nose, somehow making herself hotter, accentuating the freckles there. She looks like a TikTok filter. "But I thought you said you write books."

She's the first person I've talked to this about. Period. Outside of my agent, editor, and the licensors themselves, of course.

But those conversations were email and over the phone.

The bartender's the first person, in-person, that I've spoken the words 'Angel Wings' aloud to.

It feels like the pop of a cork. I'm both burdened and unburdened.

Before I could even be briefed about the project, I had to sign an NDA. A non-disclosure agreement.

NDAs are legal documents to ensure writers don't tweet out company secrets. Which I'd never do. Which I've never done, I've never broken a single NDA. Not even to tell my mom what I'm working on. Which is probably taking things too far.

What can I say? I'm a rule follower. Usually.

You have to agree to sign one any time you work on established IP. That's Intellectual Property. Which I don't do as much as some of my contemporaries, fantasy writers who make their living doing tie-in novels for television shows and video games. It's good money and reliable work, if you're a faster writer than I am. Someone who cares a bit less about…

And then the dread hits me.

I've broken my NDA.

It hasn't been a challenge keeping the Angel Wings book a secret, thus far. There's nobody in my life who's heard of these films. Who I'd even *want* to tell about the project.

I shudder.

The Angel Wings films.

Thinking of them as 'films' might be overstating it. Even calling *Angel Wings* and its sequels 'movies' is a stretch. They were all made in the late Nineties. They were all shot on video. And there's ten of them, all produced over a three-year span, because the Japanese work quick.

"Those are movies," she repeats. "You said you write books."

"I do write books," I explain. "But sometimes—not all the time, mostly I do original stuff—but *sometimes* I'll take jobs writing the book versions of movies. Novelizations."

"Oh, that's cool," she says. I think I'm losing her, my nerd stink has finally wafted up to her shapely, freckled nose.

I take a sip of my drink.

Next round I'll go for something without fruit juice. My tongue hurts, like when I was a kid and would get bags of Atomic Warheads and eat too many of them too fast. Like my tongue's going to crack. Or break out in sores.

"Wait. I'm confused. The Angel Wings movies are… books? In English?"

Yeah. I was confused too, when my agent came back with the offer.

"Why me?" I'd asked. "Isn't there, like, a horror guy who can do this?"

"Hey. I was wondering that too, but it's not an audition situation. You don't need to write a sample. You just need to say yes. I imagine they…" he pauses, "I imagine they tried the horror guys first and they were all busy."

"Thanks."

"Not a slam! I just pass along the offers. Easy money. Bang it out in a weekend."

He's always saying stuff like that, downplaying how much work writing a book is. "Bang it out in a weekend." Like each book doesn't take me three solid weeks of doing my laundry and staring at my hands before I get word one onto the page.

But my agent's right. The ElsePlanes series is between publishers, on a hiatus, and the offered advance to write a 70,000-word novelization is very nice.

I stare back at the bartender.

I've already broken the NDA.

Why not tell her the whole thing?

Explain it to her.

"This is all secret," I say, lowering my voice, trying to put a little gravity into what I've said.

I mean it, it *is* a secret, but also: who's she going to tell? I'm being silly.

The bartender leans in. The bat's fangs drip blood.

"They're doing an American remake of the first Angel Wings," I say. "Well. It's structured more like an anthology, because they're using material from the sequels. Big budget kind of thing. And I'm writing the novelization to that."

She's shocked. Needs a moment before she speaks again.

"Big… budget? That," she scratches her neck. Cut here. "That's… I'm sorry. But that doesn't sound like a very good idea. How are they going to do an American version of *those movies*?"

I shrug.

She's not wrong.

And I haven't seen it, so I don't know.

"Not my job to decide if the movie's a good idea. I'm getting paid to write the book."

"No offense but… not sure if there's a big audience wanting to *read* those movies as a book."

That cuts a little deeper. Because, sure, a decent advance with no royalties, on work like this. But I want to be read. Or at least it'd be nice. It's why I do what I do. It's why I'm not using a pseudonym, even for something as potentially embarrassing as this.

My expression must have soured, reflected the sudden melancholia I feel, because the bartender touches my arm.

Her hand is cold, damp from the condensation of her glass of cola.

"Not *me*. I'd want to read it. I love that shit. I am the audience. But…"

I smirk up at her. I wish I didn't smirk so much. It keeps me celibate. "You mean to tell me fans of the Angel Wings series aren't typically big readers?"

She pulls her hand back. It's her turn to be offended.

"Hey. Don't act like we're all perverts and dummies."

Fuck.

"I didn't mean to say that… I…"

But she's smiling back at me. Less of a smirk. Cuter than a smirk.

"I got ya," she says, pow goes the finger gun. "But really. Some of us, I go to a lot of horror events, *are* dummies. And *all* of us are perverts."

I smile, unsure if I'm allowed to laugh at what she's just said.

She steps back, elbow nearly touching a bottle of Grey Goose, and looks me over.

She hasn't checked on her other patrons in a minute. But none of them have approached, looking for fresh drinks.

"This kind of writing," I say, "this genre… it's not my usual thing."

I imagine she can see that, from where she's standing.

The scrunch of her adorable nose seems to say that, no, I don't have any tattoos. That I'm in a dive bar wearing a button-down shirt from Marshalls.

"Not a horror guy," she says.

She laughs at me. The sound's kind of mean, kind of sexy.

And it doesn't seem like that's make or break for her. Or maybe I've already broken. So I frown and nod.

I admit it.

I'm not a horror person.

"A not-a-horror-guy," she continues, "hired to write about genital mutilation and infanticide."

I nod again, imagine that if there was better lighting in here she'd see me turning green. Because I was forced to write about all that. And worse.

"Damn. You had to *earn* that pay," she says.

"One way of putting it."

Not that I've been paid all I'm owed. My manuscript is waiting on final approval from the studio, which will trigger the second—and largest—of the three checks I'm owed.

"I like *some* horror," I say.

But I'm not a horror person like horror people are horror people.

Like this bartender is.

I enjoy heroic fantasy.

I've read all of Brandon Sanderson's books. All of them. Not just the Mistborn and Stormlight books.

And he's a Mormon. Which makes me, after reading all that, like, a Mormon by proxy.

I look down and there's a new drink, fresh, in place of the one I just finished.

"On me," she says. I hadn't even seen her hands move.

Well, not really a Mormon.

And I guess I'm drinking another one of these, even if my tongue aches.

"I'm sorry," she says, "that you've been traumatized by the Angel Wings movies. But, for me, as a fan, it's nice to hear that they're keeping them extreme. In this new version."

The first movie in the Angel Wings series is only sixty minutes, not even feature length by American standards. But, to this day, I've only seen about ten minutes of it.

That ten minutes was enough.

"I've just," I take a swig of the drink, trying not to picture fake pus weeping from fake burn wounds. "Never seen anything that bad."

"Oh, so none of the Men Behind the Sun movies are on your shelf?"

I shake my head.

"And you haven't seen *A Serbian Film.*"

No again.

"No *Slaughtered Vomit Dolls*?"

"You're making that one up," I say, pointing up at her.

"I'm not."

She's not.

"Wow." She scratches her neck. "They threw you into the deep end when they sent you the Angel Wings movies."

I nod. They did. And that's exactly how it happened too.

The studio claimed there were security issues, that, even though they had an assembly edit of the new movie, the one I'm novelizing, they could only send me the script. When I pressed them, finding the work difficult, asking to see the movie, they'd overnight mailed me DVDs of the original series, told me to use those to familiarize myself. That their version "hewed closely to the originals."

It'd been an intense few hours, as I picked through, the volume on my TV low, fast-forwarding to get to the parts of the movies I could stomach, the lulls, trying to parse any kind of plot between the prolonged sequences of sexualized violence.

There isn't much of a plot in the Angel Wings movies. There aren't even continuing characters, in each of the installments.

"Why…"

No, don't ask her that. She'll be offended. You're drunk. Stop. Lapse into silence, finish your drink, then see if you can leave here with her number.

"Why what?" she asks.

Might as well. Because as much as I'd like to feel the warmth of another human body. I truly do want to know…

"Why do you like them?" I ask. "These movies."

It feels like a very personal question, the tone I take. And she reacts in kind. "I…"

I put my hand out, nearly spilling my drink. The orange juice smells like flowers. Wilted flowers. Rotting vegetation.

"I just like them," she says.

That's no answer at all.

"Can you be more specific?" I ask. Like she said, she's no dummy. She can use her words. She can dig into this part of herself for me, help me understand her fandom. I've shared a secret with her. It's the least she could do.

Her top lip curls up at the corner. Almost a sneer.

"I'm not judging you," I say. "I just want you to help me understand. I don't get it. No part of watching them was a pleasurable experience for me. And writing the book…"

"You're writing the book and you can't even *conceptualize* why someone would like them?"

I shrug.

Conceptualize. Odd word.

"It's probably not a great book!" I say, trying to turn it into a joke. But we're past jokes.

"That's… that's not fair to the fans," she says, sad about it.

That's what I said! My fucking agent. My need to pay rent. They've put me in this position.

I take a big sip. I take a long blink and think of all the synonyms I had to use for penetrate. For stab. For rot and blood and torture and pain.

All the emails I'd shared with the licensors. The promotional stills I'd wake up to in my inbox. Passages from the script that'd float to the top of my mind any time I was trying to eat or masturbate or drift off to sleep.

Traumatize was the word the bartender had used. But it's more than that.

The Angel Wings films have terrorized me.

It's hard to explain to someone who doesn't do it, but writing isn't just the time you spend typing.

Writing is the period of time that begins when you type the title, center justify it, bold it, and then extends until you finish your final polish and cash that last advance check.

Writing is all that time, when you're living it.

At least it is for me.

"Watching those things happen to those characters in the movies," the bartender says. And she sets down her drink, hugs her arms together like it's suddenly gotten cold in here. Which it hasn't. If anything, it's too hot.

Someone at the pool table breaks, and both the bartender and I jolt to hear it.

She chuckles at that, our reaction breaking the tension.

"I've been jumpy for two months now," I say. "But go on. You were saying. Seeing the violence it—"

"It gives me a sense of control? To see people having such a bad time? To be abused? Because as good as the special effects are, they aren't *that* good. They aren't real."

"Looked pretty real to me," I say.

"But see, you wouldn't say that, if you were someone who'd seen real abuse and violence."

"Violence towards women," I say.

And, like the initial question, like breaking my NDA, I wish I could snatch at the words and drag them back into my mouth.

"Not all of it," she says, tone sharp.

I'm in it now.

"Yes. But most of it. Most of the victims in the Angel Wings movies are women."

"It's not a numbers game. Could be argued that the men get it worse," she says.

There's a sign above her head, advertising hot dogs. I didn't even know this bar had a kitchen. I haven't seen anyone order food.

She makes scissors with her finger, snips in the air at the tip of the hot dog on the sign.

I wince, but not as bad as when I remember the Japanese man lying in bed, girl parts soaked into the mattress, flies landing on open eyes. I wonder if, in Japan, these films have as much of a cult following as they do here in the US. Or if there's some level of fetishization, the exoticism of dismembered Asian bodies, that keeps American fans happy, doesn't do as much for the Japanese, especially Japanese women.

"The dick stuff," I say. "Doesn't get to me as bad as the rest of it. And that's just like two guys, in hours and hours of film."

And I remind myself that it's video. Not film.

She puts both of her hands flat on the bar, squares her shoulders.

"I don't feel like less of a feminist because I enjoy these movies," she says. "If that's what you're about to imply. Take that shit to Twitter and out of the bar, if that's your thesis."

I hold up my hands. Don't shoot.

Don't cut my dick off.

"Not what I was thinking. Like I said. Just want to understand. You were saying. The difference from real violence," I continue. "So it's a catharsis. Watching this stuff happen to these women, the sadism lets you—"

"Yes. And it's not sexual. Not purely. Not for me. It lets me own what I've—" she waves a finger in front of her face. "But this is stupid. Because I'm just one person. And there's thousands of us, and I'm sure why someone else likes these movies is not exactly why I like them."

The expression on her face, I'm not quite sure what it is. Maybe I've caused her to have some kind of breakthrough. Or am pushing her towards a nervous breakdown, which is not what I want.

"So—"

"So nothing," she interrupts. "I'm saying something. I've got a friend. A good friend. We go to cons together. She reads a lot, reads books that are similar to the Angel Wings series. Extreme horror."

I nod. "Splatterpunk," I say. It's a phrase I've picked up. "I'm familiar."

"No. Extreme horror. They're different. But this friend, we've known each other since high school. I know her parents. She's never had a bad day in her life, never had a bad boyfriend, so don't try and do that."

"Do what?"

"Suggest that I'm a wounded bird. That we're all damaged. Those of us who watch this stuff. Sometimes we just like what we like. It's a sensation. It's an interest. It's healthy it's—"

"I didn't say it was *un*healthy! Different strokes. And I like that you like it. I guess. I'm glad someone does. It just puzzles me. But thank you. I feel like I know more now, I—"

I feel like I'm going to fall off this bar stool, even though the words keep flowing. I'm articulate, for someone so sleepy.

"And that's admirable, that you're seeking to understand," she says. "I just wish we could have had this conversation before you handed your book in."

There's another strike of the cue, the clatter of pool balls broken.

Only I flinch this time.

I… I don't remember saying I handed anything in. In fact, I remember talking about the book in the present tense, as something I'm currently working on.

Her expression changes. Not so much a slackening, as a change in demeanor. An actor calling 'scene' and dropping out of character.

"I've read it," she says.

"You've—"

"I was up all night, finished your manuscript before my shift started. Maybe fifteen minutes before you walked in that door."

I don't look over at the door. I look at her.

"You read the book? *Angel Wings*?"

"It's not terrible," she says. And do I recognize her voice? From a meeting I've taken? There are so many voices on those calls with the licensors.

So many notes.

So many cooks in the kitchen.

We know it's for an American audience. But please don't skimp on the fetal barbeque sequence. We can edit back if need be.

"I. You read the book I just—"

"Shut up. You're making this more difficult than it has to be."

Is she really regretful, or is she acting again? Is she angling for a bigger tip, or has she never once tended bar?

Bar.

I look around the room.

The game of pool is over. The men are looking at me, sticks in hand.

The guy at the high top is off his phone, has his hand on the door.

I assume he's locked it.

The other man bellied up to the bar has finished his vodka and soda and sits next to the empty glass, even the ice gone... he's also staring at me.

"What the fuck is—"

As I turn back, she pushes an envelope toward me.

"The rest of your advance."

I touch it. And like I thought...

...the envelope's wet.

In a quick, smooth motion the bartender pulls a blue plastic Bic lighter from the waistband of her low-slung black jeans. There's a flower tattooed there, a vine crawling out of her pelvic bone.

She strikes the lighter and the envelope ignites, my pay going up like a magician's flash paper.

"It was tonight. The check was in the mail. But you had to break your agreement."

NDA.

Have I ever read one of those? I understand *why* I'm signing, but can I now call up one single clause, the verbiage I've put my signature on?

Bless me father, for I have disclosed.

There's the crinkle of plastic sheeting and the two men have pulled a blue tarp out to cover the green felt of the pool table.

Then the four men begin to stalk toward me.

I try to fight them but misjudge the distance to the guy nearest the door and my glass sails over his shoulder, doesn't even break when it hits the floor.

Their hands are strong.

And I wait for her to grab me as well, but the bartender never joins them.

She only watches.

She enjoys this kind of thing. But only in theory. Only on screen. Only when she can tell herself that it's fake. Stage blood and latex.

The four men hold me down.

And all the horrible things I've seen.

The things I can't imagine *why* anyone would ever want to see.

All the things that I've written.

They happen to me.

ACKNOWLEDGEMENTS

On January 1st, 2023, I was rushed into hospital with a very erratic heartbeat of 250bmp. I wasn't expected to make it, my wife told me as much when I got back home. I fell into a pretty dark place afterwards – and I can't say I've completely come out the other side yet (the day before handing this book in, I was back in hospital, heartbeat 215bpm), but I took this book on two months later, in March, mainly to take my mind off of things, and it's saved my life in a way. It's been a difficult project, but it's given me something to focus on during some extremely awful moments. But I was adamant that I would edit the best book I was able to, and somehow, I think I've pulled the rabbit from the hat. This is my best original anthology to date. The stories are some of the strongest I've read from writers so on their game it's crazy. There are people to thank, so let's get on with thanking them.

Daniel Carpenter, my editor at Titan. For whatever reason, the pitches I was pitching just weren't hitting. This was the last idea I had, and it was a throwaway idea at that. But Daniel immediately saw its worth and this book wouldn't exist without him. Create an altar for Daniel for we must all worship at it. Also, to the designers and everyone who works at the Titan offices – from those who work at the post room to those at the top of the tree. My hat is doffed to the incredible Paul Simpson for making sure any stupid mistakes I've made have been caught and corrected. And the designer: To Charlie Mann who has made the interiors of this book something I want to read, frame and marry, all at once. Thanks also to Ellen Datlow, Dan Coxon and all the authors in this book who have gone above and beyond. Christopher Priest was to write an original story for this book, however, cancer robbed us of what were to get from him. My love to Nina Allan and his family. His words remain and will be discovered by generations to come.

Finally, I'd like to thank my wife, daughter and dog. There have been some bleak moments this past year, but we've held hands (and paws) and made our way through the darkness. I love you all.

AUTHOR BIOGRAPHIES

Charlie Higson is a successful author, actor, comedian and writer for television and radio. He co-created *The Fast Show*, wrote the first five novels of the Young Bond series and the post-apocalyptic young adult horror series The Enemy.

A.K. (Alexandra) Benedict is an internationally bestselling writer of novels, short stories, and award-winning scripts. She lives in Eastbourne with her husband, writer Guy Adams; their daughter, Verity; and their dog, Dame Margaret Rutherford.

Alison Moore's stories have appeared in various 'Best Short Stories' and 'Best Horror' anthologies. She has published two collections, including *Eastmouth and Other Stories*, and five novels, including *The Lighthouse* and *The Retreat*. alison-moore.com

Eric LaRocca (he/they) is the Bram Stoker Award®-nominated and Splatterpunk Award-winning author of several works of horror and dark fiction, including the viral sensation *Things Have Gotten Worse Since We Last Spoke*. ericlarocca.com

Nadia Bulkin is the author of the short story collection *She Said Destroy* (Word Horde, 2017) and the co-editor of the ghost story anthology *Why Didn't You Just Leave* (Cursed Morsels, 2024). She has been nominated for the Shirley Jackson Award five times and the Bram Stoker Award® once.

Lucie McKnight Hardy is the author of a novel, *Water Shall Refuse Them*, and a short story collection, *Dead Relatives*. Her short fiction has featured in numerous dark places.

Isy Suttie is a writer, comedian and actor known for her Sony Award-winning BBC Radio 4 series *Isy Suttie's Love Letters* and for playing Dobby in Channel 4's *Peep Show* amongst other roles. She has written two books: *The Actual One*, a memoir, and a novel, *Jane is Trying*.

Priya Sharma writes short stories and novellas. She has several British Fantasy Awards, Shirley Jackson Awards, and a World Fantasy Award. priysharmafiction.wordpress.com

Kim Newman is a critic, author and broadcaster. His current projects are *A Christmas Ghost Story*, a novella, and *Model Actress Whatever*, a novel, for Titan Books.

Hailing from Jersey City and of Trinidadian descent, **Zin E. Rocklyn** is the award-winning writer of *Flowers for the Sea*.

Angela "A.G." Slatter is the author of six novels and twelve short story collections; her latest novel is *The Briar Book of the Dead*. She has some awards.

Amanda DeBord is a writer and editor living in St Louis, Missouri, with her husband, two children, and the ghosts of several cats.

Jeremy Dyson is perhaps best known as the fourth unseen member of *The League of Gentlemen*, the co-creator of the hit West End play *Ghost Stories*, and its acclaimed movie adaptation. He has written several collections of short stories including Edge Hill Award winner *The Cranes that Build the Cranes*.

Ramsey Campbell is Britain's most respected living horror writer. He has written over thirty novels, the latest is *The Lonely Lands*.

Robert Shearman has written six collections of short stories, and between them they have won the World Fantasy Award, the Edge Hill Readers Prize, the Shirley Jackson Award and three British Fantasy Awards. He is probably best known for his work on *Doctor Who*, writing that episode where Chris Eccleston met a weepy Dalek.

Guy Adams is made of celluloid and day dreaming. He lives by the sea with his live-in genius Alexandra Benedict and their daughters Verity (human) and Dame Margaret Rutherford (canine).

Elizabeth Hand is the multi-award-winning author of five collections of short fiction and twenty novels, including *A Haunting on the Hill*, *Generation Loss*, and *Hokuloa Road*.

Adam Cesare is the author of the Bram Stoker Award®-winning Clown in a Cornfield series, the graphic novel *Dead Mall*, and several other books. An avid fan of horror cinema, you can hear him talk movies on YouTube, TikTok, Twitter, and the rest of his socials.

ABOUT THE EDITOR

Johnny Mains is a British Fantasy Award-winning editor. His last two books were the landmark anthologies *Celtic Weird* and *Scotland the Strange* for the British Library.

For more fantastic fiction, author events,
exclusive excerpts, competitions, limited editions and more

VISIT OUR WEBSITE
titanbooks.com

LIKE US ON FACEBOOK
facebook.com/titanbooks

FOLLOW US ON TWITTER AND INSTAGRAM
@TitanBooks

EMAIL US
readerfeedback@titanemail.com